St.Valentine's Night

Novels by Andrew M. Greeley

Death in April
The Cardinal Sins

THE PASSOVER TRILOGY
Thy Brother's Wife
Ascent into Hell
Lord of the Dance

TIME BETWEEN THE STARS
Virgin and Martyr
Angels of September
Patience of a Saint
Rite of Spring
Love Songs
St. Valentine's Night

MYSTERY AND FANTASY
The Magic Cup
The Final Planet
Godgame
Angel Fire
Happy Are the Meek
Happy Are the Clean of Heart
Happy Are Those Who Thirst for Justice

St. Valentine's Night

Andrew M. Greeley

WARNER BOOKS

A Warner Communications Company

Warner Books, Inc., 666 Fifth Avenue, New York, NY 10103

W A Warner Communications Company

Printed in the United States of America
First printing: September 1989
10 9 8 7 6 5 4 3 2 1

Book design: H. Roberts

Library of Congress Cataloging-in-Publication Data

Greeley, Andrew M., 1928–
    Saint Valentine's night / Andrew M. Greeley.
        p. cm.
    ISBN 0-446-51475-6
    I. Title.
PS3557.R358S25   1989
813'.54--dc20   89-40029
                                                            CIP

For Ingrid Shafer

They say if you die in your dreams you really die
    in your bed
But honey last night I dreamed my eyes rolled straight
    back in my head
And God's light came shinin' on through
I woke up in the darkness scared and breathin'
    and born anew
It wasn't the cold river bottom I felt rushin' over me
It wasn't the bitterness of a dream that didn't come true,
It wasn't the wind I felt rushin' through my arms,
No baby it was you
So hold me close honey say you're forever mine
And tell me you'll be my lonely Valentine.

—Bruce Springsteen

Seeing takes time.

—Georgia O'Keeffe

He was overwhelmed by the belated suspicion that it is life,
more than death, that has no limits.

—Gabriel García Márquez

Chicago's Beverly Hills is real, but the story and the characters are fictional. However, the incident narrated in chapter 59 is based on an actual occurrence in that magic neighborhood.

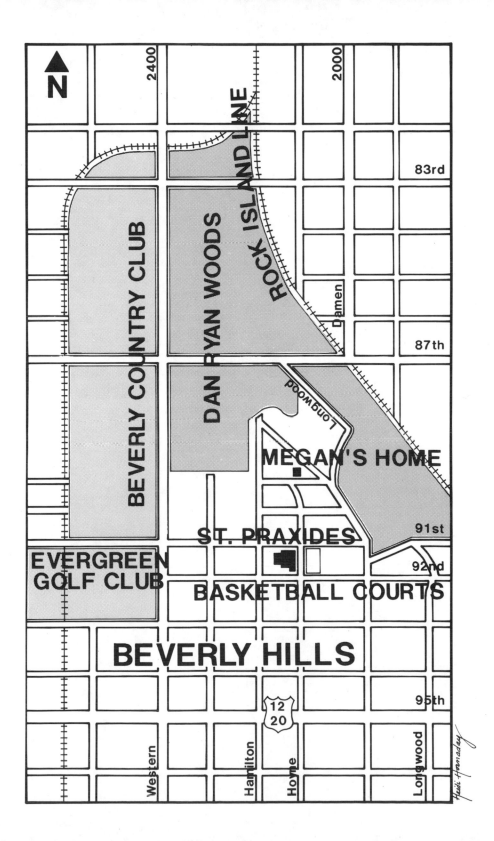

1987

1

"I hated this place when I lived here." He frowned at the little priest. "I hated it after I left, and I still hate it."

As he spoke, he savored the bile of his hatred for the neighborhood the way he would enjoy bitter nausea toward a woman he had always hated. But without intending it, he had used his "sign-off" voice—as in, "This is Neal Connor, IBC News, with the *mujahedeen* in the mountains of Afghanistan."

Once again he had cloaked deep emotion with a professional disguise.

"There are"—the cleric's nearsighted eyes blinked rapidly—"a lot of ironies in the fire."

The priest was short and inoffensive, the kind of bland and nondescript person whose presence you would not notice if you entered an elevator on which he was riding. You might not even notice that his Roman collar did not fit and that the buttons on his soiled trench coat were in the wrong buttonholes.

They were standing by the sacristy door of St. Praxides Church. The little priest had driven up in a battered and unwashed red Chevy Nova and parked next to Neal's Hertz Taurus. Moisture—part drizzle, part mist—enveloped them like a transparent shroud.

There was now no possible escape, not without looking more of a fool than he already felt for being in the St. Prax's parking lot in the first place.

"I'm here to cover Mayor Washington's funeral and the election of a new mayor," Neal explained.

"My Lord Cronin—our good Cardinal—says that the dynamics are like those of a papal conclave." The priest's round face was expressionless, his head tilted meekly to one side. "Save for the absence of white smoke."

"I met Lisa Malone at O'Hare," Neal continued his explanation, not clear in his own mind why it should be so apologetic. "She told me about this thirty-year reunion."

"Indeed." The priest was searching for his car keys with his right hand, fearful perhaps that he had left them in the car. In fact, they were in his left hand.

"I guess I was not on the mailing list."

"Hmm . . . remarkable." He had rediscovered his keys. "Oh, yes, I saw your envelope with my own eyes. We sent it to New York, not having the proper address of the *mujahedeen*."

He had pronounced the name of the Islamic holy warriors just the way that Neal did during his Afghan series. In the old days you never knew when Blackie Ryan was making fun of you. Neal had learned that when in doubt you should assume that despite his innocent face, Blackie had the soul of a leprechaun, a very intelligent leprechaun.

"I've been on the move a lot lately." Neal wished he didn't sound so pompous: more grist for Blackie's mill.

"Indeed." The little priest's eyes blinked rapidly behind his thick, mist-covered glasses.

Before driving into the parking lot between the school and the church and around the basketball court to the door of the church, Neal had steered his black Taurus through the streets of the neighborhood in the fading gray light of this rainy Friday after Thanksgiving. As much as he had hated the neighborhood when he had grown up in it, he had felt tears stinging his eyes. Not for the neighborhood, with its wide lawns and tall, if now barren, trees, nor for its movie-set beauty did he want to weep, but for his own lost youth. And wasted life. Why, he asked himself again, did it have to flow through your fingers so quickly?

"Midlife crisis," the smooth, sleek New York doctor had said to him.

"You haven't seen the bodies in Afghanistan," Neal had replied curtly.

Which did not answer the question of why a relatively small number of mutilated human corpses, Russian corpses at that, had reduced him to tears in the Hindu Kush when the mass graves in Cambodia had left him dry-eyed.

The Edward R. Murrow of his time was cracking up.

"I suppose," he said to the little priest, "Megan is in charge?"

"The Pope is still Catholic, is he not?" The priest began to search for the steps to the sacristy door, as though he had not climbed them a thousand times in his life. "And Polish at that?"

In his dreams about the neighborhood, Neal had pictured it as deteriorating into a resegregated slum, a fate he told himself that it richly deserved, just as a hated woman deserved to grow old and ugly. He had been surprised when the lovely Lisa, singer, actress, and now producer, had told him that it was still flourishing as an integrated community. "More whites than blacks moving in," she had smiled, "homes going for three hundred to four hundred thousand dollars."

Neal had been skeptical, but his quick drive from 95th Street to the Woods and back convinced him. The Dutch Colonial, Tudor, and old Victorian homes (some of them a hundred years old now) seemed as well maintained as ever. The dowager homes on the ridge above Longwood Drive still looked down superciliously on the small park next to the Rock Island station, conscious no doubt that they stood on the highest point in Cook County and that the drive was the historic Vincennes Trail.

The Ravine, a gully cut through sand dunes thousands of years ago, was still picturesque, virtually the only wooded hills in Chicago; its homes clung to the sides of the ancient dunes as if they were in a Swiss village. And St. Praxides, one of the first of the modern churches built after the war, still kept a watchful eye on the community with its yellow-brick elegance untarnished.

A magic neighborhood, the young priest had said when Neal was in high school.

"Spoiled rich neighborhood," Neal had sneered.

"You sound like a walking cliché," the priest had snapped back.

Not nearly so devious and indirect a cleric as Blackie Ryan.

"She's inside?" Neal asked that worthy Monsignor as they hesitated at the foot of the steps to the sacristy door. The light rain had started to fall again.

"Since we're both late"—the priest pretended to glance nervously at his watch—"it must be presumed that she is."

"With Al?"

Foolish question. Who else would she be with but her husband?

"Al's dead." The priest's voice was flat, neutral. "Didn't the wondrous Lisa tell you?"

"No. . . . DEAD?"

"Drove his car into an oak tree at 94th and Damen six weeks ago."

"Drunk?"

"So it is said. He was often drunk, though not, according to perspicacious members of my family, an alcoholic."

"Accidental death, then?" Neal shivered.

The young priest lifted a shoulder. "Some say so. Others think it might be suicide. Others . . ."

"Why should Al Lane commit suicide?"

"You heard about the stock market crash in October?"

"Sure, even in the Hindu Kush you hear about that kind of thing."

"Al was trading in S and P options at the Chicago Mercantile Exchange."

"The Merc."

"You have not been gone so long from among us as to forget that hallowed spot."

"I worked there one summer, remember? Biggest gambling casino in all the world."

"Indeed." The priest removed his glasses and dabbed at them ineffectually with the sleeve of his raincoat. "Al enjoyed many different kinds of gambling, as you may remember. Trading the index was his, uh, meat—I believe the term is. He could not believe that the great bull market was coming to an end. He must have been hard pressed for funds . . . as was usually the case, I fear. In a half hour on Black Monday, he traded with customer funds, confident that there would be a gigantic rebound. As you surely have heard, there was not."

"Wiped out?"

"In that half hour"—Blackie Ryan, glasses now back on his nose, put his hand on the doorknob of the sacristy entrance—"he lost his capital, his seat on the exchange, and his license. Moreover, he had to put all his property up for sale, including the three Mercedes and the house on Hoyne."

"My God!"

"Leaving his widow without any funds and a mountain of debts."

"Insurance?"

"Not as long as there is suspicion of suicide or—"

"How many kids?"

"Four. The youngest is twelve, the oldest a sophomore at Notre Dame."

"And no money?"

"Not the proverbial red cent." He opened the sacristy door and stood aside so that Neal could enter. "Al had put all her money into his capital pool. Her brothers and sisters would not be inclined to help, I should think, even if they could, which is problematic."

Neal studied the doorway, an invitation as sure as there had ever been one in his life.

An invitation to resume the unfinished history of twenty-two years ago.

There was no sign that read, "Abandon hope, Neal Connor, should you dare enter here."

There might just as well have been.

2

Smoke was gushing out the door. Cornelius O'Connor hesitated. His father had told him that smoke inhalation killed just as quickly as fire. Maybe she was dead already. Why should he risk his life for a stuck-up little brat?

Then he heard her scream.

It was 5:45 on a ten-above-zero February morning. Cornelius was finishing his paper route. Only one block of ice-coated sidewalks remained. He guided his bike carefully to the Keefe house on Hoyne, balanced it with one foot, grabbed a paper from the basket on the handlebars, and deftly spun the *Tribune* towards the door, hard enough so it would hit the door, soft enough so that it wouldn't bounce back into the falling snow.

Mr. Keefe would complain to the distributor if his *Tribune* were defiled by falling snow.

There was no disgrace in the neighborhood in working a paper route. Kids much more affluent than he delivered papers for the development of their characters, as their parents would say. But on mornings as bad as this one, their mothers usually would drive them through their route in the family Buick or Cadillac.

His father drove their 1952 Ford to the Gresham police station, where he worked.

After his route was finished, Cornelius would pedal through the snow to St. Prax's, where he would join his buddy Johnny Ryan as an acolyte at the 6:30 Mass in honor of St. Valentine. Destined for

Quigley and the priesthood, the towering Cornelius and the puny John were ill matched but reliable; Cornelius (never called "Con" or "Conny" by his classmates and friends) was the more reliable of the two.

Thinking of the relative warmth of the big and empty church, Cornelius kicked his pedals around and slithered down Hoyne Avenue toward 90th Street.

A tiny image struggled to form itself in the back of his brain, a gnawing picture tugging at his consciousness, an image from a dream or maybe a TV movie. He stopped his bike, rested his right foot on the snow-coated sidewalk and pondered.

What was wrong?

He had seen something unusual, something that ought not to be there, at the Keefe house.

What was it?

Nothing.

And if there were something, it was none of his business anyway.

"We can't afford to be involved with people like the Keefes," his mother had warned him the last time a complaint had been made to the paper distributor. "They have too much power. They can do us too much harm."

"My dad," he had replied proudly, "is an honest cop, and Mr. Keefe is a Mob lawyer."

"Don't ever say such things, dear," his mother had begged him.

"Why do we have to live in the same neighborhood with them anyway?"

"We're every bit as good as they are."

So it had always gone—first a warning about how rich and powerful the other people in the parish were, then a protest that the O'Connors were every bit as good as anyone else. And his father was an honest cop, which was more than could be said for many of the other fathers in St. Prax's.

He sighed and began to pedal his bike again. He must not be late for Mass. This would be the kind of morning on which Mrs. Ryan, who people said was dying of cancer, might not wake her son.

Then the image in his head detonated: a red glow in the basement game room of the Keefe house. As if a Christmas tree had been left on all night. Only it was the middle of February and Christmas trees had long since been dismantled.

Fire?

He hesitated. It was still none of his business. Only two of the Keefe kids were home: Pete, who was a big basketball star at St. Ignatius, and Megan, Cornelius's classmate and a spoiled, stuck-up little brat. What did he care if anything happened to either of them?

He started pumping on the bike again; then, almost as though the bike had made the decision for him, he found that he was riding back toward their sprawling white Georgian house—a plantation mansion of slaveholders, he had often thought.

But he was going too quickly on the ice. The bike skidded out of control, lurched into a snowdrift, crunched to an abrupt halt, and tossed him over the bars into another snowdrift.

Serves me right for worrying about those bastards, he thought as he lay dazed in the snow.

What was I worrying about anyway?

Fire!

His face stinging from the snow, he struggled to his feet. Sure enough there was a bright orange radiance within the basement windows.

He took a deep breath. What if it were not a fire really? Mr. Keefe would have him fired from his route. He would not be able to save money for his high school tuition.

He ran up the snow-covered walk, plowing through the drifts. The thick wet snow tugged at his feet like a marsh of taffy. He could barely move against the ferocious wind and the thickly falling snow.

It's like a nightmare, he thought. I'm trapped in a swamp and I can't move.

Somehow he pushed his way up the steps to the front door. He was on automatic pilot now, as he often was when he became anxious—working in slow motion as seconds seemed to become minutes and minutes turned into hours.

He pushed the doorbell. Not a sound inside. He pushed it again. And again. Still no sound.

He glanced through the parlor window. A dim orange color hovered against the walls. The whole house would soon be on fire.

"Fire!" he shouted. "Your house is on fire!"

There was no response. Hoyne Avenue was as silent as Holy Sepulchre Cemetery.

He pounded on the door with all his strength. "Fire!" he bellowed. "Fire!"

Maybe he should run next door to the Murray house and call the fire department. But by the time they came, it would be too late.

The Murrays could phone the Keefes and wake them up, could they not?

But first of all he would have to wake the Murrays.

He eyes lighted on a snow shovel, carelessly tossed on the front lawn and almost covered with snow.

Pete Keefe's work. A real slob.

What could he do with the shovel?

Then he realized what he could do with it.

He rushed from the doorway, grabbed the shovel by its handle, and swung it against the dining room window. The glass shattered loudly, an explosion of tiny bells.

If that didn't wake them up, nothing would.

"Your house is on fire!" he yelled through the smashed window. "Get out! Get out!"

The house was as silent as a mausoleum. What was the matter with them? Did they want to burn to death in their sleep?

What was he supposed to do now? How do you save people who don't want to be saved?

He considered the problem. There was nothing left to do except run over to the Murrays.

"Fire! Fire! Fire!"

Still no answer.

Then he realized that there was another possibility. Did he dare actually enter their house? There wasn't any other way to save them, was there?

He swung the snow shovel again and smashed the remnants of the dining room window. Then he braced his hands on the window sill, pushed hard, and catapulted himself up and through the window.

He almost made it.

His thighs balanced on the ledge, then he teetered backward and forward and grabbed a handful of drapes. He clutched the flimsy fabric for a desperate second and crashed back into the snow.

Shaken and befuddled, he heard the crackling of flames and smelled the acrid reek of smoke.

Once more he hurled himself up and through the window.

This time he made it.

Indeed, he sailed through the window so powerfully that he

smashed against the a cabinet and heard the tinkle of breaking crystal. Too bad, probably they had insurance anyway.

"Fire!" he shrieked. "Your house is on fire!"

"What the fuck are you doing here, you rotten little punk?"

Pete Keefe in his shorts, bleary-eyed and confused.

Cornelius tried to shout "Fire" but only croaked out a hoarse rasp.

"I'll beat the shit out of you"—Pete advanced toward him—"you crummy little thief."

Later Cornelius would realize that Pete Keefe was mostly asleep and didn't know what was happening.

He was, however, behaving characteristically, a spoiled country-club punk.

"Wake your mom and dad, the house is on fire!" The words tumbled out of his mouth.

Pete glanced around, saw the fire eating its way into the hallway at the foot of the stairs, screamed hysterically, and bolted for the front door.

"Your parents!" he shouted after Pete.

"Fuck 'em!" Pete bellowed, and shoved hard against the door. "I don't want to die!"

Cornelius's autopilot shifted into high gear. Without thinking about the dangers, he bolted up the stairs. Behind him Pete Keefe, unable in his panic to work the lock on the door, was kicking it and cursing it.

"Fire! Fire! Mr. Keefe! Mrs. Keefe! Your house is on fire!"

"What's going on? What the HELL is going on?"

"Your house is on fire! Run for your lives!"

In the smoke and darkness at the top of the stairs, two shapes pushed past Cornelius, down the steps and out the door which Pete had finally managed to open.

Megan, where was Megan?

What did he care about her?

Well, at least she was nicer than anyone else in the family.

"Megan!" he shouted. "Megan, where are you?"

The smoke was thicker; tongues of dirty orange fire were darting across the hallway at the bottom of the steps.

Megan slept on the first floor, in a room overlooking her garden—so she had said in an essay she had read in class about waking up to her garden.

Coughing now from the thickening smoke, he dashed down the

stairs, ducked away from the flames, and raced through the dining room and into the kitchen.

"Megan!" he yelled again. "Where are you?"

In the distance he heard fire engines. Someone had seen the fire. The station at 95th and Vanderpoel was only a few blocks away.

If only they would come quickly.

"Megan!" he shouted yet again. "Where are you?"

He heard a muffled sound from the left, a door at the far end of the kitchen, right next to the back door of the house. He rushed to it, threw it open, and saw the clouds of smoke and the darting flashes of fire.

And heard her scream.

Later he realized that he should have soaked some towels in the kitchen sink and used them as masks. But there was no time to think about that. He charged into the smoke and fire, stumbled over a bed, pushed himself to his feet, and saw her—huddled against the wall, her eyes wide with terror.

He vaulted over the bed, caught her up in his arms—noting in his head that such a tiny girl hardly weighed anything at all—and bolted out the door, into the kitchen, and out the back door of the house into the blizzard.

She cowered in his arms, a terrified little bundle of humanity, clinging to him as desperately as she clung to life. She was wearing, he noted, a thick winter nightgown. If he did not know that she was a girl just a few months younger than he was, he might have thought her a second- or third-grade boy.

Her heart was thumping wildly against her ribs. He held her even more closely against his chest, aware now that this was not just a girl, not just a classmate, but a person like himself, frightened and yet brave.

And she was his person, powerless, trusting, confident in his strength. For a brief and glorious second Hoyne Avenue and St. Praxides parish and the universe disappeared. There existed only Cornelius and his adoring prize. He loved her with all the passion of the exploding galaxies. Cleaving to him in innocent submission, she returned this passion.

We will stay here forever, he told himself.

Then the fire engines arrived. He heard the orders being yelled, the hoses unloaded, the tramp of booted feet toward the house.

"Are you all right?" he asked the handful of fluff in his arms, his prize, his girl, his conquest, his woman.

She gasped for breath, choked and gagged. "Is that you, Cornelius?" she said in a hoarse whisper. "What happened? Is it a dream?"

"It's all right, everything is all right now."

Somehow, he struggled out of his thick imitation leather jacket, draped it around her shoulders, and carried her around the side to the front of the house. He heard Mrs. Keefe shouting at the firemen about her poor baby inside.

A poor baby she thought of after she had fled the flames.

He bumped into a fireman in thick rubber coat and yellow boots.

"Are you part of the family, son?" The man reached out, as if to sustain them.

"No sir, I'm the newsboy. But this is Megan Keefe, she's all right. Tell Mrs. Keefe not to worry."

"You saved her life, then, son. You're a hero."

"No, I'm not," he replied.

"Yes, you are." Megan hugged him fiercely. "Yes, you are."

Even if she was a spoiled and stuck-up brat, those words made Cornelius O'Connor's heart soar toward the heavens.

The firemen removed Cornelius's burden from his arms and carried her out to the street where the rest of her family was huddled under fire department blankets. He pointed at Cornelius. Mr. Keefe glanced at him but said nothing.

The rest of the firemen thought he was a hero, too. So they told him when they drove him to St. Praxides to serve the 6:30 Mass. He told Blackie the whole story.

"She hugged you and said you were a hero?"

"She really did."

"So maybe she's not a stuck-up brat after all?"

"Sure she is," Cornelius had responded uncertainly, in those days not being completely certain when Blackie was kidding him.

After Mass the battalion chief drove him over to Little Company for a lung X ray and then home. His mother warned him again that he should have nothing to do with the Keefes and bawled him out for losing his coat.

In the *Tribune* the next morning, Mr. Keefe was quoted as denying that the fire was the result of a warning from the Mob about a case he did not want to take. Rather, he blamed the fire on "a newsboy just trying to get a little attention for himself. The punk belongs in reform school."

No attempt was made to arrest Cornelius, however. Later he

read that Mr. Keefe had taken the case about which he had hesitated. And won it.

A week later, during a sunny February thaw, Megan Keefe returned to the St. Praxides schoolyard, a bundle over her arm. Her face was whiter than usual and her tiny shoulders seemed thinner than usual. A gust of the coming March wind might blow her away.

She ignored the crowd of eighth-grade girls who swarmed around her, and searched the faces in the yard till she found him, standing as usual with Jim Sullivan, Blackie Ryan, and Alf Lane.

Then she pushed her way through the crowd and strode up to him.

"Here's your coat back, Cornelius. I was afraid I got it dirty, so I had it cleaned."

"Thank you," he stammered.

"I don't care what THEY say. I know you're a hero. You DID save all our lives, mine especially."

She embraced him, planted a brisk kiss on his lips, and sped off as quickly as she came.

The class of 1958—as always knowing instinctively the proper reaction—cheered.

"Valentine's Day came a week late this year," Blackie Ryan observed. "And it doesn't normally have an octave, either."

Later in his life, when he wondered what he could have possibly seen in Megan Keefe, he would always remember that scene. He loved her compassion, her intensity, her impulsive courage, her determination to heal his pain. That courage had not always been strong enough for either of them, but that was, he would tell himself sometimes, more his fault than hers.

He was fired from his newspaper route and then reinstated the next day because Mr. Ryan had intervened on his behalf.

The Ryans were at City Hall when they gave him the medal, even Mrs. Ryan, who looked terribly pale but laughed most of the time, like she always did.

The Keefes weren't there, not that he cared about the rest of them, but it would have been nice if Megan had been in the crowd.

The next day she came over to his house and demanded to see the medal.

This time, however, she did not kiss him.

But she looked like she was thinking about it.

1987

3

Afraid to face the grammar-school classmates he had ignored for more than twenty years—and especially Megan Lane, whom he had loved and lost—Neal Connor, IBC News, in the mountains of Chicago, hesitated in the sacristy.

"Do they have Mass servers anymore?" he asked the little Monsignor, who was struggling into white vestments.

"Even altar girls, though the Vatican explicitly disapproves." Blackie peered out of a sleeve of his alb. "But there's nothing much to do, not like the old days. And, of course, no prayers like the Suscipiat you have to memorize in Latin."

"You don't need any help."

"Cornelius, I always need help, but I think I can struggle through the Eucharist without your ministrations. Megan and my cousin Cathy will be ministers of the Eucharist, and Lisa will, of course, be the leader of song. It is, I think, remarkable that they are permitting me the homily."

"I don't know what some of those words mean. . . . I don't get to church much"—an understatement—"but I don't like the changes. They kind of take away the mystery."

"Spoken like a true would-be lapsed Catholic." The priest sighed noisily as he tugged at the recalcitrant alb. "A pity. You weren't around when the vote was taken, so you didn't get to vote."

"What vote?"

"You might come up after the gifts are presented, er, the wine and water, and pour the water into the chalice for me. The Pope would not approve of that, either, because you are, I strongly suspect, not a permanent deacon. But it's a long way to Rome."

He didn't know whether the priest was serious this time. Probably he was.

"Has Megan changed?"

"Aged terribly."

He heard that answer with both regret and relief. The neighborhood was the same as always, but Megan was not. Well, that would diminish the temptation.

Not that he was quite sure he wanted it to be diminished.

"Fat?"

"Horrifically."

Why, he wondered, do we have to grow old? Especially a little slip of a girl who hugs you and tells you that you saved her life. Which you did.

Once if not twice.

"I'd better go into church now."

The priest peered over his rimless glasses. "The angels will recover quickly enough, I presume."

Neal walked cautiously through what used to be the baptistry and was now, if the sign was to be believed, the BLESSED SACRAMENT CHAPEL.

He peered around the corner and into the church itself. Empty! What the hell!

St. Prax was still in her big stained-glass window in the back, wiping up martyr's blood from the floor of the Roman arena. The side windows were still the stations of the cross. The pseudofrescoes on the wall, including the priests who had been on the staff when the church was dedicated in 1954, were still clear and fresh, the rich wood walls and pews were still warm and inviting. St. Praxides church was not a Gothic cathedral surely, but not a bare auditorium or a barn or an airplane hangar like some of the Catholic churches that, for one reason or another, he had entered in the last two decades. With its subdued woods and its thick carpet and its soft colors, it was something like a living room done in Scandinavian modern, with less austerity than the Swedes would have wanted.

Neal's throat tightened at the memories that cascaded through his head.

But where the hell were the rest of them?

Then he glanced to his left. Several dozen middle-aged people were standing in the sanctuary around the altar.

Of course, that was the sort of thing they did these days.

But why did everyone seem so old!

Gingerly he walked up the marble steps. . . . The altar rail was gone now. Pity. Quietly he tiptoed up to the end of the semicircle of old folks who were the kids who he'd thought would never get old.

Blackie Ryan emerged from the door of the sanctuary, looking as though he were not quite sure why he was there or what was the way to the altar.

A beautiful woman stepped forward, turned around, and led them in a hymn he had never heard before.

Lisa Malone.

The class had done well: Lisa was a movie star, Cathy Collins a painter, Blackie a Monsignor and rector of Holy Name Cathedral.

And Cornelius O'Connor, now known as Neal Connor, a washed-up and burned-out TV journalist.

What did Blackie mean by the "vote"?

As his classmates sang a hymn they all seemed to know, he felt odd, a square peg, an outsider, an interloper. So what else was new?

Still, he should be able to hum the song anyway, it was easy enough. So he hummed softly.

A slim, pretty woman, standing next to him, turned and looked up at his six feet two inches of silver-haired celebrity grooming.

"Neal Connor, IBC News, Beverly Hills, Illinois," she whispered, mimicking him. Her delicately carved face, hinting at an El Greco Madonna, was solemn, as it usually was. But her eyes sparkled.

Megan!

In a black dress, who else would it be?

Blackie had lied in his teeth. She had not changed a bit.

Dear God in heaven, what am I supposed to do now?

She extended her hand and touched his. "Welcome."

"I'm sorry, Megan," he murmured.

She nodded acceptance of his sympathy and returned to the song. Her eyes flicked across his face once, quickly and decisive, sensitive and sympathetic eyes reading his soul, guessing at his pains, wishing she could heal them.

Same old Megan.

Cautiously he examined her, hoping that she was unaware of his inspection and knowing that, like any woman in such circumstances, she was fully aware of it. Her face was unmarked, save for a few lines at her eyes and her mouth. She seemed to be wearing almost no makeup. Her ethereally pale complexion had not required it in the past and still apparently did not. There was a softness beneath her chin and lines on her throat, blemishes—if so they were—that made her all the more appealing. Her body was as slender as ever, still the slip of a girl who, if she were any thinner, would have been thought skinny. Megan's sex appeal even as a girl had been in her intensity, not voluptuousness.

He tugged his eyes away from her. Did she know the content of his evaluation? Probably. Megan had not been an intellectual in the making like Lisa or Cathy, but she never missed much, either.

Then, as the little priest mumbled a prayer to which Neal did not listen, he felt the sting of sexual hunger, raw, imperious, overwhelming.

How sweet it would be to possess this fragile little doll, to take for his own Al Lane's widow and pleasure her in ways of which he had been incapable. She's mine now if I want her, he thought. All mine. Finally.

Slowly the tide of desire ebbed, and he felt shame and guilt. In church. A widow with four children. He was closer to the deep end than he had realized. He felt like he should apologize to someone. God?

But there wasn't a God, was there?

Maybe in St. Praxides there was.

There had been no woman in his life since Kelly MacGregor had left him. Nor had he felt the need for a woman.

In Afghanistan the rebels had offered him his choice of one of the three Russian nurses they had captured and gang-raped.

"They are Allah's gift to us and to you," Kemal, his friend and leader of the band of *mujahedeen,* had said proudly. "They should be enjoyed gratefully until we must dispose of them."

He had been ashamed of his reaction. Kemal's argument had somehow seemed persuasive. He almost pointed at the youngest of the captives, a blond with despair in her eyes.

Instead, he argued that Kemal knew better than that. Had not the Prophet written that women were to be respected and honored? Was not he, Kemal, dishonoring himself and his cause by violating women who were not combatants?

Kemal had hesitated. Illiterate and superstitious, he was a devout Moslem, the kind of pious warrior who had brought the crescent almost to the banks of the Seine in the seventh century. But he knew little of what the Prophet had actually said, though probably more than Neal Connor did.

"It is true," he sighed, accepting Neal's quote. "But these are *Russian* women, not modest Islamic women."

"That doesn't make any difference and you know it."

"We should kill them, then? Now?"

"You should leave them here for their own troops."

Kemal had sighed again. "Allah's will be done."

Neal knew enough Russian to attempt an interview with the captives—trade a sensational story for their release. Ten years before, even five, he would have done the story. Now he was disgusted with himself for even thinking of it. Instead, he whispered to them in Russian that they would be released. They hardly seemed to hear him.

The little priest was reading the Gospel now, something about ten lepers being healed.

As atrocities went, the Afghanistanis were not all that cruel. Neal thought that after Africa he was immune to the results of what the men with the guns did to the men and women without the guns. The Africans were fiendishly ingenious in the violation, mutilation, and destruction of the human body. But in the Afghanistan mountains he began to fall apart.

It was so like Vietnam as seen from the other side. The Russians had no reason to be in Afghanistan, save that they thought their vital interests were at stake. The young Russians who were being killed and maimed with American weapons no more understood the reasons for the war than did the young Americans who were killed and maimed with Russian weapons in 'Nam.

And he was a parasite, living off human suffering, just as he had been in Vietnam, just as they all were.

Kelly had believed that their world was the real world, that a NATO foreign ministers' conference was actually something important rather than an assembly of a group of elderly politicians concerned about their jobs and their digestive tracts. A presidential press conference, a debate between candidates, a hint of scandal in the *Times* or the *Post*, a hearing on the Hill—for Kelly these were historic events, the very stuff of reality, the episodes that truly mattered.

She was exultant when the press had forced Gary Hart out of the presidential race and had helped to destroy Bork and Ginsburg.

He had come to believe that it was all mirrors and shadows, tricks and illusions, dreams and visions.

He didn't know whether there was a real world someplace, but he did know that it wasn't to be found at dinner parties in George-town, weekends on Long Island, or in the pages of Bob Woodward's admittedly fascinating books.

Still, he loved her and wanted to marry her. He was lonely and she was fun—a vital, bouncing redhead with a quick laugh and sensuous willing lips. His first marriage had ended twelve years before when his wife had discovered in a women's consciousness group that he had been oppressing her—a difficult task since he had rarely been home long enough to oppress anyone.

Living with Kelly had killed the pain of his loneliness. She seemed ready enough for marriage, as long as he promised that they would not permit marriage to interfere with their careers.

"Careers are really important," she said in the tone used by ambitious TV producers when making an important statement, ev-ery trace of her native Nova Scotian accent suppressed. "Nothing else really matters, does it?"

Neal remembered that at her age, when he was covering the final fiasco of the rooftop evacuation of the embassy in Saigon, he had believed that, too. He did not disagree.

In St. Praxides Church, while Blackie Ryan fiddled at the altar in preparation for his sermon or homily or whatever they called it, he glanced again at Megan Keefe. Megan Lane. She had no career and never would have one.

What did the priest mean when he hinted that neither suicide nor accident might be the explanation of Al Lane's death? Al wasn't much, but who would want to kill him?

Megan's hair was laced with silver. Natural or artificial? Proba-bly natural. Attractive enough, but why did anyone have to grow old and die?

Once more his desire reached out to touch her, embrace her, make her his woman. Quickly he recalled it, like a man reeling in a flawed cast of his fishing rod. He did not want to become a character in a real-life version of "Dallas."

What would they call such a story? "Beverly"? Or "Beverly Hills"? Everyone would think of the Los Angeles suburb instead of the Chicago neighborhood, which had prior claim to the name.

He quickly surveyed his classmates. Not the stuff of soap opera, these aging and mostly overweight men and women. Not even of romantic comedy. What the hell was he doing here?

The little priest finally seemed to have figured out where he was and what he was supposed to say.

"One of the advantages of the aging process," his speech was as confident as his previous manner had been bemused, "is that one discovers how many more beautiful women there are in the world than one had suspected at fourteen."

An appreciative laugh. Wasn't Blackie Ryan cute? They had thought so at fourteen and they still thought so.

Neal had argued back in the days when he was Cornelius that Blackie was not cute at all but dangerous—likable indeed, irresistibly likable, but dangerous.

"We must not deceive ourselves, however, gentlepersons, as charmed as we are this evening by durable womanly loveliness. We are not as young as we once were. Moreover, to make matters worse, unlike our nearest genetic relatives among the higher primates, the wondrous chimpanzees, we *know* that we are not as young as we once were.

"So what do we celebrate and why do we celebrate? Is this day-after-Thanksgiving festival a celebration of survival? Of endurance? Of resignation? Of—heaven save us all—wisdom? Are we not in fact still too young to lay any claim to wisdom, even the all-wise Megan to whom we must be grateful for this event?"

Laughter, especially from Megan herself.

Dangerous, dangerous man, Johnny Ryan.

"Our Catholic tradition tells us that every Eucharist— That, Cornelius, is the appropriate word for Mass these days," he interrupted himself, rolling his pale blue eyes, "a change which, as I noted before, was made without soliciting your vote."

More laughter. Neal felt his face glow warmly. Megan peeked at him, shyly, it seemed, over an impish and most un-Megan-like grin.

"Every Eucharist, is a nuptial Eucharist that celebrates the passionate union between Jesus and his Church, between God and his people, between the Spirit and us. If that be so, then our gaze today is not so much backward to the graduation Mass in this church thirty years ago come June, but forward to the unending nuptials in the kingdom of God our Father.

"If such be the case—and obviously it is, or a member of the papal household with purple buttons somewhere in his closet if he could only find them would not have said so—then we look forward today to heaven rather than back to St. Prax's, 1958.

"While most of us would, I think, recall those years together around the basketball and volleyball courts in this schoolyard as a time of bliss, not unmarked by imperfections, the truth is that even

St. Prax's in the fabled fifties suffers by comparison with the kingdom of heaven.

"Thus by reasoning, which, given the nature of the homilist, is not extraordinarily tortuous, we come to my theme: What is the kingdom of heaven like?

"I put it to you, gentlepersons, that one of the better metaphors available is the honeymoon. To coin a parable, the kingdom of heaven is like a honeymoon that never ends.

"I trust I will be spared the ridiculous objection that, unlike you, I have never been on a honeymoon."

More laughter.

Two of us, Blackie. We spent the weekend after my marriage to Helen in a beach house at Montauk while Helen worked on her dissertation, a dissertation that she has even now not finished.

He knows that I almost went on a honeymoon once with Megan Keefe. We were ready to board the plane for Tucson when she changed her mind.

"Consider the honeymoon: it is a time of passionate and recurring celebration, a time of fascination with another person, a time of mystery and pleasure, a time when satiety does not seem possible, a time of challenge and promise, of hope and wonder at the beginning of each new day.

"That is our goal, gentlepersons. If our religion means anything at all, it means that. Pie in the sky when you die, does someone say?

"Not at all. The honeymoon without end in the heavenly city is not merely a reward that awaits us at the end of our pilgrimage, a goal for which we piously seek. It is a reality present among us, an opportunity for today and tomorrow and the next day. The One who invites us to eternal honeymoon invites and expects us to live with the joy and the hope of happy, fascinated lovers today.

"The best way to prepare for death, then, is to carry on our love affair today with God and those She loves with zest and enthusiasm. Our love affairs today are training fields for the heavenly honeymoon."

Silence. Then applause.

In church?

Something else I didn't get to vote on.

What was the point of all that? Was it aimed at me? Or Megan? Or someone else? Or everyone?

Dangerous, dangerous man, Blackie Ryan.

You can never tell what he's thinking.

But he knows too much about me and Megan.

1962

4

Neal O'Connor, as he had become, did not taste Megan Keefe's lips again till the spring of their high school graduation. Then he tasted them often. And learned to want to taste them forever.

Megan seemed a cool, prim debutante—a slender, self-possessed, and virtuous ice maiden—when she "bowed" at the annual presentation ball; a sober, almost somber product of the nuns' training into whose well-organized life no passionate disorder would be permitted to intrude; a serious and socially responsible young woman who made sensible and rational choices in laying out the chart for the rest of her life.

In fact, when her lips assaulted his on the beach at night, she became a reckless siren, reveling in her scorching emotions.

"I wanted to do that since the morning you saved my life," she explained, sighing complacently when she gave him a moment to breathe. "It was worth waiting for."

Like almost everyone in her class, Megan had broken the family tradition of attending Longwood Academy and had enrolled in the new Mother Macauley High School out on 103rd Street.

"I was yours that morning," she continued calmly, "wasn't I? We both knew. We both loved it. Didn't we? Neal, damn it, stop looking guilty and answer me."

"We were the whole universe," he replied, returning to the kiss.

Wanting to escape from the neighborhood and what he deemed its country club atmosphere, Neal had chosen Mount Carmel High

School in the Woodlawn district, the only one in his class to pick Carmel and one of a mere handful of parishioners of St. Prax's to make the long journey every day across town on the 95th Street bus to Stony Island and then on Stony Island down to 65th Street.

He had explained to his mother that he would be happier away from the neighborhood. One of the Carmelites who said Mass on Sunday at St. Prax's had arranged for a scholarship because Neal's father had gone to Carmel. His father, who rarely said much of anything, merely nodded his agreement.

In fact, the Carmelite had acted for the school's football coach, who was certain that Cornelius would outgrow his early adolescent clumsiness and become a star for the Carmel Caravan.

His mother disapproved of the game and would not permit Cornelius to play eighth-grade football at St. Prax's, a decision which made him even more an outcast and a figure of fun and scorn with his classmates.

He was a hero for a few weeks after he had snatched Megan from the fire.

"Be nice to them," Blackie had pleaded. "A lot of them would like to like you if you'd give them half a chance."

He responded by swinging his fist at Alf Lane during a noon-time basketball game. Al had made fun of his tattered gym shoes: "Couldn't your father steal new ones from Mage's?"

Alf had meant no harm. He wasn't very funny, but he thought he was funny and people laughed at his crude jokes.

But crude jokes about Cornelius's father were not funny.

So he knocked poor Alf to the concrete.

Later Alf came and apologized to him. "Gosh, I'm sorry, Cornelius. I admit it was kind of tasteless, but I didn't mean any harm."

Most of the fathers in Beverly were doctors, lawyers, dentists, and commodity traders. Cornelius was certain that they and their children looked down on the son of a cop. Much later in life, when he had met real snobs, he realized that most of the snobbery in Beverly was in his head. And his mother's.

Alf always wanted to be friends with him, but unlike Blackie Ryan, he had no idea how to break through the walls Cornelius had built around himself.

"Don't do it again," Cornelius had replied gruffly, knowing in his heart that he was the one who should apologize.

Soon his classmates tired of him again. He was sullen, clumsy, shy, an overgrown and resentful bull in the cheerful china shop of the eighth-grade class.

Years later he would look back in embarrassment at that year. Kids that age, he realized, were often thoughtlessly cruel, but they meant much less by their cruelty than the words conveyed. His shyness and sensitivity got in the way of the subtle and not-so-subtle attempts of Blackie and Blackie's cousin Catherine Collins to make him part of the class.

Yet he was not prepared to forgive, even on later reflection. If he had not been poor by the parish standards, much would have been excused. He still hated the neighborhood.

At Carmel he started over with a clean slate. There were other sons of policemen at the school. He was a potential football player and the son of a Carmel grad. Surprisingly, he found it easy to make friends and was elected a freshman class officer.

Blackie, at St. Ignatius before he went to Quigley Seminary, was unimpressed. "You'd be a class officer at Ignatius, too."

Blackie had been subdued by his mother's death that summer but even in his quiet grief he was still dangerous.

And Cornelius shuddered at the thought that someday he would have to face the death of his own parents.

"The Beverly guys wouldn't vote for me."

"With a Ryan running your campaign, of course they would. Even Alf Lane, especially Alf Lane. He'd withdraw from the race and throw his votes to you."

In later years he would wonder about that, too. Unable to expel from his memory the pain of ridicule and embarrassment in seventh and eighth grade, he would recall incidents from that time in strange places—in Angola when Russian jets strafed the UNITA jungle camp he was visiting; in Colombia when he was held prisoner by a drug baron. He could never quite make peace with his childhood, nor with Blackie's suggestion that if he had listened to Ryan family wisdom he might not have had to go into exile.

As it was, the only classmate with whom he associated—besides Blackie, who didn't really count—was Jim Sullivan. Like Alf, Jim wanted to be friends, too. But unlike Alf, Jim needed a friend. A slim young man with brown hair, a freckled face, and an expression that always seemed worried, even haunted, Jim also attended St. Ignatius, but he was a loner, content to listen to classical records and study for college.

"You want to hear my new Haydn record?" he asked Neal shyly after Mass one Sunday when they were freshmen.

Neal did not care for music, Haydn or Bill Haley or Elvis or anyone else. But there was so much loneliness in Jim's sad eyes that he could not refuse him.

Cornelius was astonished at the intricate and fluid patterns of Haydn's stately elegance. He sat dumbly in his chair in the Sullivan basement after the record had stopped, staring at Jim's new hi-fi system.

"Cornelius . . ."

"Hnn?"

"Did you like it?"

"Hnn?"

"You're acting like you're hypnotized."

"Would you play it again?"

"Sure." Jim was delighted. "You really liked it?"

"Another world . . . graceful, confident, intelligent. . . ."

So he learned to like Haydn and eventually all classical music. He even attended concerts at Orchestra Hall with Jim and watched, from the second balcony, the wondrous Fritz Reiner at work.

"Why don't you ever smile when you listen to music?" he asked Jim one night when they were riding home from a concert on the Rock Island.

"I don't think I know how," Jim replied.

Neal was afraid to ask what that meant.

Jim also dragged him to the Art Institute, where Neal lost himself in the French Impressionists. Jim shook him out of his trance so they could eat lunch in the basement cafeteria.

"You really fall in love with beauty, don't you, Neal?" Jim observed over their ham and cheese on rye.

"I get lost in it," Neal admitted, still not completely free from the world of soft and gentle color in which he had wandered.

"Amazing, isn't it," Blackie Ryan observed when Neal described the experience to him later, "that the son of a patrolman can have artistic sensibilities?"

Neal was about to lose his temper. Then he realized that his leg was being pulled.

"You're saying I think too much about family background?" he asked sheepishly.

"No," said Blackie, his face imitating a wise old owl, "I'm saying you think too much about money."

Oh, yes, even then Blackie Ryan was dangerous.

At Carmel, Neal began to blossom. Father Gerald assured his mother that there was no danger of serious injury in high school football—something of an exaggeration if not an outright lie. His body, which had seemed so awkward and grotesque, quickly filled out and acquired strength and grace. To his astonishment he became a quick and powerful pass receiver—all-city in his junior and senior years and honorable mention all-state as a senior.

On the football field his world would sometimes go into auto-pilot and slow motion. He'd see the plays unfold like a diagram on the blackboard and know what was about to happen in the instant before it happened. Much later he would read an article by John Brodie, a quarterback for the 'Niners, which described the same phenomenon.

He learned to trust the instincts of those moments of "flow," without ever understanding what happened in them. A couple of times such interludes saved his life. Often in front of the camera he felt traces of the same phenomenon: somehow he knew exactly what was about to happen the instant it began to happen and hence was able to do or say exactly the right thing.

He was a class officer all four years and president of the Carmel graduation class of 1962. He worked on the school paper and edited the senior yearbook. He started to read Victorian novelists, mostly because of the enthusiasm of a young Carmelite teacher, and soon became an addicted reader. Later he would leave for his overseas assignments with a couple of paperback classics tucked in a trench-coat pocket.

In his junior year he began to attend the mixer dances at Aquinas and to date girls from that Dominican high school, cautiously and quietly refusing to become deeply involved with any of them. He was amazed—and a little frightened—to discover that young women found him attractive. Megan Keefe continued to be the only girl he had ever kissed. Or rather the only one who had ever kissed him.

Halfway through his senior year he was elected "outstanding senior"; for years he kept the front page of the *Sunday Tribune* neighborhood section with his picture and the announcement of that honor.

He had shown them at St. Prax's.

The parish responded by announcing with pride that three of its members had been elected outstanding seniors at their high schools—Neal O'Connor at Mount Carmel, Alfred Lane at St. Ignatius, and Megan Keefe at Mother Macauley.

(It was not deemed worthy of note that Blackie Ryan had the highest marks in his class at Quigley Seminary: that was taken for granted.)

It was impossible to show them anything. They merely took credit for your accomplishment.

His mother warned him about the dangers of getting a big head.

Megan called to congratulate him. Bashfully he accepted her good wishes and almost forgot to offer them to her in return.

Notre Dame didn't think he was fast enough for a wide receiver. Northwestern did. Anyway, he wanted to study journalism, and Northwestern was supposed to have one of the best journalism schools in the country.

Megan called again at the beginning of May to invite him to her prom.

"Don't you want to go with me?" she asked when he did not respond to her invitation.

"I'd love to, Megan," he said, astonished at his answer. "I guess I was kind of overwhelmed."

"I'm not the kind of girl who overwhelms boys, Cornelius, uh, Neal."

"You overwhelm me."

"That's very sweet," she said pertly.

Afterward he wondered how her parents and her brothers and sisters would react. But when he came to pick her up, only Mr. and Mrs. Keefe were in the house, which had been rebuilt after the fire. They were very friendly. They congratulated him on his football honors and his scholarship to Northwestern. They did not mention the fire, which the neighborhood seemed to pretend had never happened.

Could they really be nice people?

"You look very lovely," he said to her as they walked to the car Nick Curran (Catherine Collins's date) had borrowed.

Megan was wearing a simple blue gown with wide shoulder straps and a deep vee in the back, deceptively modest raiment which left no doubt that while her figure was slight, it was deftly sculpted, a subtly seductive little porcelain doll.

"Thank you, Neal." She smiled up at him. "You look sharp too in your blue formal. We kind of match."

"No one will notice me."

"They will too."

He opened the door to the '59 Chevy for her and assisted her into the back seat.

"Those Aquinas girls have done a good job with you," she said lightly.

"The truth is," he said as he entered the other side of the car, "that South Shore girls and Beverly girls are pretty much the same."

She laughed, a soft bell chiming in the distance. "You're probably right, but you'll spoil everyone's fun if you let the word get out."

Nick and Catherine were in the midst of one of the crises of their relationship, which would end the following summer when Catherine went off to become a nun (and later a missionary and a revolutionary and a torture victim in South America). So Neal and Megan had the back of the car to themselves. She was a puzzling girl—bright and competent but unaware of such contemporary books as Baldwin's *Another Country* or Faulkner's *The Reivers* or films like *Jules and Jim*. Nor did she seem interested in the prospects for the Ecumenical Council that Pope John had convened in Rome. Unlike the Aquinas girls, however, she listened to him with attention and apparent interest when he talked about such subjects, even promising to read *The Reivers* which she thought sounded "real cute."

Intelligence was for school work, it seemed, not for life.

She was as earnest and as intense as she had been in the spelling bees in grammar school, but she also could laugh quickly and smile easily—a gossamer, faintly impish smile that seemed to contradict her seriousness and made Neal's heart flip every time its airy radiance was turned on.

"So, what's your verdict, Neal O'Connor?" she asked him on the dance floor while the band played "Love Makes the World Go Round."

"On what?"

"On me, silly." She danced closer to him than any Aquinas girl had dared.

"Oh," he pretended to ponder the question, "on the whole, I'd say you're a perfectly satisfactory young woman."

She looked up at him. "Satisfactory?"

"Yeah . . . lemme see . . . you have wonderful gray eyes and a face like one of those El Greco paintings at the Art Institute."

"I'll have to visit the place and see whether that's a compliment," she said, watching him intently.

"Believe me, it is. And your smile breaks my heart and you have fine smooth skin. . . ." He moved his fingers lightly on her bare back. "Kind of like Irish linen, though that's probably a clichéd metaphor."

"No, it isn't." She continued to regard him with the utmost seriousness.

"And you fit nicely into my arms." He drew her closer still. "And you have a neat little ass and pretty, pretty breasts."

"Neal!" She buried her blushing face against his chest. "You shouldn't say things like that."

"I know I shouldn't, but I told you I was overwhelmed. And anyway, they're true and you like to hear them."

"Sure I do. I'm a human being." She peered up at him. "Truly?"
"Truly."

"Thank you." She pressed her body against his. "I'm glad you like me. . . . You always did disconcert me."

"My turn to say, 'truly?' "

"Even before you saved my life. When you were a big, dumb lug just moved in from another parish. I had a crush on you way back then and turned tongue-tied whenever you were around."

Was there an implication that she still had a crush on him?
Sure there was. That was exciting. And also scary.
"That made two of us."

"You've changed a lot but you still disconcert me."

"I'm sorry. No, I'm glad, to tell you the truth, Megan Keefe." He caressed her back again, with such slight movement that the couple dancing next to them would not notice. "I like you disconcerted."

She shivered at his touch, and the heart he felt beating beneath her ribs pounded fiercely.

"You HAVE changed," she murmured.

"For the worse?"

The music stopped and she backed away from him.

" 'Course not. . . . I liked you the way you used to be, too."

He would learn in the years to come that such was the Megan Keefe style—blunt, direct, candid. If he had been able to respond in the same fashion, their lives might have been very different.

The band started a slow and languid version of "Moon River." They began to dance again.

He was able to maintain the pose of the masterful prince to her disconcerted maiden until the next morning at Grand Beach when the kissing began. Then she was the experienced veteran and he the novice.

A novice eager to learn.

Neal did not drink. Megan admitted that she "drank a beer now and then," but if her date was not drinking, neither would she.

Her life, he learned, was governed by a catalog of such fierce and, on the whole, not unreasonable rules.

So when the drinking began, they wandered away from the crowd and, wearing slacks and sweat shirts, walked most of the way to New Buffalo.

She kissed him as they passed a stretch of wooded dunes on which no houses had been built. It was not a tentative exercise. Rather, she assailed his lips with fierce determination, what one would suspect from this fierce and determined porcelain doll.

He was shocked by the fury of her attack. Surprised and unprepared, he responded with instant violence, matching her fury with his own.

They wrestled each other to the ground and continued to kiss. He wondered if they would ever stop, thought they should stop, and then hoped they would never stop.

They finally did, however, as if by mutual consent.

"Wow," she gasped. "You really are an expert at this, too."

"First time, Megan."

"Truly?"

"Since a girl kissed me in eighth grade."

She touched his lips gently with her fingers. "You're such a sweet boy."

He felt like a sex-crazed ape, but if Megan Keefe said he was a sweet boy, then that's what he was.

They walked back to the party, hand in hand, and spent the rest of the day psychologically isolated from the others in their own little world of young love.

Just before they left to return to the neighborhood, he saw Megan huddled with Catherine Collins in an eager conversational buzz. Surely they were talking about him. He didn't mind. On the contrary, he enjoyed it.

5

Megan was more beautiful than ever.

Not as beautiful. More beautiful.

He had indeed poured the drops of water into Blackie Ryan's chalice, sensing that the congregation was holding its collective breath as he poured.

Out of the corner of his eye, he noted that Megan was smiling benignly, like a mother whose little boy had just discharged his most difficult obligation at his first acolyte assignment.

Then on the way back to his station next to her, he realized how beautiful she was.

Whence this new and extra beauty?

"The Lord be with you," the priest suggested.

"And also with you," the congregation insisted.

It was somehow in the line of her trim figure—a hint of passionate serenity. Megan knew that she could still be hurt but that she would survive.

"Lift up your hearts."

"We have lifted them up to the Lord."

Only yesterday she had been a seventeen-year-old girl, filled with hopes and expectations for life. Now her dreams had turned into harsh realities. Her children were the same age as she had been, half-formed and vulnerable. She would try to protect them from the worst effects of the traumatic death of their father. At best she would have limited success. But she would not quit.

"Let us give thanks to the Lord our God."

"It is right to give him thanks and praise."

Thanks for genetic tenacity. Somewhere in her past there must have been a woman who survived the famine and the trip across the Atlantic and the diphtheria epidemic, too.

A woman with tenacity like that—call it character—would be a glorious lover.

He loved her more than ever. Lusted for her and loved her, wanted her and worshiped her.

We will be very civilized after Mass is over, he thought, and pretend that the hormone-driven emotions that bound us once are now only a memory of the silly past.

But that's not true. They're as strong as ever.

1962

6

The Keefes were thought to be one of the parish's perfect families, touched by a magic wand of beauty and talent and charm.

The three boys were "darlings," if perhaps a little too short. The three older girls, with their long blond hair and quick laughter, were strikingly attractive, if a bit too full-bodied for everyone's taste. And Megan, the last of them, was an "adorable little tyke."

They owned a big house on Hoyne and a sprawling summer home at Grand Beach. They belonged to both Beverly and South Shore. The women all wore mink coats, the men were spectacularly good golfers. Their homes were centers for laughter and fun, for parties and songfests.

They went to Notre Dame and St. Mary's (except for Megan); got into only small scrapes with school authorities and the law, dated and then married young men and women as attractive and as promising as they themselves.

Everyone said that the parents had done a wonderful job raising their brood. The Keefes were living proof that not all large families in the neighborhood had to be as crazy as the Ryans.

"The difference between us and them," Blackie had observed complacently one summer, "is that they're always making comparisons in their heads with us and we poor Ryans are too naive to compare ourselves with anyone."

It was an accurate assessment, like all of Blackie's owlish pronouncements. It also broke the neighborhood's unwritten code against such insights.

"Naive?" Neal had chuckled at the word.

"My late mother, God be good to her, often said that it's a shame that no one in that family ever relaxes."

"If your grandfather had been a saloon keeper and your father a Mob lawyer, maybe the Ryans wouldn't relax, either."

"The difference"—he raised a shrewd little eyebrow—"is that we would proclaim it, not run from it."

Later in life Neal would realize that the Keefes lived in an environment in which they imagined they could just barely hear the murmurs against their respectability. Oddly enough there were no such murmurs. Few families in the neighborhood were without skeletons in their closets. Few could not be accused of putting on airs. The Keefe family's obsessive quest for respectability was a doomed search for a will-o'-the-wisp not because they could never achieve it but because, as far as was possible in the neighborhood in those days, they had long since attained it.

"My mother is afraid that people will say, 'Did you see that Mob lawyer's daughter necking with that darling O'Connor boy last night?' "

Megan set her words to action and kissed him solidly and happily.

"And what will they really say?"

"Same words they always use: 'that cute little Keefe tyke.' "

"They might say," he whispered as he enveloped her in a bear hug, " 'that seductive little imp'!"

She sputtered as he covered her lips, but did not try to escape.

The demons set loose in the Keefe clan when they were kids were the creation of fears of ghosts that did not exist.

While Neal envied their boisterous, frantic family life, he also felt sorry for them. Even in those days he was aware of the ghosts that pursued all of them, even Megan. Ghosts become real if you think they're real.

But Megan was less haunted than the others. Or so he thought. Or perhaps so he hoped.

"I'm not as bad as the rest of them, am I, Neal?"

"I think your family is wonderful."

She might pretend to be critical of the rest of her clan, but she was as loyal as any of them—even to crazy obsessions, which seemed to be part of the glue that bonded them. That summer, for example, the Keefes were compelled to attack President Kennedy's wife on every possible occasion and to every audience that would listen.

It was a ritual they celebrated, it seemed to him—every day. Other participants were not constrained to agree, only to listen until the ritual was finished.

Their objection was to Jacqueline Kennedy's choice of clothes, a matter which for the Keefe women became an issue of high morality.

They were, Neal decided, just a little crazy. Fun, but slightly daft. Megan, however, was the only one who mattered and she was different.

Never once did a word against the President's wife cross her tightly compressed lips.

Although Neal realized even then that he and Megan were being swept away by first love, he did not discuss love during their summer romance. They kissed and caressed, talked and laughed, swam and danced and luxuriated in one another. The future—his at Northwestern, hers at Newton College of the Sacred Heart, near Boston College—would come in September, but while summer lasted, they would celebrate every moment of it.

Newton was a great victory for Megan, won after a family battle during which her three sisters refused to talk to her for six weeks. She had been accused of "putting on airs" and acting "like you're someone special," and of being a "spoiled little brat."

Her parents finally ruled in her favor, but Bea, the oldest of her sisters, still disapproved. "Everyone is saying, 'Who does that spoiled little brat think she is?' "

To the extent that anyone noticed Megan's fall from the virtuous path of St. Mary's of Notre Dame, their reaction was to admire her gumption.

He worked his park district lawn-cutting job just as his mother worked as an assistant bailiff at the County Court and his father drove the squad car—loyal, responsible adjuncts to the Daley organization, which in the early 1960s was only beginning to develop its great power. His weekends he spent at someone's house at Grand Beach, usually Blackie's. His mother frowned at each late-Friday-afternoon departure.

"Can't spend any time with his family anymore."

"You only graduate from high school once." His father offered a rare opinion. "Let him enjoy it."

"I suppose I have no choice but to aid and abet Megan's wanton pursuit of you," Blackie observed.

"She's not wanton," he replied hotly.

"The word," the seminarian said with a sigh, "is not meant to be critical."

"And she's not pursuing me."

"And John Kennedy is Polish."

Megan did read *The Reivers*. "It's fun," she said, "but I can't understand what they're saying all the time. What is Faulkner trying to do?"

A question of the sort which was thought to be perceptive in an English class at a Catholic girls' high school.

He tried to answer it.

"Interesting, interesting. . . . Faulkner is important, isn't he?"

"Nobel Prize."

"I suppose I should read more of him, if you'll help me. What would you recommend?"

He hesitated and took a big chance. *"Sanctuary."*

Fortunately for him, perhaps, she did not begin the book that summer.

To everyone's surprise, Megan was the first girl at Grand Beach to wear a bikini, blue with white trim and modest by later standards but shocking to the mores of the South Side Irish at the time.

She had casually tossed aside her beach robe on a Sunday morning and strolled nonchalantly toward the water.

"Hey!"

She was a demure little girl, with a woman's subtle curves, flat belly, delicate breasts, and deft hips offered as a beguiling surprise. Her pale, thin body, embraced by the two strips of blue, looked like thick cream, inviting your lips to taste its richness.

"Hey, what?" She paused and turned to him, face utterly expressionless.

"Hey, that's a bikini."

"You noticed."

"You bet I did." He caught up to her. "What do your mother and sisters think?"

"They haven't seen it and I'm sure they won't like it."

"I think you look great."

"Thank you." She inclined her head. "I hoped you would."

The implication was that she had bought the scanty garment to please him, was it not?

"Really great."

"Is that all you can say?" She held her hands behind her back.

"You know that I think you're gorgeous."

"Someone who knows as much about women as you seem to should realize that a woman can't be complimented enough."

Impulsively he seized her tiny naked waist, lifted her from the ground, and held her aloft over his head like a battle trophy.

She did not cry in surprise or protest but threw her head back in sinuous exultation. "Neal!"

"Megan!" he shouted.

He returned her to the sand quickly. It was fun, but even so slender a young woman as Megan was heavy, even in the grip of a young man as strong as Neal.

"I think"—she breathed deeply—"we both better dive in the water right now."

"It's pretty cold, I think."

"Probably not cold enough."

Her parents and her sisters did not like the swimsuit, but they had learned not to try to change Megan's mind once it was made up. (They really didn't like Neal that much, either, as he had begun to sense about the same time as she appeared in the bikini.) Within the week she was imitated by at least a dozen young women, and by a couple of svelte matrons the following week.

"You're certainly responsible for notably improving the scenery here this summer," he said as he critically evaluated one such matron who sauntered by the Ryan beach.

"You ought not to stare at her that way."

"Why not? She's for staring at, isn't she? Designed by God to be stared at."

"And you stare at all of Blackie's sisters, too."

"You bet."

"Ape." She rapped his knuckles lightly.

"But not as much as I stare at you."

"Better not."

Then she continued her catechism.

"When you look at a woman like her dressed that way"—she tilted her head, politician-style, at the woman walking down the beach—"do you imagine taking her clothes off?"

"That's a terrible question."

"I want to understand how boys' imaginations work."

"Well." He squirmed uncomfortably. "Sure I do. I mean, isn't that how the human race keeps going? She really is quite striking, like I said, designed by God to be admired. I wouldn't dream of hurting her or anything like that. If God didn't want men to imagine such women naked, he wouldn't have made us the way he did. Anyway, that's what our retreat master said last year."

She nodded, understanding what was being said if not altogether approving of it.

"And the Ryan girls?"

"That's different. They're sisters of my friend. The rules even in my head are different. They sure are pretty, though."

"And me?"

"You don't let up, do you, Megan Keefe?"

"No."

"Well, you're a kind of combination of both. I respect you. I'd never hurt you. But I have the most wonderful dreams, day as well as night, about taking off your clothes."

She gulped and nodded again. "I see. Well, I hope you enjoy the dreams."

Now what did that mean?

"I don't suppose girls react the same way."

She grinned wickedly, an expression he'd seen only once or twice before.

"Don't be so sure, Neal O'Connor. . . . Anyway, I hope I'm as attractive as she is when I'm that age. I think I'd kind of like to have young apes ogle me as I strut down the beach."

"You'll always be gorgeous, Megan," he said fervently. "You'll be able to wear the same bikini when you're forty."

"Time will tell, won't it? Come on, let's swim. It'll take your mind off THAT woman."

Although her parents and sisters—and brothers too, insofar as they were sober enough to notice—did not like the long days the two of them spent with each other on the beach, her family had fifteen years of experience with summer romances and decided—from its point of view, wisely—to bide its time.

He also realized that the control the Keefe family exerted on its members was indirect rather than direct. They ran each other's lives by laughter, good times, and subtle ridicule, not by orders and temper tantrums, although there was always the hint of the latter as a possibility lurking in the background.

Unlike the Ryans, whose sprawling family was open to and welcomed wanderers, lost sheep, strays, and anyone else who might happen to walk by their section of the beach, the Keefes were a closed corporation. Only marriage or serious dating admitted you to their boisterous and lively dinners, family parties and songfests, and ritual celebrations. Somehow Neal seemed to measure up as a serious date. As far as he could sense, there was no special hostility to him. Apparently he was acceptable—for the moment.

"Hey, Neal," Pete would yell, "have another beer."

"Thanks, but I don't drink."

"Really? Hey that's a hot one! Bea, did you hear that? Neal doesn't drink."

"He'll learn if he hangs around with us very long, won't he, Megan? You do sing, don't you?"

"A little."

"Sing something for us."

"What?"

"Something Irish, you know."

He glanced at Megan. Unsmiling now, she nodded her approval.

He sang a song by Percy French which the Mount Carmel choir had sung at their concert—"Come Back, Paddy Reilly." It was the kind of tune that everyone could join in after the first stanza. But the Keefes didn't know it and hence didn't like it.

They also didn't like the fact that he sang better than any of them.

"Too fancy for this family." Linda waved a beer can. "Come on, Pete, do 'Irish Eyes Are Smiling' again."

Megan watched him with expressionless eyes, neither approving or disapproving of his vocal abilities.

She never mentioned the incident afterward. Nor was he ever commanded to sing again.

A potential husband or a wife would have a hard time fighting the Keefes.

Neither of them spoke about the end of summer and the beginning of college. Despite the intensity of their physical affection, there was too much caution on either side to plan beyond Labor Day, much less for life.

Later he would wonder if both of them did not, deep down in their souls, already presume permanence—perhaps Megan more than he.

One fiercely humid night in August, wearing only swimsuits and T-shirts, they walked, hand in hand as always, to their favorite isolated patch of wooded beach and settled down to a long session of affection. He kissed her more violently than ever before, not merely her eager lips, but all of her body—well, almost all of it; critical places through the fabric of her bikini. She sighed and moaned but did not resist him.

Megan never tried to fight him off. "If you trust a man enough to let him kiss you, you should really trust him," she explained.

"So long as he's the right man."

"I wouldn't trust him otherwise."

Somehow they always knew when to stop.

Later he would wonder whether he could have made love to her that summer. He concluded that he could not. Still later he decided that she would not have resisted.

Should he have made love to her? He asked often, especially when he was in tight spots and dangerous places.

There was no easy answer to that. Certainly both their lives would have been very different. . . .

When they were finished that night, he lifted her again to the heavens, breasts and face and belly skyward against the moonlight, a sacred offering to the goddesses of love. They both cried out for the joy of their love and their pleasure.

Soon it was over.

Though not yet completely over.

1987

7

"The peace of Christ be with you, Neal Connor." Megan shook his hand and smiled. Same smile and same weak feeling in his legs when it absorbed him.

"And with you, too, Megan Lane," he said tentatively. "Is that right?"

The memories of all the affection they shared rushed through his mind, like a videotape on fast forward. Desire stung him again.

She nodded and turned to Nick Curran. "Peace, Nick."

"Lots of it, Megan." Nick kissed her.

Neal looked around. Was he supposed to find someone with whom to continue this rather odd practice, doubtless adopted when he was not around to vote?

Then he had an idea.

"Peace, Monsignor Ryan." He shook the little cleric's pudgy fist.

"Shalom." Blackie's pale blue eyes twinkled impishly. "And amen, too."

Whatever the hell that meant.

At Communion time, the priest stationed himself in front of the altar. Catherine Curran stood on his left hand. Megan moved toward his right hand. Neal touched her arm.

"I haven't received Communion in twenty years," he whispered.

"I'm sure God won't mind."

"I'm not sure about His Nibs' orthodoxy." He nodded at the

priest. "They must have lowered the standards for the purple, but if a pillar of orthodoxy like you—"

"We don't give absolution yet," she whispered back crisply. "But I'm sure it's all right."

So he accepted the host from Blackie's hand. "The body of Christ, Cornelius."

Were winks permitted these days?

And the chalice from the hand of his first love. "The blood of Christ, Neal."

Were there tears in her eyes or did he imagine them?

He dared not look at them for more than an instant.

Surely there was pain in them. How much did she miss Alf? A lot, probably. Maybe she had never loved him intensely, the only way Megan knew how to love. But she must have grown to be fond of him. Al was a hard man to dislike. They shared four children, experiences of conception, birth, growing up. How could she not miss him, perhaps terribly?

"If this isn't OK," he murmured mentally to a God whose existence he deemed problematic, as he sipped from the chalice, "it's not my fault."

After Communion Lisa led them in a hymn called "Lord of the Dance": lyrics he had never heard before, set to the tune of the Shaker hymn "Simple Gifts."

What, he wondered, would the Shakers think if they knew that the Papists had usurped their music?

He hummed the verses and joined in the chorus, which was easy enough to remember:

> *Dance then,*
> *Wherever you may be*
> *I am the Lord*
> *Of the Dance, said he*
> *I'll lead you all,*
> *Wherever you may be*
> *I'll lead you all*
> *In the dance, said he*

Next to him, Megan's voice, clear and delicate, flowed together with his.

Damn every shanty Irish biddy matchmaker in the group, not

excluding the Monsignor, who was combining the two of them into a couple.

"Isn't it nice to see them together again!"

He decided that he would have to leave the church right after Mass, uh, Eucharist, and return to the Channel 3 studio on the banks of the Chicago River.

They belted the last stanza with special vigor:

> *They cut me down*
> *And I leap up high*
> *I am the life*
> *That'll never, never die*
> *I live in you*
> *If you live in me*
> *I am the Lord*
> *Of the Dance, said he.*

God knows, that's Catholic enough.

What if it's true?

He considered his aging classmates. They didn't look like dancers or honeymoon couples. Well, in a way, some of them did.

"We have an Irish-American blessing for faith in times of darkness to end this phase of the celebration," the priest said, glancing at his watch, "only two minutes later than the good Megan's absolute deadline:

> *May the God of heaven's vault bless you*
> *May the God of shimmering moonlight love you*
> *May the God of sparkling stars lead you*
> *May the God of haunting songs cheer you*
> *May the God of strange shadows calm your nerves*
> *May the God of straight roads bring you home*
> *May God be watching from a familiar window*
> *And hand in hand with Him may you wait for dawn."*

Not bad poetry, Neal decided. Blackie the poet was all the more dangerous.

"Go in peace, the Mass is ended," the little priest announced with obvious relief.

Mass, not Eucharist? A guy could spend the rest of his life learning the new rules.

"Thanks be to God," they responded, and burst into applause again.

Now's the time to run.

"Neal, it's so wonderful of you to have come." Megan clasped his hand warmly. "We really didn't expect you'd have time. You look even more handsome in person than you do on the screen."

"Uh, well, they sent me here to cover the funeral, and the election of the new mayor. I never did catch up with the invitation. Lisa told me about it at O'Hare."

Which she knew already.

"I'm sure"—she smiled again—"we can find room for you. I'm not quite as obsessive as the Monsignor would make me seem."

Then deftly she turned to someone else, the skilled precinct captain working the crowd.

He found himself shaking hands with Nick Curran, unchanged in twenty years, save perhaps for a little less hair on the top of his head.

"You look great, Neal." Nick grinned wickedly. "What do you guys have on Judge Kennedy?"

"To 'de-Bork' him, you mean? Some kids saw him jaywalking ten years ago. Do you want that kind of man on the highest court in the land?"

"Only if he were a Democrat."

"Sounds like a Chicago response."

Others came by to greet him enthusiastically, as if they had last seen him only yesterday or the day before and not twenty years ago.

But, of course, they had seen him if not yesterday or the day before, certainly last week. They all had TVs, so he was in the house of many of them every night. They could say to their kids, not without some pride, "We went to school together."

They were strangers and he was not.

"Seriously," he said to Nick, "I find this new moralism among my colleagues obnoxious and a little frightening."

"And me with a wife who was a public Marxist."

"She looks great, Nick." He patted the lawyer on his shoulder.

"A real survivor, incredible resilience."

"You have how many kids?"

"Three—Nicole, who is a freshman at St. Ignatius; Jackie, in sixth grade; and Liam, who is four."

So proud of the kids. More than I have to be proud of. Now or ever.

"How bad are things with herself?" Neal tilted his head towards Megan, who was working her way smoothly through the crowd.

"She's hurting, Neal." Nick's gentle face deepened into a painful frown. "The cool, competent pose is partly true—that's the way Megan is—but it's partly a cover. They may not have had the greatest of marriages, but it had lasted twenty years and suddenly he's gone. She hasn't figured out how to grieve yet. Or maybe as Mary Kate Murphy, Blackie's shrink sister, says—whether to grieve."

"Financial problems?"

They walked through the sacristy door to the parking lot, now covered by a moist night sky.

"If she doesn't find a buyer for the house this week, his clients will take it over and sell it. She doesn't have a penny—nothing."

"No one to help?"

"The whole Ryan clan"— he shrugged his shoulders—"is poised, as usual, like a pack of benign vultures, ready to pounce, console, protect, and heal. But it's difficult to intrude, and Megan doesn't know how to ask for or accept help. She's looking for a job as a typist—"

"My God!"

"And Tommy Dineen is her lawyer—"

"Tommy the Clown!"

"Yeah, Tommy the Clown. He was Alfie's lawyer—two of a kind—and he kind of moved in on the widow. His wife walked out on him last summer, finally, and some of the women of the parish think he has designs. But you know how the women of the parish are."

"I'd forgotten. . . . Is Tommy still a pig?"

"And worse still, a dumb lawyer. Her home is worth four fifty, maybe five hundred thousand—if she could wait for a buyer with that kind of money. But the clients want the money now, three hundred thousand. If she can't sell it next week, they put it on the market at that price and collect their money right away. A good lawyer could stop that. Tommy himself is talking about buying it for maybe three fifty, so Megan will have money for the kids' tuitions."

"And he gets her as a bonus?"

"Something like that. You may imagine my wife and her relatives on the subject, especially since their virtue and loyalty are frustrated."

"And himself?"

"Blackie? God knows, maybe, what he's up to."

"Dangerous man."

"So you always said."

They had walked outside the church and were leaning against a Corvette, probably Catherine's.

"Is it true about the insurance?"

"I think Tommy could probably get something from them, if he pushed hard, but suicide is a distinct possibility. If you asked me, I'd say that he did have too much to drink and didn't care much about staying alive."

"Blackie hinted at something more."

Nick jammed his hands into his trench-coat pocket.

"FBI is interested. A lot of money has disappeared, some to politicians, some to drug families from Colombia. Alfie turned kinky toward the end. Murder? Maybe. Anyway, there's a rumor that there's a subpoena waiting for Megan."

"And then?"

"We can't help unless she gives us a chance."

Catherine Collins, a tall, elegant woman, slender as Megan, with curly brown hair touched with gray, joined them.

"Neal! Just back in the city and already talking with my husband"—she kissed him—"like an old-time political lawyer. You are coming over to the dinner at the Evergreen, aren't you?"

"I sure am."

"You've done so much with your life." Her voice was calm, objective. "And I've pretty much wasted mine."

"You were never fair to yourself, Megan." He touched her hand. "You have four wonderful kids . . . Margaret, Mark, Teri, and Joseph."

"Blackie gave you the reunion book early." She smiled briefly. "And how would you know that they were wonderful?"

"Notre Dame, Marquette, St. Ignatius, and St. Prax's," he counted them off on his fingers.

His ravenous desire for the woman next to him—naturally it had been arranged for them to be dinner companions—was like a rampaging forest fire.

Drag her into your car, take her to your hotel room, tear off her clothes— Shut up, you miserable bastard. She's just lost her husband. You're no better than Tommy Dineen.

"But you don't know whether they're wonderful or not," she persisted with her firm, literal respect for truth, her chin resting on a delectable little fist.

The program booklet had also listed her interests and accomplishments—parish societies, school mothers' clubs, alumnae organizations. And one saving membership in the Lyric Opera.

"You're their mother, they must be wonderful."

She blushed at his compliment. "Still disconcerting me after all these years. . . . I *do* think they're pretty wonderful, but I'm their mother, so I might be deceiving myself. Still, each of them is a lot better than I was at their age."

"If that's true, Margaret must really be something else."

Blackie Ryan ambled back to his table, through some miracle bearing three unspilled glasses of Diet Coke.

"A discreet preparation for the holiday season," he murmured arranging the three glasses on the table. "Neal, if one is to believe *People*, eschews the Creature."

The three of them were at the same table with the Currans and Lisa and her husband, George, all of whom were table-hopping. "Table for celebrities," Blackie had sniffed, "and papal broom sweepers."

The dining room of the Evergreen restaurant, part of a golf course that lurked, enviously perhaps, on the south fringe of the country club, had been since time immemorial the scene of most St. Prax reunions—on the borders of the parish and sufficiently reasonable in its prices as not to strain the budgets of the smaller-income members of the class. With a low ceiling, veneer-panel walls, and slightly unstable furniture, it was a fitting companion to the lower-middle-class bar which it adjoined. The Savoy or the Georges Cinq it was not. But the food was good.

His classmates, as might be expected, were professionals—lawyers, doctors, dentists, judges, accountants, teachers. Many of the women had jobs or careers of their own. A quarter of the class still lived in St. Prax's, a remarkable statistic and a tribute to the holding power of the neighborhood.

He had studied the room quickly after Blackie and Lisa and her husband, George (a computer whiz and president of her production company), had guided him to his place. Lower-middle-class surroundings, professional-class careers, lives doubtless a mixed bag. Many overweight and many of the men bald, but some men and women trim and handsome. He didn't want to trade places with any of them. But his reaction was different than it would have been five years before, had he come to the twenty-fifth reunion: he now had no illusion that his world was any more real than theirs or that his life was any happier than theirs.

He had glanced quickly through the book, searching for Jim Sullivan's entry. But he must have missed it. Clearly Jim had not flown from Los Angeles for the celebration.

Neal Connor, IBC News, was a folk hero among his classmates, even more so than Lisa Malone, who had returned to the neighborhood often.

"How's the book on Afghanistan coming?" he was asked repeatedly.

He knew nothing of them, and they knew all about him. Doubtless they had long since forgotten he had been a pariah in his years at St. Prax's.

Each time his book was mentioned, he tried to explain how hard it was to write the book because of the Vietnam parallels. "Russian wives and mothers mourn the death of a soldier as much as do American wives and mothers."

Once he said that within Megan's hearing. She turned and considered him dispassionately. "Even celebrity journalists have midlife crises?"

"Especially."

She dipped her head in the familiar quick nod of agreement and understanding.

"You're not married, Neal?" Catherine Curran began the examination almost as soon as they were seated at the table.

"Not really. I did have a wife for a couple of years back in the early seventies. I met her when I was based in New York. She was a graduate student at Columbia. Still is, I guess, probably always will be."

"Oh."

Helen would only finish her dissertation when she was able to find answers to all outstanding human problems from abortion to Zoroaster in the philosophy of Baruch Spinoza.

"She leave you?"

"I don't know how to answer that. I came home from Cambodia and she was gone. The note said that my career was a barrier to her self-respect and her own work."

Helen was attractive and sexy and a slob and, finally, quite daft in a not altogether harmless way.

"Were you married in church?"

"It's a good thing you don't work for Rich Daley in the State Attorney's office, Cathy. But, to answer your question, no, we weren't married in church. Helen didn't believe in churches."

"A position for which much may be said." Blackie had peered up from his first Diet Coke, chosen instead of the "usual Jameson's," which he had declined on the grounds that he was driving back to the cathedral.

"And the lovely Kelly MacGregor?" Megan had raised a slightly supercilious eyebrow.

"She's Catholic, Scotch Catholic from Nova Scotia. We kind of planned on a Catholic wedding. St. Paddy's and the whole thing. Maybe have the Cardinal do it. If it was a chance to appear on TV, he wouldn't miss it."

"When will it be?" Nick Curran, doubtless on some secret signal from his wife, had asked that question.

It was all being set up. He had become the designated hitter to save Megan. He would not accept the role, save for a few hours on this Friday evening. His firestorm of lust for the woman mixed with sympathy for her loss and pain. But he was not the healing medicine she needed. And vice versa.

"We called it off when Kelly was assigned to London. Well, to be honest, she called it off."

"Why?" All three women at the table had asked the question in unison.

"Reminds me of a scene from *Macbeth*," Blackie said in a stage whisper. "Boil, boil—"

"Hush." His cousin Catherine rapped his fingers.

"I'm not perfectly sure of the reason. Maybe I was too old for her. She said that her career was more important than marriage."

"You wouldn't go to London with her?" Megan demanded.

So you are a bit of a feminist, too?

"Sure I would. In my work it doesn't matter where my base is. She didn't want me to."

"Ah, but these matters have a way of rearranging themselves eventually. . . ." Blackie looked up from his roast beef and peered over the rims of his glasses.

"She has another boyfriend already. A news reader, as they call them over there, on Thames TV."

The sigh of relief around the table was almost audible.

Then the two married couples left to table-hop and Blackie scurried away to find more Diet Cokes.

They did not have to be so obvious about it.

"I did care for him, Neal." Megan hugged herself as if to keep out the cold. "I miss him terribly. I feel so sorry for all he suffered. I . . . I'm afraid I never was much help to him."

Guilt, too. In addition to everything else.

"I didn't know, Megan, until just before Mass, uh, the Eucharist. Blackie told me. You have all the sympathy I could possibly offer. It's very brave of you even to come out for a night like this."

"Thank you, Neal." She touched his hand and then quickly withdrew it. "It helps to keep busy. He wasn't a bad man at all."

Does she want me as much as I want her? Has she always loved me? Does she still love me?

The implications of those questions made Neal Connor's head spin and his stomach turn.

No. No. No.

Then she quizzed him systematically about his professional life for the last two decades, bringing herself up to date on his career, about which she seemed to know a great deal already.

"It was an exciting couple of decades, wasn't it, Neal? Arizona, then Vietnam, then the world. And you did it all really before the first decade was over." She turned her head on the swivel of her closed fist, considering him objectively. "An impressive achievement."

She's read all the articles, my two books, and probably watches me every night on the tube. Oh my God! I never should have come here.

"If you take TV journalism seriously."

"You don't?"

"Not really, not anymore."

She pondered this information silently. "Not happy?"

"I've done everything I wanted in life, Megan, and long before I thought I would. The dream has come true too soon, I guess."

"Not happy at all." It was a statement not a question.

He turned his gaze away from the affectionate sympathy in those limpid gray eyes.

"I've proved that a cop's son can be a network reporter, big deal." He was shocked by how bitter he sounded. He glanced back at the gray eyes and melted. Megan, I want you.

"What now?" she asked softly.

"I'll probably get over it and keep on doing what I've always done."

"What would make you happy?"

A deadly question if there ever was one.

Her face had changed in twenty years. It was thinner, her smooth skin more transparent over her elegant facial bones, a carved marble bust of a wise and kind little Greek goddess who had experienced life's pains and understood them.

I only want to touch her cheek and caress her determined little chin. That's all, nothing more.

"I don't know, Megan. I really don't know."

I want you so badly I can taste you.

"Love in your life?"

"Not really." He turned away again from her absorbing eyes. "I guess I'm not impetuous enough, not recklessly passionate enough."

Words of his New York shrink.

"I don't believe that."

Which was what his self-pity wanted her to say.

They were silent for a few moments, each with their own pain. I've got to get out of here, he thought, before I make a total jackass out of myself.

"Would you do me a big favor, Neal?" she asked, hugging herself again, a gesture which made her seem all the more vulnerable and all the more appealing.

"If I can."

"Tommy Dineen . . . my lawyer—you remember him, I'm sure—is supposed to pick me up here before the dancing starts, but he has meetings today about the election of a new mayor. And may be late. If he isn't here when the dancing starts, will you take me home? Teri and Mark have the car."

"I'll be glad to."

The car. Only one. And what kind of would-be lover was Tommy Dineen? Strand the poor widow at a painful party? You'd only do that if you were a pig—which Tommy was—and a pretty confident pig at that.

Where were her brothers and sisters? Had she been excommunicated from the family? She had married Al as they had wanted her to, had she not? Might they have been offended by her Lyric Opera activity? The Keefes were capable of it. Who do you think you are, messing around with those hoity-toity people from the North Shore?

People that might remember that your father was a lawyer who was owned, body and soul, by the Mob.

Then she had spoken briefly about her wasted life, and Blackie had wandered back to the table.

"The point to be remembered about papal conclaves, Neal," he talked as if he were continuing a lecture, "is that they were not always run the way the two were that you covered with such admirable skill ten years ago. Thus for several hundred years around the turn of the millennium, the parish priests of Rome would meet in St. Peter's, select one of their number to become Bishop of Rome, and then bring him out on the balcony, not for admiration as is presently the case, but for approbation. If the crowd cheered, he was enthroned. If they booed, the electors returned to try again. On the whole, one thinks that it might not have been a completely unsatisfactory process."

"I hope you're taking notes," Cathy said as she and Nick returned to the table. "There'll be a test tomorrow morning."

"For credit," Nick added.

Blackie seemed surprised. "The issue is the similarity between what goes on in Rome and what is taking place in our fair city today."

"Catherine"—Megan seemed uninterested in Blackie's lecture—"do you think it time for me to do my little talk?"

"I guess so. Get it over with."

"What about you, Neal? Would you say something for us?"

"I don't have anything special to say—"

"The good Neal knows well"—Blackie peered over his glasses

again—"that for the communicator not to communicate would be offensive. It might even be thought," he said with a sigh, as if lamenting the evil thoughts of the whole human race, "that he speaks only for a fat stipend."

"My agent has answered for me, Megan." Neal threw up his hands. "Sure, I'll tell a couple of my dumb stories."

"Thank you," she said formally and rose from the chair with the quick grace of a sixth-grade girl who has been called to S'ter's desk.

She stood by the microphone, next to the low stage on which a band was arranging itself, head bowed, arms folded across her breasts and waited for the crowd's attention. In a few moments she got it.

Presence, he thought. She's got it. And I'm supposed to be the communicator. He made a mental note to say that during his own remarks.

When they had arrived at the Evergreen, she seemed to be in charge of greeting all the guests. Neal had noted carefully the pleased smile on the face of each person to whom Megan spoke.

"Was she always that good a precinct captain?" he had whispered to Monsignor Ryan.

"If the women of the Irish race ever decide to replace their husbands in the political arena," Blackie had whispered back, "we all of us will be undone."

The little priest still answered not the question you asked but the next one you were going to ask.

Megan adjusted the microphone to her height.

"I want to officially welcome you"—she smiled lightly—"and thank Lisa and Catherine and Mary Jane for their help on the committee to plan this event. It was an easy task for me with such helpers and such talent in the class. We have already heard from the Rector of the cathedral and will doubtless hear from him again unless he is gagged, a highly unlikely event," she said, mimicking Blackie's tone. Laughter from the group.

"Lisa will lead us in singing songs from our junior high and high school years, songs which one might suspect will be in her next album, *Lisa's Class Reunion*."

More laughter. You know, you're good enough that I could actually get you a job in the industry on your own merits, and not just as my woman.

"I would imagine that Catherine is making mental sketches for more paintings, a prospect which will scare the life out of her women classmates. We admire her work, you understand, but we don't want actually to take off our clothes for one of her nude paintings."

Yet more laughter.

And she's doing it with a heart that's at least partially broken. Class act.

"One of our surprise guests has cheated Lisa and George of the prize for coming from the greatest distance. Los Angeles's Beverly may be in another world, but it's a lot closer than Islamabad.

"So we have, as you have doubtless noted, fresh from the Hindu Kush and complete with iron gray pompadour, tailor-made blue shirt, lightly tanned face, sparkling blue eyes, coordinated to match his shirt, and five-hundred-dollar trench coat, our class's own Great Communicator. We will let him talk because he swears that he is still a Democrat!"

"Six hundred and twenty-five," Neal said, after her laugh had ended.

"I stand corrected." With equally skillful timing, she waited for the laughter to die down. "It costs big money to maintain a celebrity image these days. We won't ask how much Lisa's trench coat costs. But seriously, Neal, we're all proud of you. Whenever we see you on television, we remember the big, shy, cute ape of thirty years ago, tell ourselves that he's come a long way, and add that no one ever doubted it."

So he gave part of one of his canned talks, mostly the joke part. He complimented Megan on her "presence" and rejoiced that she was not working for another network.

He wondered after he had said it whether that was too blatant a compliment, perhaps a hint at sexual invitation.

The laughter of the group and Megan's becoming flush suggested that his remark was interpreted as harmless.

Perhaps more harmless than it really was.

When he returned to his seat between Cathy and Megan, the words "Los Angeles" stuck in his head.

"Doesn't Jim Sullivan live in Los Angeles?" he asked.

Everyone's face froze.

"Jim Sullivan is dead," George Quinn whispered softly.

"He killed himself," Megan added. "With a gun. Last summer."

1964

Megan's father died in the summer of 1964, the night the Republicans nominated Barry Goldwater for the presidency.

"He would have voted for him," Al Lane insisted. "Democrat or not, old man Keefe was to the right of Ivan the Terrible."

"Alfred," Jim Sullivan protested gently, "that's a terrible thing to say."

Neal felt no great affection for Jerry Keefe, but for all his faults, Megan's father was the only one in the family, besides Megan, who had any sense of the world beyond the limits of the family. He was their ambassador to reality.

"It's true. The whole family is a waste. Except maybe Megan. And they'll ruin her too if you give them half a chance."

"If who gives them half a chance?" Neal demanded.

"Figure of speech." Al waved his hand. "But she does have the hots for you."

"They're certainly a tight-knit and affectionate family," Jim murmured.

"Like the patients in a nuthouse." Alf pounded a table. "Don't they live in their own crazy world, Neal? You've had enough experience with them to know that."

Out of respect for Megan, Neal chose his words carefully. "They enjoy one another and have a lot of fun together. I'd say they're self-sufficient, like a lot of large families."

His roommates' reactions to the news of Jerry Keefe's death had been characteristic: Jim, quiet, gentle, dreamy; Al loud, vulgar, irreverent.

Neal was often the reasonable, sensible arbiter between them.

Since they were the only three members of St. Prax's who had migrated up the Lake Shore to Evanston and Northwestern, it seemed natural, despite all their differences in personality, that they would share a tiny apartment and each other's lives and loves. Not that in either Jim's or Neal's life there was that much love.

Al boasted that he made up for them.

Neal was second-string wide-out for the Wildcats, and Al second-string quarterback. Under the skilled coaching of Alex Agasee, NU was still fielding presentable teams. Both St. Prax alumni figured to start as juniors and perhaps play on a team that might break even. They were an impressive pair on the field of Dyche Stadium, a passer and a receiver who were best friends off the field as well as on and who understood each other's moves perfectly. Even when his sense of the "flow" of the game was not operating, Neal "felt" Alf's moves before they happened.

Genial, outgoing, totally charming—and son of one of the most successful commodity traders in Chicago—Al was much smarter than he pretended to be or his grades in the business school would have suggested. He sized up the strengths and weaknesses of people rapidly. He knew just how far he could go, for example, in kidding Neal about his continuing crush on Megan Keefe and would push the razzing right up to the border of acceptability and then stop.

Megan and Neal had promised to write to one another and had faithfully kept this promise for a month. Then she did not answer his letter and he did not write again. They both had other things to do in life. Neal kept alive his hope that they might renew their relationship after college, but he knew he had no time for intense romance, and presumed that she knew the same thing about herself.

Not that he ever asked her.

He missed her at their first Christmas break. Her family, he heard, had gone off to Florida *en masse*, complete with in-laws. When you married a Keefe, you became part of the family whether you wanted to or not.

He saw her briefly at Grand Beach that summer in the Ryan house, presided over now by the new Mrs. Ryan, whom everyone seemed to like.

"You owe me a letter," she said bluntly.

"The other way around."

"Truly?"

"Truly."

"I wrote five letters," she frowned, counting on her fingers. "And you replied only to the first four."

He counted mentally too. "I got only four."

"Sure?"

"Sure."

They paused in awkward silence.

"Maybe your reply to my last reply got lost in the mail. It's been known to happen."

She tilted her head in that now familiar nod. "My fault, maybe," she said. "I owe you a letter when I get back."

"I think I owe you one, maybe."

"Let's fight about it."

At first he thought she meant it; then he realized that he had forgotten that you had to read Megan's eyes, not her pursed lips, for the first signs of laughter.

"Fine," he replied, keeping his face as straight as hers, "I'm bigger than you are."

"You sure are." She pecked at his cheek. "Let's be friends again."

They did not, however, become friends again, and they did not write to one another in the autumn. At the end of the summer and again at Thanksgiving and Christmas, she brought friends from "the East" to the neighborhood as guests—male and female Ivy League types with whom Neal did not want to compete.

Sometimes weeks went by without a conscious thought of Megan Keefe haunting him. Then a "Megan" day would come, usually a cloudy, depressing day on which Jim Sullivan would pore silently over his textbooks or brood with his eyes closed and his lips turned down while he listened to Bach (turned up to full volume). Al Lane would be absent in one of his sustained prowls around Chicago. On such days Neal could thing of nothing else but Megan. He would write letters that he never sent, make phone calls that were terminated after the first ring, and dream dreams that he knew would never come true.

He wondered if she suffered the same days, assumed that she did not, and tried to exorcise her from his fantasies.

Yet he never gave up hope that what they had begun could someday be resumed.

Only not now.

Jim Sullivan was a biochem major and premed student. His only exercise, besides turning on their stereo system, was walking to and from class and labs. When he wasn't studying, he was reading philosophy or scratching poetry. He would read carefully each of Neal's journalism assignments and offer criticisms that often were more insightful than those of Neal's professors.

"Why are you in premed when your real interest is literature and philosophy?" Neal finally asked him.

"The old man," Jim laughed nervously, "is paying the bills and biochem is what he wants."

It seemed an odd answer. When the child was nineteen, parents were not irresistible, were they? His mother had been opposed to both Northwestern on the grounds that it was a "Protestant" school and to journalism on the grounds that it attracted a "bad class of people." But a few words about the Catholic Center at Northwestern and the change in the journalistic profession ("Drunks are not fashionable anymore"—only a mild lie) reassured her.

Doctor Sullivan was a tough old geezer, but still . . .

If Jim seemed too serious, Alf Lane was not serious enough, indeed never serious. He studied only for exams and then with casual indifference. He bragged that he knew every bar from Chicago Avenue to the Wisconsin state line and that he could outdrink anyone he had ever met in those bars. His sexual conquests, according to him, were legion.

On the occasional visit with Al to a "drinking emporium," Neal observed ample evidence of his friend's abilities to consume gin and women. Charming, gregarious, handsome, with blond hair and fair skin, and already a well-known quarterback, Al seemed to bowl women over. Without the slightest qualm of conscience. Moreover, many of his victims seemed to know exactly what he was and really not to mind being the object of his conquest campaigns.

To his dismay, Neal found that women in the bars and in the classrooms at NU reacted in similar fashion to him.

"You could get as much pussy as I do," Al would tell him with a boisterous laugh. "Your baby face is even more innocent than mine. Trouble is," he would continue with another laugh, "you *are* more innocent than I am."

One night, in a glittering, slightly sinister bar, with dim lights and lots of mirrors, off Eden's Expressway west of Winnetka, Al was caught in real trouble. He had been flirting for much of the evening with a most attractive blond woman in her late twenties in the company of a lean, dark-skinned fellow in a perfectly tailored gray three-piece suit. The man finally took exception to Al's behavior and swung at him. Al ducked and pushed him away with an obscene word and a hearty laugh.

Both of them were pretty drunk by then and, their masculine egos being what they were, incapable of walking away from the fight without losing face.

The dark-skinned man—not Mob, Neal judged, but maybe distantly "connected"—struggled to his feet and swung again. His fist grazed Al's face.

Al punched back, burying his fist in the other's belly. The woman screamed, the bartender shouted, and a large man appeared from the doorway, a bouncer no doubt.

Neal prayed that he would come quickly.

The dark-skinned man smashed a whiskey bottle against the bar and with thunderbolt speed jabbed at Al's face.

Al ducked away and then froze, perhaps because he saw death in the drunk's cold green eyes.

"He'll kill me!"

Neal figured that there was no time to wait for the bouncer. He grabbed the dark-skinned man by his shirt, spun him around, and hit him, just once, on the chin.

The man's eyes glazed, and he turned limp in Neal's grasp. Gently Neal deposited him on a bar stool.

Then he grabbed Al's arm and hustled him toward the door.

"You're right," he said to the bouncer. "We're just leaving. And we won't be back."

Al was a blubbering wreck. "He was gonna kill me, I could see it in his eyes. He was gonna kill me."

"I doubt it," Neal replied impatiently. "Give me the keys. I'll drive back to our apartment."

In the car, while Al continued to blubber, Neal pondered his action. He had never hit anyone in his life, save on the football field and then with complete absence of malice. Yet his action in the bar had been pure instinct, the punch of an accomplished barroom brawler afraid of nothing and no one.

What, he wondered irreverently, would Megan think about it? Well, she would never know.

Back at their apartment, Al recovered his equilibrium and loquaciousness.

"You should have seen him, Jimmy. One-Punch O'Connor. The guy folded his tent after one punch. Even the bouncer was afraid of him."

"The guy was drunk."

"Yeah, sure, so was I, not that it matters. He would have been no match for you in a fight drunk or sober. The point is there wasn't a fight. Just one punch from One-Punch O'Connor."

"Let's hope that he doesn't come back with some of his buddies looking for revenge. He looked like Mob to me."

"Nah." Al waved his hand. "Small-time at the most. I'll call my dad. He'll take care of it. He's got more clout than anyone in town."

Al worshiped his father and bragged constantly of his achievements and connections:

"My dad made a real killing on the exchange the other day. Suckered a lot of smart guys."

"My dad told Daley he'd better do something about the niggers."

"My dad was on the phone to the President the other day, and I mean old Lyndon Baines Johnson himself."

"My dad bought a new Mercedes. He's gonna give me the old one."

Neal accepted these assertions with a grain of salt. He did not doubt, however, that Reynolds Lane was willing, indeed eager, to buy Al out of his scrapes—proud perhaps that his son was a real "shit-kicker."

While he had no illusions about Al, Neal could not help but like him and envy, just a little, the laughter and fun that seemed to fill Al's life. Years later, when he was more experienced with sociopaths, he concluded that Al was a mild sociopath, a man with little conscience but also—unlike many men with such a character disorder—little malice.

He was generous with his friends and skilled in the art of generosity so that his gift giving never hinted at patronization. He bought an expensive stereo system for the apartment "so we'll be able to listen to whatever music we want."

But Al was totally uninterested in music. The stereo was for Jim and Neal, so that they could listen to WFMT ("that goddamn Jewish station," Al called it) and Mozart and Janáček.

His car, a Cadillac and then a Mercedes, was always available for Neal's use, often with the keys tossed to him before Neal could ask.

When Neal's mother was hospitalized with a "mild heart condition" at Little Company of Mary Hospital, shortly after John Kennedy was murdered, Al insisted on driving Neal to the hospital. "You're in no shape to drive yourself. There's no point in having two-thirds of the family in the hospital at the same time."

Mrs. O'Connor was released from the hospital after a couple of days with instructions to "rest for a few weeks."

Neal tried not to worry about her, but despite his father's

reassurances he continued to fret, especially when falling asleep at night and waking up in the morning.

Al somehow understood. So the pre-Christmas season that year in their apartment was wild and daffy, eggnog parties every night (through which Jimmy continued to study) with special "nonalcoholic eggnog, if you can imagine that, for my teetotaling friend Neal."

When Neal tried to thank him, Al waved him away. "Hey, don't go trying to make me out an altruist like yourself."

On the subject of Megan Keefe, Al had mixed opinions:

"Sure she's putting out for those Harvard guys; that's what Newton is all about."

"You could do worse than her, Neal. OK, so she's kind of flat, but I bet she's fire beneath the ice."

"Someone has to protect that poor kid from those vipers in her family. She's the only one that's not sick. And I mean SICK. Everyone of her brothers is a fall-down drunk, but they still think their shit doesn't stink."

"I bet she's great in bed. Is she, Neal? Come on, tell your old friend Alfie about her."

"I'm sure she's got the hots for you. She's the kind that spread their legs real quick for football stars."

"If I were you, Neal—and thank God I'm not, by the way, you don't have any fun—but like I say, if I were you, I wouldn't let her get away. She'd make you a damn good wife."

Neal's refrain was always the same: "Sounds to me like you're in love with her, Al."

And Al would always laugh him off.

"Just the same," Jimmy Sullivan said one day, his aching eyes still fixed on an advanced chemistry text, "he's right about her, you know."

"Who's right"—Neal looked up from *The Moonstone* by Wilkie Collins—"about whom?"

"Al, about Megan Keefe. She's a super girl and I know she likes you a lot."

"Megan is busy with her Ivy League friends."

"She would make a great wife."

Well, Megan Keefe, he thought, do you realize that far out here in the prairie provinces there are three Northwestern University sophomores in the same apartment, all of whom are in love with you. Not bad for a flat-chested broad.

So the three unacknowledged lovers went together to her father's wake.

It was a classic Irish wake, genial, extroverted, with seemingly happy mourners. Two of the sons were already well tuned when Neal and his friends arrived.

The Irish, he thought and then corrected himself, WE Irish have a strange attitude toward death.

"Well," said Megan, dry-eyed but tense, "the three musketeers from Wildcat land."

"At your service, milady," Neal responded.

"So nice of you to come." Her eyes clouded. "Neal, Alfred, James. You really didn't have to."

The others were tongue-tied, so Neal became the spokesman. "You have all our sympathy, Megan. We know how much you loved him."

"Thank you, thank you very much." She gripped his hand firmly. Then, still the smooth precinct captain working a crowd, she turned to the next mourner.

Her three sisters barely acknowledged Neal's expressions of sympathy. Their bodies encased in form-fitting black dresses and their pale faces framed in long blond hair, they looked like models for a painting of classic grief—until you looked at their eyes. Then you saw something that was not grief at all: rage and hatred at the world that had taken their father from them and at those who dared to be part of such a world.

The Keefes were haters. This was a night for special hatred—almost as if they were vampires who, after the wake, would go out under the full moon and suck lifeblood from the bodies of those they hated. Including, quite possibly, his own.

Scary, scary people.

"She'll be the only sober one in the family before the night is over," Al said in the parking lot on Western Avenue.

"A remarkable woman," Jimmy agreed.

Neal breathed deeply, sucking in the humid summer air.

"It makes you wonder how you're going to react to your own parents' death."

"Don't even talk about it," Al said nervously.

"It won't happen for a long time," Jimmy agreed.

"I suppose not. You want me to drive, Al?"

"Yeah, I'm not up to it tonight."

The next day at the Mercantile Exchange, where he and Al worked that summer, courtesy of Mr. Lane's clout, Neal reassured himself that his parents both had many good years ahead of them.

He was wrong.

His mother's poor, worrying heart stopped beating on the Feast of the Assumption that summer. Two weeks after her body was laid in the ground at Holy Sepulchre, his father was shot by a pimp with whom he'd been arguing about protection money.

REVEAL HERO COP'S CORRUPTION

Such was the headline in the *Sun Times* the day of his father's funeral mass. The few mourners from the parish who heard the final salute of police weapons at the graveside were awkward and embarrassed. There were some whispers, intended to be audible, behind his back the next Sunday at Mass.

Years later his New York psychiatrist would say to him, "Of course you felt guilt over their deaths. Admit it, you still do. Perhaps if you had not played football, your mother would not have worried herself into an early grave, is that not so?"

"She would have worried about something else. It was in Mom's nature to worry."

"Especially about you, no?"

"I suppose . . ."

"And your father, naturally you feel responsible for his corruption, as guilty of it as he was."

"Certainly not!"

"Yet you know in your heart, do you not, that he was on the take—that is the proper expression, is it not?—to provide you and your mother with the life-style your community demanded."

"I guess I thought of that."

"Even then?"

"Yes, even then, damn it."

"And you also feel guilt for your anger at him because he betrayed the principles he taught you, do you not?"

"Maybe I was furious at him."

"So it was from your guilt and your anger that you ran. And you projected onto your community the thoughts you felt yourself, did you not?"

"NO!"

"Come now, Neal, you are too intelligent to engage in such denial mechanisms. Was your father's behavior atypical of police in Chicago in those days?"

"What does that have to do with it?"

"Isn't it arguable that your community took such corruption for granted and was not shocked at it?"

He hesitated. "I suppose you're right, but—"

"And for you and your parents they felt not contempt but only pity?"

"I don't want their goddamn pity!"

"Naturally. Your friend who became a priest, you do not want his pity?"

"Blackie? The Ryans didn't pity anyone. They felt compassion, maybe."

"And you ran from that, too?"

"Am I not permitted grief over my parents' deaths? I loved them both. They loved each other. They loved me. Their ways of communicating love were different, but they loved me!"

"Naturally. Otherwise you wouldn't be healthy enough to be here in this office. But you ran, did you not? And from love?"

"I don't know."

But that was many years later.

In those late-summer days, numb with emotions he could not name, Neal decided that it was time to leave. There was enough money from his father's police insurance for him to live for a year or two. He called a journalism major who had graduated the previous year and was working for the *Arizona Daily Star* in Tucson. The young man called back an hour later and gave him a number and a name at Channel 13, a CBS affiliate. Neal dialed that number and was told, sure, he was welcome to a tryout, though they really didn't need anyone just then.

Without a word to anyone—Jimmy, Al, Coach Agasee—he packed a few clothes and boarded a TWA flight the next morning.

He thought of calling Megan Keefe, who had hugged him at both wakes and stood grimly just behind him at both gravesides, but decided not to. If you're going to make a break, make it clean.

He never returned to St. Praxides. And with the exception of a brief conversation with Jimmy at the beginning of a magic, deceptive interlude two summers later, he never spoke to either of his roommates again.

Or, God help him, to Blackie Ryan.

In the autumn of 1987 he learned that the two roommates were both dead, apparently suicides.

And Blackie Ryan was still very much alive.

As was Megan Keefe Lane.

1987

10

"Still shocked about Jimmy?" The question was gentle, tentative, as though he were a mourner.

"Shocked and guilty," he admitted.

They were driving through the mist and fog to her house on Hoyne, the same house, long since rebuilt, from which he had pulled her on the morning of St. Valentine's Day almost thirty years before.

"Don't be guilty." She touched his arm. "You couldn't have helped either of them. . . . Besides, Al didn't kill himself. You know as well as I do that he wasn't the type."

It sounded reasonable.

"Sorry, Megan. You're the proper mourner, not me."

"Am I?"

They had slipped out of the dining room at the Evergreen as quietly as they could, Megan imperturbable, Neal worried that the class would think he was stealing away for a tryst.

"Don't be ridiculous," Cathy Curran had whispered hotly. "We know Megan better than that, for the love of heaven."

"But you don't know me, not all that well."

"Regardless." She waved her hand. "And remember supper at our house tomorrow night. Nicole will never forgive me if I don't bring you around to be worshiped. She wants your job, you know."

"Maybe she can have it. . . . If I don't see you, Monsignor, I'll see you."

"Indeed. I offer you the words of the Lord God as transmitted to us by Blessed Julian of Norwich."

"What did he say?"

"She. Julian, that is. . . . But Lady Wisdom too for that matter. 'All manner of things will be well.' You too, Megan."

"Yes, I'm sure," Megan agreed.

Dangerous, dangerous little priest.

"Where do you live, by the way?" Neal asked as he opened the door of his Ford for her.

She chuckled softly. "You don't know? . . . But then there's no reason you should. We bought the family house on Hoyne. The room in back is my office now."

"Call me if there are any fires." They both laughed, not too awkwardly.

"I kept in touch with Jim," Megan said in the car. "We went out to his wedding. Nice girl, poor thing. She tried, but Jimmy was beyond help even then. They had some good years before he became really depressed."

"I should have kept in touch, too."

"He would have liked it, but it wouldn't have made any difference. He talked about you often and understood why you left so suddenly. He was very proud of your success. He admired you, Neal."

"I think he kind of half loved you, Megan."

"I know." She sighed helplessly. "There was nothing I could do to help, either. Al and I flew out to see him just after he was released from the asylum. He was so happy and confident then. So was Jeannie, his wife. Two weeks later he was dead, after he had slashed all the books in their library."

"He wanted to be a teacher and a poet. His father forced him to be a doctor."

"I figured that out, too." She sighed again. "But I never did figure out why you left after your parents' deaths."

He remembered his conversation with the analyst.

"I would have thought that was obvious," he said, his voice on edge.

"It wasn't," she replied firmly. "I didn't have the nerve to ask you later. But it didn't make sense to any of us."

"Not even to Blackie?"

"He never said."

"I guess I was ashamed at my father's corruption," he said, gripping the wheel of the Taurus, "and ashamed maybe of my anger at him. And maybe guilty, too."

"Corruption?" She sounded surprised. "He wasn't corrupt, Neal. He was an honest cop."

"He was shot by a pimp," he said, his voice choked, "who had been paying him off."

"Really? But that wasn't so shocking in those days, was it? I don't even remember that part of it. I'm sure no one noticed. Or only barely noticed."

I love you so much, Megan. I want to sleep with you tonight and every night for the rest of our lives.

"Things which are big in our lives at that age"—he tried to sound like a wise philosopher—"turn out to have been small to everyone else."

"I know."

So much unhappiness. Was any of it avoidable? Time to change the subject before her sympathy sweeps away my last trace of restraint.

"I was not joking at the party, Megan, when I said you have the 'presence' to work in our industry."

"I'm too old."

"No, you're not. The industry is looking for attractive, mature women who can put together intelligent sentences and behave presentably before the camera. Talk-show interviewer types."

"I don't know enough about anything to ask intelligent questions."

"The associate producers make up the questions."

"I'd be too scared."

"You don't think I am every time the red light blinks on?"

"Truly?"

"Truly. The secret of our game is not to be relaxed but to give the illusion of being relaxed."

"I guess I'm pretty good at that," she admitted with a touch of bitterness. " 'Poor Megan, isn't she wonderful and with so much on her mind.' "

"Sincerity is what counts," he continued. "Once you learn to fake that, everything else is easy."

They both laughed again and then there was a silence, each alone with private thoughts and private regrets.

"For the first time in her life," she resumed the conversation, "Megan is no longer in control, even though she's damn good at faking it. Loss of my father, marriage, childbirth, problems, kids—I could cope with it all. Now I'm in over my head, I don't know what to do, but I still pretend that I'm coping brilliantly."

He could think of no response that would not be empty.

"I know that it will work out," she continued with a deep breath. "The insurance will come eventually. Tommy Dineen—he's been such a support—will fend off the FBI, and everything will be all right. But now it's tough. And I've got to keep up a good front for the kids, who feel like they've been hit by an express train."

She described her troubles in an objective, matter-of-fact tone of voice, still fighting for control.

"FBI?"

"There's some money missing. You know what Al was like, happy-go-lucky, generous, filled with big plans—always trying to outdo his father, poor dear man."

He thought he heard a hint of tears.

"I'm sure it's nothing I know about. But what will the picture of me going into a grand jury room do to the children? Tommy says it will never come to that, but I'm still worried."

If she trusted Tommy Dineen, she was, for all her self-possession, an innocent in the world of downtown Chicago. Tommy the Clown was not much of a defensive line against the United States Attorney for the Northern District of Illinois, the redoubtable Donald Bane Roscoe.

She should turn to Nick Curran or Ned Ryan and his son Packy.

"Is there some trouble with the house?" They had pulled up to the corner of 89th and Hoyne.

"If I don't have a buyer within two weeks, the creditors will take over and sell it, for a lot less than it's probably worth. The judge isn't very sympathetic. Too many pictures of me in mink coats, I guess. Tommy says we can live at his place and he'll move into the Chicago Athletic Club."

At what payment, Neal wondered.

He'd offer his house and not pick her up at the reunion. Why did Megan trust such a jerk?

Because she's an innocent and because she had to trust someone and had no skill at asking others for help—especially the hovering Ryans.

Help her that big and energetic clan doubtless would; but the walls of privacy and self-possession Megan had built around herself would collapse in the intimacy of Ryan affection. She would gladly give up her defenses now, but she had no idea of how to do it. Someone would have to invade the citadel and rip down the ramparts from the inside.

That's not me, he insisted mentally.

But it would be fun.

He walked with her up to the door of the house.

"What did you break the window with?" she asked suddenly. "I never did find out."

"What? . . . Oh, you mean the day of the fire?"

"St. Valentine's morning 1958."

"A snow shovel."

She laughed. "Pete never bothered to put anything away."

"I've always been thankful that you wrote that essay about your garden. That's how I knew where your room was."

"I wouldn't have dreamed that you listened to the essay. I was so embarrassed when Sister Cunnegunda made me read it. . . . Well, good night, Neal." She extended her hand. "It was very good of you to drive me home."

They shook hands firmly. Neal fought off deliciously lascivious images of undressing her in the same room in which he had found her, hysterical from fear, the morning of the fire.

"My privilege, Megan."

"You'll be in Chicago for a few more days?"

"Till after the election anyway."

"Would you ever have supper with us? The kids would love to meet you. They refuse to believe that we dated once."

"I'd be delighted. Give me a ring. I'm at the Ritz-Carlton. Or at IBC."

"I will. For sure."

She wouldn't. No more than she would write the autumn of her sophomore year.

On 87th Street, driving toward the Dan Ryan Expressway, Neal realized that he had loved her since Valentine's morning 1958. He had never loved anyone quite that way since. The mixture of mind-bending lust and paralyzing tenderness that he'd felt as they plunged into the snow, and which he still felt, was unique. Whatever his emotions had been with Helen and Kelly and the few other important women in his life, they were nothing like the way he felt now.

I've got to get out of town in a hurry, he told himself.

And he certainly would not have supper at the Currans' tomorrow night.

11

All one needs for the Chicago political situation now to be a mirror image of a papal conclave is the promise of white smoke late some evening next week. Perhaps, given the racial tensions in this city presently, it would be better to suggest that black smoke would be more appropriate.

All over the city there are meetings, quiet and not so quiet consultations—the word used during a conclave—in which veiled and indirect language is being used to hint at what arrangements would win votes and what arrangements would lose votes. Explicit demands and unambiguous promises are neither given nor expected. Understandings, however, are being reached.

The native returning after a long absence is told, often in tones of admiration, that this is typical Chicago politics, isn't it?

This returned native replies that, no, it's simply politics, no better and no worse than the variety of the game found everywhere else in the world.

What may be different here is that it's all out in the open.

This necessity imposes requirements for exquisite political skill on black aldermen: How do you court the so-called "ethnics" whose vote you need to elect another black mayor without seeming to offer them any rewards for their support?

Hence the conclavelike atmosphere of Chicago on this Saturday afternoon, as the city, and particularly its black population, mourns Mayor Washington.

Reverend Jesse Jackson, whom columnist Mike Royko still calls Jesse Jetstream, inclines to support Alderman Tim Evans, but Alderman Gene Sawyer has pledges of votes from twelve of the eighteen black aldermen. The political differences between the two, both products of the Daley Machine and both early converts to Mayor Washington, are so microscopic as to be invisible even to the most seasoned of Chicago political observers.

There is a hint that if Mr. Evans is not elected mayor, his supporters will take to the streets.

That will be different from the way the political game is played elsewhere.

And this city may resemble a banana republic.

This is Neal Connor, IBC News, Chicago.

"Man, you were cool!" John Jefferson hoisted his six-foot-four-inch, point-guard frame from behind his desk and extended a massive hand to Neal. "One real hot-shit dude!"

Jive talk was an acquired skill for Johnny who, despite his success on Colgate's basketball team, was anything but a black slum kid who made it in the white man's world because of his athletic skills. The son of two M.D.s from the Upper West Side of New York, Johnny was mostly a WASP culturally. Or perhaps, given the primary and secondary schools he had attended and his current denominational affiliation, an Irish Catholic.

A New York Irish Catholic.

The worst kind.

"New York was upset with the Jesse bit." Neal extricated his damaged hand from his old friend's solid grip. "They said I can't do that to a black folk hero. I said blame Royko, not me."

"Man, you understated the way folks around here think about the Reverend. 'Course, maybe it's our fault here at the station. We helped make him."

"I got nothing against Jesse." Neal collapsed into an overstuffed chair across from Johnny. "In fact, I kind of like him. He has as much ability as some of those other guys and a lot more charm—which isn't necessarily very strong praise. I object to a double standard.

They tell me he's not going to be nominated, and I say that doesn't make any difference. What the hell, Johnny, it's not doing black people any favor by setting up different rules for them."

"Tell me about it, as my teen-age daughter, Melinda, says."

Johnny's grin was virtually irresistible, though Neal had lots of practice resisting it.

"Where does Melinda go to school, by the way?"

"Mother Macauley, where else?"

"Glory be to God! Do you guys live in St. Prax's?"

"St. Titus, the next parish south. Quite a neighborhood." He grinned again.

"Tell ME about it."

"Anyway"—John's dancing brown eyes took on a glint that always accompanied one of his fancy schemes, schemes that had not ended when he had been named general manager of Channel 3, the IBC-owned and -operated station in Chicago—"I hear you're one burned-out dude."

"That's a fair description, Johnny." Neal drew his psychological cards close to his vest. "I'm not sure I want to continue in this rat race."

"Don't blame you, man, don't blame you at all. I say the same thing to myself every night."

They waited, two wary animals who had been through the same dance before and loved it. More or less.

" 'Course," Johnny continued, "the Kelly MacGregor thing hasn't helped."

"I'd felt the same way before she left. Afghanistan did me in. Kind of."

"Uh-huh, uh-huh." John spread his enormous hands soothingly. "Hear tell you're thinking about some kind of leave."

"Indefinite leave. I think I'll go out to Tucson—I still own a house there—and lie in the sun for a few months. Or maybe a few years."

Johnny took on a solemn pose, appropriate perhaps for a papal definition. "I am about to make you an offer you cannot refuse."

"The warning bells are all going off in my head."

"Don't jive me, man."

"I can do it better than you can."

"Regardless. Just hear me out."

"OK, but with my hand on my six-shooter."

"Janey Allen, one of our anchorpersons, is going on maternity leave in the middle of December. She'll be back on February 14. That's St. Valentine's Day, isn't it?" The station manager beamed genially, a black gombeen-man.

"It is and the answer is no."

"Hear me out, man, hear me out."

"I will, but the answer is still no. I'm a reporter, not a pretty face who can read off a TelePrompTer."

"About your face I'll say nothing, except that Clara, that's my other teenage daughter, says you're terribly cute for a white dude. But I don't want someone to read a TelePrompTer. I want a roving anchorperson, someone who can cover the city and the country as a professional reporter and still drop in and out at the anchor desk."

"No." Neal realized that his voice was losing some of its firmness. Damn Johnny Jefferson. Did he know Blackie Ryan? Of course he did. Two of a kind. Maybe in cahoots. They were both capable of it.

"There's no question of taking Janey's place permanently. When she comes back, if you like the job, we keep you on doing the same thing. Sometimes"—he shrugged his broad shoulders—"we have three anchors. No law against that."

"No."

"Janey thinks it's a great idea. We cleared it all with her first. She thinks you're cute, too."

"A wife and almost-mother has better things to do than ogle aging reporters. And my answer is still no. But I am grateful, Johnny."

"Ain't doing you no favors, dude," he said, slipping back into his artificial jive. "No favors. Big help to us. Turn the other channels white with envy. Neal Connor for the sweeps. Hot damn!"

He pounded the desk, which vibrated uneasily.

"So that's why I was assigned out here? I was trying to figure out what your subtle Eurasian mind was up to. The answer is still an appreciative no."

"Won't take it for an answer, man. Won't listen to it. No way. Think about it for a week."

"Till after the election."

Johnny widened his eyes. "More than I expected."

Neal felt the trap closing on him.

13

"I think it was neat the way you quoted Uncle Punk about elections last night." Nicole Siobhan Curran gazed admiringly at Neal. "Real neat."

Was neat still a teenager's word? Some things never changed. "Uncle Punk?"

"Monsignor Ryan, everyone calls him Uncle Punk because that's what his brothers and sisters call him. I mean they call him Punk, so we call him Uncle Punk—or when we want to make him mad, Monsignor Punk."

"I'll file that for reference."

Nicole was her mother reborn, a curvaceous fourteen-year-old with curly brown hair, energy, enthusiasm, and wit—a vibrant young woman in process. She had inherited from her father blue eyes and self-confidence. No chance that she would have to suffer what her mother suffered in Costaguana to achieve freedom and maturity.

Not that she would escape her own particular sufferings.

"ANYWAY, what you said about papal elections was real neat."

"How did you know I was quoting him?"

They were finishing the cherry pie (homemade) à la mode that Catherine had served for dessert. Jackie and Liam had already been excused to watch football on TV, the obsequies for Notre Dame after its defeat by Miami having already been performed.

"Who else would say something like that? Besides, you were with him last night. Besides, I think he's CUTE."

So, for that matter, was Nicole Curran. Decidedly. Neal could never quite understand why, but he seemed to have the ability to talk with teenagers and young people, almost like he was one of them, even though he had never really been a proper teenager himself. A lovely young girl like Nicole would have scared him off at fifteen. And he had avoided the St. Prax High Club—where such were to be found in abundance—as if it were under quarantine.

"You wanna know something, Nicole Siobhan Curran?"

"What?" She turned up her nose to indicate that he was probably cute, too. And also funny.

"I don't think Monsignor Punk is funny at all. I think he's dangerous."

"Dangerous!" She was outraged.

"He's devious and secretive and manipulative and ruthless and always messing around in people's lives—for the good, I admit—and he never lets you get away and he's mostly faking when he pretends to be so inept and confused and absentminded."

"Everyone"—Nicole lifted her pretty shoulders—"knows THAT!"

"And besides, he never responds to what you've said, but to what you're going to say next."

"THAT'S one of the reasons," Nicole shouted triumphantly, "why he's so CUTE!"

"I yield the point." He threw up his hands in surrender. "Blackie Ryan has deceived another generation of beautiful young women and there's nothing I can do about it."

"I think, young woman"—her mother, obviously proud of a daughter who could match wits with a TV newsman, intervened— "that you had better get to your homework. No homework, no Bears game!"

"Mo-THER!" She stamped the floor impatiently, knowing already that she had lost but not ready to give up without a protest.

"March!"

"You heard the boss," Nick added.

"You two just want to get rid of me," she said as she rose reluctantly and carefully folded her napkin, "so you can talk about Teri Lane's mother."

"Adult conversation." Catherine was implacable.

"I don't CARE! I think it would be just terrible if she had to marry that horrid Mr. Dineen."

"NICOLE SIOBHAN!"

"And you're just mad"—Nicole was beating a slow retreat— "because she won't take off her clothes and pose for one of your paintings."

Nick tried unsuccessfully to suppress a laugh. Nicole caught it and realized that she had a temporary advantage. She stopped her retreat.

Catherine could give it back as well as her daughter could dish it out. "Your existence, young woman, is excellent proof that I am straight, not kinky."

They all laughed at that. Nicole, knowing that her ace had been trumped, renewed her slow march toward the dining room door.

"I know THAT! But I think you like to paint women with their clothes off."

"Sure I do, or I wouldn't do it. There's a special sexual magic in painting another human person of either sex, and I happen to like women's bodies, though not as much as men's bodies."

"WELL, like, I'm glad of THAT. Fersure."

"To the books!" her father ordered.

"All RIGHT. I hope we see you at the Bears game, Mister Connor."

"Neal."

She frowned. "I don't know . . ."

"How about Uncle Neal?" her mother asked.

"Really bitchin'." She grinned and, embarrassed, rushed away.

"The child will be the death of me." Her mother sighed with elaborate insincerity.

"She's already got you figured out." Nick's eyes glinted behind his thick glasses.

"She's right about my nudes." Catherine tapped a Waterford wine goblet thoughtfully. "When a woman paints another woman, a special intimacy occurs between them. It's a giving and receiving that makes their relationship different afterwards. Kind of neat, as Her Nibs would say, and very satisfying. I can't imagine Megan Lane ever being ready to risk herself that way."

Catherine had designed the remodeling of the Curran home on Damen, an old Victorian place, the walls of whose small rooms had been torn down and replaced with, open, airy, loftlike spaces with loftlike Danish furniture. Every available wall space was occupied by Catherine's work, either a sunburst or a nude woman, the latter usually modest, misty, mysterious—and powerfully if subtly erotic. The sunbursts and the nudes seemed to fade into one another.

"The house was designed to be an art gallery," Nick observed.

"Nicholas!"

The two of them were bursting with pride that Catherine was about to have her first New York exhibit, about which she alleged she was very nervous.

An occasional woman, Neal noted, was not enveloped in misty light, but was instead depicted with candid realism that stopped just a fraction of an inch short of obscenity. Why, he wondered, would Catherine make such a decision about some women?

"I suppose she needed to build up lots of protection," Neal said in defense of Megan, "against that crazy family of hers."

"I suppose," Catherine nodded.

"Really crazy," Nick agreed. "I don't mean kind of strange like the Ryans, but off-the-wall mad. Her three sisters make up their mind about something, and it doesn't matter what the rest of the world says, they do it. One of the problems of extremely close family ties, I guess."

"Like this silly concern about the opera." Catherine refilled her husband's wineglass and her own and poured more iced tea for Neal. "I can't imagine what business it is of her mother and her sisters and brothers and their wives that Megan became active in the Lyric a couple of years ago. But it became a *cause célèbre* with them. Big family meetings, lots of fights, scenes at church on Sunday when they would encounter one another, oceans of tears, and finally a kind of excommunication."

"The opera?" Neal shook his head as if he couldn't believe what he had heard. "What have they against the opera?"

"Don't expect a rational explanation, Neal. Like Nick says, they're crazy."

Nick Curran replaced his Waterford goblet on the table, not wishing to ruin good wine while they were on a distasteful subject. "What it is, is the old Irish passion for respectability gone insane."

"What could be more respectable than the Lyric Opera. Some of my friends—"

"You're talking about the sensible world, Neal." He jabbed a finger at Neal, an attorney in court. "They live in a world in which lust for respectability has been twisted into a demonology. The demons are 'people,' as in 'What will people say' or 'People will say Megan is putting on airs.' "

"I remember that line," Neal agreed. "Do you mean that they think people will say Megan is putting on airs by working for the Lyric?"

"With all those North Shore snobs," Catherine added. "It's a seamless collective neurosis which is not damaged in the least by the fact that the 'people'—what my husband calls the demons—exist only in their heads."

"I can't believe it," Neal muttered. But remembering the hatred in Bea and Linda's eyes the night of their father's wake, he could well believe it. Or any other mad dream they might concoct.

"They're saying that what has happened to her is punishment for her mixing with the North Shore snobs." Nick extended his hands in a gesture of hopeless dismay. "Their words. And that she will have to ask for forgiveness before they'll help her."

"Which Megan will never ask?" Neal inquired.

"I don't think so." Catherine sipped her wine. "Not this time. She finally dug in her heels, but what a silly subject for the last family shoot-out."

"I suppose Al was never any help against them?"

"Are you kidding?" Catherine shook her head sadly and stood up. "Why don't you two go into the living room and I'll make the coffee?"

Nick and Neal helped her carry dishes to the kitchen. Cathy was wearing a navy dress with a paisley scarf, a combination that emphasized her slender gracefulness.

His weariness and his sexual frustrations were such that for a moment he found his lust directed toward her.

I have really become a pervert, he thought.

"I note your feminist statement, Neal." She washed remnants of the pie down the disposal.

"I'm a bachelor. I'm used to cleaning up my messes."

They all laughed.

He watched the byplay between Nick and Catherine, the nudges, the quick touches, the silent jokes shared. This was what married love was supposed to be. Were they exaggerating it a little for him? They might be. They were, it must not be forgotten, active agents of Catherine's cousin, that most dangerous, dangerous priest, Blackie Ryan.

"Nicole is an impressive young woman," he noted while Catherine filled the coffeepot. "Tea for me, please."

"I worried about her for a long time." Catherine turned to the teapot. "I thought my problems might somehow rub off on her."

"She's maybe a bit precocious," Nick observed judiciously, "but her sense of humor saves her."

"Maybe there is progress sometimes," Catherine responded. "Anyway we're terribly proud of her."

It would be pleasant indeed, Neal thought, to have a Nicole around the house, even if she did drive you right up to the brink several times every day.

Was there progress sometimes?

He wasn't sure.

"Some of your nudes," he said, as they strolled into the living room area, "are not all that misty."

"Hmm? Oh . . . don't be gross and stare at them all night. They're usually women whose eroticism is missed. So I spell it out. That's probably how I'd do Megan if it ever came to it. Of course, she'd have to accept it because the model and I really paint the picture together."

"You've asked her?" Nick spoke in some surprise.

"Hinted. Those tricky little gray eyes glinted. She was flattered but scared, so she ignored the hint. I suspect that locker rooms scare her and that she might even think that God blushes when she takes a shower. . . . Don't look shocked, Neal. I'm joking."

"If you painted the picture, I'd buy it."

"I bet you would."

He paused. In the devious designs of Blackie Ryan, there was now to be a conversation about Megan. He would be damned if he would ask the first question.

"I really wouldn't say we were close," Cathy began thoughtfully. "Not best friends or anything of that sort. I'm not sure that Megan has a best friend. Her terrible family . . . Neal, you should have seen them at the wake: pleased as punch that she was being punished. They'd die if they knew she was even tempted to pose for me."

"No room for the world outside their circle, huh?"

"Absolutely not. They made her marry poor Alfie and then dismissed him as though he didn't exist. It's the sisters that are really bad. The boys are just amiable drunks."

"Sometimes not so amiable," Nick murmured, pushing his glasses back on his nose. "Pete's a viper."

"Right." Cathy frowned, seeking her train of thought. "So we're not all that close. I mean, we've known each other all our lives practically, except when I was away playing virgin and martyr"—she dismissed the horrors of Costaguana with a flip of her fingers—"and Nicole and Teri are almost the same age and good friends from Grand Beach. But Megan keeps her own counsel. You'd learn about the marriage from her only if you listen very closely to the hints."

"Uh-huh."

"It was not what you'd call a happy marriage." Cathy paused for dramatic effect.

"Uh-huh."

She frowned at his lack of cooperation. "Not terribly unhappy, either. I don't think he hit her often—"

"Hit her!"

All right, you got your dramatic effect.

"Maybe only a handful of times in the whole twenty years. And then when he was drunk. He probably only half remembered the next day. A woman never forgets something like that." She threw her arms impulsively around her husband, sitting next to her on the couch. "Oh, Nick, you're so wonderful."

"If anyone gets pushed around in this relationship"—he snuggled supportively against her—"it's the poor lawyer."

A spasm of raw envy raced through Neal's nervous system. Lucky bastard.

"Be quiet," she said as she disengaged slowly from her lover. "You know that's not true. ANYWAY, you remember Alfie. Mostly he was a pleasant, empty man who gave her nice presents, made love occasionally and probably not very effectively, stayed away from her family as much as he could, made and lost a couple of fortunes at the Mercantile Exchange, and didn't play around too much."

"Play around?"

"Oh, sure." She shrugged as though everyone knew it. "He thought that he kept his escapades a secret, but naturally everyone in the neighborhood knew, including Megan. I imagine she never challenged him, because she knew it would be humiliating and wouldn't do any good anyway."

"How terrible."

"For a lot of women it's worse, Neal. He was normally inoffensive and meant no harm. He let her raise the kids, at which she's done a great job. He wouldn't have even thought of walking out on her."

"If you don't love a spouse," Nick joined in, "at least you can be happy that he's not a bastard."

"I think he was a bastard." Cathy frowned at her husband. "But not a bastard the way other bastards are bastards."

"Poor Megan."

"Right, Neal, poor Megan. But as the Irish put it, better the divil you know than the divil you don't know."

Was he the divil she didn't know?

"I suppose."

"She goes along in life figuring she's got forty more years of the same. It's like a mild toothache: you can live with it, after a while you don't even notice, and extraction is out of the question. Then suddenly the ache is gone and you miss it, but you feel guilty that you don't miss it more."

"Interesting metaphor."

"She's an emotional shambles, and being Megan, she has to pretend that she's in control. All that does is postpone the eventual collapse."

"And then?"

"There's always Tommy Dineen, whom the family thinks is wonderful."

"Ugh."

"Precisely."

"Nick," he turned to Cathy's husband, "what's the legal situation?"

"Murky and kinky. You've been around the game long enough to know that the United States Attorneys all over the country will do anything to get themselves a single clip on the five o'clock news. Al was front page in Chicago for two days after Black Monday. He thought that the first collapse was just a blip, so he threw his clients' money into buying and lost everything in a half hour—you can do that at the Merc if you're trading on the S and P index. Poor guy may have done it before and got away with it. Probably thought he was invulnerable."

"But how does this affect Megan?"

"If you call Al's widow before the grand jury, it's worth one, maybe two evening news clips and probably two page-five stories. You can see the headlines, 'Broker's Widow Subpoenaed' and 'Lane Widow Testifies.' For the FBI and Donny Roscoe that's pure gravy. They're not going to have anything solid on her that would obtain an indictment. Public opinion would turn against them, if they ever went for a trial. But that's not the goal. The goal is media coverage."

"And I'm part of that."

Nick and Cathy were both startled.

"The thing is," Nick persisted in his lecture, "there is a lot of money missing, not clients' money, but capital of Al's. And he did hang around with some pretty odd people in the bars over on the South East Side—high-class drug dealers and their high-class whores. There's a possibility that they might dig up a lot more publicity and that would mean more agony for Megan and the kids.

But hardly an indictment. It's evident even to Donny Roscoe that Megan is not a criminal type, much too straight."

"How do they know about the money and the whores?"

"FBI has a mole somewhere. In fact, they have moles everywhere these days. That's how they get publicity and indictments."

"Sounds fascist."

"You're the reporter."

"That's right, I am. So it would be much better if you or Ned and Packy Ryan were defending her."

"Acting for her. She's not accused of anything. But we have to be careful about that. The case could end up before Judge Kane. So it would be better if we were in the background and someone like Larry Whealan of Whealan, Bishop, and James was acting for her."

"Judge Kane?"

"Eileen Ryan Kane." Catherine smiled. "Uncle Punk's sister. Remember her?"

"Who could forget her?"

"You bet."

"She detests Donny Roscoe. And her connection to Megan is thin—grew up in the same neighborhood but don't really know each other—so there's no conflict of interest there, not if we're uninvolved." He grinned enthusiastically. "If Donny is playing games—and five will get you ten he is—Eileen will take great delight in dissecting him."

"This Larry Whealan . . ."

"Former president of the Bar Association. Best trial lawyer in town. Absolutely the best."

"And absolutely darling," his wife agreed.

So there was lots of support available for Megan—if she could crack out of her shell and accept it.

"I see. . . . There's no risk, then, that they'll indict her?"

Nick scowled. "I don't think so, but I can't absolutely promise. An indictment gets a United States Attorney another thirty-second clip on TV. Then when it's quietly dropped, no one notices."

"Except the poor family that is crucified for a night or two on TV," Neal commented.

"That little pig Don Roscoe is so hungry for publicity," Catherine added, "that he might even go for a trial."

Neal felt his stomach turn uneasily. "And a supposedly rich

woman on trial might go the way of Patty Hearst or Gerry Ferraro's kid."

"That's not likely," Nick said, without too much confidence. "God knows what Donny Roscoe might try. . . . Dineen says that Roscoe assures him that Megan is not a target."

"You don't seem so great yourself, Neal," Catherine began with tentative, very tentative sympathy.

He was surprised at how eager he was to talk about himself.

"I'm a mess, Catherine. I don't enjoy the work anymore. It's all shit, if you'll excuse my language. It's not the real world, and the way we report it is even more unreal. Afghanistan, for example. I had ten minutes to tell that story, five two-minute segments, then a half-hour special, which meant twenty-two minutes, of which we'd already used ten for the evening news. How can you describe the history and the culture, the cruelty and fanaticism of that place in so little time? I don't approve of the Russians being there, God knows. But those brave Afghan freedom fighters, whom we equip and to whom the American media are programmed to be sympathetic, are zealots, savages, barbarians, the kind of folks who swept almost to the banks of the Seine in the seventh century and to Vienna in the seventeenth century. You can't get away with any more than a hint that you would rather not have one of the *mujahedeen* to supper."

They were both silent in the face of his outburst.

"Sorry for shouting at you. None of what I say is new. Every thoughtful critique of the medium during the last twenty years has said the same thing. I guess I had to work in TV for the same twenty years to discover it for myself. Watch us foul up this election in Chicago and Gorbachev's visit next week. I don't know what's real anymore. I don't know what life is or what purpose, if any, it has. I don't know what roots are or what love is. I have no one to live for and no reason to go on in life."

He was dangerously close to an emotional breakdown. He must not let that happen.

"Don't worry, guys," he said with a smile. "I'm not a Jim Sullivan or an Al Lane. I'm not going to kill myself."

"Not all at once," Catherine said grimly. "Do it slowly, like I tried to."

"Sounds like a midlife crisis." Nick watched him anxiously.

"As Nicole Siobhan would doubtless say, tell me about it. That's what my shrink observed. Labels don't necessarily help."

"Shrink!" they said together.

"Yeah." He grinned crookedly. "In my world, unlike here in Beverly, everyone has one. But as mine says, therapy doesn't cure existential angst. Only death does."

"Or life," Catherine said promptly.

"He said that, too."

Would all this be reported to Blackie Ryan?

No way he needed to hear their report. He knew it already.

Still, they'd tell him. Probably before the night was over.

Terribly dangerous priest.

So he left an hour later, agreeing that, yes, he would come back for a breakfast and a "tailgate" barbecue and the Bears contest with the vile Green Bay Packers.

Catherine kissed him. Nick shook has hand vigorously.

As he walked to his car, the two of them stood together at the door, silhouettes outlined against the light, arms around each other's waists, a marital intimacy, a sharing of stories and of life, which would have been unthinkable in any of his relationships.

They waved good-bye as he pulled away. He waved back.

Soon they would make slow, leisurely, deeply affectionate love to one another, scaling a mountain of ecstasy in joyous combination.

That had never happened to him, either. Not pleasure of the sort which was surely routine with them by now.

And it probably never would happen.

1966

14

Neal rushed in to answer the phone, which he had heard ringing from the carport next to his town house.

"Neal Connor."

"Neal O'Connor?"

"Jimmy Sullivan?"

"That's right."

"I dropped the *O* out here. Obvious Irishness is not so much an asset in Tucson as it is back east."

"I'm glad I caught you, Neal."

Jimmy was as solemn and as gentle as ever.

"Are you here in Tucson?"

"Oh, no. Still in Chicago. Is it hot there?"

"Terrible. Over a hundred, but my town house is air-conditioned. Everything out here is. How you doing? What medical school are you attending?"

"Northwestern. Where else? It's my father's school, you know."

"Yes indeed."

"Is the TV business going well?"

"Prospering. I'm an anchorman already, not that it's any great honor here."

"The Walter Cronkite of the Gadsden Purchase?"

A faint hint of the sly wit that Jimmy usually repressed.

"Not that authoritative, I'm afraid."

Neal was enormously proud of his rapid rise in "Gadsden Purchase" TV, though it was never called that in Tucson—more likely "old pueblo TV." He had been lucky, but he'd also worked hard and outperformed all the local competition. He'd already earned himself a reputation as an anchorman who was also a reporter, a newscaster who could and would follow a story, no matter how much legwork was required.

And now the network wanted him to go to Vietnam. It would be dangerous surely, though not very dangerous. But it would be exciting and an enormous boost to his career. Maybe his dream of being a foreign correspondent would finally come true. At the age of twenty-two or twenty-three, no less.

On the other hand, he loved Tucson. He didn't mind the summer heat, and he enjoyed the slightly slower pace of life, the heated pool in his town-house complex, the mountains and the desert, the playful but not serious (yet) relationships with the pretty young women he seemed to have no trouble attracting and who were more than willing to introduce him to the delights of sexual passion.

He thought of Megan occasionally but without regrets. That was part of his life that he had left behind, almost as if it had never happened.

He still dreamed about her, but he did not think the dreams came often anymore.

Why not stay in Tucson, eventually marry the most acceptable of the pretty young women, and raise a family in the fun-filled outdoor life of the Sunbelt?

He was already on the top of the heap here and would stay there for forty more years, becoming in the not too distant future one of the most important "personalities" in the city.

Why not indeed? Was it not better to be first in Tucson than second in New York or Washington?

How long would it take to become bored?

The network would want an answer soon.

"How are things in Chicago, Jimmy? How's Al doing?"

"That's why I'm calling, Neal." Jim Sullivan hesitated. "Alfred will marry Megan Keefe the week after next."

"WHAT? Impossible!"

"I'm afraid not. Her family strongly approves. They believe that Mr. Lane is fabulously wealthy and that it's a very prestigious marriage."

"He's one step ahead of the Justice Department!"

"You and I know that, but the Keefes, as you probably remember, live in a world of their own."

"Does Megan want to marry him?"

"Megan wants to get married, or thinks she does. Her three sisters all were married the summer after college graduation. She thinks, because they have told her so, that she must maintain the family tradition."

Jimmy's voice was flat, precise, cool. But Neal, who had once known him so well, was not deceived: Jimmy Sullivan was furious.

He loved Megan, too. And he was as much bound by the chains his family had forged as she was by the manacles fashioned by hers.

"I see."

"She is not enthusiastic as a bride ought to be. One has the impression that she is going through the motions because it is her duty to go through them."

"She shouldn't marry him."

"I agree completely, Neal. You and I both know Alfred well. We admire his strong points, but we can hardly believe that it's an appropriate marriage for Megan. It will almost certainly be unhappy from the very beginning. Alfred is the kind of man who will find fidelity difficult even on his honeymoon."

"That's a harsh judgment, Jim."

"You reject it?"

"Not necessarily."

"Therefore, you will return to Chicago and prevent the match?"

"Me! How can I do that?"

"By persuading Megan that she should marry you instead, how else?"

"It's not that simple, Jim."

"It seems perfectly simple to me. . . . You are not married or involved out there, are you?"

"Well, no."

"I thought not. Hence the matter is simplicity itself."

"I can't see that."

"You've always wanted to marry Megan."

"I wouldn't say that."

"I would. . . . It's my belief that Megan is only marrying Alfred because she has given up all hope of ever seeing you again. It is my further belief that she will listen to what you say and will do whatever you wish. Her future is in your hands, Neal."

"I can't—"

"Think about it. I'll call you back in two hours. There's still time to save her."

"Save her?" Neal said to the dead phone line. "Why should I want to save her?"

He sat for an hour at poolside, watching the sun sink behind the Tucson mountains and rose light bathe the desert.

Why save Megan? What was she to him? She and Al would be well matched, two incomplete humans from crazy families. Why mess up his life with her, even if his rescue mission was successful?

If he should, for the sake of the argument, bear Megan away with him and back to the desert, he would have to forget about Vietnam. The network did not give those who turned it down once a second chance.

Ruin his career for a girl he did not love, indeed had never loved?

Absurd.

After an hour and a half of reflection, he returned to the house and dialed Jimmy's number, which he had found in an old notebook.

"Jimmy? Neal. I'll be on the morning plane."

1987

15

The Lane children did not like him.

No particular reason why they should. They saw as clearly as anyone else that a giant conspiracy was evolving to program him as the successor to their father. No kid likes a potential stepfather, even when he's a celebrity newsman.

Newsperson.

He should have realized that an invitation to the Bear/Packer encounter was part of the ingeniously orchestrated Blackie Ryan plot—so ingenious, indeed, that the devious little Monsignor probably did not have to elaborate on such minor details as a football invitation.

Megan seemed surprised when she and her brood, laden with food, climbed into the Curran minivan. "Neal, what a pleasant surprise." She turned a light shade of pink. "I didn't know you were coming!"

"Jackie was a little under the weather," Catherine cut in quickly, "so we called Neal."

Jackie had seemed fine at breakfast. Marvelously sweet-tempered child that he was, he had surely been recruited to the conspiracy and had given a willing assent.

Absolutely ruthless, these conspirators.

Megan was wearing a down jacket, still open, over a form-fitting black sweater and slacks, thus honoring the demands of custom for widows (about which her family probably had strong convictions), the requirements of warmth at Soldier Field on a chilly, rainy day, and the need to be reasonably attractive.

How could he ever have been so crude as to imply that she was flat-chested?

His fingers itched to get under that tight sweater and explore the contours of the enticing curves within it.

He reprimanded himself for having such thoughts about a widow when she was surrounded by her four grieving children.

But the hormone system of the male animal of the human species is notoriously resistant to such reprimands.

"Did you have a nice dinner at the Currans' last night?" she inquired politely.

"I was distracted by all the dirty pictures."

"They're NOT dirty," Margaret, the oldest, a sophomore at Notre Dame and a tall, lovely honey blonde, snapped irritably. Margaret reminded him of her aunts at the same age, except that her woman athlete's body, confident, erect, disciplined, would never turn flabby.

"Volleyball?" he asked her when they were introduced.

"Basketball," she sneered contemptuously.

"My second guess," he smiled, turning on his charm.

She brushed her long hair away from her face, a gesture of rejection aimed at him. "Men are not the only ones who play basketball."

"Not even at Notre Dame, I'm happy to learn." Once again he tried his charm.

She turned away from him in disgust.

"You mustn't take Mr. Connor literally, dear," Cathy interposed. "He really has quite sophisticated tastes."

Dark black clouds, so low that it seemed as if you could reach up and touch them, swept along the lake shore like hungry birds of prey. The lake itself had almost disappeared, as if it were hiding, like the sensible matron it was, from the mists and the rain and the late autumn chill.

"Mrs. Curran means, Margaret," he tried his charm for the third time, "that I like her work very much and that I'm sure her New York show will be a huge success."

The young woman said nothing, but Neal noted in the rearview mirror that she had turned down her lips in disdain.

It would be a long, hard road with her. And the set of her jaw suggested that her brother would not dare disagree. One more Irish matriarch in the making, albeit a gorgeous one.

Her brother Mark, a year younger and a freshman at Marquette, was almost as tall as Neal, an attractive young man with a slender, handsome face much like his mother's and brown curly hair. He shook Neal's hand with little enthusiasm and said nothing at all.

"You're as tall as your father," Neal said.

"Hmmn," the young man replied.

"Play football."

"Hmmn."

"He's into track," Megan explained.

A quiet boy, Neal decided, much like Jim Sullivan. Hopefully he wasn't haunted by similar demons.

Teri, the teenager from St. Ignatius, was the least unfriendly. A bubbling junior version of her mother, Teri could not be unfriendly with anyone for very long, especially when Nicole Curran had filled her ears with the wonders of "Uncle Neal."

"I think Mrs. Curran's paintings are really bitchin', don't you, Mr. Connor?"

"Totally," he agreed, happy that someone was responding to his charm.

In the rearview mirror, he saw Margaret jab a warning elbow into her sister's side. She's the enforcer of morals around here, not unlike her aunts in that respect, too. Maybe not as crazy as they are.

Joseph, the seventh-grader, was an appealing little fellow with the face of an angel, a dimpled chin, and a lock of black curly hair hanging over his face. He ignored Neal's outstretched hand and glared at him with an expression of pure hatred.

I'd never win him over, even if I tried.

"I'm sure you don't know the story," Nick tried to break the ice, "about Eileen Kane and the picture in her office—we were partners before she went on the bench."

"Tell me the story."

"She has one of Catherine's misty nudes hanging in her office, on one side and a little behind the chairs in which clients or colleagues sit. It drives them crazy, trying to figure out whether the woman is Eileen or not. She's moved it over to the Federal Building, where I guess it has the same effect."

"Is it a portrait of the judge?"

"Don't you dare answer!" Catherine insisted.

"No answer required." Neal laughed. "Neato, huh, Teri?"

"Outstanding," she replied and was the target of an instant disapproving frown from her older brother and another nudge from her sister.

They parked the van in a lot in the very shadow of Soldier Field and draped an awning from the back to protect themselves from the rain. Other vans and station wagons piled in all round them. The process of setting up for the hamburger barbecue must have been long established because all the members of the party seemed to know their tasks.

"Tell me what Jackie does, so I can help," Neal said.

"Mostly he stands around and acts like an idiot," Nicole chortled. "So it's real easy, Uncle Neal."

"I was designed for it." He winked at Teri, who giggled.

Joseph turned away from him in disgust, his little shoulders tense with hatred.

Megan, he noticed uneasily, was already on her second scotch. None of his business.

"A beer, Mr. Connor?" Mark extended a can reluctantly.

"I don't drink, Mark, never started, which means I'd have a hard time at Marquette, wouldn't I?"

"Sure would." The big kid permitted himself a tiny smile. "Terrible winters in Milwaukee."

"With nothing else to do."

"When are you going back to New York, Mr. Connor?" Margaret demanded, cutting off any warmth that might emerge between her brother and the enemy.

Megan's back stiffened, but, thank God, she didn't get into it.

"Washington this time, I think. To help welcome Mr. General Secretary Gorbachev. Probably after the election Tuesday night."

"You must find Chicago dull after all the places you've been." The girl's voice dripped with icy venom.

She was probably a sweet kid at heart, but as the oldest, she was assuming the lead responsibility for protecting the family hearth from invasion.

Perfectly within her rights.

"On the contrary, Margaret. It's one of the most fascinating and beautiful cities in the world. Every time I return, I wonder how I was ever able to leave and how I can possibly stay away. It's not only home, it's the best place I know to call home."

"Truly?" The girl's face relaxed a bit, but she was still suspicious.

"Truly."

He bit his tongue so that he would not say that the word was a favorite of her mother, too.

"I don't suppose that there ever is any chance of you coming back to stay, is there?"

Behind the girl, Catherine Curran rolled her eyes.

"You never can tell, Margaret. The trench-coat-clad itinerant knight role gets a little heavy after a while."

"You don't like being a reporter?" Teri asked, eagerly offering him a hamburger.

"No, thanks, Nicole, no mustard or relish. . . . What was that, Teri? Do I like my job? I do, or I did, but as I said to your sister, there are times when I'd like to settle down."

"But not in Chicago?" Margaret insisted crisply.

The child was beginning to be a bore. She was almost twenty and ought to be just a little more sophisticated in her hostility. So the devil took control of his lips and made him say what came out next.

"As a matter of fact, Margaret, I had an offer just yesterday from my friend Johnny Jefferson, the general manager of Channel Three. You probably know his daughters"—he groped for the names— "Melinda and Clara. The two of us knocked around in some strange places when he was my producer. He wants me to experiment for the next several months as a kind of roving reporter-slash-anchorperson here. Same salary. A few years ago I would have laughed. But in my midlife crisis I'm thinking about it."

Why did he say that? He hadn't given it a single thought since he had escaped from Johnny's office.

Catherine, Nick, and Megan all froze in the middle of whatever motion in which they were engaged.

The report would go to Blackie Ryan at the end of the game. Maybe even at halftime.

"Are you going to take it?" Margaret demanded.

"Margie, it's rude to push Mr. Connor that way," Megan spoke tersely.

The girl's face flushed and she bowed her head. Then to Neal's surprise she apologized. "Of course it is, Mother. I'm sorry, Mr. Connor, I shouldn't have pushed you that way."

So Megan ruled the roost. And the kids not only had been taught good manners, they valued them.

"No problem, Margie." He smiled his most disarming smile, restoring the girl to some of her lost dignity. "It's a good thing that someone asked me the question because that makes me think about it instead of dodging the responsibility of making a decision."

"Just like a college sophomore." Margaret completed her apology with a radiant smile.

"With less excuse."

Megan smiled proudly at her daughter's grace.

Joseph continued to glare at him, hatred both relentless and perpetual.

Margaret was a sweet girl all right and a decent one, caught in confusion and grief and under great pressure. She could be won over if he simply refused to let her make him angry. And treated her like the charming woman she was maybe half the time.

Why would he want to win her over? He had no intention of accepting Johnny Jefferson's offer.

Two couples wandered over from the next tailgate party.

"Aren't you Neal Connor the reporter? We see you on TV all the time."

The millionth time, at least, that he had been so greeted by someone.

"I look a lot older on the tube," he always replied, because it was a marvelously stupid answer that somehow seemed to please everyone.

"We really liked what you had to say about Reverend Jackson yesterday."

"Jesse is not a bad man, actually"—this too was a standard line—"once you get to know him. A lot better than a lot of them."

They would laugh then and drift away, pleased that they had talked to Neal Connor (though not as pleased as if it had been Bryant Gumbel or Kathleen Sullivan or Tom Brokaw) and a little confused by what he had actually said.

"Does that happen often?" Mark Lane asked him.

"All the time, Mark. I don't mind."

"Not much privacy." The young man was pondering, analyzing, trying to understand, an explorer in a foreign land that was both fascinating and baffling. Less impulsive than either of his sisters, Mark was a young man whose passions, still problematic even to himself, ran deep—and probably strong.

He was also doubtless troubled by his new role as the man in the family.

"If that bothered me, I'd have left the business long ago. I suppose I'll know I'm over the hill when they don't recognize me."

"You did it real good. I mean, they have no idea what you said, but they're pleased that you said it."

He poked the big kid's arm. "You got the whole picture, Mark."

He sat between Teri and Nicole during the game, an arrangement that he was certain Nicole had engineered.

They both urged him repeatedly to stay in Chicago, Teri with anxious glances at her brother and sister, who sat in front of them and several seats away, to make sure they did not hear her.

"We'll see," he said. " 'Course, if I could sit between two such lovely women every home game, I'd certainly take the job."

They giggled uncertainly.

A ready-made and charming, if somewhat contentious, family.

The Bears were not spectacular and barely tied the score at 10 in the first half.

At halftime, a huge, rumpled man in an expensive fur coat and an orange Bears muffler descended about the Curran/Lane seats, beer can in a beefy paw.

"Hiyah doing, Neal, old buddy." He pounded Neal on the shoulder. "Great to see you again. You sure stuck it to that nigger Jesse the other day. Keep it up."

"You remember Tommy Dineen, of course," Cathy said, her voice glacial.

"Of course. Actually I rather like Jesse, Tom. He's better than most of them."

Dineen laughed enthusiastically as though it were a great joke. It was, but on him.

He hugged Megan. "Good to see you here, kid. Shows you got a lot of the old spunk. Hey, I got you another week from those vultures, so maybe we can still pull something out of it, huh, Nick?"

The implication was that Nick and he were legal colleagues, working hand in hand for Megan's welfare.

Tommy the Clown Dineen had been a bear of a man even as a kid, when he was already the neighborhood's favorite jester at parties and dances, a kind of overweight South Side Bob Newhart without much talent. He was at least two inches taller than Neal's six-one and now maybe a hundred pounds heavier. Everything about him was big, his hands, his feet, his nose, his balding head, his voice—everything except his small, shrewd, hard eyes.

It was hard to evaluate Megan's reaction to him—a mix of warm smile and careful restraint.

"Hiyah doing, kids?" He hugged Teri and Margaret like a bear playing with cubs; neither of them tried to hide their disgust. "Both yah looking great. Real class under pressure. Like I always say, you can tell class under pressure, isn't that true, Catherine?"

Neal felt his hands ball into fists.

"Sure is, Tommy." A voice from the tundra.

Well, the kids like him less than me, if that counts for anything.

"Hey, I'll be seeing you. Looks like we're going down this half. I tell ya, that punk McMahon has lost it all. Be good, Neal, don't take any wooden stock options, hah hah!"

"Pleasant fellow," Neal said lightly.

No one responded.

Tommy the Clown was wrong about the second half. The passing of Jim McMahon and the kicking of Kevin Butler gave them a 23-to-10 triumph.

"Better than we did against Miami yesterday," the Notre Dame girl said with a sigh. "Maybe next year."

Except next year she wouldn't be at Notre Dame or anywhere else if the money from her father's insurance policy was not released.

"Yeah," Mark agreed, "but these guys don't look like they can do too much against the Vikes next week."

Since Neal had taken the Metra train (as the old Rock Island was now called) out to Beverly, it was decided that they would drop him at the Ritz-Carlton, perhaps because wisdom said that luck with the Lane children had been pushed too far as it was.

"Is it a nice hotel, Neal?" Megan, who had been quiet and withdrawn through the game, asked.

"One of the nicest in the world. The Four Seasons chain runs only nice hotels, even if they are Canadian."

"Will you stay there long?" Margaret asked softly, trying both to be polite and to get at the facts.

"If I take the job Mr. Jefferson is offering me—and I don't think I will, but if I do—they'll probably move me into the station's apartment at the Mayfair Regent over at Oak Street Beach. At least until I make up my mind whether I'm going to stay permanently."

Again there was dead silence in the group.

He slipped out of the van in the driveway between the hotel and the Water Tower Place mall, conscious that he had stirred the whole crowd of them up in a whirlpool of conflicting emotions.

I didn't even try and it serves them right.

I couldn't possibly stay here. I'm too old to play such silly games with adolescent girls.

Even if I do kind of enjoy it.

1966

16

"Come with me, Megan," he pleaded, holding her fiercely against his chest. "Don't marry him. Run away to Tucson with me."

She clung to him for protection and salvation. "Oh, Neal, dearest, dearest Neal, if only I could."

His plan of action, concocted on the 727 flying from Tucson to O'Hare, was simple. He would phone her, ask to see her, tell her that the marriage was absurd, and invite her to come back to Arizona with him.

Defy your family, he would plead, run off with me, get married in Arizona—he would arrange matters with a Franciscan friend at San Xavier Mission out near the airport—and then tell your family what has happened.

He did not bother to calculate the odds. He knew they were not very good. He was not sure he even wanted them to be very good. Failure might not be so bad at all. But Jimmy Sullivan was right: he had to try. If he tried and succeeded, well, Megan would certainly be a good wife and mother and her family would have been definitively routed. If he failed, then Vietnam and a soaring career would hardly be just a consolation prize.

He was, he argued with himself, in a no-lose situation.

He had made reservations for himself at the Drake—he could afford a nice hotel now and he was not sure where else he might stay.

Despite the confidence of his plans, his palms were wet when he dialed the Keefe number.

What if she were not home? What if they had gone to Grand Beach for the weekend, even though it was June? What if one of her sisters answered? Megan was the only one living in the house on Hoyne with her mother, but perhaps the hated sisters, overweight and crude, were hanging around to make sure Megan did not try to escape the trap in which they had bound her.

"Megan Keefe," the voice on the other end of the line said tersely.

"Neal Connor."

"Truly?" she sounded excited.

"Truly."

"Haven't heard from you lately."

"I've been down the road a little way."

"So I heard."

"I'm in town for a few days. At the Drake. Can I buy you lunch tomorrow? Or brunch?"

"You know I'm going to be married, Neal? To Al?"

"I've heard. I . . . thought I might apologize for my disappearing act."

Silence while she pondered the possibilities. She didn't seem terribly happy about the prospect of her marriage. Or was he imagining that?

"That will hardly be necessary, but I'll be happy to have brunch with you at the Drake. You must be very successful in Arizona to afford such a nice hotel."

She seemed delighted with his invitation.

"We'll talk about my career tomorrow, after I've apologized."

"What time?"

"Ten-thirty?"

"Make it eleven. That way I can go to the nine o'clock Mass and not be afraid of being late for brunch. Can't keep an important anchorman waiting."

So she knew he was an anchorman? Who had told her?

He didn't sleep much that night, caught between conflicting hopes. He woke early and, although he had stopped attending church regularly in Tucson, strolled over to the cathedral in the pure crystal air of a Chicago Sunday in June with a light lake breeze sweeping away the pollution of the city and a cloudless blue sky smiling benignly on his mission.

The Mass didn't mean much to him and the sermon was terrible. They'd changed a lot of things in the Mass and he didn't particularly like the changes.

He wondered if Blackie Ryan was still in the seminary. If he was, how many years did he have to go to ordination? And was his pretty cousin Catherine Collins still a nun? How had all the changes in the church affected her? And what had happened to Nick Curran, her loyal—and from Neal's viewpoint, much put-upon—swain?

He returned to the Drake, donned his freshly pressed light brown summer suit, and descended to the lobby to wait for his first love, still uncertain whether he really wanted her or not.

As soon as she walked into the lobby, all his doubts vanished. Certainly he wanted her. If he had to take her away from Al Lane, he would do that eagerly and enthusiastically.

"Megan," he whispered to the lovely young woman in sleeveless white dress with matching shoes, gloves, and hat. "You're even more beautiful than you were."

"Neal?" She gasped as he hugged her. "I didn't recognize you, you look so professional and successful."

They filled their plates high from the brunch tables and, sitting by the windows overlooking the drive and the lake, eagerly filled each other in on their lives, while most of the food went untasted.

"I am sorry," he said finally, "more sorry than I can possibly say for running away. I was hurt, humiliated, angry—angry even at people like you who had never done anything to me but love me."

"I understood, Neal." She touched his fingers. "I felt so badly for you. I knew what your father meant to you and how sensitive you were. I didn't blame you for running away. I wished you had written after you were settled down, but then neither of us was ever very good at writing to each other, were we?"

Absolution and remission of all temporal punishment in a few quick sentences. Neal began to feel confident about his mission. She loved him. They both loved one another. Life stretched out ahead of him toward the desert horizon on a path of happiness and love that would never end.

"Afraid that letters could so easily become love letters and then where would we be?"

"Exactly," she agreed.

She talked about her wedding plans, not listlessly but automatically—flowers, dresses, reception, the enthusiasm of her mother and her sisters, Al's prospects at the Merc.

Megan was going through an act, the truth of which she had almost persuaded herself. But not quite.

"It's such a wonderful day, I'd invite you for a walk on the beach, but it would be hard on your shoes."

"I'll kick them off," she said as she smiled her quick, radiant smile, "and walk in my stocking feet."

So they strolled down the beach as far as the point that separated Oak Street from North Avenue. Then they sat on a park bench and watched the pastel Chicago skyline and the gentle blue rollers that danced up to the shore and playfully slapped the waiting beach.

Finally he said it. "You don't want to marry him, do you, Megan?"

Her face hardened. "You have no right to say that."

"I won't debate my rights. I'm simply saying that you don't want to marry him. You're caught in something you would give anything to escape."

"And where would I escape?"

"Elope to Arizona with me."

"Elope? With you?" She tried to make the prospect sound absurd, but somehow she seemed intrigued, even fascinated.

"I love you, Megan. I'll always love you." He folded her into his arms. "I'll never run away from you again."

She collapsed completely, surrendering herself to his embrace. Then he repeated his invitation.

She pulled away from him, examined his face intently, took a very deep breath which sent a shiver of delight through him, and then nodded solemnly.

"All right, Neal. I will elope to Arizona with you. It's what I've always wanted." She leaned submissively against him again. "Even before you carried me out of that burning house on St. Valentine's morning."

It shouldn't have been that easy.

17

"Someone could have been killed." Nick Curran, arms akimbo, stood in the midst of the debris in the living room of the Lane home.

"It looks like an amateur job." Neal glanced at the books thrown on the floor, the overturned chairs, the cushions pulled out of the couches.

"Pros don't panic and kill someone when they're surprised." Nick scowled. "Suppose that one of the kids—Teri, let's say—became ill at halftime and Megan drove her home."

"Oh," Neal caught his breath as an icy tremor raced through his body. "We lucked out."

"This time."

"Will there be a next time?"

"Probably—unless they found what they wanted."

Neal had settled back in his suite at the Ritz, glass of iced tea in one hand, chocolate chip cookies ready at the other, to watch the 5:30 network news. Nothing much was happening outside Chicago, so they were using the normal Sunday night filler—violence in Northern Ireland. You could always count on the Irish to provide news when the rest of the world was quiet.

The phone rang. "Neal? Nick. They've torn apart Megan's house. Searching for the money, I suppose. No one has been hurt. They found the mess when we came home from the game."

"I'll be right out."

As he drove down the Dan Ryan Expressway in the continuing

rain, Neal wondered why both he and Nick assumed that he should be summoned. I met the woman for the first time in two decades only forty-nine hours ago and already I'm on call for family perils.

He did not, however, turn around and drive back to his hotel. He did not even seriously consider doing that.

Her name began to pound in his head when he turned off the expressway at 87th Street.

Megan!

Megan!

Megan!

I love you. I want you. I must have you.

The pounding stopped only when he plunged into the living room, just as he had done thirty years before.

"They're shook up," Nick continued. "As far as they can tell, nothing valuable has been damaged or taken. But once something like this happens you worry about the next time."

"Megan?"

"She's out in her office with Catherine and the kids. It's through that door."

"I've been there before."

The bedroom from which he had snatched her on St. Valentine's morning in 1958 had been converted into an office—since it was Megan's office, presumably pin-neat.

Now it was a shambles, papers and manila folders strewn about the floor, books pulled off the shelves, desk and file drawers piled high on the antique desk, drapes pulled off their rods, bedclothes torn from the twin bed in the corner.

Megan, still in black sweater and jeans, sat behind the desk, dry-eyed but clutching a tissue, shocked, dismayed, paralyzed. Her children surrounded her in a tableau of impotent sympathy. Catherine Curran was pouring coffee and serving Dunkin' Donuts.

"You've changed the place, Megan."

"Neal!" She struggled to her feet and grabbed his hand. "How good of you to come!"

Her quick movement, the delicate and graceful rhythm of thigh and waist and shoulders, like a bird soaring from the smooth waters of a lake, unleashed a spasm of desire so fierce that he almost swept her into his arms.

"I didn't have much of a chance to see it the last time." He laughed and held both her hands in his. "The smoke was pretty thick."

"It's almost as messy now," she said as she swept her hand around the room.

Again he realized how almost incorporeal was her sexual appeal, as sheer and subtle as new-made lace, tantalizing black lace.

There was no turning back now. He would protect her, come what may. She was irrevocably his to protect.

Margaret was glaring at him. How dare he intrude! Little Joseph turned his back. Mark frowned uneasily.

"Was she cute in eighth grade, Uncle Neal?" Teri tittered as she asked the question—and was rewarded with a glance of the purest malevolence from her older sister.

"Teri!" her mother protested—and turned purple.

"That was so long ago, Ter"—he bent over and began to collect manila folders—"that boys didn't even notice whether girls were cute. Besides, nightgowns were so thick then that it didn't make any difference."

"NEAL!"

"Some of the other kids, like little Johnny Ryan, told me she was cute, so I guess she was. . . . Yes, Mrs. Curran, I'll have two Dunkin' Donuts. . . . Come on, crowd, let's get this mess cleaned up."

Joseph left the room. The others set to work. Megan led them in sea chanties. He thought that Margaret had smiled at him once, however faintly.

I'm hooked, he told himself.

18

You've just heard Vernon Jarret, columnist for the Chicago Sun Times, *urge Chicago blacks to kill their fellow blacks who are supporting mayoral candidate Eugene Sawyer before the white people of Chicago kill them. Such is the wild rhetoric here at the University of Illinois pavilion at what was supposed to have been a memorial for the late Mayor Harold Washington. Earlier, Hispanic Alderman Luis Gutierrez warned the highly emotional crowd that Alderman Sawyer had sold them out by making a deal with white ethnic aldermen who had opposed much of Mayor Washington's program.*

As a native returned to Chicago after a long time away, I'm frankly scared. There have always been ethnic tensions in the city, but the last race riot here was in 1919. This is no longer just another Chicago political game; it's a deadly serious conflict, a volcano which could erupt.

There is talk tonight of violence in the streets tomorrow. Activist "Slim" Coleman, a white from the Uptown district but an ally of Alderman Timothy Evans, the other candidate for the position of acting mayor, has spoken of war. Attempts will be made to prevent or disrupt the meeting of the city council tomorrow night. In the name of the late Harold Washington, blacks of Chicago were urged tonight to take to the streets.

Moreover, while no one has said it on camera yet, there is a strong strain of anti-Semitism here tonight. Why the Jews should be blamed for Harold Washington's death, I do not know. But I've heard several people mutter that the only thing wrong with Mayor Washington was that he surrounded himself with Jews.

There is something terribly wrong in my hometown when a Christian burial service can be turned into a ritual of hatred.

In Mr. Jarret's words, Mr. Sawyer's supporters must be done in before the white man does in Chicago blacks. And in Mr. Coleman's words, tomorrow there will be war in the streets.

In the pavilion of the University of Illinois at Chicago, this is Neal Connor, IBC News.

19

They made it to the boarding gate.

The wedding was scheduled for Saturday. They would leave on the evening plane Wednesday, check Megan into the stately old Arizona Inn that night, see the priest at Saints Peter and Paul parish the next day, and celebrate their marriage on Saturday.

Same date, different man.

Megan would phone Al on Thursday morning and tell him that there would be no marriage.

"I don't think it will bother him all that much," she admitted. "My mother and sisters have been driving him crazy. You know poor Al, easy come easy go."

It was not easy go for Megan, however.

As the sun set on Sunday afternoon and she rushed to her car to hurry back to Beverly Country Club for another prenuptial party, she fretted about how to tell them what she was doing.

"Wait till we're married and there's no turning back," Neal advised her. "They'll hear from Al, directly or indirectly, that the marriage is off. They won't know where you are for a couple of days. Then you call them and tell them you're all right and on your honeymoon with me. They won't like it, but they'll get over it."

"I suppose you're right," she agreed. "It will hurt them terribly."

He thought that it would anger them more than hurt them, but he said, "To marry Al would hurt you worse."

"I know that. . . . He's not a bad person, it's only that . . ."

"I understand. I lived with him for two years."

Back in his room in the Drake, watching the black and purple shadows of night discreetly cover the peaceful lake, Neal was not certain that his love had the courage to break with her family. She was not worried about Al, who would surely get over whatever trauma he might feel. Intellectually she knew that she should not marry him. She was apparently perfectly ready to trust herself to Neal. But the ties of family loyalty, so important to the Keefes and so irrationally deep, a subtle and complex mixture of affection, dependence, and fear, still stood in the way of her elopement.

Nor was he certain that he wanted her to elope with him. Their passionate embraces on the beach were satisfying and promising. He had always loved her and she had always loved him. It made sense for them to marry. There was no possibility of the marriage being a serious mistake of the sort he might make if he married one of the pretty poolside girls he hardly knew.

Yet he realized that he was acting out of a curious mixture of duty and passion, which in combination made him less concerned about the outcome of their plot than he ought to have been.

"It's fifty-fifty," he told himself. "Maybe even sixty-forty against."

They agreed that if the plan were to work they would not see each other till Wednesday afternoon. Megan's family had scheduled every hour of the week before the marriage. She would call him at the Drake each day, rather than run the risk of someone becoming suspicious about a strange male voice on the phone.

Neal worried and wondered. The girl was so self-possessed, so poised, so apparently mature and competent. But the elaborate pose of deception to escape from her family was bizarre. Would she ever be able to cut her ties with them?

In his arms, her breasts pressing against his chest, her own arms clinging to him, she seemed uncertain, defenseless, a woman in desperate need of protection.

Would it not be better to confront them, tell them that the marriage was off and that she was taking a long vacation in Arizona—with him? She was of legal age, she had money of her own from her father. There was no reason, legal or moral, why she should not do whatever she wanted.

She listened carefully to him on the phone Monday night, weighing her words, considering her decision as she always did.

"You're right, Neal. I should do it that way. I just can't. Not now. It's hard enough the way we're doing it."

"I don't want to force you into something—"

"Come on, Neal! That's not the issue and you know it. I love you and I always will. The problem is breaking away."

Tuesday he thought about buying her a diamond ring in a jeweler's on Michigan Avenue to replace the one she would return to Al with her note.

He decided against such a purchase. Later, after they were married and the separation wounds had begun to heal, he would buy her a really big diamond.

All right, what about a wedding band? You're going to need one on Saturday.

He realized that he was not at all confident that the wedding Mass at Saints Peter and Paul, across the street from the university, would ever occur. If they did indeed elope, he could always buy a gold band in Tucson.

In their Tuesday evening phone conversation she seemed jumpy.

"I think I'll leave a note for my sister Bea. I'll tell her that I'm all right and that I'm going away for a while and they shouldn't worry about me. She won't find it till our plane has taken off."

"That's up to you," he said guardedly.

Beatrice was the oldest of the Keefe daughters, the "Queen Bea" of the clan, a dour woman with a terrible temper, a disintegrating figure, and a biting tongue. Neal had no doubt that when she found out where Megan was, she would fly to Tucson, trailing sulfur and brimstone.

"I'm not losing my nerve, Neal," Megan insisted, "really I'm not. I love you."

"I love you too, Megan. And I trust you."

"Six-thirty in the lobby of the Drake?"

"Right. We'll take the six-fifty limo to O'Hare. That'll give us plenty of time to catch the plane."

After she had hung up, to hasten to yet another dinner at the club, he wondered what more he could have or should have said. Megan prided herself on her moral toughness. She had made the right decision and she intended to stick with it. She could not admit to him or to herself the turmoil within. How then could he help her? Was there anything he could do before they arrived safely in Tucson?

He could think of nothing. He could not even speak with her save for a few moments of stolen time on the phone.

Elopement, he thought, ought to be more fun than this.

He packed his flight bag and his garment bag, deposited them with the doorman, and waited nervously for her in the lobby of the Drake.

He glanced at his watch. Six twenty-five. If she did not come on time, he would wait till seven-thirty and then take a cab to O'Hare.

Megan would not, however, be late. She would either appear punctually or not appear at all. Nervously he waited for a page to call him to the phone.

At six-thirty she walked up the steps to the lobby, unbearably lovely in a light blue suit, her eyes shining, her face aglow.

How had he ever doubted her?

She dropped her two bags and rushed to him.

"Neal!"

"Megan!"

She kissed him eagerly, pressing fiercely against his chest. For the first time since he had flown to Chicago his head filled with delightful sexual fantasies. He circled her with his arms and held her in a prolonged, passionate embrace.

Reluctantly they finally separated.

"Is that the way you are going to be in the bedroom?" She smiled and raised an eyebrow.

"Only a faint hint, woman."

"I can hardly wait."

"Tonight at the inn?"

"Why not?"

He kissed her again, squeezing her furiously.

"I think you may do," she said, catching her breath. "I'll probably keep you as a roommate."

On the ride to O'Hare they laughed and giggled as only lovers do. She asked a few questions about the town house in Tucson, his job, the heat, whether she would be able to find work, who were his friends—a careful catalogue of information points. Dizzy in love Megan might be, but she still wanted the facts.

In the big lobby at O'Hare, swarming as always with people, she sobered.

"This is it, isn't it, Neal?"

"The last mile?"

"Don't be silly." She gripped his hand. "It's life, not death I'm walking to . . . but do you mind if I have just one drink to steady my nerves?"

There was no need to check in because they were both using carry-on luggage. So Neal led her out to the bar near gate K-5, from which they were leaving. Now he really wanted her. The closer to the plane they were, the safer he would feel.

He ordered his usual soda water. She ordered a "J and B and water," her purse open for the driver's license that she knew would be required. The bartender glanced at it, shrugged his shoulders, and served her the drink.

"Will I ever look like I'm not a child any longer?" She gripped Neal's arm and drew close to him.

"You'll never look anything less than beautiful." He extended his arm around her waist, let it slide in the general direction of her superb rear end, and imprisoned her passionately.

"I'm not running," she said.

"That's not what I have in mind."

They both laughed.

She was certainly inexperienced in bed. The most Alfie would have been able to accomplish, despite his boasts about his many conquests, was a few gropings and pawings.

"I'll always love you," he murmured.

"Truly?"

"Truly."

"And I will always love you."

She ordered another drink and gulped it convulsively.

"I'll be sober by the time we arrive in Tucson," she said, defending herself from his unspoken doubts. "I'm not a souse, really I'm not."

He tightened his embrace.

Fifteen minutes before plane time they walked to the gate, obtained their seat assignments, and sat in the lounge to wait for boarding.

The public address system announced a fifteen-minute delay in boarding "to service the incoming aircraft."

Megan became silent, thoughtful, perhaps troubled.

What do I say now? he wondered.

He could think of nothing.

Then the PA said that boarding was about to begin.

He stood up, lifted her garment bag and his, and walked toward the door to the jetway.

She hesitated.

"Megan?" He put both bags on the floor.

"Neal—her face was contorted in agony—"I do love you, but I can't do this to my family."

The world of happiness that had begun two hours earlier, when she walked up the steps to the lobby of the Drake, vanished.

"I love you, Megan. I want you to come with me."

"I know that." She seemed to want to cry but not to know how. "I love you, too, but I can't come with you."

"I won't try to force you." He extended his arms helplessly.

"You deserve better than what I'm doing to you, Neal." She picked up her garment bag. "I hope someday you will forgive me. I'll always love you."

"I forgive you now, Megan."

"Don't come out to the cabs with me, please. I've got to do this myself."

He watched her stride briskly down the concourse, a dream fading from view.

Later, during the most dangerous times in Vietnam, he wondered if he should have run after her.

1987

20

The election of Chicago's acting mayor last night was like the papal conclaves in the tenth century. After the pastors of Rome elected a new bishop, they would bring him out to the balcony to present him to the Roman mob. If the mob cheered, they crowned him; if the mob booed, they returned and tried again.

It's one way to do it.

There were some precious moments during this all-night drama here in Beirut-on-the-Lake. Alderman Helen Shiller, a young white "radical," called Alderman Anna Langford, an authentic black reformer and a veteran civil rights activist, a string of obscene names that no television channel could repeat save with several minutes of beeps. Alderman David Orr, the Reform acting mayor, attempted to manipulate the proceedings in a fashion which would have made the late Mayor Daley blush.

The night's adventures reminded one observer of the old saying: Patriotism is the last refuge of the scoundrel. Whoever said that did not appreciate the possibilities of the word "reform."

In City Hall, Chicago, still under siege at six o'clock in the morning, Neal Connor, IBC News.

21

"Crazy night." Tom Dineen blocked Neal's path in the Daley Civic Center Plaza, just as the sun peered over the rim of Lake Michigan to see if it was safe to rise. "Looks like the niggers are taking over the city."

Neal was too spent to want to talk to Dineen, whose breath smelled like a locker room after a golf game.

"I would have said that the machine won last night. If I were Rich Daley, I'd be thinking about running for mayor."

He ducked around Dineen and, in front of the Picasso sculpture, began to search for a cab.

Tommy had earned his nickname when he was a spectacular forward on De Paul's basketball team. He had been called a "white Globetrotter" because of his comedy acts on the court. A potential pro career had been destroyed when he broke his leg the last game of his final season—his fifth, according to sportswriters who didn't like him. It was only after that disaster that Tom Dineen went to law school and began to hang around with shady and dangerous characters.

"You figure out things quick for someone who has been away so long," Dineen said as he trailed after Neal to the edge of the curb.

"I never left."

"I don't get you."

"I'm too tired to explain." He would not ask Dineen why he was hanging around City Hall at such an early hour.

"Too bad about those nigger punks ripping up Megan's house, huh?"

So he was hanging around to see me. He wants to know what's going on between me and Megan, wants to find out if I was summoned and he wasn't. Keeping track of the rivals.

"From what I hear, they're not sure who did it."

"Oh." Dineen's massive paw pulled down the arm with which Neal was signaling for a cab. "Weren't you there?"

Neal shook off the paw.

"You so much as lay a hand on her, Dineen"—his voice was neutral, even, soft—"and I'll kill you."

He had no intention of stopping at the Lane house, the old Keefe place, on Hoyne Avenue.

He merely wanted to walk through the streets of the neighborhood one more time before leaving the next day for New York.

He had, he told himself, abandoned the romanticism that had assailed him Sunday night. Megan was an admirable woman. Her family was a piquant mixture of challenge and appeal. The neighborhood still had a touch of magic about it.

It was not, however, his world. He should escape from Chicago before farewells became painfully difficult.

He had not been able to sleep after the madness in the council chamber, gave up the effort, ordered breakfast from room service, and walked down Michigan Avenue to the Chicago Athletic Club, which had exchange privileges with its New York counterpart. He worked out with weights and swam a mile, challenging muscles that had been dormant since he had flown into O'Hare.

As he basked afterward in a comforting shower, he realized that a man's body, properly challenged by exercise, begins to wonder whether it is not time to be properly challenged by a woman. He thought of Megan and turned the shower to "cold."

Those emotions, however, sharp, delightful, and blessedly fleeting, had nothing to do with his decision to have one last look at Beverly. He walked through the Loop, admiring all the new buildings, and then found himself at the Metra station, not that he intended to be there. Why not have a last look? He might never come back again. It would not do any harm, would it?

So he boarded the first train on the Suburban Line.

When it pulled into 93rd Street, the rain had stopped, the clouds had finally lifted, the sky was clear and crisp, the air cold enough to be brisk but not so cold as to be unbearable.

He strode up and down the empty streets with confident steps. It was surely a picturesque little place for Chicago, a Disneyland version of a typical affluent American neighborhood, an image not ruined by the Irish faces on hordes of children, because the children were still in school. The neighborhood was more attractive perhaps than it was when he was growing up. By returning for the reunion, he told himself, he had faced the demons from the past, exorcised them, left them behind, purged them from his life.

He no longer hated the neighborhood or its people. Beverly was not the real world, but it was no worse than a lot of the other places which everyone thought were real. It was part of his past, not of his present. He could leave it behind now with pleasant memories.

And suddenly he was on Hoyne Avenue and in front of Megan's house.

On St. Valentine's morning 1958, there was a red glow in the basement. Now the basement windows were dark. There was no car in the driveway. No one home, obviously.

He continued to wander through the community in the general direction of the school and the church. He glanced at his watch. Twelve-thirty already. The kids would be in the yard for the lunch-hour recess.

Sure enough, plaid uniforms peeking out from the girls' down jackets, the kids were running and shouting just as kids always did during the lunch recess. Nothing at all had changed. Nothing.

The kids were exuberant. Christmas holidays at hand. They'd drive the nuns crazy during the afternoon. Not that many nuns anymore, he had been told on Friday night.

The exuberance of the kids depressed him. He had rarely been happy in his days in the same yard.

Or maybe he didn't remember the happiness.

On the basketball courts, a group of boys, sixth grade probably, were playing basketball with a male adult in military fatigues. Marine fatigues to be exact.

He recognized the man at once. Not changed much in seventeen years—a little more gray in his curly blond hair, a little more weight, but not much. Same manic grin and crazy laugh.

Neal was no longer in Beverly in 1987. He was back outside Pleiku, South Vietnam. And the year was 1970.

1970

23

The war in Vietnam does not stop for American congressional elections. Marines like these men on patrol outside Pleiku know that they can die on Election Day. The region is supposed to be secure. They move through the underbrush wary but relaxed, joking and singing and thinking about maybe being home for Christmas, after the congressional election. A couple of them joke about the time off from school to work for the election granted to their contemporaries in America, the moratorium with credit that college young people won during the demonstrations last spring. Someone says that wouldn't it be nice if there were a moratorium on infantry patrols.

Then there is sound like the popping of firecrackers. Automatic weapons. We all hit the dirt, the dry, sticky Vietnamese dirt, and return the fire, not sure where or who the enemy is. Then shadows materialize out of the brush, not just a few snipers, but a line of Charlies advancing through the dust and the smoke. Our officers scream orders, yell for artillery and air support, curse the enemy.

They ought not to be here but they are.

Strangely the men in black pajamas retreat in the dust. Then they charge again. IBC cameraman Tran Duc shoots some of the finest film of the war, a picket line of Viet Cong charging a marine patrol. He is critically wounded by a shell fragment, but he continues to operate the camera, a little less smoothly now because of his wound.

Then our artillery, more prompt than it often is, finds the range, the enemy retreats, the marines win this one. Tran Duc is our only casualty.

Here at a field hospital waiting for a report from navy surgeons on whether Tran—a man exactly my own age, with a new wife expecting their first child—will survive his injuries, I wonder what it all means. What am I doing here? What are the marines doing here? What are the Viet Cong, mostly North Vietnamese main force now, doing here? I don't ask what Tran Duc is doing here. Pleiku is his town. He's doing his job. He's working a camera for IBC News. He is a complete professional, getting footage even as his lifeblood slips away.

Tran is a Catholic. I find a priest, a tough, laughing Irish-American who anoints my colleague as mortar shells dog our retreat. Now I wait and I wait and I wait.

I know only one thing. As God—should there be a God here outside Pleiku—is my witness, Tran and his wife and their child will survive this foolish war, if it be in my power to save them.

Neal Connor, IBC News, with the marines, Pleiku, South Vietnam.

24

"You didn't say that you carried him out with AK-47 fire buzzing by your head." The priest hunched forward as two jets roared over the field hospital.

They were sitting on upturned crates in front of the surgery tent as the setting sun turned the western horizon an appropriate blood-red.

"You can count on network publicity to get that out." Neal, as weary as he'd ever been in his life, sighed. "I'll be the folk hero of the month. . . . What's your name, Father?"

"Dick McNamara."

"Neal Connor."

"IBC News."

They both laughed wearily.

"Where you from?" the priest asked.

"Chicago."

"Really? That's my home, too. What part of Chicago?"

He had found the chaplain playing basketball with a group of corpsmen and had dragged him on the dead run to the surgery tent. The priest had administered the last rites with astonishing gentleness, even though Tran was unconscious.

"What do you think, Father?"

"I'd guess fifty-fifty." The priest lifted his hands. "Only a kid."

"My age."

"Like I say, when you're pushing forty, only a kid."

So they sat on crates and waited and waited.

And discovered they were both from Chicago.

"Saint Titus," said the priest.

"Really? I grew up in St. Prax's."

"Yeah? When did you graduate?"

" 'Fifty-eight."

"Sure, you were the guy who went to Carmel and was all-city football. You probably knew my little sister Marie, she graduated from St. Titus the same year."

"Sure. Pretty girl. Married now?"

"What else? Two kids already." The priest paused to count years on his fingers. "You were in Blackie Ryan's class, weren't you? He was ordained this year."

"I think I got an invitation to his first Mass. I've never been back to the neighborhood."

"Lemme see." The priest pondered. "Sure, lot of pretty girls in that class. Lisa Malone, the singer who was over here during the summer entertaining the troops; Catherine Collins who married some crazy ex-priest; Megan Keefe . . . she married the football player from Northwestern, didn't she? Al Lane?"

"Al and I played on the same team at NU. I left after my sophomore year."

"Now I got you." The priest patted his knee. "You kind of specialize in carrying people out of danger, don't you?"

"You know, Father," Neal said as he rubbed the sweat and the dust off his face, "I'd forgotten about that. It was so long ago. I'm surprised that anyone else knows about it."

"Talk of the neighborhood. Crazy family, the Keefes. Mob lawyer but they put on lots of airs. Daughters especially. Guys are all drunks. One of the girls was in my class, total snob with not much to be snobbish about."

"To be fair to her, Megan wasn't that way."

"Hard not to be in that environment. Crazy place, the neighborhood."

"Since I left it, I've always been in places where everyone is from somewhere else. No one lives anymore where they and their parents and their grandparents grew up and where their cousins go to the same schools they go to. Except in the neighborhood."

"It's like a village here. But see how strong it is. Two guys who don't know each other meet at a field hospital, discover they're from Beverly, and immediately begin comparing notes. My father must have known your father. Both were cops."

Neal was too tired to worry about whether his father's scandal made any difference. Probably it didn't.

"It's not the way people live anymore."

"A lot still do, even in America. The question is whether it's a good way to live."

The priest was at least an inch taller than Neal, curly blond hair, impish blue eyes, and a quick, mischievous grin. As he yanked the priest unceremoniously away from his basketball game, Neal had noted that the man was also a better shot than the kids with whom he was playing.

"I don't think so, Father. Anyway, I don't want to live that way. I'm never going back. It's a terrible place. Remember all the fuss about the playground on the Kellog schoolyard? People were afraid that blacks would dump their kids there and do their shopping at the plaza?"

"And before that they complained about the plaza itself? They objected to the first shopping mall in America because they didn't want blacks shopping near their neighborhood."

"And they rejected the branch public library because they were afraid blacks would use it."

They both howled with laughter at the crazy parochialism of the community.

"Give the place its credit, Neal"—the priest did not stop laughing—"the complainers were not typical and it's racially integrated now."

"Really?"

"No problems at all. 'Course it helped that Mayor Daley said that all employees of the city have to live in the city."

"Integrated?" He could hardly believe it. "St. Titus and St. Prax's schools?"

"Great basketball teams. St. Titus always wins, naturally."

"The hell it does!"

And so, in minute detail, they went over the basketball records of the two parishes from 1950 to 1970. Father McNamara had to admit that St. Prax's had a slight edge.

"Remember 'Two-Week Nora' on the Rock Island?"

"I don't think so," Neal said, searching his memory.

There was a lot of activity around the surgical tent. Dear God, if you're there at all, please let him live.

"She rode the Rock Island every morning, probably to a job at City Hall, though no one was sure about that. And always read the *Chicago Tribune* very carefully."

"Nothing wrong with that."

"Except that it was always exactly two weeks old!"

They both laughed again.

After they'd gone through a long list of neighborhood characters, Neal said, "You know them better than I do. I was only there for two years of grammar school after we moved from the apartment in Sabina's. I never was part of the neighborhood."

"The hell you weren't."

"And I have no intention of going back. Ever."

"The question is whether any of us can ever get away from the neighborhood."

"I can and have."

"And do a neighborhood thing like that?" He gestured at the news tape Neal had played.

"What do you mean?"

"How many people are that loyal?"

"He was my cameraman."

"That's the neighborhood talking."

"Not necessarily."

The priest laughed and poked Neal's ribs. "In this case, yeah, necessarily. Just like carrying that sexy little kid out of the flames. . . . The guys all wondered what she was wearing."

"A very thick winter nightgown, worse luck for me. Blue, as I remember."

They laughed again.

153

"Can you really get your friend"—the priest nodded toward the surgery tent—"out of the country?"

"That was some of the best footage of the war. IBC damn well better get him out. I made sure of it. The clip will be in every home in America tonight. Or tomorrow night. Or last night. However it works."

A young medic emerged from the tent, his gown soaked in sweat. He looked around for Neal, spotted him, grinned, and shoved his thumb up.

Neal sobbed in the priest's arms.

"I'm ashamed, Father. I haven't cried since I was a kid."

"Women have the advantage, they can do it more easily," the chaplain replied. "In your case it's probably long overdue."

"Thanks, Father."

"I'll see you again."

The two men rose.

"I hope so. Someday."

"Maybe at the basketball courts at St. Prax's."

"No way."

25

"Hey, gyrene, aren't you a little old to be playing basketball with kids?"

The tall priest sank his jump shot before turning to Neal. He rebounded and bounced the ball over to where Neal was standing. "As long as I'm bigger than these sixth-graders, I'll keep on playing. . . . Hey"—he extended his hand with the usual genial grin— "didn't I use to see your younger brother on TV?"

"I didn't know you were an associate pastor here." Neal grabbed his hand warmly.

"Associate?" Father McNamara pretended to sputter. "Man, I'm an oh-six, that's a chicken colonel, I've got rank!"

"You're the *pastor*?" Another one of those changes in the Church on which he was not around to vote: now they made navy captains with Ph.D.s and wit, pastors!

"That's an affirmative," the priest snapped with mock military precision. "Hey, kids, report to Mr. Connor here."

A bunch of sixth-grade boys and girls drew themselves up into a ragged military line.

"Fiona One, how do you deal with the Captain pastor?" Father McNamara barked out in drill-instructor tones.

"When he says jump," an adorable little wisp of a lass replied, hand over her face to hide her snigger, "you say, 'HOW HIGH?' "

"How high WHAT?"

She struggled without much success to contain her giggles.

" 'HOW HIGH, SIR!' " Now she was convulsed with giggles. She spun around to hide them.

"And Kevin, is there anything wrong with the way the Captain pastor runs the parish?"

"That's a negative, SIR!"

Kevin and the whole ragged line of recruits were sniggering loudly.

"Fiona Two!" He pointed at another little girl, this one black. "Is Father Ace the best pastor in Chicago?"

"That's an affirmative, SIR!" She saluted briskly.

"Right! Now how do we greet Mr. Connor, troops?"

"Welcome aboard, SIR!" They all saluted Neal.

"Now, troops, let's sing the St. Prax hymn."

With voices in various degrees off-key, the sixth-graders sang,

From the halls of Montezuma
To the hills of Beverly
Father Ace we all obey
Them and you and me!

"DISMISSED!" the priest shouted.

The little ones scurried away, with enough laughs to survive till the evening TV shows.

"You gotta work at respect," Father Ace said, now George C. Scott playing Patton. "You gotta earn it, you gotta DEMAND it!"

"I see that."

A school bell rang, and silence descended on the yard; another bell rang, and the kids rushed quietly into the school—not in the orderly ranks of the past but still with decorum. Some things had changed only a little.

"It took them about five minutes after I arrived to figure out the game." The ex-chaplain sighed. "Better to be a comic figure than an Irish Monsignor with a thorn stick."

"Especially because comic figures usually get their way more effectively than guys with thorn sticks. . . . What's this Father Ace bit? I heard it from my friends at the reunion, but I didn't link it with you."

"Your friend Blackie, aka Uncle Punk, got on the phone to his nieces and nephews as soon as my appointment was announced and told them my seminary nickname. . . . You gonna move back for a time?"

The priest palmed his basketball, drove toward the basket, and attempted a dunk. He missed.

"No." Neal drove under the basket, grabbed the rebound, and sunk it on a fall-away jump. "I'm just here for the mayoral show."

"Just as well," Father Ace grumbled, "with a shot like that. Bad enough that the teenagers make me look old." He made an easy, very easy, lay-up. "Anyway, I told you that you'd come back."

"Just an accident, Father. I met Lisa Malone in the airport and she told me about the reunion."

"And today?"

"Seeing how much the neighborhood has changed. Not much, huh?"

"Not much? You saw those black faces among my troops? And more than twenty people can match my Ph.D., a third of them women. It's changed a lot."

"Still the same."

"Like Blackwood says," the priest said, putting on a heavy down jacket, white with a maroon monograph that said "SP," " *'Plus ça change, plus c'est la même chose.'* That's French. It means—"

"I know what it means."

They both laughed, as they had at Pleiku but now with more serenity.

"What about you and Megan?"

"Me and Megan?" He felt his face turn hot.

"Hey, reporter, everyone in the parish knows that you showed up for the reunion and sat next to her for supper. They draw their own conclusions."

"They're wrong, Father."

"The odds are one to two, I'm told, that you will be with her at the St. Valentine's dance. I want a point spread. . . ."

"St. Valentine's dance?"

"Yeah, he's the patron of romantic love, you know. So the laity have a romantic dance, after a Mass and renewal of marriage vows, on St. Valentine's night. It's called locally Father Ace's St. Valentine's Night Dance, because I let them do it. And that's odd because I'm the only one who doesn't have a wife to renew vows with. Still . . ."

"You're kidding."

"That I don't have a date for Father Ace's Saint Valentine's Night Dance?"

"NO! That people are predicting that Megan and I—"

"You have been away from the neighborhood for a long time."

"I guess I have."

He shook hands with the grinning priest, promised to be in touch with him, and started to walk away.

"Should I ask about Tran?"

"He's in Boston working on CBS local. The kid his wife was expecting, a girl by the way, is a freshman at Notre Dame."

"Some stories"—Father Ace grinned like a manic leprechaun—"do have happy endings, don't they?"

"Maybe." Neal shrugged. "Or maybe only happy chapters."

As he walked back toward the Rock Island station, he pondered the ironies in the fire. The neighborhood was determined to reclaim him without bothering to ask his permission. What it did not realize was that it never possessed him in the first place.

Somehow his feet had carried him not to 93rd and Longwood but to 88th and Hoyne. No car in the driveway. No one. Telling himself all the while that he was not doing it, he rang the doorbell.

He waited. No answer. She wasn't home. Just as well. No reason to see her. The past was dead. He turned to leave.

"Neal! What a pleasant surprise."

She was hugging herself again, cold, lovely, defenseless.

"I was ambling through the parish for old times' sake, and I thought I knew where I could find a cup of tea."

"I think we could arrange that. Do come in. Don't mind the glasses. I wasn't quite up to struggling with my contacts."

According to the usual Megan standards, she looked mussed—jeans and a wrinkled white blouse, sandals, no makeup, hair in slight disarray. Mussed and delectable.

Megan!

Megan!

Megan!

I must have you, Megan. Now and forever.

Al Lane's woman and she's mine for the taking.

"Any special kind of tea?"

"Earl Grey?"

"Margaret's favorite. Just give me a minute to put the kettle on."

She returned shortly. "Watched pot never boils. . . . Was it as bad at City Hall last night as it looked?" Chin on fist, she looked like a first-year graduate student in the presence of a world-famous professor.

He loved it.

"Worse, Megan. Worse. Scary. Think about the howling mob, the manipulation of grief into rage, the threats, the intimidation, the stirring up of racial anger, the 'Big Lie' strategy, the manipulation of the process with the aid of staff, the creation of hate objects, the demagoguery. Then play some videotapes put together from nineteen-thirties newsreels of Benito Mussolini prancing around in the Piazza Venezia."

He realized that he was doing his foreign correspondent role, but her wide-eyed admiration stimulated his performance.

"You mean . . ."

Ah, the woman is a perfect foil.

"The name, Megan, is fascism. It's scary, not because it will work in Chicago—Sawyer will be judged by whites and blacks alike on performance or nonperformance, not charges. It's scary rather because respectable clergy, columnists, and political leaders were willing to use it—and against a man who had always been their ally, who had a large majority of the black aldermanic votes. Chicago may not have seen the end of it."

"How terrible. . . . Let me get the tea pot."

The tea was duly poured—silver service, probably a wedding present. And chocolate chip cookies, homemade, were properly served.

He gobbled down the cookies, drank the tea, and continued to perform for her. Her admiration was even more welcome because it was not completely uncritical.

"Don't you think"—she cocked her head to one side—"that an outsider should be a little less positive about everything in Chicago?"

"What, woman"—he pretended to be offended—"Neal Connor, IBC News, ever devoid of confidence in his opinion? No way. The *persona* does not permit it. The private Neal—well, that's another matter, as you of all people know. Anyway, what do you mean an outsider? I'm a Chicagoan."

"I guess you are." She laughed. "Maybe against your better judgment, but incorrigibly."

He lusted after the woman, he loved her, he wanted to take care of her.

One thing at a time.

"Megan, I propose to buy your house. That way I can even become a voting resident again."

"What?" She jumped to her feet. "Whatever are you talking about?"

"I understand"—he was taken aback by the violence of her reaction—"that Al's creditors are forcing you to sell it at a loss. I'll buy it for its full value—what is it, four and a half? You buy it back from me when you get your insurance money. In the meantime you and that wonderful brood continue to live here. No one needs to know."

"Absolutely not," she snapped, turning away from him.

"Absolutely." He grabbed her shoulders and shook her.

"You're hurting me!"

"I'm sorry." He released her shoulders.

"You really didn't hurt me." She leaned against the fireplace. "You scared me, but you'd never hurt me."

"You deserved to be scared," he insisted, tilting her jaw up so she had to look at him.

"Am I part of the deal?"

"Pardon?"

"Do you buy me with the house?" Her eyes were cold and hard.

So that was indeed Tommy Dineen's game. The bastard.

Neal threw himself back on the sofa.

"It's been a long time, Megan, but you knew me pretty well once. Am I that kind of person?"

Head bowed, she sat across the table from him and refilled his teacup, slowly, carefully, as if she were afraid of spilling a single drop.

"I'm sorry."

"I don't treat women that way. Anyone for that matter."

"I *said* I was sorry."

"Mind you"—he relented—"the possibilities in an arrangement that gave one access to your bed are enormously attractive and would be to anyone with the normal supply of hormones, but such matters ought to be negotiated separately if they are to be negotiated at all."

"I think I'm flattered." She raised her head and peered at him, a confused little girl child.

"You should be. . . . Now what's the real worth? Four fifty?"

"No, Neal," she said slowly, hands folded piously on her lap, "I can't let you do it. I'm terribly grateful to you for the offer. But I can't accept it."

"No strings attached," he said lightly. "None at all."

He was hurt and angry—and smart enough to let neither emotion show.

"I can't be dependent on you, Neal. We'll be all right. The insurance money will come through any day now."

"In time?"

"I'm sure"—she bit her lip—"it will be in time."

"Can't be dependent on anyone, Megan?" He put down the teacup and stood up. "Or just not on me?"

"I have some family pride left."

"No one need know . . . except maybe Nick."

"I'll know. . . . Forgive me, Neal." Her eyes filled with tears. "I'm sure you think I'm rude."

"No." He paused and grinned. "Just a little stubborn, but you always were just a little stubborn. . . . Is it because we were lovers once, more or less?"

"Certainly not, Neal." She extended her hands in a meek plea. "It just wouldn't be right. Not from anyone."

"I'll charge rent, interest and rent. Make some money on the deal."

"No," she snapped, suddenly and without warning angry. "I said no and that's final."

"OK, Megan," he said as he picked up his trench coat. "It's an open offer."

"I'll never change my mind," she shouted as he reached the doorway.

He hesitated then turned and smiled his most captivating smile.

"Like Harry Truman said, never say never because that's a hell of a long time."

Only as the double-decker, aluminum Metra train pulled out of the old station at 91st Street, bound for the Loop, did he begin to feel anger. By the end of the train ride, he was furious at her.

Nevertheless, he was still determined to protect Megan and her family.

He canceled the plane reservation from his room at the Ritz-Carlton.

And phoned Blackie Ryan.

I'll show the bitch.

Chicago's new acting mayor, Eugene Sawyer, looks like a man who has been run over by an errant snowplow that he never saw coming. He seems not to be quite able to believe that he has been trashed by a substantial segment of Chicago's black leadership, men and women who until a few days ago were his friends and allies. After all, eleven out of eighteen black aldermen had put their names on a piece of paper endorsing him for mayor: the canny Alderman Ed Burke would not deliver white votes save to a candidate that purported to have, signed, sealed, and delivered, the black majority.

Then his allies, their names still on the paper, began deserting him. He was threatened with war in the streets, political destruction, even death. He lost some of them, it is said, because of a single phone call from Black Muslim leader Minister Farrakhan. He was booed in the council chamber and denounced, sometimes in marvelously obscene words, by his erstwhile allies.

Still he will surely be judged on his record, a record which he has not yet started to make.

If, as he starts to create that record, Mr. Sawyer has the bemused look of a man who can't quite make up his mind whether he is still in a nightmare or whether he is really awake, one can easily understand why.

Neal Connor, IBC News, City Hall, Chicago.

27

The troublesome priest moved a stack of computer copy from the least-crowded chair in his office.

"I knew we would find a place for you to sit, to which heaven knows you are entitled after the siege of City Hall."

"You watched?"

"I enjoy Greek drama. Ed Burke is kind of an Agamemnon, isn't he?"

"I'm sure he wouldn't get the reference."

"You err, Neal. He would, which may be part of the problem. What happens to the Irish when they begin to produce literate aldermen?"

"They prolong their power?"

"Precisely."

The Monsignor's suite looked like a slightly modernized caricature of the offices of one of Charles Dickens's clerks—musty, dusty, cluttered, chaotic. Piles of books, magazines, papers (some of them yellowed) littered almost every available flat space, including the floor. The furniture probably had been in the Cathedral rectory since its construction and most likely survived the Chicago fire in some other rectory. On one wall were tattered and aging posters of men to whom Blackie referred as "the three Johns of my childhood—the Pope, the President, and the Quarterback."

"I'm surprised that you haven't replaced Unitas with Jim McMahon."

The little priest's eyes twinkled at Neal's recognition of the Colt quarterback. In response he closed an open closet door and revealed the McMahon-as-MacArthur poster in which the fabled Bear quarterback promised, "I shall return."

"An accurate enough prophecy," murmured Blackie Ryan, who was wearing over his clerical shirt a jacket that also must have dated from before the Fire.

Once Neal was ensconced in the vacated chair, Blackie produced an enormous glass of Diet Coke for him.

"I assume"—Neal leaned back in this chair—"that you now include me among the North Wabash Street Irregulars and want a report on my investigation among my fellow journalists of the circumstances around the death of our classmate."

What am I doing here? Neal wondered. He didn't ask me to investigate and I didn't offer to do so. Yet here I am reporting to him, just like I'm a part of some great secret intelligence organization playing the Great Game. Strictly from Kipling.

"Avenue."

"Sorry." He had scored a point against Blackie with the title for his group of snoopers and do-gooders. "In any event, the circumstances surrounding his death are many and confusing. Let me list them:

"Item. Money in the amount of several hundred thousand dollars is missing from various accounts which Al kept in Chicago banks and S and Ls, money that his clients would certainly have claimed instead of his house.

"Item. Al was into the Outfit for gambling debts, amount considerable but unknown.

"Item. Al died a violent death, presumably in an accident when he drove his car into an oak tree a block from his home. He left the exchange at the usual time that afternoon, not visibly troubled by the disaster that had afflicted him during the final half hour. He drove to Beverly Country Club, where he played nine holes of golf, ate supper, and joined an all-night crap game. He left at approximately one-thirty, drove across Western Avenue, turned the corner at 89th and Hoyne, and smashed into an oak tree that has been there since long before the beginning of the neighborhood. He died shortly thereafter of a skull fracture and brain damage—before the accident was noted and some time before anyone called the police. He was pronounced DOA at Little Company of Mary Hospital, the same place, be it noted, where he was born into the world in 1945—as were we all.

"Item. According to an FBI mole, name unknown, Al had certain dealings with the Garcia family from the South East Side, a group specializing in the distribution of drugs.

"Item. The FBI and the United States Attorney persist in harassing the widow about Al's finances.

"Item. It is my impression that there are strains within the Garcia family—more than the usual strains, that is."

"Capital summary. You may indeed eventually merit inclusion in the North Wabash Street Irregulars, as you have, with considerable lack of reverence, dubbed my little band of colleagues."

"Avenue."

"Indeed. And your information confirms what I have learned from, ah, other sources. But is it not possible that these phenomena are only loosely related and that there is no pattern to be found in them at all. There is no evidence of foul play in our classmate's death. The insurance investigators are searching desperately for some hint of suicide and have found none." The priest lifted his pudgy hands. "The grieving widow will eventually receive her money from them. The other money will never be found and life will go on."

"Any suggestions?"

"I have here . . ." He felt in the pockets of his jacket, then his trousers, then his clerical shirt. He rose from his chair, stumbled over to his littered desk, shuffled through several stacks of paper, and triumphantly produced a small pink telephone-message slip. "As I was saying, I have here a list of three names of people you might wish to interview, all of whom could have some interest in the case. Let me see . . ." He tilted the paper at several different angles, peered at it through his thick, rimless glasses, and then turned it over. "Aha, here they are."

"Associates of Al?"

"In one sense or another." The priest returned to his chair and sunk wearily into it. "First of all, there is a gentleman named Cosmo Ventura, alias Cos the Card, who has information about the gambling debts, which certain people out on the West Side have no objection to communicating to the proper person, so long as that person does not work for the United States of America."

"Why would they tell me?"

"They have certain hints that you are interested, and they think you are the proper recipient of the information, doubtless for reasons which seem good and proper to them. Cos the Card is not to be feared. Our friends on the West Side do not go after reporters, unless as in the case of Jake Lingle of happy memory and so long ago, the reporters are actually working for them."

"Cos the Card?"

"Indeed yes. I have here in my hand, in the difficult code which is considered to be my handwriting, phone numbers of all these people. Let me see, ah, yes. The second person is one who, for some curious reason, everyone has overlooked—a certain Brian Neenan, business partner to our late classmate."

"Partner? I didn't know Al had a partner!"

Blackie continued to peer at the pink slip. "Partner in the sense that they shared the same office and some of the same investments. A kindred spirit I take it."

"Which is to say one should not trust him for a moment."

"And that despite his not inconsiderable Gaelic charm. Our classmate was a likable man, not notably encumbered by conscience."

"And ultimately empty."

"Terrifyingly empty. I suspect he did not cling to life too desperately at the end."

"Remarkable children."

Blackie did not ask how he knew the children. "Their mother's work, clearly. And at very high cost, one must presume. In any event, Neenan doubtless can be of some assistance if he wishes to be, especially since it could be called to his attention that the Honorable Donald Bane Roscoe might soon be poking about his records."

"And a TV journalist could ask questions in deep background mode which he might want to answer."

"Indeed. Now finally there is one Maureen Kennelly, a runner at the Mercantile Exchange, a young woman of perhaps twenty-eight summers with whom our classmate was reportedly involved."

"A mistress? Al had a mistress?"

"It is so alleged. He is supposed to have visited her before he went to the golf course the afternoon of his death. My information"—he sighed—"is not from the police, who, if they know about the relationship, have chosen not to probe it."

"Does Megan know?"

Blackie shrugged. "Not that she would admit to herself, I think. Our classmate would probably have found the forbidden and dangerous aspect of such a relationship more rewarding than the actual physical pleasure, such as this might have been."

"He loved danger?"

"Surely. As you yourself must remember. Even when he played football for St. Ignatius in our youth. I remarked earlier that I don't think he clung too vigorously to life at the end. But I don't see him as the kind who would do away with himself, do you?"

"No. Accidental death or murder."

"Precisely. I think Ms. Kennelly is a witness who will require all your fabled charm to be persuaded to talk."

"And I don't even know what I'm looking for, do I?"

"The problem with this problem"—Blackie Ryan sighed again—"is not that it is so deep but that it is so diffuse. Indeed so diffuse that it might not be a problem at all. . . . Incidentally, as you might have surmised, these three worthies—Cosmo Ventura, Brian Neenan, and Maureen Kennelly—are all from the neighborhood."

"Naturally, isn't everyone?"

Blackie peered over his glasses. "You have interacted with my colleague in the Lord Jesus, Richard McNamara, Ph.D., late Captain in the United States Navy?"

"Aka Father Ace?"

Blackie beamed. "So I am told he is called."

"Yeah. He thinks the neighborhood is some kind of magic place that has a hold on people from which they cannot escape."

"Tsk tsk." Blackie stared at a piece of paper that seemed to have materialized in his hand. "Remarkable. . . . What? Magic? Most unscholarly of Doctor McNamara. Obviously it is merely a sacred place, nothing more."

"And I'm in it," Neal said ruefully, "because I am entranced by a woman."

"Entranced?" The priest smiled innocently.

"Captivated, enthralled, driven half-mad." He couldn't be making these intimate and personal admissions to the head of the North Wabash Avenue Irregulars, could he?

"You merely demonstrate good taste as well as gallantry," the priest purred soothingly.

"Or obsession."

"Our species seems designed for obsession."

"Not like I am now. Dear God, Blackie, I hear her name pounding in my head all the time."

"Astonishing."

"My head is filled with lecherous thoughts about her."

"Remarkable. Even shocking."

"What kind of a pervert has lewd thoughts about a widow?"

"One whose hormone supply is intact."

"I feel I can't keep my hands off her. I mean, I have so far, but I don't want to."

"Unheard-of."

"If I don't get out of town, I'm sure I'll drag her into bed with me."

"A possibility beyond belief."

"I don't think she'll protest all that much."

"Words to which I refuse to listen."

"You're making fun of me!"

Blackie's eyes blinked in meek innocence. "Surely not. Have I ever in all our lives been guilty of such an offense?"

"I'm acting likely a horny adolescent."

"To call the mating instincts of the species 'adolescent' does not diminish their power."

Neal struggled out of his chair. "Men and women don't marry their grammar school sweethearts anymore. And they don't come back thirty years later to reclaim them."

"Happens all the time."

"In the neighborhood," he said as he struggled into his trench coat. "I'm not part of the neighborhood."

"I'm glad to be reassured on the point."

"I've never wanted anyone so badly in all my life."

"You've never been forty-three before and had such a woman as the virtuous Megan dependent on you."

"Maybe you're right." He jammed his hands into his pockets. "I don't know how it will all end. What chances do you give me of making it out of the emotional mess I'm in?"

"By yourself?" The priest seemed to be calculating. "Oh, perhaps five percent."

"Not very consoling."

"I presumed you wanted the truth."

"With someone else?"

"Depending on the person, the chances might go up somewhat."

"Megan."

The priest sighed, a great West-of-Ireland sigh that might have been interpreted as an onslaught of a serious asthma attack. "At the present, insufficient data."

Well, he wasn't pushing the relationship very hard, was he?

"It was all so long ago, Johnny."

"Was it? Perhaps. But the grief survives and that must be experienced and exorcised."

"Grief?" He leaned against the door.

"Consider those for whom we must mourn. Minimally. The little boy from another parish who moves into the allegedly affluent precincts of St. Praxides. He is big and bright and not unattractive, but he is shy and awkward and embarrassed by what he considers his inferior social status, a phenomenon to which the kids of St. Prax's pay no attention at all, whatever their parents might think. But he does not understand that. He wants to be friends, he wants to be accepted, he wants to belong. But he does not know how. So he is ignored and sometimes laughed at. He seems able to relate only to unusual types, a frustrated poet, a troublesome priest in the making. . . ." Blackie glanced at him, shrewdly, over the rims of his glasses and folded his hands again on his belly. "From a far distance he admires a girl whose cool self-possession dazzles him, but he dare not even talk to her. Oh, yes, we must grieve for this little boy. One says he will get over it—and he will—but the pain will never quite go away. Most of us cover the similar pains of childhood with a patina of nostalgia, but this little boy is too clear-eyed—and perhaps too hurt—to be able to do that."

"I've had worse grief since then, Johnny."

"Hmm . . . ?" He seemed surprised that there was anyone in the room listening to his monologue. "Perhaps. Now consider the other actor in our story: a little girl of the same age, the final fruit of a very odd tree. For reasons of nature or grace, not too distant perhaps from the miraculous, she has partially escaped the family subculture which has been built up to protect their dignity against the image of working for the Outfit. They are silly people. The little girl knows this dimly and resolves not to be silly like the rest of them. She becomes very rational, controlled, candid, self-possessed, responsible. The exact opposite of the rest of the family. But she must struggle every minute of her life against them. Alas for her, she tumbles into a crush almost upon the arrival of the other actor. Then one morning he hurls himself into her bedroom, carries her into the snow, and saves her from certain death. Now the crush is incurable. In time she finds that she can neither exorcise him nor give herself to him. Must we not grieve for her, too?"

"Yes." He swallowed. "More for her, perhaps. Because she has to pretend to be happy."

"Precisely. Now, given your cosmopolitan experience, you perceive that we are grieving for unfulfilled and unexorcised dreams and the pain they cause. The little boy seeks happiness in a career at which he is quite successful. The little girl marries a man whom she thinks is like the one she has lost. He turns out not to be, but as women are wont, she makes do. Neither has quite been able to experience the simple but often profound grief that comes from the end of childhood dreams, the termination of childhood crushes."

"I suppose you're right. We're not the only ones—"

"Surely not. But then an opportunity occurs again—much later in life. The mutual crushes persist, but so does the wisdom which says that such crushes are childish folly—"

"Exactly."

"—and," Blackie went on, ignoring the interruption, "the romantic passion which says that they are occasionally in fact a higher wisdom."

"Most improbable."

"And neither wisdom can defeat the other until both are able to grieve for the pain which has survived along with the romance."

"Alone or with each other?"

"Sounds like a question from the old confessional manuals. . . . I don't think THAT matters."

"Very dubious prognosis, I would say."

"Surely. But not yet meriting despair."

"With a whole neighborhood watching."

Blackie raised his shoulders and then permitted them to slump again. "Waiting to cheer or weep."

"I wish they would go away and leave us alone."

"That they will not do."

Clever, dangerous, troublesome priest.

And unlike the English king, no one would rid Neal of this troublesome priest.

28

"Ms. Lane to see you, Mr. Connor," said the polite black voice at the switchboard, hinting oh, so subtly that "Ms. Lane" was some dish.

"Send her back." Neal's heart jumped into his throat.

He had not told Blackie Ryan about his offer to Megan, ashamed of his generosity and not sure about his own motives.

Megan!

Megan!

Megan!

Dear God, Megan!

She was still in black, but a miniskirt this time and with black stockings. Hunger for her hit him like a blow to his gut. One could peel off her clothes so very quickly and then . . .

It would not be, he was sure, the first time someone had made love in one of these offices.

"I thought you'd have a bigger office." She glanced shyly around his cubbyhole. "I suppose some people's prestige is so high that they don't need fancy offices."

"If I'd known you were coming"—he tried to smile cheerfully—"I'd have borrowed John Jefferson's office to impress you."

"May I sit down?"

"Please do."

He swept wire-service clips off the only chair in his office, an uncertain tube-and-plastic affair that shook in dismay whenever contacted by a human body.

"You didn't finish your chocolate chip cookies," she said, reaching into her leather purse.

She placed the wax-paper parcel in front of him, in the only empty place on his desk.

"Peace offering," she continued.

He opened it eagerly. "You made more."

"I might have."

"I'll get us two cups of tea. No choice here."

"That's all right."

He returned, breathless, with two plastic cups of tea. She nodded her gratitude and reached for the cookies. "May I have one?"

"Only one." He grabbed two for himself.

"I have been told," she began shakily, balancing the teacup awkwardly in her left hand while she took a small bite out of her cookie, "that I behaved with singular lack of grace. I'm sorry."

"Who told you that?"

"Catherine . . . and that terrible little priest."

"I didn't tell him!" Neal insisted.

"I know you didn't. I told him."

"What did he say?"

"A lot of things." She was staring at her tiny shoes. "It came down to the sin of pride. Refusal to be dependent on anyone, even God."

He wanted so badly to take her in his arms, he felt for a moment that he had already done so.

Better open the door to let some air in.

"He thinks God sent me to help you?"

She looked up at him, her eyes wet, her face miserable. "Something like that. I'm still struggling with it, Neal. I know I've been terrible, but there's a barrier inside me . . . like I was selling myself into slavery. I know that's silly."

The strife in her soul, torn in two opposite directions, was reflected in agony on her face.

Megan! Megan! I love you! I want to take care of you!

"I want to take care of you, Megan, that's all," he spoke softly, trying to help. "You know the Chinese custom: if you save someone's life—"

"You're responsible for providing for the rest of his life!" She clasped her hands tightly together. "I know, but it doesn't seem fair."

Sexual tides were flooding the room, racing, swirling, surging. We're both in danger, he thought.

"I won't consider you dependent on me," he tried again. "Let's just use the convention of our native city"—he brightened, seeing a way out—"and our neighborhood. I'm doing you a favor."

"And I owe you one?" She smiled wryly.

"You owe me one. Someday."

"That way . . ." she began.

"It makes sense—a deposit in the favor bank?"

"A deposit in the favor bank it is . . . I *am* sorry, Neal. Truly I am. It's almost as hard to say that as it is to say I accept your offer."

"Because you want to," he asked bluntly, "or because people have told you that you should?"

He imagined their two bodies locked together in the agonized, pleasurable surge up the mountain of pleasure. Dear God, how much I love her! Help me to stay in control until we straighten this out!

She paused, considering. "Because I need help, Neal—desperately."

Blackie had probably been candid: Do you trust Neal less than Tom Dineen?

Good argument.

"All right," he said, brisk and efficient so as to ease her embarrassment, "what's the house really worth? Four hundred fifty thousand?"

He wanted to touch, fondle, caress her, play with her forever—her breasts, her belly, her thighs, her loins. All of her wonderful self.

I must have her!

I love her! I love her! I love her!

"No, nothing like that." She began to relax. "I mean the equity in it is about two hundred, if you just assumed the mortgage payments. . . . Megan Keefe Lane, the widow with the mortgage problem." She grinned crookedly. "I can't quite believe any of this."

"Believe it." He wolfed down two more cookies. "Call Nick and make arrangements with him today."

"Dear God, Neal, why do you want to do this?"

He slumped back in the chair, loosened his tie, and threw up his hand in despair.

"I'll be damned if I know, Megan. I'm an emotional mess. Fed up and disillusioned by my work. Morally worn out by what we do in the national media, afraid of death, I suppose. Wondering what's real and what isn't, what life is all about."

"Poor Neal!" Her marvelously etched face softened in sympathy.

And his heart almost broke in response.

"Yeah, well, I'll be all right, I suppose. Anyway, this is something I can do to help people I like. I pulled you out of that house once."

"I'll never forget."

"And I like your kids. They're a neat bunch."

"They like you."

"The truth is," he said as he leaned forward, "they have reservations about me. The jury is out. OK. You'll call Nick and start it working, right?"

"No, Neal. I can't let you do this." She stood up, her courage drained. "I've changed my mind."

"Damn it, Megan!" He jumped up and grabbed her thin, fragile shoulders. "Do I have to shake you again? You WILL let me do it, is that clear?"

She examined his face solemnly, as if searching into his soul. "All right."

"What?"

"ALL RIGHT . . . Oh my God, I sound just like Teri, don't I?"

"You could do worse." He eased her back to the chair and sat her down gently. "Moreover, you send me the college and high school tuition bills, even the one from St. Prax's."

"I can't!"

"Do you have money to pay their first-semester bills?"

"No, but—"

"How do you propose to handle them?"

"I don't know!" she cried out. "Dear God, I don't know! Leave me alone!"

"All right, then."

"Maybe I can stall them till the end of the year."

"And embarrass the kids?"

"A little suffering won't hurt them."

"Not that kind of suffering. . . . Don't worry—it will all go on my tab and I'll collect interest till the insurance money comes. An extra deposit in the favor bank."

The phone rang. Johnny Jefferson. Didn't want to interrupt anything, slight laugh, but he would like to see Neal as soon as he was free.

"In a few minutes, Johnny."

"Neal, I . . ." Megan was not quite ready to give in.

"That's an order, woman. If I'm going to take care of you and the kids, I'm going to do it deluxe."

"All right"—she nodded her brisk little sign of consent—"another favor . . . but can't I ask one question?"

"Sure," he said guardedly. When a woman from the neighborhood asked permission to ask a question, it was likely to be a dilly.

"Can you afford it?"

"That is a vulgar South Side shanty-Irish question."

There were three cookies left. He took two of them and gave her one.

"Thank you . . . I know it is, but I want an answer."

Stubborn bitch, but oh, it would be so sweet to possess you. Forever. And to be possessed by you. . . .

"Megan, I don't drink, I don't waste money, I don't buy expensive homes or clothes, I don't keep company with expensive women, I don't make crazy investments. And I earn a salary that is so big that it's almost immoral. I could do this three or four times over and still have enough left so I would never have to work another day in all my life."

"Truly?"

"Truly."

"I'm so happy for you . . . and for me, too, come to think of it." She breathed deeply, and the motion of her ingeniously sculpted bosom clutched at his heart. "I am very grateful for your help, and within reason, I'll do whatever you say."

"I like the qualification, Megan. Now"—he stood up—"I better go talk to Mr. Jefferson, lest he send out patrols to find out who is the classy broad who's been in my office."

And before I lose all my restraint and assault the poor, dear, wonderful woman.

She departed quickly, fearful also perhaps of what might happen if she stayed any longer.

"Thank you again, Neal"—hand outstretched at the door, tears still in her eyes—"I think I've lucked out in my personal guardian angel."

Neal Connor, IBC News, was exhausted from his struggle with his inner demon and hers. He also felt very satisfied with himself as he strode to his boss's office.

One look at Johnny's anguished face made him forget momentarily about Megan Lane and her mortgage.

"Three more death threats," Johnny Jefferson handed an audio-tape cassette to Neal. "Reverend Scott's people presumably."

"Fuck 'em."

Reverend Jeremiah Scott of the Hope Tabernacle Church had taken exception to Neal's kind words about Mayor Sawyer. No outside white reporter, he told his congregants, had any right to tell Chicago blacks how they ought to think about the mayor who had spat on Harold Washington's grave. Black Chicagoans should call Channel 3 and warn them to send the honky Neal Connor right back to New York. Otherwise, they would have trouble.

Reverend Scott, who did not sound all that literate, had been interviewed on a black radio station. Some of the listeners, not necessarily from his congregation, took him to mean that they could continue the death threat epidemic that had plagued Chicago all week.

So now there was a squad car in front of the IBC Building,

another in back, a crowd of cops in the building and two at the door of the tiny cubbyhole that served as Neal's office.

"They're just a bunch of guys in a bar showing off, like as not honkies themselves." Johnny Jefferson tried to sound soothing. "Did you get any comment from Evans's camp?"

"They're still denying the existence of death threats. And defending Reverend Scott's right to express his opinion."

"Bad times, Neal." Johnny slumped into the hard chair next to the desk. "Bad times."

"Fascists."

"And like you said before, people that are sick with grief. Understandably. What's the network saying to you?"

"What do you think? They're warning me to be cautious. They don't want no martyrs."

"Neither do I."

"You think the Callels will try to kill me?" Neal stared at his old friend in disbelief.

" 'Course not. The really dangerous ones are those who don't call."

"Are you getting calls?"

Johnny nodded. "Happened before. No problem."

"Threats on your family?"

"A few. Neal, it's all right. We've got our own security people as well as the police. NO PROBLEM."

Neal brooded for a moment. Then he knew what he would do.

"The hell it's not a problem. Fuck them all."

"What are you gonna do, man?"

"You ever know me to make a mistake in this kind of situation?"

"Nope," Johnny replied promptly. "Seen you do some pretty crazy things that turned out to be real smart."

"Then trust me. Once more."

Johnny stood up. "You bet."

After he'd left the office, Neal phoned Nick Curran.

"Nick I want you to draw up a new will for me. It's simple, no trusts or anything. Leave everything to Megan. Don't argue, Nick, do it. Now. Send it over here by messenger within the hour. Am I going to do something crazy? Wait and see."

The losers in Chicago's election drama on Tuesday night have refused to take seriously the death-threat epidemic that has become a way of life here in Chicago. They still cast doubt on the reality of the threats and then hint that those who didn't vote their way, even if they be black women who are long-time veterans of the civil rights movement, may have only themselves to blame if one or two irate people phone them to protest.

Well, I'm prepared to testify from personal experience that the threats are real enough. Yesterday I had the temerity to express some sympathy for Mayor Sawyer's astonishment at how quickly friends became enemies when the mobs invaded City Hall. A certain Reverend Jeremiah Scott suggested on a radio station that Chicago blacks ought to—I quote the Reverend—"run that honky outsider out of town."

First of all, I was born and raised in Chicago and consider myself a Chicagoan even when I'm in the Hindu Kush. Secondly I'm Irish, not Hungarian.

In any event, after Reverend Scott's broadcast, IBC News received a number of calls like the following:

"If you don't get out of town, you bleep honky, I'll cut off your bleep, you bleep bleep, and stuff them down your bleep throat."

"I'm gonna blow out your bleep brains, you bleep bleep honky."

"You gonna wake up tomorrow morning, you bleep honky, and find you done been blown all the way to heaven and back."

Leaving aside the implication that God would reject me at the heavenly gates, I think I might say that these seem to be bona fide death threats. And they might just as well be from whites as blacks, from ethnics as from disciples of Alderman Shiller, who affects the same kind of language.

A spokesman for Alderman Timothy Evans told me that most death threats were imaginary and that Reverend Scott had the right to express his feelings. Reverend Scott would not speak to me. A spokesman for him said, "You do yourself a favor, honky, and get out of town."

He did not give me an opportunity to assert my Irish identity.

The people who make phone calls like that are cowards, drunks, crazies, bums. I'm not particularly afraid of them. If one of them does take a shot at me and by some mischance hits me, then you have to die sometime and freedom of the press is as good a cause as most and better than some.

This does not seem likely because, as you can see, I'm protected by three of the finest—Chicago cops, as my father was.

I resent, however, threats to the lives of members of the staff of Channel Three, who are not responsible for my loud shanty-Irish mouth. I say again that those who make such calls to innocent people are offscourings of the human race, not to use more scatological language which would force our bleeping mechanism back to work.

I'll make an offer to such garbage. I'm in room nine-forty of the Ritz-Carlton Hotel. Leave your guns home and come fight me man-to-man instead of hiding in your refuse heaps and toilet drains. If you are not willing to take the chance that I'll beat the living daylights out of you with my bare hands, then crawl back to your garbage dumps and leave decent people alone.

Neal Connor, IBC News, under police protection in Chicago.

A knock at the hotel room door.

"Sayonara, Mr. Connor. Superintendent Casey to see you, sir."

The right code word.

"Send him in, of course."

Neal Connor was inordinately satisfied with himself. He was, no doubt, a washed-up has-been; a foreign correspondent who, like Walter Payton, had lost a step; an emotional mess in a midlife crisis and plagued by thoughts appropriate for a dirty old man.

Still he knew how to deal with the kooks.

Even if responding to them was interfering with his hunt for the truth about the death of Al Lane—a hunt that was the real reason for staying in Chicago.

Well, in addition to his lust for his late friend's wife.

Did Blackie tolerate distractions interfering with the work of a candidate Irregular?

"Man, you are CRAZY!" Johnny Jefferson had exploded when the feed went out live.

"Come on, John, you've gone middle-class."

"You don't make our work any easier for us," the soft-spoken, intelligent young black (woman) lieutenant had protested.

"Corrine, believe me, there won't be a single taker for my crazy offer. And the calls are finished. Bet?"

"Not on duty, ma'am." She frowned. "There's nothing like this in any of the manuals."

"When you write yours, you can put it in."

The police were monitoring all calls to him at the Ritz-Carlton, part of Chicago's Water Tower Place complex. Neal gave them strict orders to refuse all calls from IBC Network News. Let them stew.

At a quarter to ten, the lieutenant rang his room. "The calls are tapering off now, Mr. Connor."

"No threatening ones, I presume."

"No, sir. Only calls of support. There was even one from your network a few moments ago. I guess I will have to put it in my manual, sir. I'm not sure what chapter it belongs in, however."

"Try crazy reporters or crazy Irishmen."

"Yes sir. Speaking of the latter—Irishmen, I mean—Superintendent Casey is in the lobby and would like to see you, may I send him up?"

"He's not superintendent anymore, is he?"

"No sir, not really, but we call him that because he is so revered."

Was she kidding the former top cop?

"I'll be happy to see the revered former acting superintendent."

You throw in the "acting," just so she knows that you know his history.

"I'm Mike Casey," said the tall, slender, silver-haired man, in brown double-breasted suit, brown tie, brown shirt, and brightly polished brown shoes.

"Aka Mike Casey the Cop, cousin of a certain troublesome priest and charter member of the North Wabash Street Irregulars."

The former policeman, kind of an Irish Basil Rathbone playing Sherlock Holmes in the old movies, smiled genially.

"Avenue . . . and you sound like my wife. I won't deny the connection."

"Sit down, Mr. Casey."

"Mike."

"OK, Mike, order a drink? No? My first problem is how I

persuade that young lieutenant that she is not breaking rules and regulations if she calls me Neal."

"You tell her that male patrol officers call you Neal?"

"Sure. She says that's all right for them."

"I think Lieutenant Day has a book of yours to autograph. You sign it Neal and that should do it."

"And the watch will be over then."

"I don't think so. My former colleagues, some of whom are very able indeed, are taking no chances with you. And I, er, I have taken certain precautions of my own."

"On the instructions of the North Wabash Street Irregulars, I assume?"

"Avenue."

"I stand corrected. What if I decide to stay in town?"

"We will all rejoice." Mike crossed his long legs and folded his slender, artist's fingers beneath his chin. "And keep you protected till we think there's no danger. Needless to say, whether you want to be protected or not."

"I understand how the Ryan clan works."

They both laughed.

"You don't think there's any real danger now, do you?"

"I think you rather brilliantly defused most of it with your outrageous comments tonight. Very clever indeed."

"Thank you. But why, then, are you here?"

"Mostly to indicate my availability."

The phone rang.

"Yes, Corrine?"

"A Ms. Lane on the line for you, sir. You said you wanted to know if she called."

"Put her through, Lieutenant."

"Yes SIR."

She sounded like one of Father Ace's troops.

"Neal Connor."

"Are you all right?" A quiet, frightened voice.

"Sure. Fine. Surrounded by gorgeous women cops, not a single taker for my offer, and no more death threats."

"I was downtown at Tommy Dineen's office and I didn't hear about your broadcast till I came home. Teri was worried sick about you, and both Margaret and Mark keep calling from school. We're all worried."

Perhaps an exaggeration. Well, Megan and Teri were worried.

"Tell them not to worry, everything is fine."

"You were so brave, Teri said."

"I bask in her admiration. But it was a ploy, Megan, nothing more."

"Be careful."

"Have you talked to Nick about that, uh, matter we discussed yesterday?"

"I have. He's taking care of it."

"I've made a new will, Megan, to cover that. Just in case. Everything's all right, but life is fragile."

"I know that now. Please, please be careful . . . and I won't say you should change your will back because you're not here to shake me and that would frustrate you. So I'll just say thank you again and thank you forever."

"God bless you, Megan."

Mike the Cop's face was bland.

"Women," Neal murmured admiringly.

"Nothing better."

"Truly."

The Cop hesitated. "I married my grammar school sweetheart."

"Oh?"

"Almost forty years later."

"Better late than never."

"Precisely."

The Ryan clan had the custom of adding a title to the name of a friend or relative. Presumably he was Neal the Newscaster. The title seemed to be designed to distinguish the person from someone else with the same name but a different occupation. However, there was only one Mike Casey in the family.

And only one Neal the Newshawk—better—on which the family was attempting to close in.

Adrenaline was still being pumped into Neal's veins. His mind was still racing. Tomorrow morning, when the crisis was over, his bones would be stiff, his muscles would ache, his brain would be exhausted. He was getting too old for such emotional binges.

But now that he was on a roll, he would ask Mike the Cop some important questions.

"Tell me about the Garcia family."

"The drug dealers?"

"Right."

The silver-haired former acting superintendent spread his hands. "They're a typical group, pretty much like the early Mafia gangs—murderous, greedy, reckless, dangerous. Like Capone, not like the cautious old men who run the Outfit now. They bring the cocaine in from Colombia and distribute through their own wholesalers to the street dealers; life expectancy for the dealers is about six months. They've made vast profits, which, like the Outfit, they've poured into legitimate and semilegitimate businesses. They routinely bribe police and federal agents and brag they're above the law, just like the Outfit dons, after whom they're modeling themselves."

"Some of the dons are in jail now."

"The Garcias will tell you that they are old men who have lost their manhood."

"Are they and the Mob going to fight it out?"

"Probably not. The Mob is prudent these days about gang wars and the Spanish families are still afraid of them—though not of anyone else. More likely they will make informal agreements, dividing up territory. There's more than enough drug money to go around."

"Are they untouchable?"

"Not at all. The Garcias have lost a lot of members of their family in the last eighteen months—internal fights among factions, raids from rivals who are defending their own turf, affairs of honor with the Colombian kingpins who think they've been cheated, punishment from their 'council' for those who endanger the whole enterprise. You wouldn't want to be a Garcia, Neal."

"How was Alf Lane involved with them?"

"So that's your interest?" The Cop's thick silver eyebrows lifted ever so slightly.

"More or less."

"Personal or professional?"

"Maybe both."

"I see. . . . Well, the United States Attorney, with characteristic poverty of imagination, thinks that Al was investing money not only in the Standard and Poor's index but in cocaine futures, so to speak, and that he was killed because he tried to buy too much too quickly."

"And?"

"There seems to be almost a quarter million dollars missing from various accounts that Lane maintained around the city. Mr.

Roscoe and Mr. King, the FBI agent in charge, think that the money was turned over to the Garcias, who then executed him for a failure to pay as much as they had expected."

"Why would Al play that game?"

"He was badly in debt to the Mob—gambling debts."

"He played the horses?"

"And football and baseball and basketball and everything else he could bet on. He was, as you might imagine, a loser."

"He bet a little on the horses when we were at college."

"More than a little even then."

Dear God, poor Megan. Did she know?

Of course she did.

"They executed him by banging his car into the oak tree down the street from his house?"

"After first filling him with whiskey so that it looked like he was killed accidentally."

"Doesn't sound like 'Miami Vice.' "

"Indeed not. But there are lots of murky things in the Lane case."

"You spoke of the U.S. Attorney's lack of imagination?"

"A more imaginative analysis would suggest that the flow of money was in the opposite direction, that the Garcias were investing in the S and P future index and that Al was acting as their broker."

"Wow! Has the Outfit ever done that?"

"They're much too conservative to gamble on commodities. They only go for sure things. If the Mercantile Exchange would give them a cut off the top of the house's take it would be another matter. Till then, they'll be content with Las Vegas and Atlantic City. But the Hispanics? It's possible. Mind you, I have no evidence to sustain this model, but it is interesting, is it not?"

"Why is Roscoe hassling Mrs. Lane?"

"To suggest the possibility that she knows where the money is hidden and that thus the death of her husband is the result of his withholding sums that he owed to the Garcias."

"And what will come of all this?"

The Cop regarded him carefully.

"Nothing, I hope. The United States Attorney has no case. He will get some publicity, not much, and then find a new game to play. The Garcias are not acting like they've missed any money they think is rightfully theirs. And since no attempt has been made by them or by anyone else—save Donny Roscoe—to question Mrs. Lane, it's safe to presume she doesn't know where the money is. Finally the insurance company will almost certainly have to pay on her husband's insurance policy. There is no real evidence of either suicide or murder."

"And the quarter million?"

"Lost, probably forever, most likely in the Black Monday crash, perhaps in accounts which the Merc or the CFTC will never discover."

"No case, no story."

"Probably not. I emphasize the first word. Mr. Roscoe is unpredictable when publicity is to be gained. Indicting those who are thought to be rich is always a good way to reap a rich harvest of that precious commodity."

Long after Mike the Cop left, Neal's body finally slowed down, about four A.M.

As he drifted off into sleep, with images of characters from television cop shows storming the peaceful streets of Beverly, he knew that there was one detail the sometime acting superintendent of police had missed.

But he couldn't quite remember what it was.

32

"I tell you, Neal, it ain't right." Johnny Jefferson tossed a stack of telegrams on his desk.

"It shouldn't have worked, but it did?"

"Man, you're a frigging folk hero—Neal Connor, defender of the First Amendment. Network is ecstatic, everyone in Chicago is proud of you. Royko writes a column saying you're the last of Chicago's great white folk heroes and probably the only one that doesn't drink."

"I called him already to thank him."

"Eugene Kennedy has an article that'll be in the *Trib* tomorrow analyzing the psychological interaction between you and those who threatened you."

"Without interviewing me or them? I can hardly wait."

"You're a big frigging deal!"

"I told you I'd take care of it. No more death threats?"

"Not a one. Nowhere in town."

"Any offers to fight me?"

"Bare-handed? No way, man!"

"Great. I'm not much of a fighter anyway. I only knocked one guy out in all my life."

He remembered Megan.

I must call her. Dear God, how much I want her.

"Now about the job here?"

He sighed. "I've thought about it, old buddy, and I can't do it. All kinds of reasons, personal more than professional. Just can't do it. Appreciate the offer and the concern, though. More than you could know."

"Definite?"

Just the way she said "Truly?"

"Definite."

"You win some and you lose some. Thanks for thinking about it."

"I really did that. But I gotta get out of town by the middle of next week. One or two more stories about the healing of wounds, then I'm off to Washington for the Gorbachev gambit."

When Johnny finally left, he reached for the phone to call Megan. Her line was busy, so he turned to the telegrams. He was interrupted several times by anxiously reassuring calls from network vice presidents.

Then he remembered Megan and dialed again. This time she answered.

"Megan Lane."

"Neal. I hope you got some sleep last night."

"After you said not to worry I did. What about you?"

"Eventually."

"Did you see Royko's column?"

"You better believe it. Talked to him. Thanked him. Kids OK?"

"Teri wants to know if there are any posters of you."

"Not yet. Tell her to buy a Bruce Springsteen poster and kind of squint."

"One of those we already have."

"Have you talked to Nick?"

"Yes."

"Sorry if I sound like a catechist."

"Sister Superior, actually. . . ."

She was laughing at him.

"I'm sorry I sounded like I was giving orders."

"To quote my daughter Teri, you're so cute when you pretend to be dominating."

He felt his face turn warm. "I said I was sorry."

"Three times. No need to be—not so long as you don't expect any woman around this house to be dominated just because you're cute when you give orders."

"God forbid."

"Actually I've been a good girl. I'm going down to Nick's office tomorrow to sign some papers."

"Good. Let's have lunch. Do you want to take a cab up to Water Tower? It's a great place. I'll probably be leaving the day after for Washington."

"I was hoping you could come out for dinner before you left."

"No such luck, I'm afraid. Twelve-thirty tomorrow?"

"Fine."

All very businesslike and efficient. Protect the widow from those who would foreclose on her mortgage and then get out of town. Shane rides over the mountain—while Joseph Lane stares at him hatefully.

"Neal . . ."

"Yes?" He should start working on a report for tonight. Network probably would not want to use it, but they'd want the option.

"I'm not sure whether to tell you this or not. I haven't told anyone else."

"If it's important, tell me."

"I've been getting calls at night—from a woman with a Spanish voice. She wants to know where the money is."

"Oh?" He jerked himself upright in his chair. "Does she make threats?"

"No . . . not really. She kind of begs me to tell her, but, well, I don't know—there's something a little threatening about it."

"Do you know where any money is, Megan?"

"Certainly not. Al never told me anything. He felt women couldn't understand money. I tell her that and she hangs up."

He thought for a moment, heart pumping rapidly again.

"I don't think it's worth worrying about, but it's a good thing you told me. If you don't mind, I'll drop a word to someone who will be able to take care of it."

"Please do. I worry about the kids."

And I worry about you.

After they confirmed the twelve-thirty lunch and hung up, Neal drummed his fingers thoughtfully on his desk for several minutes.

He pulled a business card out of his wallet and punched in a number on the phone.

"Reilly Gallery."

"This is Neal Connor, Ms. Reilly, is Mike there?"

"Mike the Cop of the North Wabash Street Irregulars?"

"Avenue . . ."

When Mike came on the phone, Neal told him about the apparently Hispanic phone call. Mike said he would "look into it."

Does Blackie Ryan have his own private police force, really?

Then he sighed and rose from his chair and walked down the corridor to Johnny Jefferson's office.

"Have I ever said 'definite' and not meant it?"

"Nope." The manager began to grin. "Not so far."

"Well, I've just done it for the first time."

"Hot DAWG!" He jumped to his feet and hugged Neal. "We're really gonna kick the shit round this town."

"If you keep talking that way, you're not going to be able to do white English when you get home!"

"Hush your mouth, white man!"

Johnny insisted that Neal move into the Mayfair Regent. The suite was waiting, it was nicer even than the Ritz, and it was his until his final decision in February.

"St. Valentine's night, huh, Johnny?"

"Yeah, will Channel Three be your Valentine? How about that!"

"Where is the Mayfair, by the way?"

"On East Lake Shore Drive, down the street from the Drake, real class."

"Facing the beach?"

"Nothing but the best for our celebrity!"

"Is there a good restaurant there?"

"Ciel Bleu, one of the best in town, three meals a day, plus tea in the lobby."

He called Megan back and changed their luncheon date to the Ciel Bleu. He had to tell her where it was.

"They're conservatives." Cosmo Ventura played gently with his expensive fountain pen. "The friends of my friends out on the West Side do not like trouble. There's been too much trouble lately. Too many elderly men who have been community leaders all their lives sent off to jail. They all have bad hearts and they're not getting proper medical attention."

He meant the Mob bosses who had been recently convicted, and he was saying in fact that the Outfit was in disarray and wanted to avoid publicity till it got its house back in order.

"I understand that your friends, ah, the friends of your friends"—the elaborate euphemisms annoyed Neal—"would want to avoid trouble particularly at this awkward time. But would Alf Lane really constitute trouble?"

Neal wished he had bitten off his tongue. His question had been far too direct. It violated the protocol of the conversation. Cos Ventura winced at his gaucherie.

Perhaps he was too eager to have lunch with Megan.

They were sitting in Johnny Jefferson's spare, tasteful office, lent for the sake of privacy. Johnny and Cosmo apparently knew each other—both active in the Mother Macauley High School Fathers' Club.

So maybe the neighborhood had changed—Outfit accountants and black television station managers were a new addition.

"You don't understand." Cos spread his tiny, jeweled fingers expressively. "Take, say, a casino in Jersey. If the friends of my friends, let's say, have a small business interest in that, it's strictly a blue-chip matter, you understand? The house takes its cut for rendering a service to the client. My friends' friends take their cut for rendering a service to the house. No one loses."

Cos was a tiny man, no more than five feet two inches. Immaculately groomed, impeccably dressed—manicured fingers, razor-cut hair, flawless gray suit—he looked like a model for *Esquire* instead of an ambassador from the West Side who happened to live on the South Side.

"Except the customer."

Cos's smile was mild, self-deprecating; his small brown eyes sad; his fingers anxious.

"And not all of them. Even those that lose are entertained. But now you take this Mercantile Exchange . . . that's gambling. There's no house, no one in charge, no one to maintain law and order. A man could lose everything there."

"You're telling me that the people on the West Side, the friends of your friends, think the commodity exchanges are dangerous gambling establishments?"

Cos missed the irony of the question.

"They think the whole business is irresponsible, worse than these Hispanic kids who market cocaine. There's no respect in either business, if you understand me." He delicately lifted a teacup. "The friends of my friends are appalled."

Well, that was a twist.

"So they don't like any of their money going on S and P futures, for example."

"My friends tell me that their friends want only the most conservative blue-chip investments. If some of the younger guys—you know, the MBA kids—want to play the game, well, the wiser men won't stop them, but they're not ready to bail them out when they lose their shirts, like a lot of them did back in October."

Younger Mob members with M.B.A.s? Well, why not?

"Which brings us to my friend Alf Lane, about whom you called me."

"Yeah." Cos leaned forward on his leather chair and rubbed his hands as if they were dry. "See, the word is out on the street that you're interested in Alfie's death. Nothing wrong with that. Hell, he was your friend, right? If we don't stand by our friends, who we gonna stand by, right? But I get a call from this very good friend of mine, and he says that his friends want me to tell you that they had nothing against Alf. After all, his wife's father was a lawyer for some of these men when they were all a lot younger, right?"

"Right."

"So, OK, Alf had owed them some money because he didn't know how to bet conservatively on the ponies. But he paid all that off, right? He was clean. No problem."

"I see."

"And Al and I were personal friends, right? His kid Teri and my daughter Rita go to the same school." Cosmo rubbed his hands again. "I ask some people I know—as a personal favor—to ask the bookies not to take any more of his bets. It's not right to take your friend's money, right?"

A wonderful ethical principle. One which would not normally disturb the Outfit. Somehow there was a message beneath all this, but Neal could only comprehend that the Outfit wanted him to understand that its hands were clean in the death of Al Lane.

"I understand."

"All right, some of the young fellas put money into the commodities game through Al. I'm told he gave them excellent service. Never a question of anything shady. They made a few dollars and then lost a few dollars, OK? What happened to Al, I'm told, is that he got caught up in that insanity back in October and made a mistake or two. Who wouldn't under the circumstances? But none of our friends were involved. They got out a few days before. One of the older men passed the word down that the market was going to collapse, so all our friends got out."

"Wise man."

"Been around a long time. Shouldn't be in jail. Bad ticker." Cos tapped his own heart. "Right?"

"Al invest any of your money?" Neal fired the question like it was an AK-47.

Cosmo Ventura winced as if he had been hit by AK-47 fire.

"A little bit now and again, you know? He was a great broker, God rest him. I made a few dollars, too—help to pay for the kids' college. That's really expensive these days, you know. A crusher. But I got out when all our friends got out. Al told me it was a mistake, but I turned around and told him that I had it on the inside that the Dow was headed for a nosedive."

"He suggest you go short?"

"Yeah, he said that if I thought that was going to happen, I should make like a bear. But I just wanted out."

It would be an interesting investigative story: How did an Outfit don in a federal penitentiary somewhere know beforehand about the October meltdown?

It was the kind of story that could get you a one-way boat ride on Lake Michigan.

"So you were one of the lucky ones? You made a few dollars and got out with all your money?"

"Absolutely."

Then why was he so nervous? And why were his friends and their friends so nervous? He didn't get all his money back, Neal was willing to bet. He'd been one of those clients that Al had robbed in the fatal final half hour of his career as a trader. The big guys had warned him to take his loss like a man. They also insisted that he report to Neal that they had no interest in Al Lane even if he was a welsher and a cheat.

That was unlike the Outfit. In the good old days they put guys like Al in the trunks of autos and left their bodies to rot on obscure side streets.

"I see," Neal said tentatively, not really seeing anything—except that unlike the Garcia family, the Outfit elders were cautious men who did not kill capriciously anymore.

When they did kill, however, you were just as dead.

"Look, Neal"—Cos squirmed in his chair—"sure, some of the friends of my friends were involved in the past in some illegal operations—gambling, vice, that sort of thing. No drugs, not usually anyway. But they're essentially businessmen now, concerned with sound investments and responsible management, right? And are they any worse than those crooks over at the Federal Building who use a guy's lawyer as a mole? They're officers of the court and they violate the lawyer-client relationship all the time. I mean, who's more corrupt?"

"I think your friends, excuse me, the friends of your friends probably have some principles they honor. I'm not sure Don Roscoe has any."

"Yeah, and he's on TV every night looking pious."

"He's not from the neighborhood, is he?"

"Nah, North Side. Evanston, right?"

"I've heard of the place, but I'm not sure it exists."

Cos the Card, doubtless so called because he was devoid of wit, tried to figure out what Neal meant and then abandoned the effort. Neal began to understand, however dimly, the message: Some of the friends had played the S and P with Alf, possibly because he still owed them money. They had taken a bath like everyone else on the day of the crash. But they had also taken their medicine. They did not want Donny Roscoe and his crowd launching yet another investigation of their activities. So they were prepared to grin and bear their losses. Cos confirmed Neal's conclusion.

"The last thing in the world they wanted was for Al to die. He had too many friends."

Which translated that they did not want a headline on the front of the *Sun Times* which announced:

INVESTIGATE MOB LINK WITH MERC

What conservative businessman would want to see that headline about his business—maybe with a stereotypical "Cosa Nostra" name in the story. A name like Cosmo "Cos the Card" Ventura.

And would you—if you were a businessman interested in blue-chip purchases—would you want a dangerous national celebrity like Neal Connor poking his nose around your involvement with the Merc?

No way.

"Who would want him dead, then? Your Hispanic friends?"

"They're no friends of ours," Ventura said bitterly. "They have no class, no style, no respect."

"You gotta teach it young." Neal sighed, thinking of Father Ace and his amused troops.

"You're right, you're absolutely right. That's what I tell my wife all the time. Anyway, if I told Al once, I told him a hundred times to stay away from those people. Poor guy—meaning no disrespect to the dead—couldn't get enough excitement. He never would listen. And he was a great guy, Neal, a great guy. But you knew him, didn't you?"

"A long time ago. . . . So you think he might have offended some of his friends over on the South East Side?"

Dear God, he was talking like a native.

Of course, he *was* a native, wasn't he?

"You want to know what I think, Neal? I think he did what a real man does when he's caught in all the binds that poor Al was caught in."

"And that is?"

"He clears away all the dishonor by dying honorably. That way, his debts are paid and his wife and kids are taken care of, right? That's a man's way out."

Was it? Neal wondered. He would never take that way out himself. He might rush into a firefight to pull out a wounded cameraman, but take his own life directly? Not very likely.

"But Mrs. Lane doesn't collect any money if it's suicide."

"Not if they can prove it's suicide." Cosmo supplied a big wink.

Neal was not sure that Cosmo believed the message he had finally delivered for the friends of his friends. In fact, he was not sure that Cosmo believed anything anymore on this subject besides what the friends of his friends told him to believe. But the message was finally clear: the Outfit firmly believed . . . no, it *said* that it firmly believed that Al Lane had killed himself to provide insurance income for his family.

And would Neal Connor, please, as a personal favor, not stir up any embers which would bring the troops of Donny Roscoe in yet another investigative charge against the Outfit?

No threats. Only the very vague hint that it was in the interests of Megan Lane and her kids that the lid be kept on that particular Pandora's box.

Which the mole might open anyhow.

But if you were an elderly don in prison with your whole empire under plea-bargained assault, you did what you could.

"I understand," he said tentatively to the anxious Cosmo. "I wouldn't be surprised if that's exactly what happened."

Cosmo beamed enthusiastically. "I told my friends that everyone said you were a smart man and would understand. They'll be glad to hear I was right."

"The only thing is," Neal spoke very cautiously, "that the Al Lane I knew wasn't much concerned about things like honor, not the way you or I would be, Cosmo."

The Outfit emissary paled. "A man changes with time, Neal." His tiny shoulders seemed to go limp. "He has responsibilities, things like that. It's not all just fun and games."

"I suppose so," Neal said as he stood up. Just enough doubt had been planted to keep the West Side elders a little nervous. He might need their help later on.

Neal knew that Alf would not fake his own suicide. The Outfit might do so easily and skillfully, given its resources, if it wanted to cover up something else. But they were probably no threat to Megan and her children, not as long as the elders who remembered her father were still alive.

"That guy's scared shitless," Johnny Jefferson said when Cosmo Ventura had departed.

"What's he doing in the business if he can't take the heat?"

"I've been known"—Johnny grinned—"to raise the question about certain anchormen."

"But IBC doesn't terminate aberrant anchorpersons with extreme prejudice."

"Not yet anyway."

Enough about Al Lane for a while. It was time to meet his widow for lunch.

34

"Mary Kate Murphy." The handsome, statuesque woman with gold and silver hair held out her hand at the corner of Chicago and Michigan, oblivious to the cold wind. "Mary Kate *Ryan* Murphy."

"You're not the kind of woman a man ever forgets, Mary Kate." Neal kissed her enthusiastically. "And I hear you're the resident psychiatrist of the North Wabash Avenue Irregulars these days."

Neal wondered if the dangerous and troublesome priest had suggested that his eldest sister, the top matriarch of the Ryan clan, ambush him on his way to lunch with Megan.

"Wrong person," she said with a laugh. "My husband, Joe Murphy, has that job. He talks funny, you know, 'cause he's from Boston. A Celtics fan even, poor dear man."

Even as a girl Mary Kate had been a warm and irresistibly gregarious person. A quarter century of marriage, four children, one grandchild, and a couple of decades of psychiatric practice had only enhanced her charm. Almost as dangerous as her brother, the little Monsignor.

"Congratulations on all the good things that have happened in your life since I last saw you at Grand Beach."

"You must come down next summer to see me and my kids and my grandson, a little pirate named Joe Maher."

"I'm afraid I'll be long since gone by then."

"The neighborhood won't let you go this time." She looked him straight in the eye. "No way."

"Fair warning, I guess."

"I'm delighted"—she sailed like a racing boat running with the wind right into business—"that you've persuaded poor Megan to turn her legal affairs over to Nick Curran— 'cuse the pun on 'affairs.' "

"Mary Kate, you're as outrageous as ever. And it's not an affair."

"Not yet anyway, worse luck for the two of you. . . . Anyway, I don't like that Dineen. He's a child molester, you know. Fairly standard pattern. Man marries a young widow with pretty daughters, more for the daughters than for the widow. Not that he wouldn't brutalize Megan just for the fun of it before he went after the girls."

"Mary Kate, that's slander!"

"The hell it is. Why do you think his marriage broke up? And if it hadn't been for clout and payoff to the girl's parents, he might be in jail now, where he belongs."

"They're two very attractive young women," he observed cautiously.

" 'Course they are. Any man with hormones in his blood and eyes in his head would find them disturbingly appealing. No problem. Not unless a man wants to hurt and exploit them. And that's all Dineen sees in a young woman—someone to hurt and degrade. Nice way of getting back at his mother, you see. Remember her? One of the all-time great hags of the Irish world."

"Does Megan know?" he asked in horror.

"She's probably heard vague rumors. Doesn't believe them. That couldn't happen in the neighborhood, right?"

"Anything could happen in the neighborhood."

"Too true. Anyway, take good care of her. Like I say—I did say it, didn't I—she's a real doll and a fine woman besides."

"I have my marching orders, ma'am."

She poked his arm, smiled cheerfully, and sailed away. "If I don't see you," she called over her shoulder, "I'll see you. And if you need help, yell."

Lucky man, Joe Murphy.

They've all made up their minds about Megan and me.

Megan is mine for the taking if I want her.

The tender trap is closing.

35

"What a beautiful place!" She looked out of the window on the glistening lake, a quiet, reflective mirror at peace with itself and the world. "It looks like a spring day!"

Did she remember the spring day twenty-one years ago when they planned to run off with one another? If she did, she gave no sign of it. Megan would always be a mystery. She had hidden too much in her life ever to be transparent.

"You've never been here?"

"Al didn't like to go to restaurants at supper, except for the club, of course. And I haven't gone out much for lunch in a long time."

She had replaced her widow's weeds with a simple gray suit, a white turtleneck sweater, and discreet makeup. She was, however, still wearing her wedding ring. She looked simultaneously delicate and sexy, vulnerable and provocative.

"Good old club."

Neal's hunger for her was like a fever, disorienting him, making his head light, interfering with his thought processes and his appetite. His imagination touched her and kissed her, stripped her and played with her, took possession of her and loved her forever.

"It's a nice place, Neal—for the kids to swim and for men to play golf. Just a little narrow, I guess, but then I'm a little narrow."

"You still go there, then?"

"Oh, no, I'm estranged from my family, you see, and I don't want to encounter any of them."

"Really?" The waiter brought a scotch and water for "madame," which he served with an elaborate bow, and a Diet Coke for Neal. She deserved the bow: no, definitely not flat-chested. She glowed with happiness. Her first date in how long?

"I'm tired of them trying to run my life. They have drug problems and alcoholism and homosexuality in their families and my kids are fine and still they want to tell me how to raise them."

"Attempts which your kids welcome, naturally?"

She rolled her eyes. "They're pretty fierce when they want to be, aren't they? But they DO like you."

He would not debate the matter.

"Was there anything special that led to the family fight?"

Could the opera story be true?

"It's the silliest thing." She was sipping her drink very slowly, thank God. "Margaret got me interested in opera when she was a junior in high school. Took me down to the Lyric. I started to love it. I met a classmate of mine from Newton. She asked me to serve on some committees. My sisters became violent about it, for no good reason. I kept going to the meetings, so they cut me."

"Why did they object?"

She placed her drink neatly on the tablecloth to the right of her plate, precisely where the books said it should be. "I'm not really sure. Sometimes they don't need a reason. As they—we—get older, their demands become more unreasonable. You know what Irish families are like, Neal. Their quarrels last for thirty years over things like who should have bought a newspaper. At Grand Beach, lifelong friendships end because someone who owns a ski boat is accused of discriminating against the kids in one family—as if the mother of that family and not the owner of the boat should be in charge of the schedule. Why the opera? Why not?"

"They're down on you about something else?"

"Maybe. I don't know. Maybe because I still have my figure, such as it is, and they don't. That's what Margaret says, she doesn't miss much, you know."

"I noticed."

"At first it was kind of a joke between Lin and Bea, but you know how they egg each other on. So one day the joke became serious. They said that I was pretending to be someone that I wasn't. No, that's not quite right. They said that people would say that I was pretending to be someone I wasn't."

"Always what others will say, isn't it? The Irish fear about respectability."

"I'm not sure about that." She considered the possibility thoughtfully. "Anyway, I said to hell with them."

"Good for you."

"And this time"—her eyes flashed dangerously and she picked up her drink—"it sticks."

"Better late than never" was the answer he didn't give.

"Better late than never," she said it for him and gulped half of her drink in a single swallow. "But why have you moved over here? Are you staying a little longer?"

"I'm flying back to Washington tonight for the end of the summit. Then"—he inhaled—"I'll be back here till after the first of the year. Johnny Jefferson, the general manager, is an old buddy and he wants me to work out of Chicago for a while."

"How wonderful!" Her face was flushed with excitement and joy. "You'll be here for Christmas?"

"I guess."

"I'm so happy." She pushed her drink aside. "The kids will love to have you for Christmas."

It was a big jump, but he didn't protest.

"You working out our arrangement with Nick?"

"Yes." She turned deep red as she opened her purse. "As you commanded, here are the tuition bills for the second semester."

"You're making fun of me again."

"I said you were cute when you became dominant. You really are."

"Cute but not to be taken seriously?"

"Of course not. Do you mind being laughed at when you're cute?"

He considered. "When you do it, it's embarrassing but kind of nice."

"Like I say, so long as you don't expect me to be dominated."

"I'd be terribly disappointed." He put the bills in his jacket pocket without looking at them. "Don't tell the kids."

"If you say so, but they should be grateful."

"I say so."

"Yes, Neal." She smiled at him like he was an amusing little boy.

They both laughed again. He wanted desperately to cradle her in his arms.

Could it be that this woman was more of a comic than she had been twenty-one years before? Or had he brought out the comic in her? Well, that was more than he had done in the past.

"Have you told Tom Dineen about this, uh, arrangement?"

"Certainly not." Her back stiffened a little. "No one knows. It's between you and me and Nick, and Catherine of course."

"He won't tell her unless you tell him to."

"I told him to. I hope you're not offended."

"Not at all."

Did they count Blackie Ryan, the troublesome, dangerous priest, as someone?

Probably not.

"I am so grateful, Neal. I don't deserve . . ."

He felt himself fill up with love for her.

"You do, Megan, and you can argue with me about anything else but that."

They did not, however, argue. Instead, Megan asked him about his adventures, and God forgive him—as he thought when they left the table—he performed outrageously for his charming and attentive, not to say worshiping, audience.

"You're a great audience, Megan," he said as he helped her on with her cloth coat.

"I'm glad I've pleased you, Neal."

She was still mocking him.

He'd better get used to it.

"You're not going to let go of that, are you?"

"Nope, it's fun. Unless you object."

"Never to your having fun. I'll get you a cab."

"I drove down, didn't want to keep Nick waiting. I parked over in the lot behind Bloomingdale's."

"Bloomingdale's? In Chicago?"

"It's the 900 North Michigan Building that's going up around the corner. Every woman in Chicago calls it Bloomingdale's even though they haven't moved in yet. The garage in back is open already."

Their arms linked, they walked down East Lake Shore Drive,

huddling together against the lake wind, turned the corner at Michigan, crossed the street at Walton, and walked to the elevator inside the massive garage which occupied half the block at the Rush Street end.

Still holding her arm, he rode up with her to the third floor. The silver Mercedes with sunroof looked like it had seen better days.

If I'm keeping the woman, however innocently, I should see that she drives a new car. No sunroof, I don't like them. And this sunroof seems unlocked.

"Sunroof doesn't work?"

"Never did." She laughed. "Kids make fun of it all the time." She seemed genuinely happy for the first time since the reunion. "I suppose you don't own a car."

"And if I did, it would be American."

They laughed together again, laughter utterly out of proportion to his remark.

We're falling in love again.

Megan, Megan, Megan.

He held the door as she climbed into the car. Beautiful legs and thighs, he decided once again as those nylon-covered appendages briefly revealed themselves for him.

"You'll call me when you come back?" She was suddenly diffident.

"Sure. We have to get this deal signed and sealed before the bailiff comes."

"Thanks again, for lunch and for everything. . . . If those tuition bills are too high—"

"Megan!"

"Sorry!"

The kiss that followed seemed the most natural gesture in the world, something that happened at the initiative of both and of neither.

It was not a passionate kiss, not quite; but it was sweet and tender and warm.

"Take care," he said as he closed the car door. "I'll talk to you soon."

"You take care, too."

Instead of going back to IBC or to his room to pack, he strolled down the drive to North Avenue, back along the beach to the bench on which they had once embraced, and sat there for a few moments.

The relationship wasn't out of control yet. He would not permit it to get out of control. But its present delicate balance was most satisfactory.

Then he walked back to Oak Street, crossed Michigan in the underpass and turned down Oak Street to the Reilly Gallery.

He was introduced to its lovely owner and then discussed at considerable length with her husband why a woman member of the Garcia family would ask about lost money and not threaten.

There was no immediate answer. "We'll take care of her while you're away; don't worry about her."

"I appreciate that."

"Neal . . ."

"Yes, Mike?"

"You're obviously impressed by my wife?"

"Who wouldn't be?"

"She's a distraction when I try to paint." He smiled ruefully. "But otherwise she's nice to have around."

"I should hope so."

"She was an old love lost and then found again."

"So I understand. Lucky you. Lucky her, for that matter."

"A cardinal rule—you should excuse the expression—of the North Wabash Avenue Irregulars is that you get second chances."

"A consoling theological principle."

"Sometimes they're even better than the first chance."

"Even more consoling. Thanks for the discretion of your advice."

They shook hands warmly. The troublesome priest chose his aides well.

He called the studio and was informed that the network would not require him in Washington till Monday afternoon. "You can stay in Chicago and watch the Bears play the Vikes on TV," Johnny had observed. "Unless you want to fly up there. We can probably get you in, even find some roller skates for you so that you can skate around with Mike Ditka."

"No, thanks."

He walked down to the Chicago Athletic Club and worked out for an hour and then swam for a second hour. Gotta be in top condition to cover Mikhail Sergeyevich.

As he swam, he remembered how radiant was her smile and how contagious her laughter.

Naturally she'd seem that way, he insisted to himself: I'm falling in love with her.

He discovered again that a male body, satisfied with itself after intense exercise, manifested a deep desire for a female body.

Megan was less than three inches away from him on the Currans' TV-room couch. Instead of watching the war in heaven between the Bears and the Vikes, he often concentrated on the outline of her trim legs and nicely curved thighs beneath designer jeans, the rise and fall of her pert bust, the lines of her bra beneath a not quite opaque white blouse, two buttons of which were invitingly open.

Moreover, in the sensual TV room, radiant with sunbursts and nudes, such carnal emotions seemed part of the natural rhythms of the cosmos, not only not wrong but somehow right and proper and necessary.

He had accepted the invitation from Nick Curran to watch the TV of the game at the Hubert H. Humphrey Rollerdome (as Mike Ditka was calling it), fully aware that Megan and her family were likely to be present. In fact, he had accepted the invitation because he wanted her to be present. Looking at her, absorbing her with his eyes, dreaming about her as a naked lover—all of these admittedly adolescent activities seemed, for the moment, to make life worthwhile.

He would not, in fact, try to take her to bed. It would be impossible in the Curran home anyway. Besides, it would be unfair, exploitive and cruel.

And it would involve him in a future he did not want.

As he sat next to her during the first half and watched the Bears blow a shutout in the last minute, he thanked heaven, in which he found himself believing again under the pressure of the neighborhood and the ever-present North Wabash Avenue Irregulars, that he did not drink. Deprived of even a bit of self-control, he might be pawing her before the game was over.

Nor was it his fault that she had sat next to him.

Only Margaret accompanied her mother. Joseph was not feeling well, and Teri was staying home to baby-sit. Jackie Curran had been dispatched to keep Joseph company and Nicole Curran to support Teri.

Such family confusion because Joseph, adorable little boy that he was, hated Neal.

Thus it became an adult party. Margaret's quiet presence, aloof, reserved, a trifle supercilious, surely entitled her to an adult's privileges.

Just as he had a hard time keeping his eyes off her mother, so Margaret, long golden hair wrapped around her fingers, seemed determined to watch his every move. Her penetrating gray eyes warned him not to move an inch closer to her mother, not even to think about it.

Well, kid, you can prevent me from touching her, but you can't prevent me from thinking about it.

At halftime, two Kevin Butler field goals, his twelfth and thirteenth in a row, were all that separated the Bears from the Vikes.

"A thin margin for a division championship," Neal mused. "They're not quite as intimidating as they used to be."

"Neal Connor, IBC News," Megan said, sniggering, "at the Rollerdome in Minneapolis, Minnesota."

Everyone laughed, even Margaret.

"Let me strike back in self-defense," he said, "with a trivia question. We all know that the new Twin Cities entry in the NBA will be called the Minnesota Timberwolves. I don't suppose you can tell me, Ms. Margaret Lane, the name of the last Minnesota NBA team."

"The Minnesota Lakers," that young woman responded promptly. "Now the Los Angeles Lakers. Before they went to Minneapolis they were the Chicago Stags."

"Remind me never to play Trivial Pursuit with you."

"No danger of that."

A blast of ice from much further north than the Twin Cities swept across the room and enveloped Neal.

"Margaret . . ." her mother raised her voice in warning.

"I meant"—the girl smiled sweetly—"that Mr. Connor has to go to Washington to welcome General Secretary and Mrs. Gorbachev. If he comes back, I'll be happy to beat him at Trivial Pursuit."

The poor kid was caught between her natural sweetness and good manners on the one side and her distrust of him on the other.

If she knew the kinds of thoughts I've having about her mother, she'd be convinced that she has good reason to distrust me.

"You've interviewed him, haven't you, Neal?" Nick stepped in to ease the tension between the Lane women. "What's he like?"

"Interviewed him and spoke with her. . . . They're both dedicated Communists, albeit of a somewhat dissident variety. Their theory—one might almost say, their theology—is that Marxism *ought* to work. If it doesn't work, there is something wrong with the way it is being applied. He may be the first really sincere Marxist in that job since V. I. Lenin."

"Not much hope, then, for peace with him?"

"More than with any of the others, I think, because he really wants to make the system work and needs peace to do it. And he really believes that if the system works, they can win any economic competition with us."

"He's wrong?" Megan asked, her eyes once more wide with admiration for the wisdom of his analysis.

Gosh, woman, I can fake like that without half trying.

"Sure, but it will be a long time before they find out."

During the halftime, various members of the group brought snacks from the "kitchen area" to the "media area" as these were properly called in the Curran house.

As luck would have it, he and Megan were alone in the kitchen area for a few moments. She leaned against the fridge and looked at him, eyes soft in invitation.

Again the kiss was as natural an event as breathing, something that happened without plan or intent. This time, his hands descended to her shoulders as they did when he had shaken her. One of them managed to brush against a firm and defiant breast.

"Part of the agreement?" She rubbed her tongue along her lips.

"I said no access to your bed. I didn't mention your lips. Especially when there is invitation in your eyes."

"Was there? Truly?"

"Truly."

She sighed. "And my breast?"

"Accident."

"I bet. . . . Come on," she said, pushing him lightly, "if my duenna finds us alone out here, we'll both be in trouble."

"Very nice breast, by the way."

"I bet." She blushed and turned away from him.

"Nifty ass, too," he said as he patted that quite spectacular part of her anatomy.

"Neal!" She jumped away, not at all displeased.

"I'd better watch out for Margaret, huh?"

They both giggled like conspirators—a safe alternative to much more passionate conversation and behavior.

Horny adolescents, both of them.

They carried plates down the stairs to the media area, at more than a sufficient distance from each other. Megan preceded him, allowing him to marvel at her tidy posterior. His fingers yearned to reach out and touch her—with affection and love as well as desire.

Margaret, her brow furrowed in suspicion, passed them on the steps. "I'll bring the cake," she said lamely.

Only if the girl was more skilled at reading eyes than anyone her age ought to be were they in trouble.

But the brush in the kitchen area had been reckless. Megan had been reckless as a young woman and still was. Was he now the pursuer or the pursued?

"Mrs. Curran," Margaret asked when she returned, "you really paint two different kinds of pictures of women, don't you?"

Women, not nudes: a maiden's shyness.

"Most misty and vague and some quite explicit, you mean?"

"Well, like, you know, some are almost *Playboy* pictures."

"*Playboy* should be so lucky to have such erotic pictures," Catherine said with a laugh. "You see, dear, they're all celebrations of the erotic, the sacramentality of the erotic, as Father Blackie says. Some women I celebrate in mists, others quite explicitly, mostly because at first they don't seem very erotic at all, even though people who know them think quite correctly that they are terribly sexy. So it's my job in the picture to explain why. If you're wondering about yourself, you'd be surrounded by mists."

"I was thinking about my mother."

"MARGARET!"

"Mo-THER, if it's all right for Mrs. Curran to paint those pictures, it is all right to ask."

"I'm sure Mrs. Curran does not want to paint me." Megan was

acutely embarrassed. She put at least a foot between herself and Neal on the couch.

"Mrs. Curran never said that at all," Catherine replied with a wink. "When your mother finally lets me paint her, Margaret, she's not likely to be shrouded in mists."

"I agree," Margaret said solemnly.

"MARGARET!" her mother exploded again.

"It's true, Mo-THER. I never thought of that before, but you are a pretty sexy bitch. Isn't she, Mr. Curran?"

"I'll reserve comment, Margaret."

"You're all embarrassing me!"

"You'd have no trouble selling that picture," Neal chimed in. "Men would line up to buy it."

"NEAL!" She was now acutely embarrassed, but again not displeased. "You're as bad as Margaret."

"Arguably worse. Fortunately for all of us, the Vikes are about to kick off."

What was that all about? he wondered. Is the kid trying to understand why someone like me would find her mother attractive? I suppose that's understandable. Poor child, it's all confusing and painful for her—especially because she is smart and sensitive and is well aware of the chemistry between the two of us.

The Bears scored on the first series of downs. Then Anthony Carter caught two Wade Wilson passes for touchdowns and the Vikes led 21 to 20. A field goal made it 24 to 20. In the closing minutes of the fourth quarter Kevin Butler, now almost as automatic as the rising sun, booted another. Bears down by one point.

McMahon went out, sick with the flu and hurting in both his elbow and his hamstring. Mike Tomzack came on and made his usual mistakes, including a fumble on the four-yard line.

Astonishingly the Bears held, Todd Bell sacking a runner at the six-yard line on fourth down.

Then Tomzack led the team down the field, ending the drive with a short pass to Dennis Gentry, who broke into the clear and ran thirty-five yards for the winning touchdown.

The pandemonium in the Curran basement was doubtless being repeated in almost every home in Chicago.

Everyone hugged everyone else, except that Margaret made no attempt to hug Neal. She did not, however, seemed displeased by the very brief and exceptionally chaste embrace between Neal and her mother.

There was no opportunity for them to embrace again when Neal left for the lonely drive back to his luxurious apartment in the Mayfair Regent.

Probably just as well.

Mikhail Sergeyevich Gorbachev had returned to Russia, and the world was marginally a safer place. An "expert" on Russia because he had worked there two years back in the early seventies, Neal had been interviewed by Fiona Sweeny, the black-Irish beauty on the "A.M. Program," about the meaning of the meeting.

Fiona was a good deal more spectacular than Megan, if not quite so sexy, but once you're charmed by an Irish woman, they all are a threat.

The result was that Neal performed with astonishing wit and wisdom and insight.

"Fiona," he concluded, "if someone had told us in Moscow sixteen years ago that what Russia needed to increase personal freedom and decrease world tensions was a truly dedicated Communist and that such a man would reach major understandings with California's governor Ronald Reagan, we would have suggested that he needed a long vacation in the sun."

"Thank you, Neal Connor." She beamed. "As always, you've summarized with poetic precision."

"Comes from being Irish," he said with a grin.

Was Megan watching? Only if she knew he was going to be on. Did she know?

Unless Teri was sick with a fever.

Would she mind his flirting with Fiona?

You bet. Well, good enough for her.

He sighed as he walked down the street to the Hay-Adams, still his favorite Washington hotel.

I kissed the woman, a forty-three-year-old mother of four children, once—well, twice—and I'm acting like I'm besotted by her.

I don't dare go back to Chicago.

I have to go back. I promised Johnny. I must take care of her.

I want her, dear God in heaven, how much I want her.

Sure, a voice in his head responded (not necessarily of the Lord God), and after you've had her a couple of times, you'll be bored, just like you were with the other women.

No way.

I'm falling in love with her again. Or maybe for the first time. She's an obsession now. She wasn't that twenty-five years ago, was she?

You weren't as lonely then as you are now. Or as hungry. Or as old.

Several times he had almost called her, even dialing the 312 area code. Instead he called Mike Casey and asked him to stay in touch with Megan in case the calls from the woman with the Hispanic accent grew more threatening.

Casey responded that he would be happy to do so.

After he hung up, Neal felt kind of foolish. Surely Mike had already been in touch with Megan. The Wabash Avenue Irregulars would not miss that one.

He spent the rest of the day at the Treasury Department, pondering a file a friend of his had put together on the Garcia family.

Their net wealth, almost all of it laundered somewhere or the other, was estimated at twenty million dollars. The current "captain" was Luís Garcia, the second youngest son of Antonio and Rosaria Garcia.

Both deceased. Killed in a gun battle with a rival gang in 1975. Twenty-two automatic-weapon bullets removed from the mother's body. Reportedly victims of the Suarez family.

Which in turn was completely destroyed two years later, grandmother, grandfather, three sons, three daughters-in-law, five children. South Florida shoot-out.

Both families had come from the South East Side of Chicago and had maintained businesses there even when their empires spread over the country and reached into South America. Garcia owned a neighborhood tavern. Suarez operated a small grocery store. Typical American success story.

The Garcias blew up the grocery, just to keep the record straight.

They were reported to be responsible for the death of two narcotics agents who had set traps for them.

The two older Garcia sons had died mysteriously, Hector found floating in the Calumet River with his throat cut. Rosario blown up in his car.

Luís (Lou) and Ricardo (Rickie) were the two survivors, apparently peacefully exercising joint power. Suspected of bribing several federal narcotics agents. Involved in a scandal with Chicago police narcotics agents.

Nothing proved.

A cop or a narc finds a courier with a half-million dollars of coke. The cop is earning maybe thirty-five thousand a year. The Garcia operator offers him half the take.

A few months later the cop retires.

Violent people. But they killed by knife and machine pistol and bomb, not by staged accidents.

And would they really try to play the commodity markets?

Wasn't there a lot more money in drugs?

And would they politely ask a woman where the money was? They seemed to be untroubled by torture and murder of women as well as men—unlike the more gentlemanly Outfit.

Presumably some of Mike Casey's people were keeping a discreet eye on Megan. And, hopefully, the kids too.

But her husband had died seven weeks ago. If the Garcias wanted their money, would they not have moved more promptly?

And who was the woman on the phone?

Neal sighed and returned all the folders to the file box in which they had been placed. It was "Miami Vice" in real life, every bit as violent, if not on a once-a-week basis. Not even a good story there. The specials on drug gangs had already been done.

Alf Lane was a likable and mildly psychopathic nut. That he might drop into the Garcia tavern and talk big was utterly believable. But would he really get involved with them, even for money to pay his gambling debts?

Not very likely.

Then he saw that one interesting question remained un-answered, mostly because unasked: Who was the mole who had suggested to the feds that Al was dealing with the Garcias?

As he would learn later, it was not yet quite the right question.

He held the phone in his hand, hesitating to punch in the number.

Ten o'clock at night. Too late to call her?

Not if you're obsessed.

"Lane residence."

How much she sounded like her mother.

"Teri Lane speaking, I bet?"

"Uncle Neal? Outstanding! Are you back in town?"

The bubbly voice hinted at the glowing enthusiasm on the teenager's face.

"I guess I am, Teri. Sorry to call so late."

"It's NOT late. We're watching *Rocky II* on the VCR."

"Someday you will have to teach me how to operate one of those things. Is your mother home?"

"Sure. I'll get her."

"Good evening, Neal." She sounded hesitant, uncertain.

"Hi, sorry for calling late, but I just got in."

She might have said that they did have telephone communica-tion between Washington and Chicago. Instead, she said, "I don't sleep too well at night, I'm afraid. This is still early."

Somehow the spirit had gone out of her.

"Are you all right, Megan?" he asked gently.

"A little discouraged, I guess. Two men from the FBI came today to ask me questions—about Al's gambling and investments."

"You talked to them?"

"I called Tommy Dineen, and he said there was no harm in answering because I didn't know anything anyway."

"Did he?"

The fat bastard.

"Well, I wasn't any help to them, because I didn't know what they were talking about most of the time. Poor Al was so confused. . . . I did care for him, Neal. I mean, I can't hide it from you that there wasn't much love between us. You've figured that out. But there wasn't any dislike, either. I felt sorry for him and tried as best I could to take care of him. He wanted to be a good man. . . ."

She sounded close to tears, the grief that had to come and yet would not.

"Next time, call me."

"I didn't have your number."

Oh, damn, I blew that!

"I'll give you my number. Did you talk to Nick about it?"

"Well, I had to sign some more papers about the house, so I did mention it. He seemed very angry, but when I told him what the conversation was about he didn't think I should worry. So I guess Tommy did give me good advice, didn't he?"

"If you can't get me, promise me you'll call Nick."

"All right." She sounded confused and tired, just barely keeping her head above water.

"Any more calls from the Spanish woman?"

"Last night she broke down and cried. She said that she just had to have the money."

"What? She cried?"

Garcias didn't cry, did they?

"I tried to calm her down and told her again that I didn't have the money and I didn't know where it was. I think she half believes me and half doesn't."

"Did a Mike Casey speak to you?"

"Yes, he's a very nice man. He seemed puzzled by the calls, too."

"Any more harassment from the family?"

"Bea and Lin came over to see me today, right after the FBI men left. Mom's sick again. Her heart is real bad. They told me I was killing her with this opera nonsense."

"What did you say?"

"What could I say? I told them I was very sorry for Mom and would love to see her and be friends with her again, but I don't understand why I should give up something that I enjoy. It was pretty bad, they both had something to drink before they came and more while they were here. I was afraid to let them drive back to their homes—Mom lives with Bea, you know."

"You didn't give in, then?"

"No way, Neal, but it hurts."

"Good girl. . . . Are the papers ready for the house?"

"Tomorrow or the next day at the latest. I'm going to see Nick in his office tomorrow. And, Neal, I'm embarrassed but I need advice and then maybe a favor."

"You shall have both, milady."

She tried to laugh, without much success. "Well, the Lyric is doing *The Marriage of Figaro* tomorrow night. I suppose you know it?"

"With von Stade as Cherubino?"

"Yes, and she's so good. Teri and I watched the tape last night. Well, anyway, Artis—Ms. Krainik, the general manager—has asked a couple of us to have supper in their green room before the performance. With her and Maestro Bartoletti. And I'm not sure that it's right, with my being a widow, and I don't know what people will think."

"In the neighborhood in the old days, they would be shocked, but it's not the neighborhood and these aren't the old days and the opera crowd wouldn't bat an eye."

"Truly?"

"Truly."

"Not even if I brought a date?"

That bastard Tommy Dineen!

"Not even if you brought a date. They'd probably be more shocked if you didn't."

"Really and truly?"

"Really and truly."

"Well, now the favor . . ."

"OK." He tried not to sound angry at her. "What's the favor?"

"Well, I kind of need the date and thought that maybe you—"

Cornelius O'Connor, you're an idiot.

"I wouldn't miss it for the world. Really and truly."

"I feel so funny. I mean, like it was a prom or something."

"We did that once before, didn't we?"

"And you hesitated that time."

"Only because, like I said, I was overwhelmed. Which I still am. Look, you ride the Rock Island—"

"Metra."

"All right, you ride it down to the Loop and your appointment with Nick. I'll drive you back after the opera."

"That's so sweet of you, Neal. I'd be afraid of the Dan Ryan Expressway at that hour. The bank is going to send over the final papers tomorrow afternoon. So maybe you can sign them and we'll be all set."

"Sounds like a great idea."

"Thank you for calling."

He almost said "I love you" before he hung up, but he wasn't sure that he would mean it.

Not yet.

A date with a woman who turned away from you the last minute at the airport twenty-one years ago.

Maybe you should have run after her.

39

Neal was astonished by Maureen Kennelly. He had expected a voluptuous beauty, the kind of woman that had flung herself at Al Lane during their two years as roommates at Northwestern.

In fact, she was quite plain—medium height, chubby, lusterless black hair, dull gray eyes behind glasses even thicker than Blackie Ryan's. She lived with her parents, she told him, in an apartment a half block from the 99th Street Rock Island station.

"We're valley people," she said with a touch of bitterness, "not ridge people."

"Pardon?"

"I thought you said you were from the neighborhood," she muttered, a trace of contempt in her tone.

They were sitting in the coffee shop of the Bismarck Hotel for a late-morning snack, Ms. Kennelly wolfing down calorie-rich sweet rolls while Neal nursed his cup of tea.

"A long time ago. And from North Beverly."

"The ridge"—she curled her full lips—"is up on the hill, Longwood Drive and west. It's where the rich live. We ordinary people live east of the drive—a buffer against the niggers."

Then Neal remembered the distinction between the two halves of the neighborhood. It dated back to the time when the community was an exclusive residential preserve for the titans of the packing industry, the owners on the top of the drive and their servants on the bottom. In St. Prax's the distinction didn't mean much because most of the parish was west of Longwood.

"I grew up on Vanderpoel, so I guess we're in the same category."

She curled her lip again, as if to tell him that he would not score any points with her by claiming the same class background.

"The woman killed him," she said, chewing on a cinnamon raisin roll that made Neal's mouth water. "That's what I told the police, and it should be obvious to the media, too."

Despite Blackie's prediction, Maureen Kennelly had been ready, even eager to talk to him. "I want to see justice done," she had whispered ominously on the phone.

Now she was sitting across from him in a lumpy, baggy business suit, looking perhaps like a nun in lay garb. Neal considered her carefully. She was not completely devoid of sex appeal. Undressed, she might reveal a classic full figure, but she was either unaware of her possibilities or condemned them.

"The woman killed him?" he repeated her charge as a question. "What woman?"

"His wife, naturally. She gets everything. All the money, the insurance, the house, everything."

"There isn't any money, is there?"

Maureen Kennelly shook her head patiently. "Not that they've been able to find. But it's there. He told me that he had saved a bundle his clients would never take from him. And she'll get the insurance, two million dollars. She never loved him, she saw their precious life-style slip away, so she hit him over the head and then faked the accident. It's not hard to do such things, you know."

Neal pondered the possibilities of Megan bashing her husband over the head with a hammer, dragging him to the car, driving it against the oak tree, slipping out, and then shoving his body into place. Small wonder the police didn't take the charge seriously.

"She certainly could have done it that way," he said, keeping his tone of voice neutral.

"Oh, I don't think she actually did it with her own hands." Maureen finished her cinnamon roll and reached for another. "But her family has the underworld contacts to get the job done for her. Why, her brother Pete, when he's not drunk over at the club, hangs around with underworld characters and their women."

"Women" was said with a sneer suggesting cheap prostitutes. How, he wondered, did Maureen define her own role in Al Lane's life?

"I never did like Pete very much."

"She was no wife to him, Mr. Connor, I can tell you that. She wore her fancy clothes and stuck her fancy nose up in the air and walked around, proud as punch, with those spoiled kids of hers, but she was no wife."

"Why don't you tell me about it."

He must strive for objectivity about Megan. If he did not see her role in the decline and fall of Al Lane as others could see it, he might miss something important.

"I don't mean just sex." She waved her hand, oblivious to the butter smeared on her fingers. "That wasn't a big thing in Alfred's life. He was good at it"—she essayed a lewd smile—"when he wanted it and I don't mind admitting I enjoyed him as a lover, but it wasn't all that important to him."

Even in college Neal had suspected that in this area of life Al was a barking rather than a biting dog.

"I see."

"I suppose she didn't even sleep in the same bed with him. She's frigid, you know. But that didn't bother Alfred as much as her indifference. She's a tight-assed little bitch, cold, calculating, unsympathetic. I was more of a wife to him than she was. When he was with me he had some fun, some laughs, some good times, some encouragement when he was down."

"What kind of fun?"

"We'd watch TV together, have a few drinks, maybe send out for some pizza, rent a videotape, cuddle on the couch, maybe knock off a few beers. He'd tell me about his work, and since I'm in the same line of work, I'd know what he was talking about. . . . Doesn't that sound like a husband and a wife together?"

"It certainly does."

"Is that too much to expect a wife to give to her husband?"

"I shouldn't think so."

"Would he have been getting it from me if he was getting it from her?"

"It doesn't seem likely."

"See what I mean!" she exclaimed triumphantly. "She was no wife and I was!"

"It certainly sounds that way."

"I loved him"—her eyes filled with tears—"I miss him so much. . . ."

She dabbed at her nose.

"I'm sorry." His sympathy was genuine. The woman was unattractive and angry, but she was also hurting, more painfully perhaps than Al Lane's wife.

Would Megan cuddle with a husband in front of the TV screen and drink beer and eat pizza? Sure she would, if asked. She would do anything a husband asked. But it would never occur to her to offer such affection, especially to a distant and apparently self-reliant husband.

And her own aloof elegance would discourage a request for that kind of consolation, especially from a man who, for all his talk, was uneasy with and threatened by women.

Not a Greek tragedy, but tragedy nonetheless. An Irish tragedy. Classic, in fact.

Maureen controlled her tears. "He was generous, that's what he was, the most generous man I've ever known. We became friends when he offered to carry my big bundles of charts from the station over to the exchange. No one else even noticed."

She started to cry again.

"That's how I remember him, too."

"Anything she asked for she got," Maureen sniffled. "And she never gave him anything back."

The portrait of Megan emerging from Maureen's perspective was incomplete perhaps, but accurate as far as it went. She and Al were a mismatch from the beginning.

"You make her sound pretty selfish."

"Selfish? Worse than that! Al told me that it never occurred to her to think about what he might like."

The comment had probably been delivered in a different tone of voice and with a somewhat different meaning than Maureen Kennelly imposed upon it, but he had little doubt that Al would say it.

"Do you think he would have left her eventually?"

"Sure. He cared about his kids, though they're stuck-up brats as far as I can see. Once they were raised, he would have walked, believe you me."

"And married you?"

"I don't know." She put her crumpled tissues in her expensive leather purse—a gift from Al, perhaps?—and folded her hands on the table. "We never talked about it. And I never made any demands. I figured it was up to him. . . . Well, it's all over now, I guess. Anyway, it was a lot of fun while it lasted."

"And he didn't leave you anything?"

"Some jewelry. I didn't expect anything. You see, the way it was, he left the exchange the day they took away his license, and stopped by my office to have a word—bright and cheery as ever. Then he drove straight out to the club to play golf with Brian Neenan, his partner. They played golf every Wednesday afternoon till the first snow, regardless. They ate a late supper, I guess; he stayed around to play craps, won a little bit, Brian tells me, and drove home. He never made it."

She opened her purse again and reached for a fresh pack of tissues.

"I see."

"Everyone said he was his usual happy-go-lucky self. You know what he was like?"

She was crying again. Perhaps blubbering would be a better word.

"I certainly remember. Nothing would ever really depress him for long."

"You got it exactly," she said, as if Neal had spoken a brilliant insight. "He says to me, 'Don't worry about it, Little Mo'—he always called me Little Mo—'don't give it a single thought. I'll bounce back from this like everything else. Minor setback. The way the cookie crumbles'—his exact words: 'The way the cookie crumbles.' And then he says, 'And I'll take real good care of you, too. Never fear.' "

"You believed him, naturally?"

In Neal's recollections a promise from Al was no more than an expression of benign feelings.

"Sure, why not? He would have bounced back, too, if she hadn't stopped him. Does he sound like the kind of man who would have killed himself?"

"Hardly. But wasn't he the kind of man who could have an accident on the way home at four o'clock in the morning?"

A man whom the newspaper clips said had been drinking heavily at the club.

"He never had an accident before, did he?"

After Maureen Kennelly had put her tissues away again and lumbered out of the coffee shop of the old German hotel, Neal ordered another cup of tea and pondered its darkness for a half hour more.

Accidental death still seemed the only possible verdict. Sure, there were loose ends, like the missing money and the connections with two different crime mobs. But no one had any reason to kill Al Lane.

He was not the suicidal type, not the kind of man with enough depth for despair.

And those who might have decided to kill him would have had to lie in wait for him to leave the club, follow him home, and dispose of him down the street from the house. What reason could there be for such an elaborate hoax?

Two million dollars of insurance?

Which would benefit Megan.

Try as he might he could not imagine her involved in such a crime.

Her brother, who was apparently "connected" now himself?

In hopes of borrowing money from Megan later on?

Maybe. It was a remote possibility that ought to be checked out. But not very likely.

Al had skated across the surface of life for forty-three years and had finally hit the thin ice. There wasn't any story here. And no threat to Megan, either. A lot of smoke and no fire.

Yet Al's affair—if you could use the word—with Maureen did not fit the image. Twenty years before he had not been a lower-middle-class homebody seeking someone like himself with whom to drink beer and cuddle at halftime on "Monday Night Football."

Neal shook his head and rose from the table. You couldn't understand another human being perfectly.

He passed a public phone in the hotel lobby. On impulse he dialed Mike Casey.

"Mike, how much alcohol was in Al's body that night?"

"Enough to get him a ticket if he had been picked up, not too much more."

"Enough to put him to sleep?"

"After losing his broker's license, eighteen holes of golf, and a night of crapshooting? Sure."

"Anything else."

"Coke."

"Cocaine, you mean?"

"Not too much of it. That never got into the papers. Everyone who was with him at Beverly claims that there was no cocaine used that night."

"Do you believe them?"

"Not necessarily. They'd lie about it if they had been using it, but the club is pretty strict about coke. They already eased a couple of younger members out. Quietly."

"So he sniffed some on the way home?"

"Could be."

"What do the cops think about the possibility of murder?"

"They haven't closed the case."

"Neither has your little friend at the Cathedral rectory."

"When he gets his teeth into a case, it's never closed till it's solved."

Oh yes, a very dangerous and troublesome little priest.

"Everyone waiting for something to happen, huh?"

"Kind of looks that way, doesn't it?"

So the North Wabash Avenue Irregulars had activated him to make something happen.

From the IR—Injured Reserve list.

40

"Our humble store is honored by such a distinguished guest." The young man was of medium height, dark-skinned, handsome, with a thin mustache and long black hair. He was dressed as if he was about to appear as a villain on "Miami Vice." Fact imitating fiction, once again.

To complete the picture, a young woman with deep cleavage, in a red cocktail dress, lurked behind, seventeen at the most and with despair in her sad brown eyes.

"Is it really?" Neal asked evenly.

On the outside the Garcia place—South East Tap, it was called—looked like any neighborhood bar. Inside, it was vest-pocket Las Vegas—glitter and chrome and expensive imitation leather and mirrors and high-priced teenage whores like the one Luís Garcia had in tow. The clientele, affluent and a little shady, were hardly from the South East Side. Mostly men like what he imagined Al would have been in his last days—overweight pretenders to a macho image that they thought would be enhanced by skirting danger, the pseudo-danger of Garcia's bar, much too public a place to be really danger-ous.

With expensive foreign cars parked outside.

"*Hombre,*" Luís hissed, "do you know who I am?"

"Lou Garcia."

"A man could get himself killed in here if he does not treat me with respect."

Why, Neal wondered, was it necessary to maintain the presence in this old, worn-out neighborhood when the family had homes in Florida and Maine and North Carolina (on one of the Sea Islands)? Probably part of the culture they had inherited from their parents. Neighborhood people, just like the folks in Beverly.

"Come on, Lou, drop the phony accent. You're third-generation Chicago, just like I am."

"You either have *mucho* balls, *amigo,* or you are crazy."

"I'm as safe here as I would be in a convent," Neal said in Spanish, just to prove that he could do it. "Half the people in this place are moles of one kind or another. The FBI has to keep its people busy."

"Outside, *amigo*"—he grinned thinly—"in the alley it might be another matter. . . . But you speak with a Mexican accent. You are not pure Castilian, then?"

"Pure shanty Irish," Neal said, returning to English. "It's a Sonoran accent, actually. I learned it when I was working in Tucson."

"You have come a long way, *amigo.* Why risk it all by defying Luís Garcia?"

"I'm not defying you, Lou. That'd be crazy, because there would be no point in it, would there? I'm merely saying that I'm not afraid of you."

"You want to fight me with your bare hands, like those poor *hombres* who make the death threats?"

"Not especially, Lou. I'm not really a very good fighter. I've only knocked out one man in a bar in all my life. But if you want to fight . . ."

"With one punch, I bet."

"He was pretty drunk to begin with."

"But I could have your throat slit one night"—he made a cutting motion—"you would be dead before you knew it. One minute walking down the street, thinking about a woman perhaps. The next minute before God."

"We both would be startled by such an encounter, I suppose. . . . Look, Lou, it's easy to kill someone, as you well know. You could cut my throat, blow up my car, fill me with bullets from an Uzi. No problem. I'd be dead. But you'd be dead, too."

"So?" Garcia lifted his eyebrows. "Why would that happen?"

"Lou, you're a big man in your world and I'm a big man in my world. Sometimes I'm not sure that there's all that much difference in the two worlds, but the point is that my world comes into everyone's home several times a day. If it is known that I'm talking to you—and believe me, Lou, I wouldn't drive out here without making it known—and I am sent to face God, every cop in the country will close in on you. Even if they don't get you, your buddies in the other families will dispose of you as a liability to their industry. I'd give you a week, *amigo*."

"So." Garcia studied Neal coldly. "Now we have both made our little acts, perhaps we talk."

"All right."

"*Chiquita*"—he waved at the girl—"get lost. My *amigo* Neal Connor and I must talk."

Obediently the voluptuous child walked away.

Such a slave was part of the television villain image. Neal despised Garcia for the way he treated her.

"So." Garcia folded his arms on the table. "You want a drink?"

"Diet Coke."

"Huh, a funny Irishman who doesn't drink more than that."

He signaled for the girl, who almost ran back, gave her the order, and dismissed her with a wave.

"Nice, isn't she?"

"Of course."

"You want her?"

"Thanks, but no thanks."

"So, what *do* you want?"

"A story."

"And what is in it for me?"

"Creative control. That means—"

"I know what it means." Garcia eyes flared dangerously.

"Touché, Lou. That fake accent makes me forget that you are at least as American as I am."

"So I win a point. . . . You let me veto everything that goes on camera?"

"We talk through the show beforehand. We don't do anything on camera you don't want. We let you watch the whole show before it airs and cut whatever you want. I destroy the notes and the outtakes so that Donny Roscoe can't subpoena them."

In fact, the specials on the cocaine trade had already been done. And the myriad cop-shows on television had created an image that no special could change. There were, however, some angles which perhaps might interest the blasé public.

"You don't normally give those things, do you, Neal, if I may call you that?"

"Why not, Lou? And no, of course we don't normally give them. But I'm not so dumb as to think there's any other way you would cooperate."

"And what's in it for me?"

"Your side of the story. I don't know what it is, but I'm sure you have a side to tell which you wouldn't mind telling—especially if there were no risk."

"So Mr. Roscoe can come and arrest me?"

"I don't work for him, Lou, like I said. And I don't like him. I can't imagine you letting anything go through that would help him in the slightest."

"And he calls you before the grand jury?"

"And messes with freedom of the press? Not twice, *amigo*, not twice."

"Interesting, interesting," Garcia reflected thoughtfully. "You want an answer now?"

"I'll take one, naturally, but I don't expect one."

"Good." Garcia slipped out of his chair with the dangerous grace of a tiger. Or a sidewinder. "I will call you, one way or another."

"I appreciate that."

"Hey, *Chiquita*, come here. My *amigo*, Mr. Connor—you see him on TV every night, no—he likes you. You want María Anunciata, Neal? I guarantee she has no AIDS. She gets herself infected, I cut off her tits. Nice tits, huh?"

"As I said, Lou, very nice indeed. Again, thanks, but no thanks."

"Suit yourself." Garcia shrugged. "She's much fun. She has to be or I put her out on the streets."

Neal's fantasy was concerned with a woman old enough to be María Anunciata's mother, and a much less voluptuous woman at that.

But I'm old enough to be her father, he thought as he drove away in his rented car.

If I could salvage that child, I would.

Then he reprimanded himself for being an incorrigible romantic. You did not salvage women from the world in which she lived. He had not thought such an absurd thing in fifteen years, not since he'd stopped being a romantic.

Was he becoming a romantic again, under the influence of his dreams about Megan's shapely little white limbs and curves?

If he was, it was a dangerous delusion as he played a game of "chicken" with Luís Garcia.

41

Sluggish and dirty, the water of the Chicago River reminded Neal of a sewer.

"You'll never know for sure, Neal." Brian Neenan sighed. "That was the kind of guy Al was. I knew him as well as anyone, better than most. And I could never figure him out. Wheels upon wheels upon wheels. Towards the end I think he was running on empty. He himself probably didn't know till the last second what his next move would be."

Brian Neenan was perhaps ten years older than Neal, a chunky little man with thick silver hair, a Tip O'Neill face, an expensive leather coat. He had suggested to Neal that they walk along the bank of the river and talk.

"No Donny Roscoe bugs out here," he said with a wink and a grin—a fiftyish leprechaun.

"Do you really think they're bugging you?"

"Donny is trying to figure a way to get some publicity from the crash. A dead broker looks like a good lead. So naturally his gum-shoes are stumbling all around. . . . It would help if someone over there understood the commodity game. Now that they've heard me insult them, let's take our walk."

Neal was not sure that the trader was joking.

Or that he was any less opaque than his late partner.

They were standing on the riverbank across the street from the green glass 333 Wacker Building, facing the Merchandise Mart and hunching their shoulders against the fine drizzle that was falling.

"He was a hell of a lot of fun, a never-a-dull-moment kind of guy. But what if anything went on behind those blue eyes of his I could never tell."

Brian Neenan talked in short bursts, like an automatic weapon, spitting out strings of words, then pausing before he fired another burst.

"That's the way I remember him."

"One of my kids, Notre Dame grad, is a psychiatric resident over at Northwestern Hospital, working with Joe Murphy, you know, the guy from Boston. She told me a year or so ago that Al showed 'antisocial' tendencies. I say, 'You mean that he's a psychopath?' And she says they don't use that word anymore."

"It's a word which had occurred to me."

"But then she thinks about it and says his antisocial tendencies are unusual. I guess that means he was not a psychopath like other psychopaths."

"A hard man to work with?"

"You'd expect that, wouldn't you?" He dug his hands into his coat pockets. "But you know, Neal, he never lied to me, never once in the fifteen years we worked together. Lots of times he didn't tell me everything he was up to, but when I asked him directly about something, he always told the truth. You couldn't say that about a hell of a lot of other traders."

"I guess that's the way he was when we were in school, though I never thought of it that way."

"He was totally honest about our joint ventures, too. You see, we occupied the same office, used the same staff, backed up a lot of each other's bids, worked jointly for some clients, kept some of our capital in joint accounts. I never worried about him cheating me. It was just not going to happen."

"You didn't do everything together, did you?"

"Hell, no!" His red face squinted up at Neal. "Each of us had our own ventures. Me? I was cautious and conservative. Al? He was always a gambler."

"How so?"

"Well, he was mixed up with the guys out on the West Side"—the required nod up the river toward Taylor Street—"and they're poison, if you ask me. Lately he was hanging out in some of the bars over in South Chicago and those guys are even worse poison. He seemed to thrive on the danger."

"And on the floor?"

"You gotta understand"—Brian bit his lip—"that Al was afraid of death. He went into a terrible funk on his fortieth birthday. Wanted to stay young forever. Wore sports clothes like the young fellas, made plays for the young broads, dyed his hair, spent a lot of money on cosmetics—all that sort of thing."

"Really?"

"Yeah. So he thought he could use the same strategies on the floor that the young guys did, mix computer programs with high rolling. They made a lot of money that way trading on the S and P index. I don't know. I figure you can't teach an old dog new tricks, so I stick with my T-Bills and Fannie Maes."

"And you weren't wiped out on Black Monday."

"The young guys—and some of them are women—never knew a bear market. They thought it was like Santa Claus or the Tooth Fairy or the Great Pumpkin Spirit or something like that."

"They weren't ready?"

"They didn't believe it. Some of them still don't know what hit them. Al had been around a long time. He lived through the Hunt silver run-up, made a bundle in it. He ought to have been ready. But he panicked just like the kids."

"Odd."

"Fucking odd. I could have sworn he had more sense. Still, I didn't know—and don't know now—what the other pressures were. You wanna walk towards Michigan Avenue?"

"Sure, why not? Did you lose some of your money when he went under?"

"We had about a million in partnership capital. Half of it was mine. Every penny went down the drain."

"Wow!"

The older man would not look up at him. "What am I supposed to say? No big deal? That's not true. It's a big deal. That kind of money always is a big deal. But it doesn't change my life-style much. A few pinches here and there . . . only a week in St. Maarten this winter instead of two. I can't complain. The kids are all raised, finished college and graduate school. I'll make it back in the next few months if I feel like it."

"Not sure it's worth it?"

"I don't know what the hell is worth anything anymore. With Al gone, the fun is gone, too. Funny thing. I saw his casket like everyone else. Still, when the office door opens, I half expect him to come waltzing in with that big Irish grin on his face."

"I know what you mean."

"I'll say this for him: he took it all like a man. Laughed it off and said he'd be back. But what does a trader do who's lost his seat? A broker who's lost his license? I don't know how he planned to earn a living. Still, off we go to Beverly that afternoon and play our usual eighteen. He shoots four above par and I guess wins a bundle in the crap game that night."

"You didn't stay?"

"Me? I got a wife I love, and we have an empty nest now. I was home at 92nd and Leavitt at nine o'clock—and that's later than I'd stay out any other night except my night with Al. . . . That's all gone now, of course."

"How does she feel about the money you lost?"

"Easy come"—he lifted his shoulders—"easy go."

They paused for the stoplight at Dearborn.

"I couldn't ever figure that out, either," Brian Neenan murmured. "The Megan business, I mean."

"Oh?"

"He adored the woman, absolutely worshiped the fucking ground she walked on."

"Really?"

"Yeah, and still he played around. And I mean played around a lot. Somehow the two of them weren't on the same wavelength. She tried hard, God knows. It just never did work out, God be good to him."

"Uh-huh."

"She had to raise the kids. He would have spoiled them rotten. She's done a hell of a job, too, if you ask me. Had to pretend a lot, I guess, but then she learned that growing up in the Keefe family. You know them?"

"Oh yes. I know them. Megan and Al and I were in the same class at St Prax's."

"Yeah, that's right. Anyway, they had to pretend that their old man wasn't in bed with the Mob, so they all ended up kind of funny. All except Megan. And I worry about her now, with that Tommy Dineen hanging around all the time. I wouldn't be surprised if he tries to rape her."

"Rape her?"

Every muscle in Neal's body tightened.

"Sure, widows are easy targets. Megan is in shock. Can't figure out what happened and how she ought to feel. I see the look in Tommy's eyes."

"Bastard."

"Worst kind. I could never see why Al messed with him. Liked the danger, I suppose. I kept telling him that Tommy was trouble and he just laughed, like he always did when he knew I was right and intended to ignore what I said. Figured that if you hung around with dangerous people you stay young."

"How dangerous is Dineen?"

"Pretty damn dangerous! Don't let the clown image fool you. There are people in the ground that Tommy put there."

"A murderer?" Neal could hardly believe that Dineen was *that* dangerous.

Murderer, rapist, child molester? Yeah, Al had always teamed up with some odd ones. But not for long.

"Not with his own hands, maybe."

"I see."

"I never liked the way he looked at Megan even when Al was alive. I told Al that. Tommy, I said, is the kind of man who likes to ravage the innocent. Al just laughed it off."

"That was his way when faced with problems he didn't like: laugh it off."

"Men would say to him, 'Hey, Al, are you married?' and he'd reply, 'My wife is.' That about sums it up."

"Did you ever talk to him about his attitude towards Megan?"

"Yeah, a couple of times." Neenan shook his head, unhappy even at the memory. "He'd laugh and say something like she was too good for him. I suppose he meant it, but it was no goddamn answer."

"You wonder, don't you, why he ever married her?"

"Nah." Brian took his hand out of the pocket of his coat long enough to wave it. "I don't wonder at all. For some reason, her crazy sisters decided that it was a good marriage, and she went along. They dropped Al as soon as they had landed him. Treated him like dirt. So poor Megan is caught between her family and Al, and she's gotta protect the kids from both of them. Amazes me that she pulled it off."

"And now between her family and Tommy Dineen."

"Five will get you ten that they're already pushing her to marry Tommy, though I guess they're not talking to her right now. My wife says that it's something about the opera, which is the damnedest thing I've ever heard. Fits them though."

"Irish families fight about odd things."

Neenan glanced up at him, a knowing, sideways look. "Yeah. Tell me about it."

What would the Keefes think if they knew that he and Megan had a date for the opera after the five o'clock news that evening? He imagined that there was no way he fit into their plans to rehabilitate their wayward daughter.

"So they never paid much attention to Al."

"Nah. Except Pete in the last year or two. You know Pete?"

"Well enough in the old days to hate his guts."

They had paused at the Michigan Avenue bridge, above the landing where the lake excursion boats parked in the summer. The drizzle was turning into rain.

"Showed good taste on your part," Brian grunted. "Drunken moron. He and Al were tied up in some kind of kinky stuff I didn't want to know about. I think it was almost over, but you never could tell with Al."

"So how did he die?"

"Like I said when we started our walk, I don't think we'll ever know for sure. My guess is that he just said to hell with it all. Al was the kind of guy who could do that, you know, if the mood hit him. I heard him say once that it was better to die young and have a beautiful corpse instead of turning into an old man with leaky kidneys."

42

"Got a minute?" he asked Mike Casey the Cop.

The handsome silver-haired man laid one of his watercolor crayons at the end of the neat line on the table next to his painting.

"The North Wabash Avenue Irregulars always have a minute." He smiled benignly. "Anyway, I'm not sure this painting of the 900 North Michigan Building going up around the corner quite conveys my distaste for it. . . . Hey," he said, glancing at his watch, "don't you have to do the five o'clock news?"

"If I get there at ten to five, it's all right. The terrible secret of our trade is that it doesn't take much work at all."

"No good job does. So tell me how it feels to be a cop."

"My head is spinning. I've talked to Kennelly, Garcia, and Neenan today. I'm more confused than ever."

"What are their theories?" Mike the Cop wiped his fingers on a rag.

"Garcia doesn't have one, or if he does, I don't know it because I'm walking very slowly with him."

"That's wise."

"Cosmo Ventura, whom I saw before I went to Washington, thinks that Al killed himself to keep his honor clean—which I take it is the official Outfit line. Kennelly says that Megan killed him, or rather that her brother Pete had a West Side connection who took care of the matter for the Keefe family. Neenan says we will never know for sure, but probably Al said to hell with it on impulse and piled up the car instead of facing the cold, gray dawn."

"Aided by the booze and coke?"

"As good as any explanation."

Mike nodded sympathetically. "You don't buy any of the theories?"

"As I remember him, he was not the kind who would choose self-destruction. I can't see Megan involved in some sort of plot, though her brother, I guess, is crazy enough to do anything. The Outfit doesn't want to find itself accused of meddling in the commodity exchanges. But they lost money to Al, at least I'm pretty sure they did. Maybe Garcia did, too. Neenan certainly did. And Tommy Dineen is hanging around on the fringes oozing slime. By the way, Neenan is afraid that he'll try to rape Megan."

"We're keeping an eye on her," Mike was tapping a crayon thoughtfully against his work table. "I agree that she's in danger. Widows tend to be in danger."

"I'm glad the Irregulars are watching her."

Mike smiled easily. "Naturally. Enjoy the opera tonight."

"I think I should be angry that you know, but I'm probably relieved. Anyway, what do you think? Why are you asking me? You wrote the book on detective work."

Mike the Cop's eyes narrowed, making him look even more like Basil Rathbone as Sherlock Holmes. "My gut feel is that someone killed him and that the killing isn't over yet."

43

"*Ciao*, Maestro," Neal extended his hand to Bruno Bartoletti.

The maestro's handsome face was startled and then exploded in delight. "*Ciao*, Neal! So you are back home again!"

Bartoletti pulled Neal into a typical Tuscan embrace and kissed him on both cheeks.

"I told you we'd meet in Chicago someday."

"But I didn't believe you. I say you will never come home. Again I misunderstand the Irish. Hey, Rosanna, Neal is here finally."

Signora Bartoletti pecked him on either cheek. *"Buona sera,* Neal."

"Buona sera, Signora. Megan, may I introduce Maestro and Mrs. Bartoletti. Rosanna, Bruno, this is Mrs. Megan Lane."

"Signora." The maestro kissed her hand with a marvelous Florentine flourish. "I have always said Neal has excellent taste in everything."

"Thank you, Maestro." If Megan was flustered—and he would have bet his last penny she was—she certainly did not show it. One classy broad. "I enjoyed *Trovatore* so much. . . . *Signora,* it's wonderful to meet you."

Presence, wonderful presence. And here in the gracious green room of the Civic Opera House, Megan Keefe Lane was a woman who could move anywhere in the world with easy charm, more so than she could in the dining room of the Beverly Country Club. The Big World was her element, even if she didn't know it yet. Then, when she found that out, Beverly would be a pushover. Even her crazy family would come running.

I'll tell her, but she won't believe me till she finds out for herself. Strange that her instincts brought her just to the right spot to leap off into the Big World.

"Hey, Bruno"—Neal picked up the lull in the conversation—"I see you on television, eh?"

"But no, I'm supposed to say that to YOU."

"But yes. The videotape of *Onegin. Magnifico.*"

"Grazie. This year we do *Trovatore* on video. I send you a copy."

"With an autograph, please."

"And one for the signora." He bowed formally to Megan.

"I'd love to have an autographed tape."

When the maestro and his wife drifted away to talk to the other guests in the green room, Megan turned to Neal. "You know everyone," she said with a sigh. "And everyone knows you. I guess I should have expected it, but it surprises me every time."

"And disconcerts you?"

"No. . . . YOU disconcert me, as always. But that these people know you only surprises me, and delights me, too."

She was wearing a black dress, widow's color still, but with suggestions of festivity in a low back, bare arms, a moderate display of throat and chest, and a hint of deliciously pretty little breasts, one of which had been so firm to his touch in the Curran kitchen.

And tonight no wedding ring.

By now he was almost used to the surge of desire that he experienced whenever he considered her sexual appeal.

He told himself that tonight could be dangerously romantic if he did not exercise the most stringent control on his imagination.

Al Lane had at least three women Neal had seen today, Maureen Kennelly, María Anunciata or someone like her, and this diminutive archduchess standing at his side.

None of them made him happy, not for long anyway. Poor man.

"Yet, Megan Keefe Lane, you are sensitive enough to how people react to know that people are looking at you more than they are at me."

"Wondering who the old woman with the famous reporter is."

"You don't really believe that, do you?"

"No, but the alternative scares me."

Still candid, still blunt.

"You can make it in this world, Megan—in fact, anywhere in the Big World that you want. I'm not saying that you should or that the stage here is finally any better than the stage at the country club. I'm merely saying that you can have this stage if you want it."

Her gray eyes pondered him thoughtfully. "I'm not sure quite what that means yet, Neal. But I'll believe it if you say so. I'll believe anything you say."

"That's a little risky."

"No way." She colored and turned her eyes away from him.

Before supper was served, she drank only part of one glass of sherry. And with the roast beef, a half glass of red wine. "Can't fall asleep during Mozart, can I?"

"He won't let you."

"Neal, I don't mind if you stare at me that way. I mean, I'm flattered that you like my breasts, but what will the others say?"

"You heard what Bruno said: they'll think I have good taste in everything."

A blush started on her chest and crept up to the roots of her hair.

"If I didn't want to be disconcerted, I suppose I wouldn't have asked you for a date. Thank you."

"I may continue to stare?"

"If I didn't want you to stare, I guess I wouldn't have worn this wicked dress, would I?"

"Among your many admirable qualities, Megan, your candor is one of the most admirable. . . . By the way, did you get all the papers from Nick?"

She nodded. "I called home from his office, and Teri said the package had come from the bank. We can sign them all when you drive me home and you'll finally be a Beverly property owner."

"I'm sure it will be an excellent investment."

He would be in her house after midnight.

With two children in their bedrooms on the same floor as hers. Small chance of any chemistry getting out of hand there.

Did he want such chemical reactions?

His head told him that it would be folly. But his head was not in complete control and had not been in control since he stood next to her in the sanctuary of St. Prax's.

And had, without realizing what was happening, fallen under the sway of that troublesome priest, John Blackwood Ryan.

Their seats were in the fifth row at the aisle. The folks at the Lyric obviously knew that they had a prize in Megan and were taking good care of her.

At the familiar opening notes of the overture of *La Nozze* he took her tiny hand into his large one. It came unprotestingly.

"My hand is part of the arrangement?" she whispered.

"Hand and lips."

"But not my breasts?"

"Only by accident."

They both chuckled softly and settled down to enjoy the opera even more, because finally they were next to one another.

By the time of the single intermission, between the second and third acts, she was leaning against his shoulder. In the atmosphere of the marvelous music, the ingenious comedy (made delightful by the English "supertitles" flashed above the stage) and the spontaneous enthusiasm of the audience, the physical contact between them seemed to replace lust with affection. How nice it would be, he thought, if the relationship between man and woman was not impelled by the gonadal hormones to go beyond affection.

Affection with Megan for the rest of their lives would be

wonderful—light, gentle, kindly, and without passion, involvement, commitment, responsibility.

They returned to the green room for intermission wrapped up in a dreamy glow that the rest of the crowd seemed to share with them.

"Isn't she wonderful?"

"Frederica von Stade? Sensational. The perfect adolescent boy."

"She's German?"

"American as you are. Americans are taking over the opera world. Our political and economic imperialism may be slipping, but in culture it's our world now."

"How does the Lyric stack up with the Met?"

"Now I hear Chicago imperialism! Actually the comparison isn't fair, because the Met is much more a repertory company, like Covent Garden or La Scala. But the Lyric is still one of the best in the world. I knew it was good because Bruno was involved—I met him at the Teatro Colon in B.A., Buenos Aires, that is. But I'm surprised at how good it is. No one in the world could do *Nozze* better."

"Do you know her?"

"Frederica? Yeah, I've met her. Nice lady."

"You know everyone." She was sipping a Diet Coke, too. Give the woman affection and she doesn't need booze.

"The grass is always greener, Megan. . . . You don't have to be a celebrity to know special people: the Currans, Mike Casey and his wife, the crazy Ryans, that troublesome priest."

"You're right, Neal. I guess you have to go away so you can come home."

That bit of wisdom hit him hard.

"The end of all your journeys is to return whence we started and know it for the first time."

"That's very nice. Yours?"

"T. S. Eliot, following G. K. Chesterton, I think."

"Can one do it without going away?"

"There has to be a psychological break, anyway, I think. One doesn't have to be a damn fool and stay away twenty years, though."

She threw back her head and laughed, a richer and fuller laugh than he had ever heard from her.

"How lucky you bumped into Lisa at the airport."

"Given my confusion, I probably would have returned soon, anyway."

"Poor Neal." Her fingers reached out to his and remained on top of them. "You're so smooth and articulate, I keep forgetting that you have your own little hell, too."

"Not as bad as yours," he said gruffly.

"I'm not so sure." Tears formed in her eyes, tears for him.

He looked away before she could.

As they walked back to their seats for the third and fourth acts, he was happy that Teri and Joseph would be in the house on Hoyne Avenue. Alone with the woman, there was no telling what he might do.

No, that wasn't true. There was in fact little doubt about what he would do.

Will I put my hand on her thigh during this act?

Dear God, no! It would scare the hell out of her.

All right, let her be scared.

Now why would I think something like that?

Then he realized, in a new insight to his own tangled emotions, that in addition to desire and longing, there still remained a lot of anger. Toward her and toward her family and toward her late husband.

His first assault on her might be violent and harsh, a settling of old scores. He shivered. Was he, after all, any more civilized, any more decent than Lou Garcia?

44

"Come out in back to my study." She led him through the dining room, turning on the light as they went. "I told Teri to put everything out here. We can finish in a few minutes and let you get home. Goodness, it's late."

The arteries in Neal's temples were throbbing. His hands were clammy. Once again he thanked a kind heaven, or whatever, for providing the two sleeping children upstairs as guardian angels to protect him from his baser instincts.

"You've only been here once before," she said as they flipped on the lights in her "study"—identical to the bedroom from which he had snatched her on St. Valentine's morning 1958. "And you didn't stay very long then."

"Not counting last Sunday night."

"Oh Neal!" She gasped. "I've forgotten that already. What a dummy!"

The study, now completely restored to its pristine neatness, was Megan—small, quiet, tasteful: feminine without being frilly or girlish. An antique desk with a matching chair stood in the center of the room, with a halogen light in the center of the desk. Several stacks of papers were arranged in neat symmetry on the otherwise bare desk. Thick green satin drapes blocked the windows facing the garden. A period easy chair (American Colonial) and a matching sofa created a conversational nook with its own halogen light in one corner, a single twin bed with a spread matching the drapes occupied the other corner. Against the opposite wall were several shelves—matching the decor of the desk—with books and notebooks, the former seeming to be every Literary Guild and Book of the Month Club selection for the last twenty years: books that she probably "meant" to read when she had time and had dutifully arranged in neat chronological order against that day when there was time.

A snug, sensible little area of serenity—with a bed on which she could sleep when she wanted privacy from her husband. How often had she used it? he wondered.

Perhaps also a place from which children were barred when mother was working.

"Pretty, Megan," he murmured.

"What? Oh, the study. Thank you. It's kind of an island of peace. Now why don't you sit down on that sofa, while I get all the papers in proper order. Here, let me take your coat."

His coat and hers were deposited on a coatrack by the door. She closed the door carefully. "Don't want to wake up the kids."

He sat on the sofa, gray and soft, and watched her remove a thick envelope from her purse and, standing at her desk, shuffle the papers into a a neatly stacked pile.

"Let me get rid of my contacts. My eyes are exhausted." She ducked into a bathroom next to the bed.

He was indeed tired. Mozart wrote for an audience who had nothing else to do at night and not that much to do during the day—an audience, moreover, which was not given to two hours of exercise before strolling down to the opera house.

Megan emerged from the bathroom, reading glasses in hand. "Now to work."

She put on the glasses and bent over her desk.

The performance had been a triumph, most particularly the final act, in which the composer gives all his main characters splendid arias to sing. The audience had given an enormous ovation to each aria, especially to von Stade, "the Cherubino of her generation" as the program notes called her.

Their ride down the Dan Ryan to 87th Street had been mostly silent, each of them with the memories stirred up by a comedy in which the bittersweet was so subtly implanted that you realized it was more than a comedy only when you found yourself thoughtful as well as satisfied at the end. Thoughtful and perhaps a little puzzled about your own intimate relationships.

Such as they might have been.

He felt his eyes closing as Megan fussed with the papers. He wished she'd hurry, so he could return to the Mayfair and snatch a little sleep.

Nothing like physical weariness to stifle sexual hunger.

Finally she brought the papers over to the coffee table and placed a fountain pen in front of him.

"You sign them first, then I'll sign them. You write your name at the red *x*s."

While he was signing, she opened a cabinet at the bottom of one of the bookcases, removed a Waterford tumbler and a half-empty bottle of J&B. She poured herself a stiff shot and swallowed it in a single gulp.

"Don't worry, Neal. It's only my nightly sleeping potion. I never drink more than one."

He continued signing the papers. She stood next to him, her arms across her chest in her familiar defensive position. Then he added the check on Citibank that Nick had told him to write, and reversed the papers so that she could sit on the easy chair and sign them herself.

"OK, Megan. Your turn."

She sat across from him and rushed through the signing ceremony. "I'll have these notarized in the morning. I'm afraid I'm bothered by all kinds of guilts and hesitations just now."

"Repress them."

"Yes." She tried to smile.

"Here's the check."

She glanced at it quickly, embarrassed but still careful and responsible.

"Thank you, Neal. I am very, very grateful."

She took off her glasses and folded them on the coffee table.

"I'm sure I'll have it all back," he said cautiously, "when the insurance money comes through."

"Please God." She carefully put the meticulous stack of documents into a large manila envelope.

"Now, woman, if you'll excuse me for running, I have a long day tomorrow, much as I enjoyed this one."

"I enjoyed it, too, Neal. I'm so glad you agreed to be my date."

He stood up, turned toward the coatrack, then glanced back at her. She was standing by the coffee table, dejected, weary, and oh so vulnerable.

It was the vulnerability that did him in. It demanded tenderness. And tenderness generated lust.

Then something seemed to snap inside Neal's head. His good intentions dissolved, his resolutions vanished, his restraints collapsed.

All the longing and frustration, all the loneliness and disappointment in his life merged in a terrible tidal wave of desire.

His "flow"-altered state, as he now thought of it, had not taken over in any of his previous encounters with women. He had been, on the contrary, hesitant, wary, always ready to step back. Now, and without warning, his world wound down to slow motion. He saw her responses to his actions at the moment of the action. He was as confident and as certain as he was in the old days when he would see the pass leaving Al's hand at a frame-a-second speed.

So relaxed and assured was he that he even noted to himself, almost casually, that it would be interesting to see how the slow motion worked in bed.

He grabbed her and pulled her toward himself. Then he attacked her lips with a furious, violent, devouring kiss that drew her whole being into his possession.

You are mine now, the kiss said. You dare not resist. I am bigger and stronger than you. There is no help anywhere. Deliver up your body and soul for my amusement.

She acquiesced in his assault, accepting it, but not cooperating. Her hands against his chest were no more than a tiny plea for release. She was so frail—a weak, a slight, defenseless doll. Her helplessness poured gasoline on the flame of his passion. Every inch of you, woman, now belongs to me.

I'm no better than Tommy Dineen, he thought. Surely he has tried the same thing in this room.

But I'm a better lover than he is. And a more determined one.

"Neal," she pleaded when he paused for breath.

That word destroyed all his controls. Desire, savage and implacable, affection, anger, tenderness, the need to conquer and possess—all surged in one mighty thrust toward union, and still at a frame-a-second speed.

His fingers found a zipper and a bra hook. With a few, quick determined movements, he despoiled her of her clothes and held her in front of himself, a naked prize in which to exult.

She glanced down, astonished to see herself suddenly naked. Terrified and ashamed, she tried to cover herself with her hands and her arms.

Imperiously he pulled her limbs away and extended them as he pushed her against the wall, the more easily to devour her with his furious eyes.

She was all he hoped she might be, a slender, gossamer girl with soft flesh and pale skin, exquisite little breasts, milk-chocolate nipples, trimly turned legs, and a rear end that was designed for the shape of a man's hand. A faint line, a touch of extra flesh, a mark of childbearing here and there only made her more appealing.

"Neal," she begged, eyes closed in shame.

As he had done long ago, he seized her tenuous waist and swung her high above his head. She seemed lighter than before.

A hoarse cry of triumph escaped from his lips. He was the victor, he had won finally, he would now enjoy the fruits of his conquest.

She replied with a cry of her own, not of protest, nor even of surrender, but rather a shriek of animal release.

He lowered her to the bed and with hands and lips and teeth hurried her toward readiness for lovemaking. There was no resistance left in her. She was pliant, submissive, subservient—ready to accept meekly whatever was done to her.

Then, in the leisurely recognition of his altered state, he realized that his conquest would be complete only if her pleasure matched his. She ceased to be a captive and became instead a friend to be freed from the constraints and the burdens of the past. He gave himself over completely to the task at hand: not merely taking her but making her his own for the rest of their lives.

She seemed surprised by the sudden gentleness of his onslaught, but she arched her back in response, moaned with pleasure, and opened herself up to him.

She cried out several times, a piercing shout of joy as he finished his triumphant journey and their bodies merged in spasms of wanton pleasure.

Then, fighting off exhaustion and the need to sleep, he soothed and caressed her, praising her beauty and her responsiveness.

Finally, he said the words that had to be said, even if they were on his lips before he knew what they were.

"I love you, Megan."

45

"If you dare apologize, I'll hit you." She nuzzled close to him, her sweat-drenched body adhering to his.

"How did you know I was going to apologize?" His fingers sought a pale breast.

"I know the look."

"I'm afraid I was pretty violent."

"Were you ever." She sighed contentedly. "Scared the living daylights out of me. It must have been a new world's record for undressing a woman. Didn't even rip anything. You certainly have had lots of practice."

"Not that much."

She covered his mouth with her hand, stifling the apology springing to his lips again. "I said no, and I meant no. I knew what I was doing when I brought you back here. Kind of dimly anyway. It wouldn't have happened unless I was willing to let it happen. . . . I'll admit I was terrified when it started, which serves me right for being such an inexperienced prude."

"I don't think you're a prude, Megan. And not inexperienced, either. Certainly not unresponsive."

"You're only my second man, Neal." She huddled closer still to him. "I don't know what this is all about. But I liked it, even if I was frightened silly at first."

"There haven't been all that many women for me, Megan. None as glorious as you." His fingers continued to frolic with one of her pretty little breasts.

"Anyway"—her fingers rested on his marauding hand, not to stop it exactly but to influence its assault—"don't give me ever again that New York psychiatric stuff about not being recklessly passionate."

"How did you know—"

"It didn't sound like anything you'd say."

"Actually he was pretty accurate." He annexed her other breast. "This is the first time I haven't been a very hesitant lover."

"Truly?" She frowned skeptically.

"Truly. I always lost my nerve at the last minute before."

She threw back her head and bit her lip. "Neal . . . please."

"I'm not hurting you," he insisted.

"Let me catch my breath." She squirmed away. "What was I saying? Oh, yes, you certainly didn't lose your nerve tonight."

"Too hungry, I guess."

She slipped further away from him, put her hands on his shoulders and sighed again. "You are a solid ape." She touched his chest. "Strong enough to tear a woman apart. I felt like I was being carried off in the jungle."

"I work at exercise."

"Keep it up." She traced the outline of his body with her fingers—chest, belly, thighs. "I like you solid and hard. Big, strong beast . . . do I embarrass you, dear, by enjoying you as a sex object? Too bad if I do. What's sauce for the goose is sauce for the anchorman."

He was indeed embarrassed by the candor of her appraisal. The women in his past had not been so frank in their admiration. Male bodies as such held little interest for them. "Hey," he protested as she pinched his flank.

"I've wanted you for so long. . . ." She paused and changed her mind. "I should exercise, too. The girls are after me all the time. Aerobics, they say, if nothing else."

"A body like yours doesn't need much maintenance, which is all the more reason why you should provide it."

"Sweet, sweet Neal. I will, I promise. I've never had any time. . . . That's silly, isn't it? What have I had to do during the last twenty years except raise children and take care of myself? Al didn't much believe in fitness and kind of made fun of it when I tried it. All he cared about was golf. Poor man"—she drew in her breath—"he'd even play in the snow. He played the day he died."

A vagrant thought teased at his brain, but he was too busy with other activities to pay much attention to it.

"I didn't give you much choice when I started." He still felt guilt pangs.

She sighed patiently. "Will you stop trying to apologize. If I really resisted, you would have stopped. What's the word for my modesty? Perfunctory?"

"I admit I enjoyed it all, but still—"

"But still . . . I said to myself he's stripping me and I should be fighting him off, but I love what he's doing and I don't want to fight him off. He's holding me up in the air like a trophy and that's an outrageous thing to do to a widow with four kids, but I enjoy it as much as he does and I don't want to stop him. He's turning me on like I'm a helpless captive and that's not right, except I enjoy being his helpless captive. . . . Does that little excursion into my fantasy life ease your conscience?"

"I guess."

"I've had fantasies like that all my life. I suppose most women do, though I've never talked to anyone about it before. It's usually about an overpowering and gentle lover who makes me do the things I want to do but am afraid to try. Many times you've been that lover. Do I shock you, Neal?"

She did, kind of. He wasn't sure that he liked being a fantasy object.

"You fascinate me."

"The crush never disappeared." Her tiny fingers ran up and

down his body, exploring his muscles with evident delight. "I was a faithful married woman, in fact, but my imagination committed adultery with you whenever it saw you on TV. I told myself it was all silly. And it was, but it didn't go away. I guess I didn't want it to go away. I told myself that if it ever became real, it would probably be terrible. Now it's real—" She paused, her fingers digging into his flanks. "Or at least I think it's real—if this isn't just an erotic dream—and I have you and it's not terrible at all."

"I thought I had you." He chuckled and nibbled at her breast to reassert his possession of her.

"Same thing. I don't know why I'm pouring all this out now. Maybe since you've taken so much of me, I want to give you everything. Do you like having so much of me?"

"I'll never have enough, my darling."

They clung desperately to one another so that they would never again be separated.

Neal was filled with a tenderness that slipped easily once again into a tender desire. He reclaimed one of the breasts he had fondled so delicately, enveloped one with his mouth and closed his teeth against its skin. His other hand gently sought the luxuriantly forested mountain between her thighs.

"Neal . . . twice in a night!"

She seemed more scandalized than displeased.

He freed his mouth temporarily.

"Doesn't your fantasy assailant want more?"

"No. . . ." She reflected carefully on the question. "I suppose that he's so satisfied with me that it never occurs to him to try again. We both just fall asleep contentedly, and then when I wake up, he's gone."

"Well, we didn't fall asleep and I'm not gone and I don't propose to leave until I've enjoyed you again. Is that clear?"

"Are you sure it's all right?" She was a virtuous high-school sophomore again.

"Why wouldn't it be all right? Have you had enough of me already?"

"Oh, no." She sounded frightened that she might lose him. "I don't think I'll ever have enough of you."

"So stop talking." He jabbed a finger at her ribs. "I have to catch up on twenty years of fucking."

"And I have twenty years of fantasy." She laughed happily, drew his mouth back to her breast, and gave herself to him again.

This time, every movement of his on their journey was sensitive and light, a sweet nostalgic invocation of joy lost and joy found. Her cries of delight were more uncontrolled than before.

Poor dear woman. Twenty-one years of marriage, four children, and she was still almost virginal in her innocence.

Not anymore.

Finally, she insisted that she must dress herself and show him to the door. "It's four o'clock in the morning."

"I hope we didn't wake the kids."

"Not much fear of that." She dressed with neat womanly efficiency, black undergarments going quickly and firmly into place. "I had this place soundproofed so their rock music wouldn't drive me crazy."

Now she tells me. Not so reckless after all.

"How convenient. Come here and let me fasten your bra. It's a service we offer."

"Thank you." She stood stiffly as he closed the hooks.

"There we are." He permitted his fingers to linger against her ribs, gliding over the thin film of moisture that coated her flesh.

He marveled once more at her warm skin, slender frame, and diminutive rib cage. She's not used to a man who enjoys watching her dress almost as much as he likes undressing her. He slowly zipped up her dress and then patted her rear end, compact and firm.

"Thank you again."

"My pleasure. And I mean that."

I think I might have been seduced.

"I was part of the deal after all," she said as she leaned back against him. "Wasn't I?"

He extended his arms around her waist. "Was it a good deal?"

"You bet. I get the money and the man I need. . . . Blackie was right. God sent you."

"That terrible priest." He was not sure he wanted to think of himself as an angel in the pay of God.

"Horrible."

He cupped her breasts in his hands.

"You always liked them, didn't you?"

"I'm only human."

"Come on, lazybones," she said, slipping away and turning on him, "get dressed."

"Yes ma'am."

She kissed him at the door. "Thank you for everything."

"Not quite St. Valentine's night, I'm afraid."

"I thought it was, Neal. It sure seemed that way."

"I'll call you later. . . . This, uh, I mean this isn't intended to be—" He stopped, wondering how to say what was so obvious: it would not be a one-night affair.

"I'll be waiting." She brushed her lips against his, one last time.

As he drove down 87th Street toward the Dan Ryan, Neal debated whether he should feel guilty or triumphant.

So he decided to feel triumphant.

A voice in the back of his head observed that he might also be well advised to feel trapped. She seduced you, the voice insisted, and what's more you know it. This time she won't let you get away.

Dearest Neal,

I love you.

Did you notice that I didn't say that last night? I'm not sure whether it even dawned on you, you were having so much fun.

I wanted to say it, but somehow couldn't.

That was very foolish of me.

But I do love you. I've always loved you.

And I always will.

Megan

47

Complacent, perhaps even happy, perhaps happier than he had ever been in his life, Neal Connor arrived at Channel 3, IBC, in Chicago, at one in the afternoon. Despite the nagging voice which insisted that he had been seduced by a clever and determined woman, had he not performed as a man ought to perform, regardless of who had initiated their dance of love? Whatever the future might hold—and he did not want to consider that on this rainy December day—the night had been magic. Indeed, it was magic he would never forget.

The "slow motion"—would it happen every time from now on? Why had it kicked in last night? Mozart? Could he learn to turn it on and off in bed at will?

He licked his lips at that thought.

A pink slip on his desk with a note: "Call Ms. Lane. IMPOR-TANT and URGENT."

Oh boy, he thought. Maybe I'm in trouble. Maybe I went too far last night.

He punched in the number and received a busy signal for his efforts.

He repeated the action every minute for the next half hour, waving off Johnny Jefferson. "Be down in a minute, Johnny."

Finally she answered. "Megan Lane."

A woebegone, frightened voice.

"I just got your message, Megan. The line has been busy."

"Oh, Neal, I'm so glad you called. I'm frightened."

"Not about last night?"

"Last night? What—" She laughed. "Oh, no, Neal, that was wonderful. That's not what's wrong. Did you get my note? No, of course not. I only put it in the mail today. Well, two notes, actually. No, but what's happening is terrible."

"What IS wrong?"

"A man from the government brought a piece of paper this morning"—her voice was frayed, anxious—"I have to appear before the grand jury tomorrow. Tommy says there's nothing to worry about, but I'm so scared. I don't know anything about Al's business. He never told me a thing."

"Have you called Nick?"

"No . . . not yet."

"Megan, call him now. Tom is all right for a lot of things, I suppose. But this is a dirty game being played by dirty people. You need someone who is as strong as they are. Stronger."

"I guess. I don't know. I'm so confused."

"Megan!"

"I'll call him right away."

"And tell him to call me."

He called the switchboard and told them that a call from Mr. Curran should be forwarded to him in Mr. Jefferson's office.

To his surprise Johnny approved an exploration of the possibility of a Garcia series with the simple warning: "No extra risk taking. Remember that, Neal?"

"I am not a character from 'Miami Vice' and I have no desire to be one."

He would remember that line often in the weeks ahead.

Nick Curran was on the phone the moment Neal was back in his office.

"I talked to Larry Whealan. He will appear for her. He can't go into the grand jury room with her, but she can go outside after every question to seek his advice. Which is exactly what we will tell her to do."

"What's it all about?"

"Nothing. They have absolutely nothing. One more abuse of the grand jury process for publicity purposes. Watch Don Roscoe on your channel tonight and see if I'm not right. There is no suggestion of crime. Al cheated some of his clients. They've all got their money back—or will when your check is cashed. There's no evidence that he did anything else wrong. There's money missing, but no one claims it's theirs, so presumably it was Al's. If Megan is hiding it—and I don't believe for a minute that she is—it would only be criminal if it's money she does not report for probate or income tax, and neither issue has arisen yet. Donny's looking for media time, that's all."

"With no concern for what it does to Megan and her kids."

"Donny never worries about families."

"Bastard."

"That's what United States Attorneys tend to be."

"What about this Larry Whealan?"

"What about him?"

"Is he any good?"

Nick laughed. "Best in the city, far and away. Donny's bowels go limp when Larry shows up in court. Wait till you meet him."

"I'll be there tomorrow morning."

"No, you won't. And neither will I. If you show up, the other media people will have a field day. Not all of them are happy to have you back in town. Larry will call me when it's over and I'll call you."

"I want to be there."

"Use your head, Neal." Nick's voice was stern. "Do you want to make the ordeal worse for her?"

"Certainly not."

"Then wait for my call."

That night on all the Chicago channels, as predicted, Donald Bane Roscoe, round boyish face striving for sincerity and wisdom, was asked about the subpoena of Mrs. Alfred Lane.

"We can't talk about matters before the grand jury. Naturally my office sympathizes with a bereaved woman. But at this point in time we cannot let the abuses of the commodity system go uninvestigated."

"Fucker!" Neal yelled.

Then ashamed of himself, he slumped back in his chair. I'll get him, he vowed. I'll get him if it's the last thing I ever do.

48

Darling Neal,

Two letters in one day? And I'm supposed to be worried about the grand jury tomorrow.

Actually I am terribly worried about it.

You don't even know about it yet, do you? Well, you will soon.

Anyway, I still have to write to you.

Please don't talk about these letters until I work up enough courage to mention them to you.

When I was a very little girl—oh, first or second grade—I began to realize that I was different from the rest of my family. I don't think my mother really wanted me; I was kind of a mistake. I didn't look like the others. I didn't act like them. I was tiny and dark and quiet. The other kids ridiculed me a lot—silly little brat.

So I spent a lot of time in a dream world. I'd skip off to school. My head filled with great visions of how I'd be a wonderful person the whole world would admire and live a spectacularly happy life.

If I became good at pretending to be in control of everything, the reason was that control was part of my plan to achieve power and fame and happiness.

My family gradually wore down my dreams. I gave most of them up.

Last night one of them came true, for a few minutes anyway.

I won't let you get away from me, Cornelius O'Connor. You're my dream come true.

All my love,
Megan

WIDOW TO TESTIFY IN MERC PROBE

So the *Tribune* announced in a headline on the first page of its Chicago section.

Damn!

Repeated calls to Megan the night before and this morning had provided the information that

a) Tom Dineen advised against bringing in Larry Whealan as being unnecessary and too expensive;

b) she had asked him to appear for her anyway;

c) he seemed to be a very nice man. Cute, too;

d) the kids were pretty good. Margaret and Mark were, respectively, at Notre Dame and Marquette and not likely to be hassled. She was keeping Joseph home from school and sending him over to Catherine's. Brigie Murphy, Trish Ryan, and Nicole Curran would run interference for Teri at St. Ignatius.

And heaven help anyone, Neal reflected, who messes with that bunch of future matriarchs. Talk about triune Irish goddesses.

The next generation of the North Wabash Avenue Irregulars.

On that thought the phone rang again.

"Connor."

"Yes indeed, how can I help you?"

"Blackie?"

"I believe so."

"You called me."

"Did I really? And your name is Connor what?"

"I'm Neal Connor, your classmate."

"Fascinating. I was just thinking of calling you."

"You just *did* call me."

"What a convenient coincidence."

Was it all an act? Was it a mask behind which that very dangerous and extremely troublesome little man hid? Or was it real and perhaps irrelevant?

Or maybe all of the above?

"You wanted to talk to me."

"Yes, so I did. About the matter of the inestimable Larry Whealan of Whealan, Bishop, and James."

"Indeed." Use his own word on him.

"Indeed yes." Blackie paused. "I thought it might be important to observe that one need not fear for the good Megan with that gentleman involved. Our friend Don Roscoe may try once more for publicity out of this case, but he will do so only at very great risk."

"I'm happy to hear that. Actually he's in trouble now."

"With IBC News?"

"One could do a nice series about his years in office."

"One surely could."

"I suppose it has not been done because of sources that no one wants to disturb. But a new man has no sources."

"There might be something to be said about the unethical contacts between his office and judges sitting on cases that Mr. Roscoe is trying."

"You don't disapprove of the series?"

"Not at all. . . . But the purpose of this call is to say that while the wondrous Megan may have to suffer a little more, she ought not to have any fears that it is a serious matter."

"This Larry Whealan is one of the North Wabash Avenue Irregulars."

"An auxiliary, shall we say. Well, good of you to call. Give my best to Megan and her children."

Good of me to call.

And how much does he know about my relationship with Megan and her kids?

No point in trying to figure that out.

I'm sure she hasn't told anyone.

And they've all probably guessed.

He began to take notes for a series on Don Roscoe. Half the lawyers in town would want to talk. The secret would be cutting it to ten minutes of air time—two minutes on five nights. Maybe three minutes a night.

He threw his pencil away. Fifteen minutes to wreck a man's career. That's the game we're in and it disgusts me.

On the other hand, he uses us for a minute or two a week to ruin people's lives.

Poetic justice.

At twelve-thirty the phone rang again.

"Nick. They kept her for three hours. Idiot questions according to Larry. They're heading for his office. One twenty North Wacker. He's having lunch sent in. Some of your colleagues were there with cameras. Megan was wonderful."

The office of Whealan, Bishop, and James was in a loft-type building in the shadow of the glass skyscrapers on the Wacker Street canyon. There were perhaps some lawyers in the corridors who were not Irish or Italian, but Neal didn't notice any.

He was shown promptly into Mr. Whealan's office. He heard Megan laugh as he came through the door.

"Neal, come in." A tall, thin, handsome man with laughing brown eyes and curly brown hair waved at him, then rose and stretched out his hand. "Good to meet you. We were just saying here that Megan is so good before the cameras that she could have your job if she wanted to work for it."

Larry Whealan was at least two inches taller than Neal. Not as solid perhaps, but with a handshake that suggested enormous personal and moral force.

"I couldn't agree more." He patted Megan's shoulder, not wanting to embarrass her with a kiss. Not yet, anyway.

"Have some pizza. And Megan says you use Diet Coke. This is Anne Marie Flynn, my colleague."

"How do you do, Ms. Flynn."

It was perhaps a tribute to Neal's affection for Megan that he had not noticed Anne Marie, a black-Irish beauty that you had to be almost blind not to notice instantly.

"Shall we do it for him, Megan? Nick, you be the reporter. Megan, you be yourself. Lights, camera, action."

"Ms. Lane, do you expect to be indicted?"

Megan put on a straight, formal face.

"No, I do not."

"What might you be charged with?"

"Nothing that I know of."

"What did they ask you about?"

"I'm told the proceedings are secret."

"Did your husband discuss his business with you?"

A puzzled look. "What do you mean by that?"

"I mean did he tell you what he did with all his money?"

"No, he did not."

"Did you ask him?"

"No"—quick smile and flash of gray eyes—"but then he didn't ask me what I did with my money. Does your husband ask you?"

"Fade out!"

Applause.

"The bottom line, Neal," Larry Whealan said, his hands resting behind his head, "is that Donny made a fool out of himself before the grand jury by asking those kinds of questions. Each time she was quizzed Megan came out and talked to me and Anne Marie— incidentally you may notice that almost every woman in our firm bears one or the other of those names, and several of them both in variant forms—and went back in to respond with wide and innocent gray eyes that, no, her husband never told her about his margin accounts or his speculation in the S and P index and that, no, he never explained his income tax return to her and that, no, outside of insurance he had not left her any money."

"She won the jurors' sympathy," Anne Marie continued crisply. "Donny isn't smart enough to know that he created the impression that he is a bully. His assistants will tell him before the day is over."

"And with any luck," Nick said, "we'll never hear from him again."

"No clips," Larry Whealan concluded, "on the five o'clock news and no headlines in the paper tomorrow."

"The accusing hints are dropped and then never refuted. . . . I guess I know that. It's where I work."

"But you never do anything like that," Whealan insisted. "I don't judge my profession by Donny Roscoe, and you should not judge yours by those who play ball with him."

Neal decided that he liked Larry Whealan. Naturally. Nothing but high quality for the North Wabash Avenue Irregulars. Even for the auxiliaries.

"He's right you know, Neal." Megan bit into a very large chunk of pizza.

"You're right, he's right, but a man has to engage in some self-pity during his midlife crisis."

They all laughed.

Megan was on a high. There'd be a letdown later in the day. Still, she knew now that she could handle a courtroom situation. One more step toward the new Megan.

"Proud of you," he whispered as they rode down in the elevator.

"Thanks. I'm kind of proud of myself. . . . I'm coming down to the Lyric tomorrow morning. Face the music, if there is any, right away."

"Give me a ring and we'll get together."

"I will," she said as she patted his arm. "I hear from my daughters that high tea at the Mayfair is totally outstanding."

Did I really make love with her twice the other night? And was it as great as I remember it?

Did I have to come back to Chicago to find a lover like her?

Back at Channel 3 there was a phone call from Nick.

"Whealan and I are a little bit more concerned than we let on at the office. The questions Donny asked looked like an attempt to get an indictment on a conspiracy charge."

"Conspiracy to do what?"

"To defraud investors."

"But the money has all been paid back."

"That doesn't mean that a crime wasn't committed. According to Dineen, Don Roscoe told him that Megan wasn't a target. But Dineen may be lying."

"Or Roscoe."

"It won't be the first time. They have no case, no evidence at all. But that hasn't stopped Donny before."

And, before he could worry about Megan being indicted, there was yet another call.

"*Amigo.* Lou. You got a deal."

50

My darling Neal,

I used to think that only men lusted explicitly after bodies of the opposite sex. I don't believe that anymore, but I'm too shy to ask a woman. I do know I lust after your body with as much desire as I see in your eyes for mine.

That last sentence ought to have been hard for me to write, but it wasn't.

I get excited even thinking about you.

You're wonderful. I'll love you always.

Unblushingly,
Megan

"The critical question that remains unanswered"—Neal poked his chili cheese dog at Luís Garcia—"is what happens to all the money that the drug families earn."

"You expect me to indict myself, my friend." Garcia folded his arms—a posturing *caudillo*. "You cannot be serious."

They were eating lunch in a McDonald's at the Halsted Street gas stop on the Tri-State Expressway. Garcia was wearing a black leather jacket and black leather slacks, looking like a chic motorcycle-gang leader. María Anunciata also wore black leather slacks. And a white mink coat worth perhaps thirty or forty thousand dollars. That's where some of the money went.

She sat at a separate table, sipping 7-Up and chain-smoking. Was she a mascot who traveled with Luís all the time?

"Certainly not, Lou. I don't want to ask what banks launder your money or where you hide it. I accept your premise that people want to use cocaine and that you are merely offering a service, of no more inherent evil than a brewer who makes and distributes beer. . . . Incidentally, what if we should follow Professor Gary Becker's recommendation and legalize certain drugs?"

Luís raised his hands expressively. "He's right, *amigo*. As a taxpayer, I deplore the money that is wasted on foolish attempts to stop the importing of cocaine. It's as foolish as the prohibition law, just as Becker says. All it does is raise prices. If you legalize it, our income declines, but our lives become much safer. I have lost too many of my family to like the violence."

"All right, that's the kind of question I want to ask. I want to get your viewpoint on these issues. Now, you live very simply, in the flat above your store. OK, the store is a little flashier than you expect in your neighborhood. I'm sure the flat is very comfortable. Your friend over there is well dressed and wears expensive jewels. Still your life-style is hardly what one would expect of someone who makes as much money as you're alleged to make. Why do you stay in the South East Side?"

"It is home." He shrugged. " 'Where else should we live?' my father always said. Would we be safer in Flossmor or Lake Forest? Would our children have any more friends? Would our wives be treated with more respect? In the neighborhood we are someone important. Elsewhere we are dirt."

Neal scribbled rapidly. He was less interested in a program than in solving the mystery of the death of Al Lane. But these were good quotes.

"And," Lou continued, "we have many expenses to pay if we are to render our service. All along the line, we are not as rich as those who make TV cop shows seem to think."

"Do you want this life for your children?"

Lou waved his hands again, the jeweled rings glittering in the artificial light of the restaurant. "Do I want death for them? Certainly not. Every new group in this country makes its start by offering something that people want and that is thought to be corrupt or immoral. The Irish did it in politics, the Italians in booze and later gambling, the WASPS"—he laughed—"they stole the whole country. But because we are Hispanic, what we do is supposed to be wrong. I tell you, *amigo*," he said, leaning forward intently, "I would like nothing more than to see drugs become legal and my children do respectable things like yours do."

"I don't have any kids, Lou."

"You don't?" He seemed surprised. "That is a shame."

"I agree."

He must know that. He must have checked me out completely. Probably part of the act.

He was tempted to ask Garcia how his kids felt about their father's mistress, who was no older than some of them.

He decided that it was an offensive question, the answer to which was none of his business.

He almost asked about investments, the real reason for the enterprise.

But, no, not yet. I want to keep his trust.

And I won't betray his confidence. After all, he is not the one making the threatening phone calls that aren't really threatening to Megan.

He waited for Megan in the lobby of the Mayfair. High tea in the lobby was safe. Their interlude the other night had been sensational. His body longed for more. But he realized that each new romp would bind him more tightly to her.

How did I get involved in all of this in the first place? he wondered.

It's all Blackie Ryan's doing. That troublesome, dangerous priest.

His head was spinning from the interview with Garcia. He didn't buy the drug boss's self-serving arguments, they had been used by every crook before him, too. But would it be possible to say something about American society, something important, if he juxtaposed Lou Garcia and Donny Roscoe? Who was the worse crook?

Somehow Megan and Al were tied up in it all, too. He would have to protect them, but there were themes that tied everything together.

If he could find the principal themes, he might be able to explain what had happened.

He pulled out his notebook and jotted down the puzzles:

1) How had Alfred Lane really died?
2) And why had he died?
3) What link, if any, was there between him and the Garcia family?
4) What happened to the money he had drawn from his many bank accounts?
5) Why were the FBI and the United States Attorney so interested in hassling Megan?

He paused at that one. Publicity, everyone said. OK, that's probably the truth. But why select her unless there was a remote chance of digging up something more important?

6) Who was the mole in the Garcia organization who tipped off the government about Al's connection with them?
7) Who was the woman who called begging for the money, not threatening but begging?

8) Could Maureen Kennelly tell him about Alf's dealings with the Garcias?

He considered the list. Written out that way the complexities looked even more daunting than he had realized.

Then he scrawled another question.

9) Might Maureen be the mole?

Why might she be? No reason. Brian Neenan and Tom Dineen were the more obvious choices. But hell hath no fury . . .

He closed the notebook.

So far he had rushed about impulsively, flailing for clues.

Hell, he was a reporter, not a detective.

Nonetheless it was an exciting puzzle, as much a challenge as anything he had ever done before, if perhaps not a matter of major news.

On the other hand, it might be.

And it also might end up being a matter of life and death.

He needed a handle, a key, a hook to hang it on, a map to chart his way through the swamp. So far he hadn't even come close.

The Garcia project was as impulsive a caper as he had ever tried.

Impulsively screwing a woman and impulsively chasing a drug boss.

Romance is where you find it, he thought with a sigh, putting away his notebook. But you're supposed to find it in Stevenson or Conrad novels, not in visits to class reunions.

"Finished?"

He looked up. Megan in an open trench coat, navy blue jersey dress, and a rain hat, smiling down on him.

"Sorry, Megan, I was jotting down ideas."

"So I noticed. You work hard, don't you?"

"Sometimes." He stood up and brushed his lips against hers. "Do you want tea here in the lobby or in my suite?"

Give her a chance to make the decision about what happens next between us.

She glanced around the lobby. "I haven't seen your suite yet."

"Well, then"—hormones began rushing excitedly into his blood—"come on up."

She seemed amused by him, a mother smiling at an errant, if appealing, boy-child.

They rode up in the elevator. "You seem in a good mood today, Megan."

"Do I? I guess I am. I've started my Christmas shopping. I always enjoy that."

He made a mental note that he would provide her and her daughters with a Schwinn exercise bicycle for Christmas. The kids would sandbag her into using it. You kept the body of your mistress in good shape.

"The worst is over, I think."

He didn't really believe that.

"My Hispanic friend has not called for the last two days. I felt really sorry for her, she sounded desperate."

"Does she ever say what money she wants?"

"I ask her, and she says that I know what money it is—and of course, I don't."

The elevator door opened and they walked across to his suite. He opened the door, bowed her in, and helped her off with her coat. She was wearing a navy blue shirtdress, lambswool and nylon perhaps, with a black and white neck, a white handkerchief in the breast pocket, and white stockings. Still a widow, but a widow who was moving beyond the worst of her mourning.

"What an adorable apartment!" she exclaimed. "Everything a spoiled bachelor needs and in excellent taste."

"Not quite everything." He laughed as he ordered high tea for two.

"You can see our park bench from here." She was standing at the window, looking out on the fog-covered lake. "Just barely when the fog moves a little."

"You remember then?"

"How could I ever forget?" she said sadly. "I was wrong, Neal. Does it do any good now, after all these years, to say I was wrong?"

He gulped. "Now who's disconcerting whom?"

"We both wonder about that week, don't we? We've always wondered, haven't we?"

"It would have never worked, Megan," he said, sinking into a chair.

"I'm not so sure about that. If it hadn't worked, it would have been my fault, not yours."

She continued to stare out at the lake, seeing nothing perhaps and at the same time seeing everything.

"What's done is done, Megan. We can't undo it."

"I suppose not. Still, maybe if we can understand it, we can learn something. . . . I was a coward. I was as afraid of you as I was of my family."

"Afraid of me?"

"You would tear down my walls, Neal, all my carefully prepared walls. You were ripping them away already . . . getting close to my most private dreams."

"That would have been bad?"

"I thought so then. Al, poor, sad, well-meaning man, didn't even realize that I'd put them up."

"What if I had run after you?" he blurted.

A knock on the door: a pretty young woman in black dress and white apron with tea, which she served with Gallic charm, arranging even the pastries in perfect symmetry.

Neal began to munch on a cucumber sandwich even before the waitress had left the room. Megan blew on her Earl Grey tea and sipped it.

"You didn't answer my question, Megan."

"I was hoping you'd forget it.

"I've wondered about it ever since. Thousands of times."

"Oh, Neal, how horrible for you."

"You melt my heart when you look at me that way, woman."

"I'm glad of that. I'll try to remember just how I looked at you."

"Please answer my question."

"So you can feel guilty and angry at yourself and mourn for what might have been? Even if what might have been could easily have been a terrible tragedy for both of us at that stage in our life?" She was suddenly angry at him, for the first time since his return, and she was devastatingly beautiful in her anger.

He put down his teacup.

"I can't argue with that."

"Suppose you had come running after me? Suppose I gave in to that part of me that wanted to be with you in the Arizona Inn that night? How do we know we would have been happy? It could have been a terrible mistake. You wanted to go to Vietnam—face it, you did. I was still tied up by my family. We might have hated each other within six months. Who can answer those questions? They're not the important ones now, anyway."

"Do you get hot under the collar like that often?"

"Not nearly often enough, I'm afraid. Why?"

"I've never seen you look more beautiful."

"Blarney," she said, not displeased with it. "But thanks. . . . You do understand what I'm saying?"

"I do, Megan, I do. And you're right."

"Not completely right. Anyway, you did come after me."

Gulp.

"Eventually."

She waved that off and finished her cup of tea. "Maybe at just the right time."

He seized two strawberry pastries and downed them one after another. "So we work through it again?"

Megan stood up hesitantly and folded her arms across her chest. "I guess so. It scares me more this time. It seems like we've stumbled into it again, and we're more like children than we were before. Still . . ."

"Still what?"

"Still, do you want to make love to me this afternoon?" She undid the top three buttons of her dress, down to and beneath her bra—still black, but sheer and with the hook in front this time. She undid the hook. "I don't know exactly how this game is played. I guess I'm still mostly a virgin. So I'll be dumb old Megan and rush right in, bluntly and clumsily."

He stood up, closed his hands around her upper arms and pulled her near him.

"Certainly I want to make love to you. Why else did I bring you up here? And you're neither blunt nor clumsy. You're rather elegantly and devastatingly seductive."

"Truly?"

"Most truly."

"I'm glad. That's what I want to be."

"And I will not be the maniac forest ape that I was the other night."

He began to kiss her eyes, her nose, her chin. One of his hands slipped into the warmth between her breasts.

"I didn't mind." She giggled. "It was different. Anyway you weren't an ape the second time."

"Which did you like better?" In each tender kiss there was an agony of joy for him that made him want to kiss her forever.

"I like anything you do with me, Neal."

"Do you have time?"

"Till seven-thirty. I got ahead of my Christmas shopping schedule because I thought you might want me to stay."

He finished unbuttoning her dress and let it fall to the floor. "A leisurely afternoon in bed?"

"Oh yes, how wonderful." She helped him ease the bra off her shoulders. "No hurrying. Warmth in bed, cold outside."

She picked up her dress and arranged it neatly on the couch. Then she placed the bra on top of the dress and turned back to him, holding out her hand for him to take.

He led her into his bedroom. "Should I pull the drapes?"

"Can anyone see us here?" She glanced out the window at the fading light of a chill winter sunset behind the tall buildings of the Gold Coast.

"I very much doubt it."

She sat on the edge of the bed, kicked off her shoes, and gazed up adoringly at him. "Leave them open then."

He sat next to her. They embraced and began to kiss.

It was indeed a leisurely afternoon in bed. Megan was still the mostly passive recipient of passion; however, she had begun shrewd and calculating little experiments, testing what a woman might do to arouse a man.

When their interlude was over, he realized that he had discovered a woman who might develop extraordinary talents as a lover.

One part of his troubled, anxious soul made up its mind:

Never let her go.

The other warned him that, given half a chance, she would bind him and never let him go.

53

"I don't know anything about Hispanic clients," Maureen Kennelly insisted, attacking one of her favorite cinnamon rolls. "He didn't talk much business with me. But he hated drug peddlers."

They were in the Bismarck coffee shop again.

"He never mentioned a bar on the South East Side?" Neal was matching her roll for roll this time.

"Not a word. Like I say, the poor guy had a lot of things on his mind, but some of them he couldn't talk about, not even to me. He was afraid the government was bugging his office, I know that."

"Uh-huh." The woman was lying, contradicting herself in every other sentence. "But you're sure—"

"Look—" She sighed impatiently as she smeared butter on yet another roll. "I don't have to talk to you. Like I said, I know he had no contacts with any Hispanic drug pushers."

Neal apologized for pushing too hard, signaled for the check, waited till Ms. Kennelly had finished the last roll, and then paid the bill as she tramped out the door of the coffee shop, her body quivering its displeasure.

Blew that one, he thought.

Brian Neenan was more forthcoming when Neal found him in the small, colorless office he had shared with Alf for so many years, an office with harsh fluorescent lights and no windows.

"Everyone on the street knew he hung out with Lou Garcia. But invest money for him?" Neenan shrugged his stooped shoulders. "I don't know about that."

Neal assumed that he was telling the truth. Why lie about the matter? Unless Neenan was in on the deal, too. That did not seem plausible.

Back in his office he called Cos Ventura.

"Investing money for the Garcias?" Cos asked with fastidious dismay. "Neal, my friend, those savages don't know what commodities are. Or even where the Board of Trade is. I don't think they can find their way to Lasalle Street."

"Your friends have heard nothing about Alf laundering money through commodity accounts?"

"You mean the friends of my friends?"

"Right."

"First of all, there are easier ways to launder money. Even the savages know that. Secondly, if my friends, ah, the friends of my friends found out that one of their friends was doing something like that, maybe even mixing their money with dirty money, they'd be very upset."

After he hung up, Neal wondered whether the fact that commodity accounts were a difficult way of laundering money might not make them attractive. Not the place where the feds would look.

But they were looking now, were they not?

Cos wasn't telling the truth. Neither was Maureen Kennelly. Brian Neenan probably was telling the truth, or at least most of it. He had seemed to clam up when the question of Garcia money in the Merc was raised.

Tom Dineen told the truth.

"Hell, Neal," his big voice boomed on the phone, "you don't think Alf hung out over there just to mess around with the broads, do you? Sure he was putting their money into phony accounts. Everyone knew that. Nothing illegal, by the way. If someone wants to open a couple of savings and loan accounts with cash and then use the money for hedges, what's wrong with that?"

"To launder the money?"

"Nah! To make more money."

So Alfie was speculating with Garcia money and Outfit money. A sure way to get yourself dead real quick.

Especially when you lose the money in a meltdown.

How did you die, Al? How did you really die?

And why?

Dearest Neal,

I want to write you a love letter.

The other letters weren't real love letters, only letters from a lover.

Is that a fair name for me? What am I—mistress, concubine, friend?

I'll define myself as a love and leave it at that.

Being sensible, self-possessed Megan, I will write one draft and send it to you. I won't even reread it. Please don't mention this or any other letter I might write until I work up enough courage to raise the subject with you.

I'm writing, obviously, because I'm not sure that I can tell you in person all I feel.

Now, says sensible Megan at a loss for words, what do I want to tell you?

I love you, but you know that.

I am out of my mind with love for you. Do you know that? I'm not so sure.

My body is so crazy hungry for you that whenever I think of you, it absolutely refuses to do anything besides preparing for lovemaking.

I'm not ashamed, either. To tell the truth, I am fearsomely proud of myself for having seduced you.

When I see your eyes turn hard as I undress, and know you must have me, I go crazy with pride and joy.

There are so many other things I want to do with you.

I understand now that a crush is really something physical, a longing to be possessed by another. I am possessed and I possess and I am insanely happy.

I exult in your physical strength and my own physical weakness. You can overwhelm me anytime you want and I love that.

Please overwhelm me often.

I want all I can get of you. As I said before. I don't intend to let you go. Ever. Ever. Believe that, Neal. I really mean it.

Dear God, I love you so much.

I'd better stop now.

Megan.

PS. What I wanted to say was this:

That little girl skipping off to school that I mentioned in one of my other letters, remember her?

She faked being cheerful and bright. Inside, she always felt cold, even in the summer. Probably because she was left out of her family (a blessing, I guess, but it didn't seem so then).

I have felt chilled all my life. I even saw a doctor about whether I had a circulation problem. He suggested a shrink and I was mortified.

I was cold in that burning room. I thought I was going to burn to death, but I was still cold. Then you came and carried me out into the zero weather and I felt warm.

Just like I did at the class reunion in church when I looked up and saw you next to me.

You melt me, Neal. Even by standing next to me.

And when you are inside of me, igniting me with your flame, the ice melts and turns into water. Then the water begins to boil and consumes me with its fearsome heat.

I become your flame.

Oh, my darling Neal, I love you so.

55

"Nipples like sweet milk chocolate."

Beneath him Megan stirred sleepily. "You and Blackie are obsessed with chocolate. Breasts, too," she added, giggling, "though he never says."

"Must that troublesome priest intervene," he protested as he continued to stroke one of her nipples with his tongue, "even on my marriage bed?"

Megan's eyes were wide with remembered satisfaction and renewed desire.

"This isn't a marriage bed, Neal." Her voice was soft with submission. "At most it's a bed of love."

Their early afternoon interlude in her office had not begun so well. Crazed by the invitation in her letter, he had, against better judgment and common sense, left the Dan Ryan on his drive back from the session with Garcia. Megan, rumpled and clad in a thin white robe, opened the door for him dubiously.

"Catching up on laundry," she murmured. "Want to help?"

"Not with the laundry." He reached for the belt of her robe.

"Neal!"

Quickly he pulled off her robe and the plain white bra beneath it.

She twisted away from him.

"You bastard!" she shouted. "You think you have the right to come into my house and assault me whenever the mood is on you! Get out!"

Thus rejected by other women, Neal would have fled in disgrace and humiliation. He almost retreated this time, too.

Instead, he grabbed both her hands and spun her around.

"Yes!" he shouted back. "I have exactly that right! Try and stop me!"

Her face contorted in anger—lips tight, eyes flashing, skin white with fury. She struggled to free herself, her champagne-glass breasts twisted away from him in exquisite defiance.

Then she stopped struggling. Her shoulders went limp. Her body crumpled. She sagged toward him.

"Oh, Neal, I'm sorry. Of course you have that right. I lost my nerve, that's all. I'm such a little bitch. You scared me."

"I'm sorry that I scared you." He gathered her into his arms and searched for the elastic on her panties.

"Nice scare." She huddled against him. "Please burst in here whenever you want."

All right, he had handled that problem. Now what was he to say about his "marriage bed" slip of the tongue.

"Let's say that it's a bed somewhere between the two."

His hand reached for her thigh. I did say "marriage bed." For a moment I thought she was my wife. Maybe she is already and I don't realize it. . . . Could a wife taste so good? Why not?

"I wonder," she said thoughtfully, drawing away from him.

"About what do you wonder?"

"About you. I love you, but I'm not sure that I trust you completely. Oh, I don't mean that quite the way it sounds, Neil." She touched his shoulder. "What I mean is that we have lived so long in completely different worlds."

"So?"

"So I wonder if you can ever have any private life at all. Does your public life demand everything? What would you not sacrifice for your career?"

"Haven't I told you that I'm disillusioned with my career?"

"It doesn't follow," she said, resisting his attempt to absorb her back into his arms, "that you can ever give up its habits."

"Like what?" he demanded impatiently.

"Like picking up remarks made in ordinary conversation and then using them on your broadcast."

"Huh?"

"Everything, everything, is grist for your mill."

"Like this?" He started to kiss her breast.

She offered no resistance. "Like Blackie's crack about the city hall vote being like a papal election save for the white smoke."

"Blackie didn't mind."

In truth he had never thought of the possibility that there might be anything wrong with stealing the troublesome priest's wonderful crack. Maybe Megan had stumbled on a half-truth that he ought to consider.

"I know. But still . . ."

He touched her nipple with his tongue.

"Maybe you're right," he murmured. "I'll have to watch it. I'll ask that troublesome little priest what he thinks."

Despite her anticipation of more pleasure, she examined his face very carefully. "You love Blackie more than the rest of us," she said, almost an accusation. "You take him seriously all the time. We laugh at him."

His fingers paused. His mouth rose from her breast.

"I bet he'd like to be where I am now."

"I hope he would." She sighed. "He is human, isn't he?"

"Sometimes I'm not so sure."

They both laughed.

"Does it always have to be twice?" she protested at his renewed play.

"There's never enough time for thrice."

"That would be interesting."

So for another half hour he forgot about Garcia and Donny Roscoe. And he forgot about his central assignment: How did the husband of this astonishing woman die?

Well, he almost forgot about that.

In the pool at the CAG, recovering from Megan and Garcia, Neal figured out who the mole was.

It was absolutely simple. And it might well be the key to everything else.

No, it need not be that. At most it would be useful. He'd have to find proof before he could tell anyone.

The last quarter mile of his swim was an agony of effort. He was running on overdrive and such effort took a toll—especially, he told himself, on a man over forty.

Garcia was being skittish.

They met at their usual rendezvous spot. This time Luís also wore a white mink coat. María Anunciata was permitted to sit at the table with them. Despair continued to lurk in her eyes, but Neal also noticed for the first time, a feral shrewdness. The child might be a survivor, might, for example, end up as a successful madam.

Irrelevantly he wondered what she was like when she had made her First Communion.

"I need some deep background information from you, Lou, if I'm going to get this picture clear in my own mind. I won't insult you by telling you what deep background is."

"So?"

"So I need to know how you run the family. You and Rickie share power, is that right?"

"Rickie does what I tell him. If he wants to give the orders, he has to get rid of me."

"I see. Does he want to do that?"

Lou moved his right hand indifferently. "Who knows? Perhaps he understands that there are others who will kill him once my protection is removed. I hope so. If he tries to kill me, I will find out first and I will kill him. I have already killed two brothers. I do not want to kill another."

"You killed your two older bothers?"

"Of course." He smiled.

"Everyone knows that." María Anunciata spoke for the first time. Standard American English free of accent. Neal's notion that she was an illegal went down the drain.

Lou did not try to silence her.

"Could I ask why?"

"What is that to you?"

"Let's get this straight, Lou, once and for all. I ask only the questions I need to ask. I am not motivated by morbid curiosity. I don't work for the narcs or for Donny Roscoe. Personally, I don't give a damn why you blew away your brothers. But if I'm going to put together a picture of your world from your perspective, I've got to know more about your world."

"He had good reason to kill them," the girl spoke again.

Again Lou ignored her.

"Look, *amigo*. I like you, huh? You've got talent and balls. You don't bullshit. I trust you, more or less." He grinned crookedly. "Hell, more than most of my family, which isn't very much. I'll answer your questions, because like the *chiquita* here says, everyone in the neighborhood knows, but that's all for today and I want to think more about what you're doing. First, tell me again, why you are on this track of questions?"

"I haven't told you once. But the answer is that I'm trying to figure out whether some of your family—I mean the whole crowd, not just you and Rickie—work their own independent deals."

"I see what you mean. What do you think? They do it all the time—we're criminals, eh, *amigo*? We cheat on each other, just like we cheat everyone else. I let them get away with it so long as it stays small. If it gets big, or if they get in my way or if they create problems with some of our allies, I warn them once. Always I give them the warning. Then"—he snapped his fingers—"poof."

"And he knows everything," María Anunciata announced somberly. "Everything."

Was it admiration or fear in the girl's voice?

"I don't doubt it."

"So I find my brother Hector cooperates with the Suarezes to kill my mother and my father and my sister. So, poof, that is the end of Hector. He is a pig anyway. My other brother, Rosario, he doesn't mind that, but he gets worried about me. If I blow away Hector so easy, maybe I try to blow away him. I wouldn't do that because I have respect—"

"More respect than anyone," the girl interrupted, as if she was reciting a line she was expected to recite.

"Right, more respect than anyone. I tell Rosario I won't waste him if he leaves me alone. I tell him if he tries to kill me, I send him to heaven real quick. He doesn't believe me. He thinks I am dumb. So he tries to kill me. Poof! He's gone, too. That answer your question, *amigo*?"

"Avenging your parents and defending yourself?"

"Sure. I'm not proud of it, but what am I to do? Now, *amigo*, we leave. Don't call me. I'll call you."

"*Adiós,*" said the teenage girl, smiling at him as if she would like to blow him away. Poof!

Charming folks. It still sounded like an episode of "Miami Vice." Maybe that's just what it was. Pure fiction. Next time, if there was a next time, he'd begin by asking bluntly about Al Lane.

And why the change in the girl's demeanor—originally a slave and perhaps a battered one, now she was something altogether different. Was that part of the act?

Or did it amuse Lou Garcia to order his mistress to change roles?

Lou could be using him just as easily as he was using Lou.

Was María Anunciata the woman on the phone? She didn't look like the one for tearful pleadings. And she spoke with no trace of an accent.

And why would she plead?

He pondered all these questions as he struggled through his exercise. No answers. Just more craziness. Everywhere.

And then there was Megan. He was caught now. In a tender trap. A wonderfully tender trap, but still a trap. Did he want to stay in the trap forever? If he didn't, he'd better slip out of it while the slipping was good.

He pulled himself wearily out of the pool and wrapped a towel around his naked and aching body. "Telephone, Mr. Neal." An attendant handed him a portable phone.

"Neal Connor."

"Nick here. We've got another puzzle. The FBI visited Megan this morning. Harassed her for two hours. No warrant, no right to push their way into her house, no charges. Lot of browbeating. Reduced her to tears. Of course she didn't think of refusing to answer without a lawyer. And they didn't read her any rights, which makes whatever questions they asked useless in court, not that there's anything to go to court with."

"What kind of questions?"

"About you mostly. Apparently they've found out somewhere that you two were once romantically involved so they're working that line—hinting, I'm afraid, that maybe the two of you conspired to kill her husband."

"The bastards! I was in the Hindu Kush ducking Russian gunships."

"So you did it from a distance. It's all crazy. Larry Whealan is shouting at Donny, threatening to get an injunction against him. I think he's scared him. He damn well better be scared. This is not Nazi Germany yet."

"He'll regret it, Nick."

"That's what baffles me. Why mess with a powerful media person like you? By the way, I hate to ask this, but—"

"Yes, we are and I don't intend to stop it. You can tell your wife, too, though I suppose she knows it already. Am I under surveillance, do you think?"

"I doubt it. I think they're just guessing. Putting a tail on you would be one hell of a dangerous thing. Incidentally, congratulations."

"Another victory for the troublesome priest."

After Nick hung up, Neal promptly called Megan. She was fine now, she insisted. Learning to cope with these terrible men. They would not catch her off guard again. She was looking forward to seeing him tomorrow."

"So am I," he grinned.

Finally he called Blackie Ryan. "Can I talk to you sometime in the next few days? No rush. I want to check out something. . . . End of the week? Fine. . . . About what? I struck your curiosity, huh? Well, I've got an idea—no, more than an idea, a fact—and I want your opinion on what to do about it."

He smiled contentedly. That would give the devious little priest something to think about.

57

Another letter from Megan. She is trying to seduce me by mail. As well as in the flesh.

Dearest Neal,

I bet when you saw this letter you said to yourself, This crazy woman is trying to seduce me by mail.

I wonder if I am. Probably I am. By mail or by any other way.

I don't want to bind you. I want you to be completely free.

But I do want to bind you. I don't want to lose you.

I know those are contradictions. I don't care; that's the way I feel.

It's hard for me to keep writing. Putting down your name in the salutation sets me on fire. I want to have you inside me now.

What kind of a wanton woman would write that horny line in a letter to her lover? Certainly not a widow with four children.

I use to think that lust and love were two completely different emotions and that I was born without much of the former. Now I know that when a woman loves a man (and vice versa, I guess) they're the same emotion. How wonderful!

And I also know that my poor little body, in which you take so much pleasure, thank God, has more than its share of lust.

Thank God for that, too.

I'd better stop now.

All my love,
Megan

58

"Three young persons here to see you, Mr. Connor." The concierge's very proper voice did not altogether approve of the three young persons.

"Their names," he said with a sinking heart, knowing what their names would be.

"Mark, Margaret, and Teri. They apparently do not have a surname."

"Tell them I'm finishing some work, but I'll be happy to see them in five minutes. I'll phone down when I'm ready."

"Very good, sir. . . . They say they'll be happy to wait."

The work was cleaning up the traces that their mother had left only a half hour before. He jumped out of bed, yanked on his clothes, threw open the windows to exorcise any trace of her scent, made the bed as neatly as he could, cleaned up the bathroom, did a quick reconnaissance of the kitchen, and glanced in the closet to make sure she had not left anything.

He swept through the apartment once again, no scarf, no gloves, no telltale tissues, no lingerie, no raincap. Megan was a tidy woman, even in her sexual romps. Still, he couldn't take any chances. Not with old eagle-eye Margaret. No way.

He ordered high tea for four. Arranged some papers on his desk, and turned on his Toshiba portable computer.

Then he closed the windows and donned an Aran Isle sweater, so that he could explain that he liked the apartment cold if anyone asked.

He took a deep breath. Was there the smell of lovemaking? Margaret was undoubtedly a virgin but not so innocent a one as to miss that unmistakable aroma.

No, winter air had cleaned it out.

He glanced at his watch. Six and a half minutes.

He picked up the phone. "Connor here. Would you send up the three surnameless young people, with my apologies for being a minute and a half late."

"Certainly, Mr. Connor." There was only a hint in the poor man's voice that he thought Neal was around the bend altogether.

In fact, Neal felt that his soul was caught in a tug of war

between contestants whom he did not know. The Chicago TV reviewers were now assaulting him almost every day—"hot dog," "showboat," "ham," "pompous phony" were some of the kinder words they were using. Johnny explained that they were always hostile to someone new, especially when that new person was famous to begin with. They had virtually driven Jane Pauley out of Chicago when she came from Indianapolis, and had never really apologized after her move to "Today" and national acclaim.

"Our ratings are up fifty percent and the letters and the calls are favorable. No one pays any attention to the critics except a few yuppies and lakefront liberals, and they don't watch TV news anyway."

"It's been a long time since they went after me, back in Tucson."

"Ignore them, don't change your style in response, and, Neal, for the love of heaven, don't offer to fight any of them with your bare hands."

"Don't worry, Johnny. I do that only once a year."

He was nervous and jumpy and sometimes irritable with the producers and the technicians, who were sullen in his presence. He always apologized after his outbursts, a show of contriteness that seemed to astonish them. Some of the reporters and the other anchors also seemed to resent him.

Neal had been around long enough to understand these reactions. They would pass away in time, melted by ratings if these continued to be high.

He was uneasy with his new job. He wrote his own material twenty minutes before air time and played the anchor role with ease. It was a job, but for him it wasn't work. His ideas for special stories were only a stack of notes or a file of ideas in his head. He realized that nothing would be expected of him till after the first of the year and that he could put together a good series with a few hours' work; but it all seemed both too easy and too confusing.

Maybe he was simply not designed to settle down in one place and work at one kind of job.

He had heard not a word from Garcia and knew that it would be futile and counterproductive to try to call him.

He had not seen Blackie Ryan at the appointed time because he had another flash of insight—during lovemaking actually—which he wanted to examine and ponder before "our superpower summit," as he informed the troublesome priest.

He thought for a moment he knew where the missing money was—there was, in fact, money and it was hidden in a place he saw.

But after he woke from a nap, his sleeping woman still cuddled in his arms, he couldn't quite remember what the insight was.

He'd have to work on it.

The greatest anxieties in his life and also the richest rewards came from Megan.

"I didn't think," she said as she lay peacefully in his arms, "that pleasure like this was possible, except in storybooks."

"I didn't think women like you were possible except in storybooks."

He spoke the strict literal truth. With the single-minded candor that seem to be her stock in trade, Megan had thrown herself into sexual play. She was astonishingly good at it. Indeed, while the word "aggressor" did not fit either one of their roles, she was often the pacesetter.

Neal drifted through his days in a pleasant afterglow that sometimes, and a for a few minutes, dimmed all the worries that ought to have preoccupied him.

He knew the pattern of the relationship was changing when he rang the bell at the house on Hoyne one morning—when the children were in school—and Megan answered the door. She peered around the outside.

"Come in, Neal. I'm too embarrassed to open it all the way. Don't worry, I won't fight you this time. Unless it amuses you as it did the last time."

She disappeared behind the door. He slipped in and discovered that she was wearing a silver lace teddy.

"Megan!"

"Don't you dare laugh."

"I wouldn't think of it. I'm staring, not laughing."

"You're supposed to stare." She leaned against the wall, hands behind her back. "I can't believe I'm wearing it."

"You won't be wearing it for long," he replied, reaching for her.

It was the turning point. Their love sessions now were relaxed and delicious comedy, with Megan not infrequently directing the show with delicate and determined refinement.

Yet she continued to worry about his inability to protect his private life from his public life, a problem which, he argued, if it existed at all, was minor.

"I suppose," he said, trying to sound philosophical, "it's a problem that affects everyone who is recognized on the street."

"That's not what I mean, Neil." She slipped back from his embrace as she often did when she worried. "I don't mind you knowing everyone and everyone knowing you, even if I am a square peg in that world. I worry that there is no limit to what you would sacrifice for a story or for your career."

"I haven't sacrificed anything for my career." He insisted on reclaiming her with his embrace.

She yielded to him, surrendered herself into his arms. "Only your life."

"Oh, boy!" He held her close and thought about it. "You're a tough one, Megan Keefe Lane."

"I'm sorry," she said with a sigh. "I had to say it."

"I'll think about it, I promise." Even as he said it he knew that he wouldn't. Maybe she was right. However, he had made up his mind that those days were over, had he not? The problem was not what he had done in the past, but what he had to do in the future, wasn't it?

"I promise not to say it again." She wrapped her legs around him. "Let's love one another now, while there's still time."

"You're every man's dream of a *Playboy* lover."

"Come on, Neal." She jabbed at his ribs. "I don't look like any of those women."

"You deliver what they promise and can't deliver." He started to caress her again.

"I hope I never becoming boring."

He was too far gone even to reply.

Earlier that afternoon he had been Christmas shopping at the Water Tower mall. Coming out of Kroch's bookstore, he encountered Megan coming out of Enchanté lingerie shop, with two shopping bags filled with packages, none of them giftwrapped.

She turned crimson and stayed that color.

"You shouldn't be here." She refused to look at him.

"Do I get to see what's in the packages?"

"In due course. If you act right."

"I can hardly wait."

"You'll have to wait." She giggled, now a frequent sound from Megan. "You may even have to pay for them when my Visa bill comes due."

"Shouldn't I have a say in what you buy?"

"No." She still refused to look at him. "If you want to buy something for me, that's different."

"I bet they're all appropriate for the name of the store."

"I'm not the Frederick's of Hollywood type."

"Thank heavens. . . . Do you have a couple of free hours?"

"An hour, I suppose."

"Come on."

"I was hoping you would ask. I won't take anything out of these packages. You'll just have to make do with what I'm wearing."

"A come-as-you-are party?"

"NEAL!"

But she let him take her arm and guide her down the escalator and through the rain on Michigan Avenue.

"Are we acting like a couple of horny adolescents, Neal?" she asked uneasily.

"We're acting like lovers, which means a little crazy. Don't fight it. Enjoy it."

"I have every intention of doing so. And, Neal, I'm not imposing any obligations, understand? There's no strings attached to me."

"Next year we can worry about that."

She dragged him into the arcade at the Drake, glanced up and down the dark corridor to make sure that no one else was there, and in front of the entrance to Spalding's Jewelry, stood on her tiptoes and kissed him.

"I would have done something like that on the beach when I was a kid," she whispered, her hands were cupped behind his neck. "I'm not ashamed of doing it now."

"Megan . . ." he protested.

"Quiet, sex object." She kissed him again, her hands slipping down his back and pressing against his butt. "No one is watching."

"But . . ."

She linked her arm with his again. "I bet none of your other women do that."

"There aren't any other women," he said after he managed to catch his breath. "And you're right: the few there were in the past were not quite so . . ."

"Avid?"

"Good word."

She laughed and, at the door of the Cape Cod Room, kissed him for the third time, a long, lingering kiss, her fingers digging into his flanks, appropriate behavior, he thought prudishly, only for the bedroom.

Then she slipped away from him and ran outside to the rain on East Lake Shore Drive.

She was still laughing when he caught up.

"I WANT you," she informed him.

"So I gathered." He recaptured her arm. "Do you think you can wait till we ride up to my suite?"

"This time maybe."

Just barely, as it turned out.

In the suite there was no need to remove anything from her shopping bags. Under her black suit and white blouse she was awash in white lace.

"Thought you might meet me?" He played with a thin strap.

"If I hadn't, I would have come over here. Oh, Neal . . . how wonderful. . . . Don't stop . . . I love it."

When they were finished and Neal lay back in bed, drenched in sweat, ready for a brief nap, she sat next to him, cross-legged, her slip grasped at her breasts in symbolic modesty.

He reached for his shorts.

"Put that down," she demanded. "You know that I like you naked."

"But—"

"It's my turn to be modest."

"Anything you say." He touched the bottom of one of her breasts, reaching under the slip that was draped over it.

"No, Neal," she said firmly, just as she had warned her daughter when she was getting out of line. "I don't want to be distracted. Not now, anyway. I must say something that I've kind of said before"— she frowned—"but in greater detail."

"Fair enough." His hand retreated to her belly. Megan wanted to explain herself to him, but more probably to herself.

"I wanted you the first day you came into sixth grade. I had no idea what that meant then. I would have been horrified, I suppose, if someone had told me. But if that's what having you meant, I would have been willing to do it even then."

"I'm flattered. I think I would have been terrified then."

"I guess maybe what I'm doing now . . ."—she paused and looked away from him—" . . . is testing to see if it's love or just a crazy adolescent dream."

"What does it seem like?"

She seemed surprised by the question. "Oh, it seems like love. I mean, I don't know whether I can tell the difference. Whether I'll ever be able to tell the difference. I hope it's love. I hope I've always loved you. I hope I made the wrong decision when I turned my back on you at O'Hare. If I don't love you, I don't know what my life will mean anymore."

He groped for the right response. "Megan, will you permit me to say, lovely lady, that you are being just a little too serious about this. I don't mean about sex or about love: they're both very serious matters and on the basis of your performance you're spectacularly good at both."

"How do you know anything about my love?" she protested.

"I see it reflected in your children."

"That's a wonderful compliment." Her voice choked.

"OK. We're not sixth-graders. We're two adults who are discovering each other really for the first time. Both of us like what we see so far. We continue to explore. Nothing more than that. No heavy burdens of past mistakes."

It sounded hollow to him even as he said it. Truth enough, perhaps; but at the most, a small part of the truth.

A greater part of the truth was that he was already so captivated by that small, pretty body that he had just possessed and which had just possessed him, that he knew he would never be able to quite escape its piquant spell even if he should finally separate himself from her.

Megan is the field which is the neighborhood. Like the ancient kings of Ireland, I have plowed the field and it has absorbed me. I have fucked a whole neighborhood.

"There I am, standing in the sanctuary of St. Praxides, confused and hurt and not knowing what comes next, missing my husband and afraid I'm not grieving the way I ought, and then, without any warning, you come into the sanctuary, as beautiful as ever with your blue eyes, and your curly hair, and your quick smile, and your broad chest, and your strong arms, and I think I'm hallucinating. My legs turn to water and I want to be swallowed up by the earth."

"You didn't let on."

"Women don't," she said, waving off his objection. "Then I realize it's you and I'm terrified because you're still so handsome and I think I'm old and dowdy and you can see that and you're disappointed in me."

"I was NOT," he protested.

"Hush." She put her hand over his mouth. "I KNOW you weren't. I could tell that you were looking me over and that you liked what you saw, and then I really thought I would die of shame and happiness. Does that sound crazy?"

"No, not at all."

"I wanted you inside of me, right then and there. Does THAT sound crazy?"

"Since I wanted to be inside of you right then and there, no, it doesn't sound crazy at all."

"Did you really?" She dropped her protective slip, clasped his shoulders, and peered into his eyes. "How exciting! Anyway, since then, I haven't been able to think of anything else but you. I told myself that if we did have sex, I'd get it out of my system. My legs wouldn't turn to water every time I saw you. My heart wouldn't jump whenever I heard your voice. I wouldn't feel your hands every time I stood under the shower . . ."

"We haven't done that yet."

Her hand returned to his mouth. "We will when I'm through with this confession, all right? Anyway, all that was nonsense. The more I have of you, the more I desire you, need you, lust for you. Or the more in love I am—I don't know."

"Does it have to be one or the other, Megan?"

"Yes. No. I don't know. I just hope I'm not a horny, menopausal woman fighting off old age."

"We all grow old, Megan. . . . When you asked me if you were part of the deal—"

Hand on her own mouth now. "I was being dreadfully wicked, wasn't I?"

"If I had said yes?"

"I knew you wouldn't. You are too much of a gentleman to do that. But if you had, I would have undressed for you on the spot. That's how crazy I am. I was being ineptly seductive, that's all."

"Not so inept, Megan, not so inept at all."

He drew her close.

"So?"

"What?" he murmured into her hair.

"Are you utterly repelled by all that self-disclosure?"

"Repelled? Woman, I am utterly seduced by it."

Again she peered into his eyes, examining them for veracity.

"Truly?"

"Truly."

"Good." She grabbed her slip again, clutched it to her throat, bounded out of bed, and scampered toward the bathroom. "Now if you still want to indulge my shower fantasy . . ."

"Not quite yet." He raced after her and captured her, giggling and squirming, at the bathroom door. "I have a fantasy of my own."

"Which is?"

"Kissing you."

"Where?" she demanded defiantly.

"Everywhere."

So they indulged both fantasies and established that thrice was not too much, not even at their age.

And now she had left, leaving him with uneasy guilt feelings. Was his pleasure the result of the manic rashness of a woman pushed to the brink of her sanity? Was he exploiting a woman whom grief and confusion had made unstable?

Before he could seriously analyze this new barrage of guilts, one step behind her came her children, possibly suspicious, probably hostile.

Do they know?

Can they tell from my face?

He glanced in the mirror at the doorway as he responded to a very light knock.

Dear God, I look satisfied with myself.

The three eldest Lane children arrived at the same time as the waitress with tea. If she noticed the similarity between Teri and her mother, she gave no hint, thank God.

Margaret promptly took charge of arranging and pouring the tea—very much Megan's child though there was but slight physical resemblance.

She sniffed the air with a puzzled grimace. Then brushing the long golden hair away from her face, she seemed to dismiss it.

All three were dressed for an important event, Mark in a business suit, the girls in dark dresses and high heels, which created the impression, till you looked at their faces, that they might be twenty-five.

"Well," Margaret began, pushing aside her hair again. "I suppose you wonder why we're here?"

"I'll admit to some curiosity." He tried his most charming smile with zero effect.

"We want to talk about our mother." Mark had been assigned the first line in the scenario, which his older Irish twin had doubtless planned.

"And your relationship with her." Teri, his one possible ally, sounded miserable.

How much did they know about the relationship? He had better be careful. If the kids knew that their mother and he were routinely making love, there would be big trouble. Did Margaret even now suspect that he had thrice entered the body that had brought them into the world? If she did, it didn't seem to bother her as much as it should.

What was happening?

"You're certainly within your rights," he said cautiously. "I'm not sure what you mean by the relationship, however."

"We don't altogether approve of it"—Margaret had saved the punch line for herself—"or of you, either, for that matter."

"That's very wise, Margaret; there's much in me which does not merit approval."

Once more she brushed her long blond hair out of her eyes. "You're not very stable, your charm looks phony some of the time, your relationships with women sound like they've been shallow, you seem to avoid intimacy—"

She was ticking off the charges with her fingers, quoting from a psychology textbook description of a certain rather unattractive male personality type.

"But I AM kind of cute, I heard Teri admit that to Nicole Curran at the Bears game."

"Kind of," Teri agreed, "but maybe too cute for your own good. And for Mom's."

Betrayed by my one ally. But they haven't guessed that we're screwing. Or have they?

"Let me add to the indictment," he continued. "I have no experience of living in one place for any length of time or becoming part of an established community. I keep odd hours. I don't drink, which is suspicious. I relate too well to young people, which is kind of suspicious for an old man. I'm glib and perhaps not altogether honest—sometimes it's hard to tell. In short, there's a pretty good chance that I am simply a superannuated sophomore boy of the sort you three know all too well, and will never be anything else."

"WELL," said Margaret.

"You've been reading our minds." Mark permitted himself a small grin. Dear God, he was a handsome kid. With a little more self-confidence—and that would come with time—he could own the world. Or maybe only the neighborhood, if there was a difference.

"Just my own," Neal said ruefully. "In addition to what you've thought of, I am in the midst of a huge midlife crisis in which I have even less notion of who I am than I did even a couple of years ago. I'm a bad risk altogether, as the Irish would say. Which is why you don't have to worry about any 'relationship' between me and your mother."

That observation did not seem to please them as much as it ought. What was going on?

"On the other hand"—Mark breathed deeply, a runner at the starting blocks—"on the other hand, we have to realize that our mother is a young woman still and that in a few years she will be alone. She'll still be in her forties when Joseph leaves for college."

"And, while we don't find the idea of a stepfather, like, really neat at all"—Teri's turn—"realistically, we have to admit that it's inevitable."

"It's hard for kids to be objective about their parents," Margaret continued the recitation, "but we've thought about it and we've decided that our mother is sexually attractive."

"You'd better believe it," he said with a sigh.

"She doesn't have much money right now, but maybe she will eventually when the insurance mess is straightened out. Even without the money, she'd probably be an appealing target for lots of predatory males, don't you agree?"

"Very appealing, Margaret. But just because you've discovered that your mother is an enticing woman, don't conclude that she can't take care of herself. She can."

"She's like really messed up now, Unc—Mr. Connor." Teri was close to tears. "We're really worried about her, you know."

"I care too much about her to play the predator role."

"So"—Margaret would not be shaken from her drama—"we've decided that you're not totally unacceptable."

"Huh?" That wasn't a line he had expected.

"Among the available alternatives," Mark added, nodding solemnly, "you seem to be the best."

"What?" Neal screamed.

"We can't promise there won't be any stepfather conflict"—

Margaret was equally solemn—"but we'll try to make life as smooth as possible."

"Wait a minute!"

"You're so much better than that gross Mr. Dineen." Teri exhaled in relief. "Totally gross."

Neal rubbed his eyes. "You gotta be kidding!"

Margaret returned to the battle. "As Uncle Punk says, 'Better the divil you know, than the divil you don't know.' "

"He said that about me?"

"Of course not, but it fits."

"You don't know me," he insisted.

"We think we know you well enough."

"Look, Margaret, Mark, Teri, your mother is a wonderful woman. I've adored her since I was Joseph's age—"

"You saved her life once." Mark made it sound like an accusation.

"All right, I saved her life once. And I'm glad I'm here to support her at a tough time in her life. But I'm not planning on marriage—as attractive as the possibility of acquiring such a splendid, and candid, ready-made family is. And she's not going to marry Mr. Dineen, I'm certain of that."

"He thinks so," Margaret said grimly. "Already he acts like we're his kids."

"Bastard."

"Precisely, Mr. Connor. Precisely."

This was sitcom material. Only it wasn't funny when they were closing in on you.

"Will it keep you happy if I guarantee that your mother won't marry him? She won't, guys, I mean, *really* she won't."

"Maybe we'll have to tell him," Mark said to his older sister.

"I guess we don't have any choice."

"He'll think that we're like total geeks," Teri protested.

"He already does." Margaret smiled thinly. "Look at the expression on his face. But we have to tell him, regardless."

"Tell me what? . . . And I don't think you're geeks and I won't no matter what you tell me."

They looked at one another. Mark shrugged and asked the first question.

"Mr. Connor, you saved our father's life once, when someone was trying to kill him with a broken bottle, didn't you?"

"Well, that's a bit of an exaggeration." He extended his hands, palms down, minimizing what he'd done. "Your father always made more of it than he should. The guy was pretty drunk. I just hit him and he kind of folded."

"Our father never talked about it, Mr. Connor."

"Then how did you know? It was a long time ago."

Three anxious, youthful faces scrutinized him.

Suddenly he felt cold. A shiver coursed through his body.

"Look, guys, I said you're not geeks. Let's hear all about it."

"It's like Joseph, you know," Teri whispered. "I mean he really didn't like you."

"That's understandable." Neal began to relax. Joseph could be counted on to reject their plot.

"Now he like totally adores you."

"What?"

They all shook their heads. "Totally."

"Why?"

Again the hesitation and the exchange of glances.

"WELL—" Margaret took up the baton. "Like, last Saturday, Mark and I are upstairs in our rooms studying and Joseph is downstairs playing with his computer. And the doorbell rings. Three times. Like, each time we shout down that Joseph should answer it."

"What's the point in having a little brother if he doesn't answer the doorbell, right?"

They relaxed a little.

"So, you know, he answers it and we don't hear anything for a few minutes, then he runs upstairs to my room crying—no, babbling. I call Mark and we both try to calm him down. But he's so happy that you'd think he was going to explode, you know?"

"What was he so happy about?"

"Because of you. He said you had to marry Mom and make her happy and that we'd all be happy and that you'd be a totally excellent father."

They stopped. "Geeks?" Margaret asked ruefully.

"Certainly not. But why the change in Joseph?"

"He said that Daddy was the one at the door, in his golf clothes, just like he was coming home from the club, and he bawled Joseph out for not answering the door when we told him to and especially for hating you. And he said that you were a wonderful man and had always loved Mom and would take good care of us and that if it hadn't been for you when a man tried to kill him with a broken bottle he would have never known us and that he's happy and that we should stop worrying about him and that you were the best friend he ever had and that if we loved him even just a little we should love you too."

Neal felt the color drain from his face and his jaws tighten.

"Joseph was upset because of everything," he said tonelessly, "and imagined it all."

"Even the story about the man with the broken bottle?"

"And if Joseph made it up," Mark asked, "why did we hear the doorbell?"

Neal's throat was very dry. When he spoke, his voice sounded hoarse. "I don't know."

"There's only one explanation, Mr. Connor," Mark said, his handsome face wrenched in a concentrated frown. "Dad came back from the dead to tell us to love you."

"There's lots of other explanations."

"Like?"

"Like Joseph wanted to believe that it was all right to like me."

"The story about the man with the broken bottle?"

"Your father told him that once after the two of them had seen me on the tube. Joseph forgot about it."

"Dad didn't tell stories like that about himself."

"Maybe he did once."

"We heard the bells," Margaret insisted. "Both of us."

"I understand."

"So you just gotta take care of Mom." Teri extended her arms in appeal. "And us, too."

"I'll do that," he said mechanically. "I promise you that I'll take care of all of you. No one's going to hurt you, no one."

"I mean," Margaret tried to sound reasonable, sensible, "we wouldn't mind if, well, if you, like, moved in."

"Margaret!"

"I don't care." She blushed. "It's not like you and Mom are teenagers or something. If you, like, love one another, why shouldn't you—"

"MARGARET!"

"Yes, NEAL?"

They all laughed.

"I care deeply about your mother. If there's anything more than strong friendship between us, I'll make her more than my mistress, understand?"

Do I really mean that? I did call it a marriage bed, didn't I?

"Yes."

"OK."

"As I said before, she's a VERY appealing woman, even more appealing right now than at the beginning of this conversation. About what the two of us might work out, I can't say anything right now." His mouth was sandpaper dry. "It's too soon. But regardless of that, I'll take care of her and of you. No ogre stepfathers in your house, only somewhat unsatisfactory guardian angels."

"Unsatisfactory some of the time, NEAL."

"Yes, MARGARET!"

"You will come to our house at Christmas?" Teri begged.

"I'd be in so much trouble if I didn't that I'm afraid not to."

He and Mark shook hands firmly. Teri hugged him fiercely. Margaret tentatively pecked at his cheek and then hugged him, too. "Neal, you HAVE to save her."

"I will, Margaret, I really will, but let me judge the best way."

They agreed to that proposal, although he thought their agreement was reluctant.

They don't want to take any chances of my running away.

He poured himself a second cup of tea after they had left—most of the tea service was untouched—and stared out the window at the gray, rain-specked lake.

Alf Lane had always been a showboat. Coming back from the dead to offer you his wife—no, to insist that you take her.

The kind of trick you'd pull.

And despite all the distractions, pleasant and unpleasant, my main task is to find out how you died.

As he stared at the lake, Neal saw the solution to the missing money again.

This time the solution didn't fade away.

"I hear you been asking questions."

"That's what reporters do, Tommy." Neal eased away from the shaggy lawyer, who had been lying in wait for him in front of the new IBC building on the riverbank. "That's how we earn our living. I even asked you a question or two, and you gave me a straight answer."

"I didn't know you were talking to others."

"Now you do."

"It can be dangerous," Tommy the Clown said, struggling to be both genial and ominous.

Cos the Card, Tommy the Clown—comedians all.

Neal was in one of his rare grim and angry moods, the kind of mood in which he might easily lose his temper—as he had with a deliberately inept cameraman on the ten o'clock news—or even slug someone.

Tommy Dineen would be a perfect target.

In the surrealistic lights of Candlestick Park the 'Niners had routed the Bears forty-one to nothing, Mike Ditka had been arrested by the San Francisco police for throwing his gum at a woman who had thrown ice cubes at him, and the team and its entourage of journalists had been delayed for a day at San Francisco International Airport by an early winter storm that had dropped a foot of snow on Chicago and closed O'Hare.

Neal was among those journalists because he had assumed that the Bears would rout the hated 'Niners and that an anchorman report from Candlestick would be a nice touch. Johnny Jefferson had enthusiastically agreed.

Neal had lost interest in pro football long ago. But his loyalty to the Bears had reappeared intact when he had returned to Chicago.

What is it Adlai Stevenson, the REAL Adlai, said when he lost the 1952 election? "I'm too old to cry, and it hurts too much to laugh"? This is Neal Connor, IBC News, Candlestick Park.

He missed Megan desperately during the two days in San Francisco—her shy smile, her intent gray eyes, her delicious white limbs, her luscious little breasts, her warm thighs, her quick laugh, her decisive nod. Maybe that which bound them was no more than adolescent infatuation. He still ached when she was not with him.

Before he had left for O'Hare they had stood in the parlor of the house on Hoyne and gazed at the painting of Al that she had hung over the fireplace.

"He never liked it," she mused. "Said it made him look old."

"He doesn't look any more than thirty." He extended his arm around her thin shoulder.

"I know. But for him that was old. Actually he looked much older." She leaned against him.

"Poor man."

"I miss him. He tried to be good to me and he was most of the time. He would cheer me up with his laugh when I was down from a fight with my sisters or Pete. I don't think we ever knew one another."

"I'm not sure anyone ever knew him. Or vice versa."

"He was kind of caught behind a wall. . . . Does that make sense?"

"It does. . . . Are you feeling guilty?"

"Because of you and me?" She considered carefully, fist under her chin. "I suppose so. It's unconventional behavior for a widow, isn't it? But Al wouldn't mind. He used to joke that if anything should happen to him I ought to try to find you."

"WHAT?"

She snuggled closer to him. "He didn't know about us, I mean that we almost ran off before the wedding. Or that we were in love." She hesitated. "Is that a fair description of what we were, Neal?"

"I'll buy it."

"The thought that we were would never have occurred to him. Probably wouldn't have bothered him anyway. He was so proud of you. Bragged about you whenever he saw you on TV. I think those days in college were the happiest years of his life. He never quite got over the fact that you left without saying good-bye to him."

"I would not have dreamed that it mattered." He put both his arms around her and drew her against his chest.

"It did, though. I don't mean he brooded about it. But you were special in his life. He told wonderful stories about the crazy things you and he and Jimmy Sullivan did when you were at Northwestern."

"Mostly fictional, I'm afraid."

"We all knew that, but they were so funny."

"Did he ever tell a story about a man trying to kill him with a broken bottle?"

"No," she murmured into his chest. "I can't remember that. I'm sure I would."

"He wasn't serious when he said you should find me if he died?"

"Who could tell when Al was serious? I think he half meant it."

"Recently?"

"You mean right before the crash? No."

He tilted her head back for a lingering farewell kiss.

"But he wouldn't mind our making love. He said once that I was probably one of the few women in the world who were good enough for you and that I'd have no trouble beating out Kelly MacGregor."

"REALLY?"

"Crazy thing to say, huh? But Al said some crazy things. I think he kind of enjoyed thinking about my seducing you away from Kelly. He was wrong, of course."

"No, he wasn't." Reluctantly he disengaged from her, wishing that he had just arrived at her house.

"You see. . . ." She stopped, searching for words.

"Yes?"

"Well, he brooded a long time when Jimmy died. He told me every day that you would never do anything like that, like he wanted to reassure himself."

"Why, Megan, in God's name why did he care about me?"

"I think he loved you more than anyone else in the world. You and Jimmy Sullivan. But especially you."

Enough to come back from the dead and offer you his wife? Is Al getting off in heaven on that kink?

Well, Al, I've taken her whether you like it or not. She's mine now, all mine.

But did you really love me?

And what does such a love mean?

Images of Megan haunted him obsessively on the plane to San Francisco, as the DC-10 raced above the storm that was closing in on Chicago.

Megan in the shower, body taut and eyes jammed shut as his fingers and the hot water kneaded her flesh.

"I could stay here forever." She opened her eyes, round with

293

ecstasy, and sighed contentedly. "Don't stop, my dearest darling, please don't stop. It's so wonderfully warm."

What demons of ice was he exorcising? Probably she couldn't give them a name. Probably, too, they would come back.

Or Megan after a shower in a loosely tied white robe, fresh and scrubbed and smelling of soap and smiling diffidently at him. She knew she turned him on that way but could not understand why.

Or Megan lying facedown while he systematically covered every inch of her body with kisses and nibbles, her satisfied sighs driving him to a paroxysm of love.

Megan's darting eyes never missed a turn-on. Soon there would be no secrets left to him.

Not that such a fate would necessarily be bad.

He would think of her whenever he smelled shower soap for the rest of his life.

He was thinking of her when Tommy Dineen sidled up to him in front of the IBC Building.

"I think my record shows I'm not afraid of danger, Tommy."

"Sure, sure, I know that." The fat man grabbed at his arm. "No one could call that into question. My point is there aren't any answers to the questions you're asking. No one is ever going to find Alfie's money. And no one will ever know for sure why or how he died."

Neal shook off Dineen's arm. "I've about come to the same conclusion myself."

"Yeah"—Dineen seemed relieved—"I mean there's just no story in it."

"There certainly does not seem to be a story."

"None at all. Megan will get her insurance money eventually, I promise you that. And the other money, however much it might be, that's gone. I mean gone."

"Is there other money, Tommy?"

They turned on to Michigan Avenue, splendid in its white jewel Christmas lights blazing against the piles of shoveled snow, a sound set for Santa and his elves.

The big man shrugged his shoulders elaborately.

"Who the hell knows?"

"I hear on the street"—Neal was learning the vocabulary—"that maybe it's as much as a half million."

He had heard no such thing.

"At least, if you believe some of the stories, but like I say, who the hell knows? Alfie was a hard man to read. He made up a lot of it as he went along, you know? There could be a million or there could be nothing at all, and it wouldn't make any difference to him."

"But no one is going to find it?"

"Let's put it this way"—Tommy was glancing nervously up and down the street—"if it's going to be found, it's been found already."

"I suppose so."

Neal didn't buy that explanation. He was certain that he knew where the money might be found. But he had unfair sources of information, unavailable to Tommy Dineen.

A voice from beyond the grave, a voice that offered another prize that Tommy wanted, more precious than the money.

"So there's no point in asking questions, is there?" Tommy Dineen prodded at him.

"Until tonight I had only one reason to keep asking them. Now I have two."

"Yeah?" Tommy stopped walking and turned to him anxiously. "What are they?"

"The first reason is that our mutual friend Donald Bane Roscoe, the United States Attorney for the Northern District of Illinois, is still asking questions."

"You know Donny—"

"And the second reason"—Neal's temper snapped—"is that if a scumbag like you wants me to stop asking questions, it's a pretty good sign that I shouldn't stop."

"Whaddya mean?" Tommy tried to pretend that he was surprised, shocked, offended.

"I mean your presence is polluting the snow. Get lost!"

"You think you're hot shit, don't you? Well, let me—"

Neal walked away from him. Then he paused and turned back.

"And if you so much as touch Megan Keefe, I'll break your fat neck."

Tommy Dineen scurried away, a large, frightened rodent rushing back to his hole in the ground.

I really scared him, didn't I? What did I say that for? I wouldn't really break his neck if he did anything to Megan, would I?

Well, yes, I might very well break his neck.

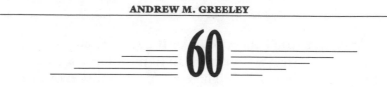

Pete Keefe grabbed at Neal's throat. "You stay away from my sister, you filthy media bastard. Or I'll have you killed."

It was getting to be risky walking out of the IBC Building after the news broadcast. Last night Tommy Dineen, tonight Pete Keefe.

He should have virtuously denied that he was involved with Pete Keefe's sister. But his temper was still frayed, and the harassment from colleagues and technicians at Channel 3 was beginning to annoy him.

He swept Keefe away with one quick motion of his arm.

"What I do with Megan is none of your business, Pete. Get lost."

He had been impatient with her at his apartment that morning, impatient and insensitive.

"Neal!" she had exclaimed in surprise when he had snarled at her for being a few minutes late and grabbed her and kissed her as though he were punishing her.

Instantly he was contrite. "Forgive me, Megan! Forgive me!"

"No problem." She followed him to the window of his apartment and embraced him from behind. "It's nice to know that my knight in shining armor, my cute lord and master, has a few faults."

"A lot, Megan. I'm thoroughly ashamed of myself."

"That's nice. I like you when you're thoroughly ashamed of yourself."

Her breasts were a light pressure on his back. Forgiveness should not be so easy.

"What if I hadn't stopped?"

"Silly man. You did stop."

"And the next time?"

"One word from me will stop you then, too."

"Just like one word stops poor Margaret."

"Poor Margaret indeed." She laughed into his back. "Actually the kid is a pushover, a pussycat. Just like you. No wonder she's starting to adore you. I could even become a mite jealous."

"The line between brutality and passion is so thin," he murmured.

"No, it isn't. It's as broad as that gray lake out there. And you weren't brutal, just a little angry." She tightened her embrace. "If you ever even approach the line, buster, you'll hear about it from me."

He realized that he would indeed. Compliant she might be, but a doormat she was not. That thought made him feel better, but not better enough.

"Jet fatigue, the wait in the airport . . ."

"And those evil 'Niners, as Blackie calls them."

She was unbuttoning his shirt. Delicately but persistently.

"Troublesome priest . . . and troublesome temptress, come to think of it."

"Right."

"I'll never hurt you, Megan. Never."

"Damn right. . . . Now don't try to get away from me. I have designs on you."

She did indeed. As she hovered over him on the bed, he decided that they were the most wondrous designs a woman ever had on him.

"Am I driving you mad with desire?"

"To put it mildly," he managed to breathe out the words.

"Good, that's what I hoped I was doing. Hold still, I'm not nearly finished with you."

So he added to Pete Keefe, slumped against the wall of the IBC Building, "And what she does with me isn't any of your business, either."

A stern feminist position. Woman the equal aggressor.

God knows Megan is claiming that role anyway.

"You fuck," Pete murmured, trying to clear his head from the impact against the wall.

Pete Keefe was a mess, gray, bloated, haggard—the cute and spoiled little boy of forty years ago now a dissipated wreck. Neal felt some sorrow for him. Not much but some. He thought about calling the security guard from the door of IBC and asking him to take care of Pete, who was very drunk as well as very angry.

But Pete launched himself from the wall, head down, and lurched into Neal's gut.

Neal stepped aside. Pete's assault became a glancing blow. Neal lost a little bit of wind from the impact. Pete collided with a lamp post and then toppled into the gutter.

"In the gutter where you belong, Pete. Boy hero turned fall-down drunk."

I shouldn't have said that, he told himself. But he didn't feel much guilt.

"Some friends of mine don't like you snooping around," Pete shouted after him.

"Too bad for your friends." Neal was walking away. "Tell your friends I'm not interested in them. I don't think there's a story in any of it."

Why had he taken Pete Keefe off the hook?

He had no idea why. Maybe because he felt sorry for the poor bum. Despite his wealth and popularity when he was growing up, Pete probably never had much of a chance for a decent life.

Later, Neal would be much relieved that he had tried to take Pete Keefe off the hook.

61

Megan wanted to talk.

The letters had stopped. Now the self-revelation was verbal. The woman seemed to love it. He didn't mind at all. Talking about herself and her life made her even more passionate.

It did distract him, however, from trying to figure out who killed her husband, a search that was currently in neutral.

"Can we spend a whole day together?" she asked with a determination that suggested he'd better not disagree. "I'd like to talk in addition to fucking."

"Megan, such language!"

"Perfectly good word, even if I blush when I say it."

She was a curious mixture of prudery and prurience, the best bedmate he could ever hope to have, but still shy and timid and at times prim. The combination made her even more desirable.

The first time they made love after the children had visited him—in her office in midmorning—he had been driven to heights of hunger that scared both of them.

"Neal . . ." she gasped when they were finished. "That was wonderful, but frightening. Are you all right?"

"Hmm . . . ?" He was so exhausted he could barely talk. He wanted only to sleep.

"Are you sure you're all right?"

He patted her rump appreciatively. "Worn out, woman, and it's all your fault for being so appealing."

But he had flipped out, gone completely out of control, lost even a remote contact with any reality beyond the act of love itself.

If it were still an act of love.

Later he was not sure, but he thought that he had never loved her more.

The kids were to blame.

"Sometimes I wonder about us." Megan, a towel around her waist when he awoke, was pouring him a cup of tea.

"Oh?" He reached up and touched a nipple.

"I can't believe the woman you fuck is me." Gently she brushed his hand away.

"Looks like you." He rested his face against her thigh.

"I tell myself before you show up"—she dodged him, but without much zeal, and handed him the teacup—"that I will not be a crazy woman again. I'm a forty-three-year-old matron and I should act my age. Then I see you and I become a she-demon. Women aren't supposed to react to men that way, are they?"

Since she was Megan, it was a serious question, even if she had asked it in one form or another before.

"If they love them."

"Oh, I love you all right." She dismissed that issue with a peremptory little wave. "I worry about whether I'm losing my mind."

"You're as sane as anyone I know."

"I'm not demented?"

"As you've said yourself, you're a woman who has discovered her sexuality all at once and is enjoying it."

"And her lover." She sat next to him on the bed. "All right, if you say I'm not abnormal . . ."

"Supernormal." He moved aside the towel and squeezed her thighs where they came together.

"Fresh!"

But she tossed the towel away and opened herself up to him again.

Afterward she pleaded for time to talk. "Fucking is fun, oh God, it's fun. But I want to get to know you better."

"Fair enough."

Now would come the push for marriage. How would he react? How should he react?

Before he left her house, she invited him formally to spend Christmas with them. "There's a guest room on the third floor with its own bath. All very private. The kids insist. Joseph has become a complete convert."

"Really?"

He accepted the invitation, not that declining was ever a real choice.

It had been arranged that she would join him at the Mayfair at nine-thirty and that they would stay together and talk until four when he would leave for the studio.

"I DO want to talk."

"No love at all?"

"Don't be silly. I couldn't spend that much time alone with you and not climb all over you."

A candid woman, Megan Keefe Lane.

After the evening news the same day, he would finally enter the summit meeting with the troublesome priest.

The news program itself was becoming more sticky. The backroom mutterings against him were increasing, abetted by the unremittingly hostile comments from the critics, particularly from the nitwit at the *Tribune*. While his ratings were still at an all-time high for a Chicago anchorperson, his enemies at Channel 3 were whispering that he was a novelty and that soon the ratings would plummet to rock bottom, endangering their jobs.

Johnny Jefferson rejected this analysis. "Pure envy, Neal. Forget it."

However, only the weatherman spoke to him off-camera.

Some of his colleagues were making minor attempts to embarrass him on the air, tossing questions at him without warning, cutting him short, not responding promptly to his feeds to them.

One night the sports reporter tried to sandbag him. "Art," Neal asked him, "do you think Jim McMahon will be able to make a difference during the playoffs? He's been out a long time. Will he be quick enough against, say, the Redskins?"

It was standard anchor patter.

"You want to place a bet," the sportscaster said with a sneer, "with a bookie on the Washington game?"

Neal laughed easily. "I don't gamble, Art. My mother never did like it. You take big risks, you might lose."

It was a neat put-down. Johnny Jefferson chewed Art out after the program was over. The others shot dirty looks at Neal. He was apparently not supposed to defend himself.

Neal had not experienced such harassment from other journalists since his promotion to anchor in Tucson. It required no great effort on his part to fend off such attacks. If Russian rockets scorching over his head could not faze his on-the-screen cool (which, of course, was fake), amateur harassment was not likely to perturb him. He brushed off the assaults as if they were harmless gnats.

But if they persisted, Channel 3 might not be worth the effort.

Still no word from Lou Garcia.

Megan showed up promptly at nine-thirty.

He gestured at an elaborately wrapped box on the sofa.

"Early Christmas present."

"Oh! Can I open it?"

"Absolutely."

She clawed at the wrappings. "From Bonwit's! How exciting!"

She unfolded the prize, an old-fashioned, long pink nightgown and a matching robe, the latter with a furry collar. "Neal, how gorgeous! Am I supposed to wear it today?"

"I thought it was suitable for talking rather than instant lovemaking."

He could no longer bring himself to use the word *fuck*, despite Megan's ease with the word. For him it implied lovemaking without love.

"It's marvelous. I'll feel much better in this than in those flimsy things. They embarrass me."

"You don't have to wear them, Megan."

"I LIKE being embarrassed for you, and you like me being embarrassed for you." She held the gown out full-length. "But this will make me feel like a countess, a pint-sized countess maybe, but still . . ."

"You are a countess, Megan."

"So SWEET." She kissed him. "Actually I'm a grand duchess. Back in a second."

She ducked into the bedroom and returned, if not in a single second, then in no more than twenty.

She stood at the door, arm on the frame, head tilted to one side, available for his admiration.

"I don't how much talking I'll be able to do with that kind of loveliness in the room."

"Silly"—she leaned over and kissed his forehead—"I told you it wasn't to be JUST talk."

"You changed in a hurry."

"Undressed even more quickly than you undress me, huh?"

"MEGAN!"

She laughed and slipped away from his reach for her rump. "First we talk."

She reached for her purse, removed a notebook, sat across from him on the sofa, put her notebook on the glass coffee table, and bent over it.

The gown was not so old-fashioned as to hide her cleavage in that position.

"Taking notes, fair grand duchess?"

"Sure. I'll want to study what you say afterwards. It'll be in shorthand, so the kids won't be able to read it. . . . They're showing what I can only call an indecent interest in my relationship with you."

"I'm being interviewed?"

"You bet you are."

The "talk" was not about marriage or even about the future. It was rather about his past. "I don't know what happened to you since I ran away from you like a horrid little bitch at gate K-5. I mean, I saw you on TV, but I didn't know what was happening to you as a person."

Her inquisition touched only lightly on his love life. Megan did not want to know about his women, she wanted to know about him.

"I'm good at what I do, Megan. Funny thing is, I don't know why. The very first time I did a story in Tucson I was perfect—scared stiff, but flawless. I just knew what to do. Pure instinct, like that morning I pulled you out of the fire. It's been that way ever since the first clip in Tucson. I'm a little smoother maybe and a bit more self-confident—though still scared each time the red light goes on—but basically I'm running on pure instinct. That's the story of my life. I wonder what happens when the instinct runs out."

"Will it?"

"I don't know. I suppose so. It can't last forever, can it?"

"You tell me."

"In part it's the result of my hunger for success. Now that I'm not hungry anymore, maybe it will fade away."

"I haven't noticed it on the tube."

"It's so easy these days. Too easy."

"You're bored?"

"And worried because I'm bored. As I talk about it, I realize how silly the whole thing is."

"But?"

"But one part of me has always known that TV is just a game. I wonder what I'm going to be when I grow up and become an adult."

"Do the instincts help with women?"

"They didn't till very recently."

They both laughed.

"They sure are good now." She patted his hand. "But your life has been very lonely, hasn't it? Instincts and a game, a kid's game even. And now you're almost as old as I am and you're worried."

"Terribly lonely, Megan," he agreed, acknowledging his loneliness for the first time to anyone.

Megan then peeled away most of his defenses and all of his emotional clothes with the calm efficiency of a hospital nurse helping a man to undress for examination. A therapist could not have found out so much about him in such a brief period of time.

Neal was sweating profusely. He also felt elated to be sharing himself with such a gentle but determined woman.

If she were planning to capture him, she could not have devised a more effective strategy.

So soothing was her inquiry that when she asked about loneliness and he admitted it, tears came, the tears that had welled up in his head since they had escaped across the Pakistan border.

Megan closed her notebook, astonished and dismayed by his tears.

"Neal . . . you poor dear man."

He realized that if he wanted to capture the woman forever, there was no better way to accomplish it than by shedding tears in her presence.

"I'm sorry, Megan," he said, struggling with his emotions. "I didn't mean to put you through this."

"Nothing to be sorry about." She placed her notebook on the coffee table and laid her ballpoint pen at a neat right angle beside it, stood up, and walked to him.

"I can't continue talking, Neal"—she drew him to his feet—"without loving you."

She untied his robe, pushed it off his shoulders, and shoved his shorts down to his ankles. Then she stood back, drank him in with hungry eyes, shivered with delight, and embraced him. "Neal, Neal, Neal . . . my darling Neal."

Now she was crying, too.

A fine pair of weepers we are, he thought.

Then he was pushed to the floor and smothered with healing love.

A long time later, it seemed, Neal awoke, reassured and as happy as he had ever been in his life.

His head was resting on her breasts, and she was still stroking him gently.

"I'd cry every day for that kind of love," he whispered.

"You don't have to cry for it." She kissed him. "Not ever."

They remained in each other's arms for many minutes, happy and content.

"You know what I'd like more than anything else?" she muttered into his chest.

"More of the same?"

"A little later for sure. No, I'd like a huge chocolate malted milk."

They both laughed.

"I can buy you one not ten minutes from here. But you'll have to put your clothes on first."

He watched her dress. With the other women in his life, the movements of their bodies, clothed and partially clothed, had quickly lost all mystery and allure. Megan, however, became more mysterious and alluring, the more often he possessed her.

None of which had any relationship to solving the central puzzle of the death of Al Lane.

Tonight with Blackie. Then the big breakthrough at Christmas. I hope.

"Don't I get any privacy?" She looked up from the garter she was fastening to a black stocking.

"Not so long as your put on your clothes with such charm."

"Silly . . ." She dropped her white knit dress over her head. "Now I'm finished; it's your turn."

Arm in arm, they walked down Michigan Avenue. The clouds had finally cleared away and the Magnificent Mile and the Water Tower park glittered in the sunlight, a magical fairy-tale city.

"I could fall in love with this magical city, as well as one of its magical matrons."

"I hope you do." She held his arm tightly.

Clear enough, no pressure, only hope.

They turned right on Chicago Avenue, crossed Rush Street, and entered the Chicago Ice Cream Studio.

"My brother Pete is missing again," she said suddenly.

"Pete?" he asked uneasily. No one had seen their struggle in front of the IBC Building. That's all he would need now.

"He goes missing every year or so. Turns up in Vegas or the Bahamas or someplace like that. Nothing to worry about, I guess."

"Your family called you?"

"No way. Bea phoned Margaret at Notre Dame. Indirect channels. And gets at me by upsetting Margaret. 'I hope your mother's happy now.' "

"They're blaming you because Pete is missing?"

"My family has to blame someone for everything that goes wrong. I'm the favorite target these days."

"How do they know he's missing?"

"The girl he lives with, sweet little thing actually, phoned Bea, I guess, which took a lot of nerve on her part because they treat her like a whore, which she isn't. Pete is a nice boy when he's sober."

"Except that he's a bit old to act like a boy."

"Not his fault." She sighed. "Poor dear man."

"How did my friend Margaret react?"

"You mean my rival?" She glanced at him archly. "Well, she suggested I call Neal—not Uncle Neal, mind you—and ask him for help. I told her I'd call Nick Curran, who knows more about Chicago. She didn't seem too pleased with the suggestion that anyone knows anything better than you do."

"Sweet child."

"You sure did win her over."

"Bea upset her?"

"Terribly, which is the point, you see. Margaret is very bright and very well organized—"

"Like her mother."

"—and very sensitive. So she is more vulnerable than a lot of people realize."

"Like her mother again."

"I hope she finds the right man."

"Maybe we can help."

"I hope so."

They stopped in front of the Ice Cream Studio.

"I think they built this place in the Cathedral parish"—Neal held the door for her—"so that our friend the Monsignor could have the best malts in the city a few steps from his rectory."

"Maybe he owns it. . . . Why do they call it a studio?"

"Look at the paintings."

She glanced around. "Matisse, Picasso, Seurat prints. What's so—? Oh, my heavens, they're all eating ice cream!"

"A delicious joke, wouldn't you say?"

"Shame on you." She thumped his arm lightly.

"Delicious joke, delicious ice cream, delicious woman."

"You're like totally gross," she mimicked Teri. "May I have an extra large one, please? Lent will start after Christmas."

"I hope not."

They sipped their massive delights in appreciative silence.

"OK, it's your turn."

"My turn?"

"What are you going to do with the rest of your life?"

"I was afraid you were going to ask something like that." She concentrated on her thick straw. "Better you ask what I'm going to do with next week or next year."

"All right, what are you going to do with next week or next year?"

"I have to assume that we won't ever see the insurance money. Tommy Dineen says we will. But I don't know. Anyway, what if it doesn't come? Thanks to you"—she smiled up at him but did not relinquish her grip on the straw—"I don't have to worry about the kids' tuition this year."

"Or ever."

"Oh, Neal." She struggled with her tears. "Thank you."

He touched her hand. She grabbed his.

"Anyway"—the tears were still slipping down her cheeks—"I still have to earn my keep and do something to keep myself occupied and maybe even something that challenges me out of bed the way you challenge me in bed."

"My turn to say thank you," he said, holding her hand as though he would never let it go.

"I did have this job offer to work for a real estate company out on 103rd Street and Pulaski. Typist and receptionist. Father Ace found me a job working for a PR company in Oak Lawn, I could work at home in the afternoons, which would be wonderful while Teri and Joseph are still at home. It looks very interesting, but I'm not sure I'm good enough for it."

"Megan."

"Yes?"

"Take it. At least get your feet wet with it."

"I knew that's what you'd say."

"You will take it."

"After Christmas."

"A deal."

He suspected she had already made up her mind and merely wanted his endorsement.

"Who's this Father Ace?" He decided that he would pretend not to know the former chaplain to get an unbiased reaction from one of his parishioners.

"That's right, you didn't meet him at the reunion because he had to go to some meeting. He's our pastor, Father Richard McNamara. Everyone calls him Father Ace. He's a former marine chaplain."

"What? At St. Prax's?"

"He's not that kind of marine. He has a Ph.D. in psychology."

"A marine chaplain with a Ph.D. in psychology?"

"Who plays basketball with the kids. Pure South Side Irish."

"Can't be all bad, then. Is he a friend of Blackie's?"

"Well, he's a lot older, but he laughs every time anyone mentions Blackie, so I guess he likes him a lot."

"Laughter is the only way to deal with that troublesome priest."

"Neal, shame!"

But she laughed, too.

On the way back to the Mayfair, again arm in arm, he admitted that he was not totally candid about Father Ace. Instead of being angry, she laughed at him and then laughed again when he told her about the conversation at Pleiku. He left out the part about his cameraman.

Then he asked her a question that had begun to add to his already heavy burden of anxieties.

"We don't fight, do we, Megan? Not even quarrel or bicker? I lose my temper and find it right away, nothing worse."

"Should we fight, darling?"

"Men and women in intimate relationships usually do."

"Is that what we're in?" She squeezed his arm playfully.

"It would be hard to fight with you, Megan."

"Docile slave."

"People have to fight to let off steam."

"I'm not very good at that . . . but then, I've learned lots of new skills lately, haven't I? Do you want to fight with me?"

"Not at all. I have no complaints."

"Neither do I. Maybe I'm in love."

"Lovers fight."

"They don't have to."

In his suite, he insisted that she put his present back on.

"Any more questions about me?" he asked when she reappeared, looking even more alluring. "Incidentally, woman, I like my taste in lingerie. You're made for that kind of countesslike, oops, grand duchesslike wear."

A deep blush spread over her chest and face. "Thank you, darling."

The second time he was darling.

"Have I embarrassed you?"

"Yes. I still like it. . . . Now"—she sat in front of the coffee table and opened her notebook—"let me see. Do I have all I need for the moment?"

She studied it very carefully. "A lot of unasked questions, but they'll wait. I don't think I can absorb more just now." She closed the notebook and placed it on the table. "It's been quite an exciting life."

"The best has been saved till now."

"Oh, Neal, don't be absurd. I'm very small potatoes compared to all the excitement you've had."

"I won't argue about it, but you're wrong. Anyway, come here."

"What are you going to do to me?" She walked over to him, still embarrassed.

"I haven't quite made up my mind yet, but it will be something terrible."

"I know THAT."

He drew her to his lap, held her against his chest and told her again how much he loved her.

They remained in that position of passive love for a long time. Then he carried her into his bedroom, disrobed her of her luxurious gown, and made love to her with nostalgic delicacy.

After she had left and while he was dressing for the evening news, the tears came to his eyes again.

Whatever am I going to do about her? he asked himself. As I told her kids, I'm a terrible risk for marriage. I love her so much I don't know whether I can live without her.

But she's suffered enough in life without my causing her more suffering.

"Hey, *amigo*, where ya been?"

"I've been around," Neal spoke easily into the phone. "Where've you been?"

"Funny, I've been around, too. Too bad we didn't bump into each other out there."

"Around is a big place, *amigo*."

Lou Garcia laughed. "Sure is. . . . I didn't want to distract you when you were having fun with the widow woman."

Neal's throat tightened. "What affair of yours is that?"

"Hey, *amigo*, don't get pissed at me. Anyway it's *your* affair, not mine. Not that I blame you. For a mature broad, she's something else. Me, I think it's good for you. Nothing like a challenging woman to spice up a guy's life, huh?"

Garcia meant no harm, he told himself. In his world he had just delivered two compliments, one to Neal and one to Megan. Neal decided to play along with the rhetoric of that world, which was maybe more honest, if more crude, than the rhetoric of his world.

"She certainly does that, Luís."

"Yeah, and hey, don't worry about us. We're not going to do anything to her. Even if we were thinking about it, which we're not, we'd be too afraid of you."

"Yeah?"

"I kid you not. You're a pretty heavy guy around town these days. I don't want to mess with you."

"I'm glad to hear it."

"Yeah, well, we've had some organizational problems but they're straightening themselves out more or less. So maybe we can get together and talk at our usual place. Tomorrow at lunch?"

"If you say so."

"Yeah, why not, a little wassail for Christmas, huh? But then you don't drink, do you? Well, you can wassail with Perrier, OK?"

"OK."

"And we can talk about Al Lane, which you want to talk about anyway, but haven't asked."

"A point for you, *amigo*."

"Well, yeah. I mean he was an asshole, but I don't mind talking about him. Not that what I know will solve anything."

"Fine."

"Is she really good in bed, *amigo*, if you don't mind my asking?"

A legitimate male question in his culture. Maybe in any culture if not quite so direct and on the phone.

"Best I've ever had, Lou. Far and away."

"Hey, good for you! And you've been around a lot, too!"

Not that way, but if it's what you want to think, it's all right with me.

"Yeah, Lou, I've been around a lot."

"Shows you gotta come home now and then, doesn't it?"

"I guess so."

"Well, I hope it all works out well for the two of you."

In that last sentence there was surely a threat.

Neal glanced at his watch. What would the Commander-in-Chief of the Wabash Avenue Irregulars think about that?

Another letter, this one on a small sheet of note paper:

Dearest Neal,

I love you. I'll always love you.
If it ever seems I've stopped loving you, the reason will be that I've lost my nerve.
Please, I beg you, don't let me get away with it.

Always,
Megan

Melodi Cain sandbagged him on the evening news.

Melodi Cain (a name that in its original form probably ended in a couple of lovely vowels) was his coanchor on the five o'clock news— a pretty, brittle young woman who pretended to be both tough and smart, although in fact, she was merely ambitious and ruthless. She had been one of the first to ignore him in the corridors and the newsroom and to harass him on the air.

She was, he had thought, an annoyance but hardly a problem.

He was so complaisant after his day of spiritual and physical pleasures with Megan, he hardly noticed that the air in the newsroom, as he looked over the clips and wrote his material, was even more icy than usual.

"Did you read Matt Delaney this morning?" Johnny asked at his desk.

"Nope, I've given up on TV critics. Anything important?"

"Talk of a petition among the news staff to confine you to the four-thirty slot."

"Is there such a petition in the making?" He looked up from his computer terminal.

"There sure is now."

"So?"

"So I'm running the station and your ratings are sky-high. The mail is almost entirely favorable."

"Does the inestimable Matthew describe the rationale for this petition?"

"Your taking the news programs away from people who have worked here for years."

"Too bad for them, I guess?"

"You guess right."

He pondered the situation as he finished his material. Journalists tended to be a mean-spirited and envious crowd and to be convinced that they could run their operation a lot better than their managers. Such newsroom revolts were not uncommon and never successful. This one would fade away, too, unless the ratings took a nosedive. And if they did, Neal Connor would fire himself.

Melodi did not acknowledge his greeting at the anchor desk, which should have given him a hint, but he was immune to hints in his present state of bodily and mental satisfaction.

The last feature on the program was a gory piece done by an independent Australian crew about the war in Angola, heavily slanted in favor of the government in Luanda and against the "South African–backed rebels."

It was not very good journalism; indeed, it was a classic case of reportorial bias combined with ugly pictures of death and destruction. He saw no point in commenting on it.

"You enjoy that sort of scene, don't you, Neal?" Melodi asked him, in the usual tone of cross-talk used by anchors when they were supposed to be chatty.

"Pardon?" He was surprised, but the warning bells in his head rang out loud and clear: Don't blow your cool.

"You like to see black people killing other black people, even with South African weapons."

It was the most outrageous sandbag he had ever seen or heard. He was furious at Melodi Cain, so furious that, despite the warning bells, he almost blew up.

"I don't like people to be killed with any kind of weapons, Melodi, no matter who the people or what the origin of the weapons,

Cuba or South Africa." He drew in his breath and continued evenly. "I think we have to remember that the war in Angola is not like a fight between the fourth and the sixth wards. It's between two nations, as different from one another as Germany is from Poland with their own different histories and cultures, older than ours, and with their own history of bitter conflict with each other. The so-called rebels were in control of the artificial colony the Portuguese created, until the Cubans came and drove them into the bush. They'll never give up trying to reclaim control—they are the larger of the two nations. Everyone, Cuba, Russia, the U.S., South Africa, should leave them alone. But the fighting will go on until those two nations, which are older than South Africa, older than Cuba, and older than the United States are ready to make peace between one another."

The floor director had been going mad, signaling him to wrap it up. The weatherman stood by in amazement as his final forecast was blotted out.

"And now," Neal concluded easily, "to New York and nightly news."

The producer was the first one out of the control room and onto the set: "Cain, you're fired. What the hell did you do that for?"

"Always blame the woman!" she shouted at him, "not the show-boat who hogs the camera!"

Neal sat perfectly still, fighting his rage.

The next man on the scene was the news director: "Cain, you fucking bitch, what the hell were you doing out there? Pack your things and get out of here!"

"He's the one who talked too much." She jabbed an angry finger at Neal.

Then Johnny burst in. "Be out of here by six o'clock, Melodi. You're finished here and everyplace else if I have anything to say about it."

"Cool it, Johnny."

Jefferson whirled on Neal. "What are you talking about?"

"Melodi gets another chance. . . . Now listen to me, young woman. I said what I did to protect you. One sentence would have saved me and killed you. I added the paragraph so most of the listeners didn't know that you tried to sandbag me. If you ever try it again, you really will be finished. And the same thing goes for all your friends in the newsroom. If anyone messes with me again, ever,

I'll sandbag them back so hard they won't realize what hit them. Is that clear?"

Frightened of his controlled rage, the young woman could only nod her head in the affirmative.

"Moreover—and let everyone hear this, including your friend Matt Delaney—if you want to keep me in Chicago, all you have to do is to continue to hassle Johnny and me. If you do, I guarantee I'll stay here till Judgment Day. Does everyone understand?"

He looked around the room. Other heads nodded.

"Johnny?"

"She's on probation, Neal. One more trick and we'll toss her out."

"You won't have to do that, Johnny. She'll look so bad if she tries it again that she'll run away on her own."

Now all that he had to do was face Blackie Ryan.

The troublesome priest moved several German books, which looked to be philosophical or theological, off the chair that Neal had occupied during his first visit.

"I knew we would find a place for you to sit, to which heaven knows you are entitled after your battle with the tuneful Melodi Cain."

"You noticed?"

"One could not help but notice. I assume that the admirable John Jefferson wanted to fire her."

"Indeed."

Blackie raised an eyebrow at the use of his favorite word.

"So it was fortunate for Ms. Cain that you realized such a decision would be counterproductive?"

"Why swat a harmless fly?"

"An interesting metaphor for kindness." With some difficulty the priest plugged an electric teakettle into a socket near his desk. "Now let us organize ourselves. It would seem that we have three varieties of tea, Constant Comment raspberry, Marshall Field's strawberry, and Earl Grey, which I am led to believe is your favorite."

"I'll try the strawberry for a change . . . and how do you know about me and the Earl?"

"Let us suppose, *causa argumenti* as we say in the mother tongue, that a certain person is offered tea and that at the mention of our mutual friend the Earl, that certain person gushes that his Lordship's tea is the favorite of yet another certain person. The converging probabilities for the truth of such an assertion are very high, are they not?"

So Megan had been here lately? Well, that was her business, wasn't it?

"How did that certain person seem to you?"

"Better than one might have expected under the circumstances." The priest was trying to put four teabags into a lovely Baleek Irish teapot, with only modest success.

"I would agree with the diagnosis."

"So there is some hope for her."

And that was all that would be said about Megan.

When the boiling water had been poured into the pot, Blackie settled into his chair with a glance at his watch. Neal realized that if he did not want the tea to be so strong as to bend a spoon, he would have to remember to pour the tea.

Blackie would never think of it again.

"On the less delicate subject of Melodi Cain, you salvaged her because it was easier to do so than to respond to the controversy that would have ensued if she was summarily dismissed."

"Something like that. I felt sorry for her, too. Less forthright persons behind the scenes were using her."

"You think"—Blackie folded his hands over his belly and stretched his legs on an ottoman in front of his wounded easy chair—"that this confrontation will end the sniping?"

"For a few days. Then it will start again, a little more cautiously. It will take another month of high ratings to settle them down. My colleagues at Channel Three are not all that bright, but they are not about to cut off their noses to spite their faces."

"The ratings will doubtless continue to be high." It was a statement of mutually agreed-on fact, not a question.

"We visited what I'm sure is one of your favorite places in the parish today."

"Ah?"

"The Chicago Ice Cream Studio."

"Islamic paradise. Surely a very serious venial sin. The young priests who are good enough to permit me to work with them here take it as a matter of personal affront that my frequent falls from grace in that emporium have no effect on my weight."

He did not ask who constituted the "we." Neal had no intention of telling him. Megan was not part of the discussion.

And anyway, he probably knew instantly who else had entered the Islamic paradise.

"I assume"—Neal leaned back in this chair—"that you want a further report on my investigation of the circumstances around the death of our classmate."

"Indeed."

"The circumstances continue to be many and confusing. Let me list the new ones:

"Item. The Outfit, as represented by Cosmo Ventura, officially believes that our classmate died an honorable suicide—honorable as they understand the word, of course. They also imply that they are ready to forget all debts which might have been owed them by Al rather than run the risk of another assault by the forces of Donny Roscoe."

"You believe them?"

"I believe that's what they want me to believe."

"Indeed."

"Item. Maureen Kennelly contends that Megan, through her brother Pete, arranged to put Al down. Motive? Money. Ms. Kennelly believes that her ability to provide Al with beer and pizza and cuddling for 'Monday Night Football' makes her more of a wife than Megan ever was."

"Hell hath no fury?"

"My very words to myself, but I doubt it, Blackie. Megan really loved him. I assume we agree that she is not a killer, but we are less certain about Pete, especially since he offered the other night to have me killed."

"And you pushed him aside with contempt?"

"Something like that. Now he's turned up missing, a phenomenon which seems to occur every year at Christmas. The family blames Megan."

"Naturally."

Neal found two teacups, one of them badly chipped, which matched the teapot. He poured the pleasant-smelling liquid into both of them and handed one to the Monsignor.

"Item. The night before my encounter with Pete, I was taken on by Tom Dineen with similar, if less precise, threats. Both wanted me to stop asking questions, which meant that they found the questions embarrassing."

"They or those whom they represent."

The priest glanced into his cup, seemed astonished that it actually contained tea, and began to sip it.

"Right. Item. Brian Neenan also subscribes, though with less certainty than the Outfit, to the suicide theory. He thinks that if there is any hidden money, it will never be found. Or that it has already been found. He also said that he sees rape in the eyes of Tommy Dineen. Megan the target, of course."

"And the daughters, too. Eventually. I hardly need observe that you threatened dire retribution should such attempts be made?"

"I think I said I'd break his neck."

"A modest enough punishment." Blackie's eyes flashed dangerously.

"Moreover, my *amigo* Lou Garcia emerges out of silence and is now ready to talk to me again, explicitly about Al, though I never raised the subject with him. He also knows of my, ah, interest in Megan. He assured me that he was making no threat against her. But there was something ominous in that reassurance."

"We will perhaps take certain steps."

"I would be very grateful."

"My own feeling is that at the moment Garcia means no harm, but he is nonetheless as baffled as is anyone else."

"I agree. Now do you want to know what I make of all of this?"

"Surely." The priest continued to beam over his empty teacup. Neal refilled both their cups.

"I think Al was murdered, probably by an injection of cocaine that would have killed him anyway, even if he hadn't driven into the tree. I also think there is a lot of money hidden out there someplace and that a lot of people want it. But everyone is afraid to make a move because they are aware of the circling flights of vultures from the United States Attorney's office, of the omnipresence of that worthy's moles, and perhaps of the interest of the Wabash Avenue

Irregulars, whom, if said people are wise, they fear more than they fear anyone else."

"It's quite possible that they should," the priest said blandly. "We have some loyal and skillful allies."

Neal drew a deep breath.

"I think I know where the money is and also who the mole is."

"Ah! Indeed!"

He explained his theories.

The little priest closed his eyes and looked for a few moments not only like a clerical Buddha but a sleeping clerical Buddha, with a half-empty cup of tea resting on his belly.

"Capital, capital. Very creative." He opened his eyes. "How do you propose to proceed?"

"I think I have to find the money first."

"That seems reasonable. You will do that on Christmas, I presume?"

"Any suggestions?"

"Proceed with great caution. Remember that our only goal in this matter is to protect the virtuous Megan. All other ends are secondary to that one."

Does he know we are sleeping together? Almost certainly. Is he shocked? Hardly.

Was that something else they had voted on when Neal was away?

"I agree completely." Neal rose to escape.

Should he tell him about Joseph's vision?

No way.

"One more thing." Blackie raised a hand. "It seems to me that your theory about the mole is amply supported by the data. It fits Doctor James's criteria of truth superbly—congruence, fruitfulness, and luminosity. . . ."

"*Criteria of Truth in William James: An Irishman's Best Guess?*"

The title of Blackie's most recent study.

"You are among the very select few who have heard of that neglected work. . . . But your theory of the location of the money sounds like mere guesswork."

"It's more than that." Neal sank back into the chair with relief. "Al told me where it was."

"Before he died?" Blackie raised a polite eyebrow.

"No."

"Oh, indeed?"

Well, I stirred up his interest at least once tonight.

"May I tell you a story?"

"Please do."

So he told him the story.

"How very interesting! How very VERY interesting!" The little priest's folded hands seemed to be rubbing one another in satisfaction.

"I assume you've never heard anything like this before?"

"Hmm . . .?" Blackie leaned forward, without the usual sigh that accompanied most of his movements. "Oh, contact with the dead is a common enough phenomenon. Two-fifths of the population reports it, three-fifths of those who have lost a spouse or a sibling. Quite normal, as a matter of fact. But this sort of incident, in which a third party is involved, is quite rare. I know of only one other such reported phenomenon. . . ." His voice trailed off. "And in that instance there was only one confirming witness."

"Joseph wanted an excuse to like me."

"And what better excuse could he have found?"

"His father probably did tell him the story about the broken bottle, most likely when the two of them were watching TV one night and I was on the screen."

"Highly plausible."

"But Margie and Mark hear the doorbell?"

"They too wanted an excuse to opt for you as a stepfather. Could it not have been a systematic group self-delusion with each of the participants contributing their own part to the illusion?"

"Certainly." Neal was not pleased by the priest's skepticism. "And the implicit message to me that they didn't recognize was pure coincidence?"

"What other reasonable explanation could there be?"

"Intellectually," Neal spoke slowly, trying to gain access to his feelings, "all that makes sense, yet . . ."

"It is still uncanny and hence frightening?"

"An experience which proves nothing and hints at everything."

"A comment worthy of the troublesome priest himself."

They both laughed.

"I can see you as Becket," Neal admitted, "but I'm hardly the Henry the Second type."

"I was about to make the opposite comment. . . . But the issue is not the dead friend and rival, is it? The issue is the live children and their request—nay, I should say demand."

"Does the Church approve of fornication now?" Abruptly Neal changed the subject. Well, perhaps it was the same subject.

"Fornication?" The priest frowned as if he were trying to place the word.

"Isn't that what Megan and I are engaged in?"

"I would rather limit that word to the behavior of the very young." Blackie folded his hands beneath his chin. "There was a time when some moral theologians thought of it as no more than a venial sin. I believe there was a certain fear that such a consoling doctrine would make the activity more popular. On the face of it, I think such a fear absurd. How could it be more popular?"

Neal waited, suspecting that a lecture was beginning, one which would not answer his question.

"On the other hand, in practice, even under the old moral theological principles the force of human passion is such that one must be reserved in judging each single act to be grievously offensive to the God who, for reasons of Her own, seems to have endowed us with unruly passions."

"Indeed."

The little priest's eyes twinkled. "Indeed yes. Well, to continue . . . I personally surely do not approve of sex without commitment. It does grave injury eventually to the organisms of those involved. Promiscuity as we have learned again from the AIDS epidemic is definitely not good for you."

"Definitely."

"On the other hand"—he began to tick off points on the fingers of his left hand—"sexual exchange does have the capability of increasing and reinforcing commitment. This impulse can be resisted, but as it turns out, with difficulty. Moreover—"

"You're not answering my question."

The priest seemed startled and confused by the interruption, a first-grade teacher astonished at an unruly student.

"Your question was . . . ah, whether I approve of certain exchanges of affection between you and the lovely Megan?"

"Precisely."

"It is not for me to approve or disapprove." Way in the back of Blackie Ryan's nearsighted eyes there was a dangerous gleam. "I must note that there is some question in my mind, all things considered, how free the two of you are not to engage in such exchanges. Reasons of past history, pain, loneliness, need would, I think, be judged to impede your full consent of will."

"You mean I'm not free?" Neal protested. "Of course I'm free. I can stop if I want to."

The little priest shrugged his shoulders. "You haven't."

"You won't answer my question, is it sinful or isn't it?"

"Would you stop if I said that you were offending God and risking hellfire for both you and Megan?"

"No," Neal growled. "I would not."

"Why not?"

"Because I don't think God objects."

"If you think you have access to the Dcity's position"—Blackie threw up his hands in mock dismay—"why do you need that of a lowly papal broom pusher?"

I think I was blindsided, Neal admitted to himself. Deflated and a little dejected, he tried one last time. "What would you tell me if you were my confessor?"

"What any confessor would have told you at any time in the whole history of Catholic Christianity," he said, jabbing a pudgy little finger triumphantly at Neal: "You should either marry the woman or remove yourself from her life."

"You're right, Blackie." He rose to leave, and this time he WOULD escape before he was tricked into any more self-disclosures. "They're an appealing brood. I've been sucked back into the neighborhood by a family, which is what you would have predicted. Cosmopolitan man falls into an alluring local trap."

"Alluring package."

"Alluring obsession."

"Not for that reason to be either accepted or rejected."

"You said before that Beverly was a sacred place."

"Naturally."

"Is Megan a sacred woman, a kind of temple harlot in the sacred place?"

Blackie chuckled enthusiastically. "A marvelous metaphor, which I hardly need tell you ought never to leave this room."

"Symbolically she and the neighborhood seem to be identified, at least in my head."

"Both sources of grace, perhaps."

"I thought grace was everywhere. Or has that changed too."

"For it to be in some places and some people specially, it must be radically in all places and people."

"And you don't have enough data yet to render an opinion about my fate in all of this?"

"Alas, no. Nor am I sure I would even in the presence of data."

He left the Cathedral rectory on North Wabash and walked up to where Wabash merged with Rush, then on to Oak, where he purchased some rock videos that he thought young adults might like and opera videos of *Der Rosenkavalier* (with Dame Kiri) and *Così* to complete his Santa Claus bag for Christmas.

His luxurious suite at the Mayfair seemed lonely and depressing. He peeled the cellophane off the Strauss opera, which he placed in the VCR beneath his TV.

He lacked, however, the energy to turn it on.

Instead, he called Megan's number. Joseph answered, "Lane Residence, this is Joseph Michael Lane speaking."

"Good evening, Joseph Michael Lane, this is Neal Stephen Connor of IBC News speaking."

"UNCLE NEAL! Hi! Hey, you were really great today on the five o'clock news. That mean lady won't dare try to trick you again. My mom says that she was not really trying to do that. But you know how my mom is."

Four or five times as many words as the winsome kid had ever spoken to him before. And now he was "Uncle Neal."

"Can you keep a secret, Joseph?"

"Sure," the boy responded eagerly. "ANY secret."

"This time, maybe for the first time in her whole life, your mother is WRONG!"

"I won't tell her, that's for sure," the lad whispered solemnly, half fun and full earnest. "Do you want to speak to her, Uncle Neal?"

"If she has time."

"Oh, she has time!"

"Your number-one fan tells me that after you and he talked, you still have time for me. Neal, you're an outrageous charmer with kids."

"Maybe because I never grew up. . . . How are you doing to-night?"

"I had a hard day Christmas shopping. Otherwise I'm fine."

"Christmas shopping is hard but fun."

"Lots of fun."

"Can I come out to your place tomorrow morning?"

"With evil intent."

"What else? You're driving me out of my mind."

"I can't believe that I could ever do that to a man."

"You can take it from me that you have. But I don't want to place any extra pressure on you."

"If I had a dirty mind, Uncle Neal, I could do a lot with that last sentence. Is nine o'clock all right?"

"I can wait that long, though just barely."

"Another opportunity for a pun that I'll let slip by."

Neal found himself beaming as he hung up. A ready-made family, complete with a compliant wife and an adoring son.

A trap, but such a wonderful trap. A temple and a temple harlot ready and waiting!

He turned on the ten o'clock news, halfway through a news story. Police were carrying a shrouded corpse out of an apartment building.

"With the gangland-style execution of Ricardo Garcia, his older brother Luís—the only surviving son of the Garcia family—becomes the sole ruler of the family, which allegedly controls most of the cocaine sales in Cook County."

Dearest Neal,

I'm a mess. I've never been such a mess in all my life.

When I leave you or you leave me, I feel so proud of myself, blissful and content and arrogant and ready to laugh at anyone who doesn't know my wonderful secret.

When I wake up the next day, I am thoroughly ashamed. I'm old enough to know better. Who do I think I am, anyway? as my sisters would say if they knew. (Do they know? I can't imagine they believe it possible. They certainly don't know, would never guess, how much pleasure I experience with you.) I begin to think that what happened was a silly, frivolous, romantic dream, something in a steamy women's novel. I'm ashamed of myself. I promise that I will never do it again. I will act like a sensible, adult woman and not a love-crazed little fool.

My good resolutions last about an hour. Then my hand is on the phone to call you. I don't call you all the time, but I know once I reach for the phone, I'm lost. I eventually will call you— or race to the phone even more wildly than my crazy daughters when it rings, hoping against hope that it will be you.

I lose myself for a long time daydreaming about you. I fantasize about your beautiful naked body. Then I count the hours and the minutes until your fingers and your lips drive me out of my mind with desire again.

I adore you.

Megan

She was sitting in front of the vanity mirror in his bedroom, in beige bra and slip, combing her hair, slowly, languidly, complacently. He sat next to her on the vanity bench, extended an arm around her, and cupped a covered breast in each hand, lifting and delicately squeezing them.

"Just affection," he said, drawing her back against his naked body. "Necking and petting."

"I can absorb that"—she placed her comb on the vanity—"for the rest of my life."

"I've been asking myself," he said softly, "all through this . . ."

"Affair?"

"Love. I've been asking myself whether, if we had married twenty years ago, I would be as obsessed with you as I am now."

"Not very likely." Her fingers rested on the comb.

"On the contrary." He crushed her breasts against her ribs. "I'd be as hopelessly in love with you as I am now. I will never have enough of you, Megan."

"I wish I could believe that. . . . I don't mean those words. I do believe you. I don't know why you love me so much. But I do believe you. . . . Well, you wouldn't have my silly letters if we'd been married all these years."

"If we'd been married all these years, I'd have the nerve to reply to them."

They were silent for a moment, basking in their intimacy.

"They are *silly* letters," she said, sighing.

He brushed his chin against her frail little shoulder and moved her trapped breasts back and forth. "May I talk about them now?"

"I suppose so."

"Megan." His lips met hers. "You are the most perfect woman I've never met."

"I wish that were true." She shifted uneasily in his embrace. "I have lots of imperfections."

"They're all irrelevant."

But I still must find out who killed your husband, the poor dear man who never knew you.

68

"*Amigo*, be sure you come alone."

"What the hell's the matter with you?" Neal demanded irritably. "Have I broken my word to you before?"

"I trust no one."

"Fine. Neither do I. But we have agreements for mutual benefit."

"I am very troubled, *amigo*. I wanted to warn you. I'm sorry. I know you will come alone."

Then Johnny Jefferson came into the office. "One of our Hispanic reporters tells me that the word is out on the street that Lou Garcia has gone *loco*."

"How could they tell the difference?"

"Be careful, Neal. We don't want to lose you."

"Damn it, Johnny, I don't want to lose myself, either."

Not now that I have something to live for, he thought as he glanced at his watch.

And someone.

69

Megan's scream, so loud that he feared it could be heard outdoors, drove him to yet further heights of passion. His thrusts into her became more rapid and more powerful.

She had opened the door when he rang the bell at ten minutes to nine. "You're early." She retreated uneasily. "I just got your pal Joseph off to school."

He didn't permit her the opportunity to say anything else.

She was wearing a white terry robe, her hair was wet, and she smelled fresh and well scrubbed from the shower. Underneath he found plain white cotton underwear, as he had the first time he blundered into the house at midday. He had cut short her preparations. So much the better, he thought as he undressed her.

No, this was the preparation. She had noted the effect of shower smell on him. She was deliberately seeking wild passion from him this morning.

He pulled her to the floor and gave himself over to ferocious assault, constraining her to move at his pace. She smiled contentedly, reassuring him that he had read her signals accurately.

Now he really was a raging forest ape, forcing his mate to

heights of pleasure, a journey to which, as she lay spread-eagled beneath him, she did not seem to object.

On the contrary, her smile turned into a laugh.

Then he was finished, exalted, and beginning to feel guilty. She was still laughing.

"It's all funny?" He felt deflated by her amusement.

"Neal, darling, you are so hilarious when you think you're out of control. Great big ravishing warrior overwhelming the poor timid matron."

"Well . . . it's your fantasy as well as mine."

"And I love it, love it, love it. But it's also funny."

"What if one of the kids should come home from school, surprise us?"

"We'd hear them." She laughed again. "Don't worry, mothers hear their children."

"Even when they're being ravished by the berserk warrior?"

The word *berserk* made her laugh again.

Her amusement overwhelmed him with a sweet wave of tenderness. She had not laughed much since he had returned. Probably she had not laughed much in the last twenty years. Now she was laughing again.

"Neal . . ." It was not a warning as much as an expression of surprise.

"I love you most of all when you laugh."

"Well, you are funny as Tarzan assaulting Jane!"

He picked her up. "I think Jane would like a shower."

"Would she ever!"

"I still can't believe that I turn a man on that way," she said as the water and his caresses carried her off into her own mysterious garden of warmth and fantasy.

"You do. . . . Megan, you're not an object to me. . . . I . . ."

"I don't feel used, poor dear man." She stroked his face slowly and gently. "I feel loved, passionately loved. A little surprised, maybe, and astonished, like I said, about the reaction I seem to cause in you. Right now"—she shivered contentedly—"right now I feel flattered, and like maybe I need a lifeguard to pull me ashore."

"Too bad there isn't one in the family."

"Oh, there is, darling, in my family that is. Teri was lifeguard at Grand Beach this summer. She replaced O'Connor the Cat who went to Europe for the summer."

"O'Connor the Cat?"

"Nancy Ryan O'Connor's daughter. Her mother—you remember her—writes science fiction stories, especially for kids. She was the absolute dictator of the beach, and my Teri is following in her footsteps. Even bawls me out."

"Why do they call the poor child 'the Cat'?"

"Her real name is Kathleen, after her grandmother, but she exults in the nickname. She's as quick as a cat but all resemblance stops there."

Neighborhood, community, family, kids with nicknames, lifeguard traditions being passed on. He was poised on the brink.

"But we couldn't expect her successor to pull either of us to shore, just now."

"She's not likely to walk in since St. Ignatius has exams today. So I'll make you a cup of tea."

"Thanks. . . ." They stepped out of the shower. As she scooped the robe up and wrapped it around her body, he added, "For everything."

"My pleasure."

I can't get enough of her, he reflected. I've never had so much intense sex with anyone else because I've always been sated early. Will she ever satiate me?

I hope not.

"Teri insisted on my learning some of her lifeguard techniques." Megan continued her discussion of lifeguards as she poured his tea. "She claimed that she might need help someday at the beach. So if you're drowning and I'm around, I can fish you out."

"I'll keep that in mind," he said, reaching for a large piece of coffee cake. "Though I don't think they'll let you in the pool at the Chicago Athletic Club."

"With naked men swimming"—she turned up her nose—"what woman would want to be lifeguard there?"

They both giggled foolishly.

As lovers always do.

"I thought you liked naked men."

"If they all looked like you, I'd sign up for the job tomorrow morning."

Images of the assistant-lifeguard mother and her lifeguard daughter haunted him as he drove out to the toll road: a whole package, Blackie had said. His for the asking, for the taking. Stability, roots, family—all acquired at once.

Why did the prospect not seem as appealing as it should? He was tired of wandering—so his shrink had said—and wanted to settle down.

Would the circumstances of settling down ever be any better than what was being offered him now?

Lou Garcia's face was marble-hard. "I loved him, *amigo*. Can you believe that? I loved him? I begged him not to challenge me? I even gave him a chance to kill me. The fool blew it. I had no choice."

"I'm sorry, Lou, really I am."

They were sitting in their usual meeting place, in the McDonald's near the Halsted Street interchange on the Tri-State Expressway. Plastic Christmas trees, huge cardboard Santa Clauses, bright red and green lights, and worn-out carol music testified that the "Holidays" had come to the interstate system.

"I know, *amigo*. You have kindness in your eyes."

Both he and María Anunciata were wearing old down jackets, sweat shirts, and jeans. They could be migrant workers. The girl's eyes were red. Chewing gum, she now looked like the teenager she was, a bereaved teenager at that.

"What happened?"

"I told him to take everything. Even the *chiquita* here, whom he wanted badly. Ha, she won't go. *Chiquitas* today can be pretty stubborn."

"Good for them."

"You are so right. I tell him kill me, have it all. You want everything that is mine. Take it all. But he wants to take the lives of all of my family. He fears that my sons, or even my daughters, will grow up and kill him. I love my wife. I love her more than anything.

I love my children. I will give my life for my brother, but not theirs, so I have to kill him first. Yesterday when I spoke to you, I didn't think it would end this way. . . ."

He waved his hand in a gesture of resignation and despair.

I better be careful, Neal thought. I'm beginning to buy the ethics of his world.

He loves his wife more than anything, but he travels with this kid on his arm.

"I'm terribly sorry."

"Sure." He patted Neal's arm. "Your father dies violently, too, so you know what it is like."

"I remember." But it had been so long ago that he had forgotten.

"So why didn't you ask about Lane and Dineen to begin? You did not play it straight with me, *amigo*."

A touch of menace slipped into Garcia's cold eyes.

"Come on, Lou, do we have to go through these games with each other? You're grief-stricken. I'm tired. You expect me to come blundering into your store and ask the first questions about those guys. Sure I'm interested in them. But I haven't lied to you about the whole story."

"No story." He cut his hand through the air in a chopping motion. "Not now. Not for a long time. Maybe not ever. You understand?"

"Naturally. I won't call you, you call me."

Garcia smiled thinly. "*Amigo*, I would trust you more if you understood less."

Neal was aware that María Anunciata was watching him intently, as if analyzing his responses. Exactly what role was this kid playing? Was she the voice on the phone? Somehow he felt that she was and that she was a much more important piece in the puzzle than she seemed to be.

"If we ever do the story, Lou," Neal continued smoothly, "the theme will be that the narcotics laws are no more effective than the Prohibition laws."

"I would tell them about the corruption on their own side." Garcia's face lighted in excitement. "About the judges we buy, federal judges, *amigo*. A half-million in cash will get you many federal judges. Others cost a million. If they want to be Supreme Court judges, perhaps a little more."

"Any federal judge?"

Garcia spread his hands expansively. "Not all of them, but a lot of them. No records, except those we keep for future reference. Assistant United States Attorneys, too. That little shit Roscoe thinks he has a mole in our family. Hah! We have three moles in his office, not counting the one he thinks works for him but really works for us."

"Dineen?"

María Anunciata stifled a cry. Garcia seemed to freeze.

"How did you know that?"

"It seems obvious. Who else would know a lot of traders and have contacts with you? I suppose that he brought Alf Lane over to your store in the first place?"

He did not add that only someone who was part of the action would have the nerve to admit to a reporter what everyone else knew to be true: Alf was working for the Garcias.

"You should be the United States Attorney, *amigo*."

"I'm not a lawyer."

Garcia shrugged indifferently and appeared to relax. "I was going to tell you anyhow. Dineen is a pig. I am weary of him. We have better spies in Roscoe's office. But, *amigo*, you surprise me."

"Maybe I'm a lucky guesser."

"Maybe. You love the woman, that's why you do all this?"

"Mostly. I'm afraid of people like Roscoe, too. I can see him in a black uniform with jackboots."

"The woman is your kind of woman, huh?"

Again he wanted some sort of male evaluation of Megan. Well, nothing wrong with that.

"She drives me out of my mind, Luís. I can't think of anything else."

"So." Garcia smiled. "I understand. She is not to my taste, but I can see that she would be to some men's taste. Very well, I cooperate with your love for her, OK?"

"OK."

He is not to be trusted completely, but let him set the context, Neal decided.

"It is very complicated," Garcia began. "This Dineen is a very bad *hombre*. He likes to hang around my store because it makes him feel important and because of the women and because he can talk about it to his friends. The girls say he is not much with women, right, María Anunciata?"

"All talk," she said with a sneer. "So too with Lane, but he is not mean like Dineen. He does not hurt you."

Neal fought to keep down his anger.

"So," Lou Garcia went on, "he brags to us that Donny Roscoe has him spying on some of his clients, stealing their papers, so Roscoe can follow leads in trading irregularities. . . . And I am a criminal, *amigo*?"

"I never said that."

"When I hear about Donny Roscoe, I think I am one of the good guys. He says Roscoe trusts him completely. He lets him sit in his office when he talks on the phone to judges who are hearing cases. Would you believe Judge Forest?"

"I'd believe anything."

Judge Forest, Neal had been told, was a well-known "reform" judge, a vigorous advocate of "merit selection" for county judges, a man who, according to the reporters at Channel 3, thought that "merit" rather than political friendships was responsible for his elevation from the state to the federal bench.

"So my brother Rickie says we will give you a hundred big ones a year if you report what Roscoe plans for us—a big one, *amigo*, is a thousand dollars."

"Sounds like a bargain."

"Poor Rickie had no style. Dineen says five hundred big ones and it is a deal."

"More like it."

"Me? I don't think it's worth anything, but it makes Rickie happy, and he is my brother."

"Then?"

"Then Rickie and this pig Dineen begin to invest some of Rickie's money in commodity trading. That is foolish, *amigo*. Gambling is always foolish."

"I think your friends over on the West Side feel the same way."

Garcia shrugged and spread his delicate fingers. "They are businessmen, too. They want sound investments."

"I understand."

"Rickie and Dineen and Lane—they make lots of money. They don't tell me about it, but I find out anyway. They bring Lane around the store. Him I like. He is much fun. The girls do not mind him. His stories amuse me. But, *amigo*, I tell you the truth about him: he is an innocent, eh?"

"He always was."

"He needs money. Your friends on the West Side are after him because he gambles—on the ponies, not pork bellies—and loses. I like him. If he asks me, I give him the money and he pays them off. But no, he joins Rickie and Dineen in an import order of their own. Some other traders, too. They bring in the merchandise and sell it and make lots of money. Rickie now thinks he is a big *hombre* and gets himself dead. So does Lane, but I did not do that."

"And Dineen tells Roscoe about traders working with narcotics smugglers."

"Of course. Again I do not care, because if the narcs come to arrest anyone, we buy them off. But Rickie needs one more big score before he challenges me. So they try to scrape together all the money they can find. Then it is Black Monday, and the meltdown, as they call it, occurs. Lane loses everything, except maybe a few dollars. Then he gets himself dead."

"Rickie?"

Garcia stared at him coldly.

"Perhaps. I do not know for certain. Anyway, my men pick up the merchandise and pay for it. They chase Rickie's men away. Dineen does not know what happens, but he tells the FBI that all the money goes to Lane before he dies. Actually the merchandise lands in—" He smiled ruefully. "See how much I trust you, *amigo*, I almost tell you where the merchandise lands."

"I don't want to know."

"If you know, maybe you get dead, too."

"I doubt it. But you were saying that Lane was dead before the arrival of the merchandise."

"That is true, but the FBI does not know that it's true."

"I see."

"Makes your head whirl, eh, *amigo*? I don't blame you. There are many bad *hombres*, but Tommy Dineen is the worst. Someday soon, he will get himself dead, too."

"No more killings," Maria Anunciata said decisively, "till after Christmas."

"Have a nice Christmas with la señora," Garcia said tonelessly.

"I'll try."

71

"They found Pete's body." Megan's voice on the phone was cold and distant. "In the river."

"Accident?"

"With two bullets in his head?"

"Dear God."

"They all say it was my fault."

"To you?"

"To the kids, the oldest three anyway."

"Do you think it was your fault?"

"I don't know. I'm not sure of anything anymore."

"Megan," he spoke softly.

"I know; you don't have to say it. It's crazy, like everything else in my family. Still, he was mixed up with Al. If I hadn't married Al . . ."

"Which they made you do."

"I know. . . ."

"Megan."

"The only sensible answer is that Pete has been rushing towards this end all his life and that I had nothing to do with his death. I'm merely the one to blame in this family mess. But, Neal, they can still hurt me."

"Families always can."

"I suppose I'll get over it, but now I'm so tired—so, so tired."

"Are you going to the wake and the funeral?"

"Certainly. It'll be terrible, but he was my brother. It'll be at St. Titus. Father Don Powers, a Carmelite priest, will say the Mass. Do you remember him?"

"Sure."

A fund-raiser with considerable skills at cultivating the rich.

"Neal . . ."

"Yes."

"Would it be too much to ask you to come to the wake with me and the kids?"

He had hardly expected such a request. He would be out of place. Tongues would wag. Hints would be dropped.

So what?

"Not if you and the kids want me."

"It was their idea, unanimously. Mark goes—" She laughed wryly. "See, I'm talking like them. Mark says that with Uncle Neal there, the family will be afraid to guilt me too much."

"Damn well better believe it."

Good old Uncle Neal.

After he hung up, he pondered whom he should call. Blackie? Nick Curran? No, in the implicit division of labor, it would be best to dial Mike Casey.

He knew how the media would play it:

GANG STYLE KILLING OF MOB LAWYER'S SON

A shattering blow to the Keefes' illusions of respectability.

"Person or persons unknown," Mike began tersely. "An Outfit hit. Classic. The executioner is probably halfway across the continent. The word on the street is that it was a high-level decision. Jack the Crack confirmed it from prison. Had to go that high because the old-timers owed Pete's father."

"He must have done something pretty bad."

"Probably talked too much. Long-time weakness he had."

"Your colleagues will never find the killer."

"In a week, maybe less, they'll know who did it. But no evidence with which to go to a grand jury. Like I said, an Outfit classic."

"Unless someone sings. Which people have been doing lately."

"Depends on whether the feds can keep alive the most recent snitches. Don't bet on it."

Alone in his suite at the Mayfair Regent, Neal watched the Bears ruin Walter Payton's final home game by giving away the game to the Seattle Seahawks.

An ill omen.

Then he drove out to the neighborhood. He and Megan sipped an anxious cup of tea while they waited for her daughters to finish dressing for the wake.

"Have you ever wondered what happened to my inheritance?" she asked him as she blew gently on her hot tea.

"No," he admitted. "I guess I kind of forgot about it."

"I kind of gave it to Pete a couple of years ago."

"All at once?"

"No . . . a couple of gifts. He needed it. Said he could turn around his life and his marriage with a few extra dollars. People like Pete always say that, I guess."

He nodded, letting her tell her story.

"I knew even then that there wasn't much chance of his returning the money. But I didn't need it, or so I thought. And Daddy would have wanted me to help him. None of the others would, of course. They never liked Rebecca, his wife, anyway."

"Naturally they wouldn't give him money."

"He was nice to me. Sometimes. I mean more than the others. He even told me the last time I bumped into him coming out of church that he thought the opera was a good idea."

"Uh-huh."

"Now he's dead, too. And I could use the money."

"But you don't regret giving it to him?"

"No." She placed her cup on the coffee table and folded her hands beneath her chin. "Is that wrong?"

"Not in the least."

"Well"—she stood up briskly—"my daughters have finally made themselves beautiful enough to appear in public."

"Mo-THER!"

"Make her stop, Uncle Neal," Teri pleaded.

"No way."

They drove over to the wake in somber silence. The most relevant of Neal's thoughts was that defacing the top of a Benz with a sunroof was the sort of thing Alf Lane would have done. And they ought to fix the lock on it.

The Lane family was tense and pale as they entered the Donlon Funeral Home on Western Avenue, the boys in dark suits, the three women in black dresses. None of the mourners ringed around the casket spoke to any of them, except Henry, the oldest son. He murmured, "Good to see you, Meg."

Megan took his hand and nodded. Her sisters and mother glared at Henry. He withered under their stare and drifted away, probably for another drink.

Bea, Linda, and Connie looked like Megan's aunts instead of her sisters: large, bloated, wrinkled women with hateful eyes and thin, angry lips. They were working hard at the evaluation of each new visitor to determine what level of response to offer—running from ignoring the person to kissing him or her.

The majority seemed to fall at the former end of the scale.

Their hatreds crackled through the room like lightning on a humid summer night. Their father's wake all over again.

The funeral home, smelling of mums and Chanel, was jammed with people, quieter than most Irish wake crowds would be and much more tense: a crowd waiting around for the car bomb to go off.

"A remarkably edifying display of human hopefulness, is it not?" a voice spoke next to him.

As Blackie had once said of himself, he was not only indistinguishable in a crowd; he was unnoticeable.

"What's with that touch of red at your collar? I thought you folks had given those up."

"One of the trusted young clerics on my staff keeps it in his room for those occasions when it is decided to dress me up. It will create a dilemma for the mourners, who on the one hand despise the Clan Ryan (not without some reason from their viewpoint, I presume) and on the other hand feel constrained to acknowledge the existence of a member of the papal household."

"The Clan Ryan will show up in force?"

"The Pope is not a Mormon."

"You will be at the Mass tomorrow?"

Blackie sighed deeply. "The virtuous Father Don does not believe in the concelebrated Eucharist, a position with which I do not lack some sympathy. I shall assist from a prie-dieu in my full choir robes, which, while diminished in splendor from an earlier age, nonetheless do represent some merriment. That is, I will wear them if some industrious member of the Cathedral staff can find them."

"A symbol of hope?"

"It is to be lamented that the admirable and indeed exemplary Father Ace, who will also be present and who will hopefully prevent me from snoring during Father Don's sermon, cannot appear in his dress-white captain's garb, even more hopeful raiment than my choir robes."

"An oh-six?"

"Bird Colonel." The priest sighed again. "With a Ph.D. Irreproachable. . . . You will accompany the Lanes?"

"That's what they want me to do."

"You will note Father Don's sermon. This being the Christmas season, he will celebrate the decline and fall of Caesar Augustus."

"Pardon?"

"The triumph of the Babe of Bethlehem over the Roman empire. I remarked once after such a sermon that not only was Caesar Augustus dead but so too was Innocent III, the point of which remark seemed to elude Father Don."

"Is there a heaven, Blackie?"

This abrupt change of topic apparently surprised the elfin Monsignor.

"There damn well better be."

"Is Pete Keefe there?"

"No one is born, Cornelius, and no one dies without the embrace of God's love. We are judged in the context of that with which we began. Poor Pete did not begin with much. I'm sure we'll meet him again in better circumstances . . . though in truth the Keefe family, the extraordinary Megan excepted, might not be pleased with heaven because the Lord God is reputed to admit Jews and even blacks into Her kingdom. Ah, I note the blameless Beatrice descending on Teri and Joseph Lane. Shall I or . . ."

"I'd love to do it."

"Then I shall add my sympathies to that of the rest of this worthy assembly, most of whom will miss the deceased for no more than five minutes."

There were numerous Keefe grandchildren at large in the funeral home, teens and young adults, some surly and sullen, some in punk hairdos, and some as normal-seeming as the Lane kids. Even the normal ones seemed to be waiting for the car bomb.

Bea had sunk her fingers into the left shoulder of Teri and the right shoulder of Joseph and was weeping over them.

"You'll miss Uncle Pete, won't you, sweethearts?" she cooed, a mourning dove in death agony. "Even if your mother doesn't care what happens to the family, you'll care, won't you? You'll visit your grandmother often, won't you, even if your mother doesn't love her anymore?"

The two kids squirmed uneasily, not sure how to respond to such passive-aggressive sweetness. Megan was trying to work her way through the crowd from the other side of the room. Grandmother Keefe, sprawled helplessly on a couch next to the casket, watched with hard little eyes that bulged out of the huge rolls of flesh on her face.

Car bomb.

None of my business, they're not my kids.

Then he saw the desperate plea on Teri's face.

"Cool it, Bea." He firmly removed her hands from their shoulders.

Bea Keefe Mitchell turned the color of an engine of the Chicago Fire Department.

"WHAT did you say?"

"I said cool it." He put one arm around Joseph, the other around Teri.

"I am their AUNT. I may say to them what I please."

He fixed her with his stern anchorman's glare. "One last time, Bea, COOL it."

Out of the corner of his eye he saw Megan pause in midflight, a smile playing on her lips.

"How DARE—"

"He SAID cool it, Aunt Bea," Joseph spoke up sharply. "He means it."

Wondrous boy child.

"Well, I NEVER—"

Neal turned his back on her and led his two charges to the lobby of the funeral parlor.

"Radical," said Teri.

"Totally excellent," said Joseph.

"Thank you, Uncle Neal," they both said together.

"Just defusing a car bomb."

"Huh?"

Megan and the two older kids materialized next to them.

"Let's get the hell out of here, Megan." He released Teri and put his arm around her mother. "Before the bomb explodes."

She gazed at his face, studying him carefully. "What do you think, Mark?"

"One tough son of a bitch."

"Mark!"

"That's what Father Ace said." The boy raised his hands in self-defense. "He's usually pretty right."

Then they were in the parking lot under the clear night sky of winter solstice.

"I agree, Mark," Megan said as Neal opened the door of the Mercedes for them (and winced again at the sunroof), "that Father Ace is usually pretty right."

"Me, too," said Teri.

"Me, three," said Margaret.

"Utterly radical," Joseph agreed.

"You're welcome, I think."

They all laughed.

Neal Connor now had, if he wanted it, not only a family but an admiring one.

The funeral was even more glum and sullen than the wake. Father Power, a big man with a high-pitched, almost womanly voice, did indeed preach about the triumph of the Babe of Bethlehem over the Roman empire, a triumph in which somehow Peter Keefe shared by the good fortune of dying during the Advent season. Monsignor Blackie did indeed fall asleep during the sermon. And the exemplary and irreproachable Father Ace did indeed strive to prevent him from snoring.

It was raining at Sepulchre Cemetery, but the ceremonies were inside a chapel and not at graveside as they had been when Neal's father and mother died. Only the immediate family were present. Pete's five children stood next to their mother (Pete's estranged wife)—defiantly and protectively, Neal thought—at some distance from their aunts, uncles, and grandmother.

Grandma Keefe, supported by two of her daughters, wailed hysterically through the final prayers as droned mechanically by Father Don. Al Lane's four kids were weeping softly next to Neal, remembering no doubt their father's recent burial.

When the last prayer was said and Grandma Keefe collapsed into Father Don's arms, almost bearing that far-from-frail cleric to the ground, Megan led her brood over to Pete's wife and children. The kids from each family clung to one another; Mrs. Pete shook hands firmly with Megan and smiled briefly at Neal.

"Thank you for coming," she said in a firm, clear voice.

The pitch of Grandma's hysteria soared yet higher.

"No one is born," Neal said to the widow, "and no one dies without the embrace of God's love."

"How beautiful," she murmured.

"I'll take the kids home, Neal," Megan said outside the chapel. "And call you later on. I know you have your program to do from northern Indiana."

"See you at Christmas," the children said more or less in unison.

"You bet."

The sky above the cemetery was utterly cloudless, a serene stage for the sun to scurry across in the south before slipping back into its bed for a warm winter's nap.

Neal Connor had one less day on his pilgrimage to a similar graveside scene than he did the day before.

And strong doubts about what kind of companionship he wanted on the rest of that pilgrimage.

And uncertainty about whether the doubts made any difference.

Especially when Margaret Mary Lane whispered in his ear. "It's a good thing Father Blackie didn't say the same thing to Aunt Becky last night."

"Go get your cat and broomstick," he replied. "Before the sun goes down."

She pecked his cheek and ran back to the family Mercedes.

God help you, O'Connor, she's not your stepdaughter yet, and already you have the hint of incestuous feelings about her.

If she were your daughter, would you feel the same way?

Of course you would. That's the way human nature works. Your trouble now is that you have always dreamed of a daughter like her. Now you can make that dream come true, and it scares the hell out of you.

72

You will never see in this field any shadows longer than this.

The farmhouse, the barn, the trees, that old windmill are casting their fantastic shadows this evening here in northern Indiana because it is the winter solstice, the shortest day of the year. The sun will never be any lower in the southern sky as it slips rapidly across the horizon and then sinks—with notable relief, I think—into a long winter's nap.

It's a magical day, filled with mysterious portents and promises, the day when darkness pushes its advantage against light to the outer limit.

The news is dark. Ferries sink. Helicopters crash. Trucks and cars collide on the expressway. Hostages are held in Beirut. Riots erupt in Gaza and, of all places, Bethlehem.

Here on this farm one looks at the long and scary shadows and wonders, as did our ancestors, whether all bets are off and tomorrow night, horror of horrors, the shadows will be longer and more fantastical still. One pictures mostly benign young virginal witches grabbing their cats and their broomsticks and flitting across the sky.

But tomorrow there will be a little more light and a little less darkness. The mostly benign young virginal witches will sleep late because school is out for Christmas vacation. We will have turned the corner on the march to spring.

And with it, increased marginally our hope that no one is ever born and no one ever dies save in the embrace of God's love.

Tonight one even feels vaguely confident that the Bears can win again.

Neal Connor, slightly spooked, Channel Three News, at the winter solstice in northern Indiana.

Neal smiled contentedly as his solstice tape played. During the commercial break the technicians applauded.

"That's what TV ought to do all the time," a cameraman enthused.

"It'll kick the ratings up again," a floor director agreed.

"Network wants it for late night," an assistant producer (woman) shouted in the background.

"And Cardinal Cronin is talking about ordaining Neal," Johnny Jefferson chortled.

He hoped all the Lane kids were watching, especially Margaret Mary, the mostly benign little witch. And Blackie Ryan, damn him. Troublesome, dangerous priest.

When they switched to the network news, Neal left the IBC Building and, without his coat, strolled down several blocks of Michigan Avenue, soaking up the soft white lights. He stood under the gorgeous tree in front of the John Hancock Center and felt himself floating into its delicate swirls.

You're caught, O'Connor. And you like it.

He ambled back to his cubicle at the station.

Scarcely had he settled comfortably into his chair, the aroma of Christmas peace teasing his nostrils, when the phone rang.

"Connor."

"Neal? Nick. I've been trying to get you all day."

"What's wrong?" His body froze.

"Tommy Dineen attempted to rape Megan after the burial this morning."

"She's not in the hospital, Neal," Nick spoke sharply. "Calm down. I said that HE was over at Little Company of Mary. Twelve stitches, some nasty burns, and a probable concussion."

"WHAT?"

"Our mutual friend Tommy the Clown Dineen has achieved the pinnacle of artistic success. He starred in a real-life comedy. At the denouement it was pure slapstick. He managed to get himself conked over the head with a frying pan—classic weapon, as Mike the Cop observes. But the melting bacon grease was Megan's unique contribution to the old scenario."

"Megan beaned Tommy Dineen?" He felt awe creep into his voice.

"Put him in the hospital. We'll probably be able to keep it secret. Who wants to bring charges?"

"Megan hit him with a frying pan of bacon grease?"

"Hot bacon grease. She was cleaning up from breakfast like the assiduous housewife that she is."

"Wow!"

"I don't know what your future plans with her might be"—Nick was chuckling—"but you should keep in mind that the woman is a terror."

In many different ways it would seem.

"I thought you had security people watching her."

"We do indeed, and they managed to arrive in time to save Dineen from more serious damage."

"Is she all right?" he asked softly.

"All things considered, she's fine. Catherine is with her now and, I think, Mary Kate Murphy—you know, Blackie's sister the psychiatrist."

"I know."

"The received opinion is that she'll be all right in a day or two, probably more shaken by her own reaction than by the attempted assault. She said to tell you she's fine and she'll call you this evening at your apartment."

"Tell her . . ." He hesitated. "Give her my love."

"Most willingly, as the Punk would say."

He gently returned the phone to its cradle.

Megan Keefe was ravaged only by men by whom she wanted to be ravaged: of that fact he would never have any doubts again.

He picked up the phone and punched in a number.

"Nick Curran."

"About Dineen."

"No need for you to slay him, Neal. He's well done, if you excuse the pun."

"I'll stipulate, Counselor, that the virtuous Megan can take care of herself. But there's something I've found out about Dineen which will interest you and the rest of the Irregulars. I've been saving it for later, but I think it should be played now."

"You fascinate me."

"He's the mole."

"Huh?"

"He's Donny Roscoe's mole. We all should have guessed it, but it was hard to believe that even Donny would sign on such a slob."

"You have proof?" Nick was crisp, decisive.

"Not that could be used in court, but I'm certain."

"If you're certain, we'll get the proof. Larry Whealan will love it. So, I suspect, will Channel Three News."

"That thought has occurred to me. Who knows, maybe it will leak tonight."

Silence for a moment.

"You're as dangerous as she is."

"As good old Uncle Punk might say, the Lord made us and the divil matched us."

Neal hung up, pondered for a few moments, and ambled down to Johnny Jefferson's office. He sketched a quick outline of the story.

"You'll call Donny?"

"Naturally."

"Why didn't I think of it?"

" 'Cause you black folks are too sweet and innocent to comprehend the full possibilities of human evil."

Johnny seemed bemused. Then he grinned. "I always said that when we really wanted to be corrupt, we'd have to learn to imitate the Irish."

"The story?"

"Hell, go with it!"

The name Neal Connor was magic at the office of the United States Attorney for the Northern District of Illinois—any anchorperson would have the same clout.

"Donald Bane Roscoe." A high-pitched voice trying to sound deep and resourceful.

"Hi, Donny. Neal Connor. I'm doing a story about your investigation of links between commodity traders and the drug families. Any comment for the record? I've got the tape on."

As if to confirm its presence, the recorder emitted a derisive beep.

"No comment," the prosecutor sputtered.

"Then there is such an investigation?"

There was a pause while Roscoe sought the visual signals coming from the other person on his end of the line.

"No comment."

"All right, now I'd like to ask your views in general on the attorney-client relationship."

"Absolutely sacred."

"I'm glad to hear that. Some recent incidents, as I'm sure you understand, have raised some questions—"

"They have been answered."

"I understand. Then I can take it for granted that neither your office nor the FBI is currently using an undercover agent who has an attorney-client relationship with individuals you are investigating?"

Another silence, dead and long.

"We don't comment on investigations in process."

"I understand and approve completely. But I merely want to be assured that we are not faced with another violation of the attorney-client relationship."

No response.

"Mr. Roscoe?"

"I'm still here."

"I see."

"And I still have no comment."

Better duck, Donny. Mortar incoming.

"Would you then care to comment on the information we have from excellent sources that Mr. Thomas Dineen is routinely providing information about his clients to the Federal Bureau of Investigation?"

"That's a secret!"

Neal savored the image of the other federal lawyer, speechless and horror-struck at his boss's gaffe.

"I'm afraid it isn't a secret anymore, Donny. The whole city will know it after the five o'clock news tonight. Would you want to respond?"

"No comment."

"Our sources tell us that the FBI approached Mr. Dineen and suggested that he violate the lawyer-client confidence. Your office, in other words, took the initiative. You went to him, he didn't come to you."

That was pure guesswork, but it fit the way the FBI and the federal prosecutor had operated in other cases.

"We have the right to seek help in pursuing investigations of known criminals."

What a dumb thing to say!

"Including subverting their lawyers?"

"No comment."

He should have flatly denied the right to subvert lawyers.

"Thank you, Mr. Roscoe."

What the hell am I doing? Neal asked himself. This is the kind of TV witch-hunting I despise. It shouldn't make any difference that I'm doing it for a woman I love. Did I say that? Do I love her? How would it be different now if I did love her?

Anyway, it's witch-hunting and I ought to be ashamed of myself.

Except that Don Roscoe is a witch-hunter. I'm fighting fire with fire.

The ethical issues were too dense. He already heard his closing lines:

So if you think you can trust your lawyer not to report you to the FBI, think again. Donald Roscoe claims that he can blackmail your lawyer into revealing your secrets. It's a claim they would have supported in Berlin in 1939. This is Neal Connor, Channel Three News.

Her voice distant and weak, Megan spoke to him on the phone the first thing the next morning.

"Neal," she said tentatively.

"Megan."

"How are you?"

"Shouldn't I be asking that?"

"Oh, I'm all right. I mean, I talked yesterday for a couple of hours to Doctor Murphy—Mary Kate, you know. We got along fine. I've always admired her. We're going to continue to talk, more or less on a regular basis."

"Sounds great. These have been rough times."

"I'm glad you approve. My family never approved of psychiatrists. They think we ought to be able to pull ourselves together. It didn't help Pete."

"I saw one in New York."

"Truly?"

"Truly. You guessed that."

"I was mostly kidding. . . . They don't approve of women psychiatrists especially."

"And most especially they don't approve of Mary Kate Ryan Murphy."

"You'd better believe it."

They laughed. Somehow she had sought his permission for psychiatric treatment and he had granted it. What the hell.

"Anyway," she said, "at least you know now that this woman is ravished only when she wants to be ravished."

"I sure do."

"What will happen to that poor man, Neal?"

"Dineen? Nothing much, I suspect."

"Even after what you said last night?"

"What Don Roscoe said."

"It was terrible," she said, switching back to the rape attempt. "I can't believe I did what I did. Naturally, without thinking about it."

"A fierce little woman, I guess. But then I've known that for a long, long time."

He shifted the phone uneasily from one hand to another, groping for the feel of the conversation so that he would say the right thing.

"I suppose I should be impressed by me. . . ."

"Why be in the minority?"

She laughed uneasily. "Nick says that after Christmas we'll get a restraining order but that I probably won't have to go to court."

"That should put an end to things."

"Neal . . ."

"Huh?"

"That woman called last night. She said bad things would happen to me and my family unless I found the money. But, Neal, I don't know where the money is!"

Garcia?

Maybe. What kind of odd game might that haunted man be playing?

"We'll try to find it. . . . You told Nick?"

"Sure. He said not to worry."

"He's usually right."

"I know. . . . Neal?"

"Yes?"

"I have some Christmas shopping left. I mean, I really do. I'd be finished by eleven-thirty or so."

"Do you want to go out for lunch?"

"I'd just as soon not get dressed up."

"I could have room service send something up. A sandwich and some tea?"

"Fine," she sounded hesitant. "Are you sure?"

"Sure I'm sure. Truly. Eleven-thirty."

"All right."

Now what does tenderness mean in a situation like this? he wondered.

Before he could contemplate that issue the phone rang again.

"*Amigo*, real balls! Nice going! I couldn't do it better myself!"

"Lou—"

"No questions just now, *amigo*. I just wanted to say it was fun to listen to Donny shit in his pants on national TV. *Adiós*."

There was a click at the other end of the line.

Lou didn't mention the attempted rape. Surely he would have if he had known. So his sources were not as good as he would like to pretend.

They called Chicago Beirut-on-the-Lake. They could also call it Berlin-on-the-Lake, everyone spying on everyone else. The Garcias, the FBI, the Outfit. Even the Irregulars—who seemed to know everything.

But the Irregulars had only one goal—protect Megan Lane.

Maybe a second goal: provide her with a new husband.

It might not be such a bad job after all.

The phone rang off the hook for the next two hours. Network was caught between worry about lawsuits and pride at another scoop—a typical enough position for network. Kathleen Sweeney wanted him to appear on the "A.M." program the next morning. They traded blarney as they usually did, and he agreed. Two Chicago political reporters wondered about his sources.

"Hey, don't hassle me about my sources. It's none of your business and you know it."

"But there are questions being asked—"

"Aren't there always questions being asked? And isn't that the only lead for a journalistic asshole who has been upstaged?"

"You don't have to be nasty about it!"

"Look, you guys have been kissing Donny Roscoe's tail end for years when you should have been exposing him for the little Hitler that he is."

"He's exposing official corruption."

"When he's more corrupt than anyone he's sending off to Lexington. Hell, you let Jim Thompson win the governorship by the same tactics. I suppose it's too late to have troubled consciences now."

"Yeah, but these are pretty wild charges you're making."

"You see the program?"

"Yeah."

"OK. Donny made them about himself. Now get off your rear end, get out of Ricardo's, and go do some work."

"You're an outsider—"

"Look, shit, I was born here, which is more than can be said for you."

"You're asking for trouble. You think you're hot shit and this is a hick town . . ."

"It's a great city, but you wouldn't know it from the reporters. Now fuck you!"

He hung up.

It was more barroom language than Neal would use from one end of the year to the other. But it was appropriate for the goofs who purported to be political reporters in Chicago. It would keep them off his back for a while anyway, because they knew he was mean and could fight back.

Nick called to say that Megan and Larry Whealan had searched systematically through Al's papers—both those that had been at home when he died and those which Dineen had brought from his office.

"Neal, there're cartons and cartons missing!"

"Where are they?"

"In the Everett McKinley Dirksen Federal Building."

"You're guessing?"

"We know. Larry Whealan has already sought a temporary restraining order and—guess what?—Eileen Kane has turned up on the wheel. It will be a show and a half!"

"Can we win?"

"Sticky point of law, but she'll probably grant the restraining order, which means that we win for ten days and Donny loses. That'll be the ball game."

"Why?"

"Because the media will eat Donny alive. They have no choice after you broke the rules against telling the truth about him."

"I guess I should feel proud of myself, but I don't."

Nick did not reply, perhaps despairing of ever understanding Neal Connor's strange moods.

Then Mike Casey called to say that the guards around the Lane family had been increased. "Will you and Megan be able to stop by the gallery to have some eggnog with us?"

"I think so. I'll call back."

"Just come."

Then he turned off the phone and ordered two ham and cheese sandwiches, a pitcher of iced tea, and two dishes of chocolate ice cream—doubles.

The food arrived at eleven-thirty and Neal put it in the fridge. He had just closed the door when Megan knocked.

"I didn't think they'd let me up if I asked," she said. "I look like a bum."

"You look like Teri," he said honestly enough.

She was wearing a light blue down jacket, jeans, a white Marquette sweatshirt, and white gym shoes (without socks, as is required by the teen fashion).

"Sweet." She kissed him on the cheek. "I couldn't find anything grubby enough around the house to fit my mood. Anyway"—she handed him her jacket—"the little brat steals all my things."

"Borrows," he corrected as he hung the coat up.

"She's conned you already." Megan prowled his apartment, kitchen, bedroom, parlor. "You make me very angry, Neal Connor!"

"Why?"

"When an Irish mother comes into a room in which a man lives, she expects to be obliged to bustle around straightening out his mess. You frustrate that primal instinct."

"Sorry. I learned a long time ago to keep things neat."

"Tsk-tsk, you might make someone a wonderful wife!"

Phony gaiety, but gutsy. The woman grew each time he saw her. Maybe I ought to be afraid of her.

Hell, I AM afraid of her.

"Sit down, Megan, and relax."

"OK. You do have a frying pan handy, don't you?"

"I'm bigger than you are"—he eased her onto the sofa—"and quicker."

"I suppose so. . . . Lunch?"

"In the fridge."

"I'm a wreck, Neal my darling, a total wreck."

"A brave and gallant woman."

"Thank you, but I don't feel that way."

"You'll be all right in a day or two."

"I don't know. . . . No desire." She slumped forward. "Not the slightest. Before, when I came up on the elevator, I was on fire. Now . . . nothing!"

"Can't you give yourself a day or two?"

"NO! What if it never comes back?"

"I think your hormonal glands won't atrophy."

"I lived for twenty years without much sex. I don't want to lose it now."

As candid as ever.

"You won't lose it, Megan." He touched her hand. "No way."

"Would you . . . ?" She held her hands over her face, little-girl style. "Would you, ah . . . ?"

He thought his head would explode with tenderness. "See if there's any lust left in that lovely body?"

"Well, something like that. . . . I know I don't look very appealing."

"Be quiet, woman." He sat down next to her and very gently took her into his arms.

She was stiff and awkward but yielded to his embrace quietly enough.

Dear God in heaven, can anything be sweeter than this!

His fingers were as light as snowflakes, his lips as delicate as those of a child, his affection as gentle as a nurse with a neonate.

Slowly his woman melted.

"Well, I guess maybe I still have some hormones."

He helped her off with the sweatshirt. "I propose to lick every inch of you."

"Oh, Neal!"

He continued his insidious work.

"There's nothing you don't know about me, is there?" Her serious gray eyes followed his movements as he despoiled her of the last bits of her clothing. "I have no secrets left."

"There will always be more to learn about you, Megan."

She groaned at a particularly probing touch of his tongue. "Neal, don't. . . ."

So he repeated the action several more times as she squirmed submissively.

"Please," she begged, and then said no more as he finished his labor.

Finally, at the very last seconds of his own control, he rolled her over on her belly and slipped inside her willing body.

Her cries were of joy and gratitude.

Afterward he led her to the shower.

"Make it real warm," she begged, submissively leaning naked against his side.

"Someday you'll have to tell me about your fantasies in the shower," he said.

"Heaven!"

After the shower he made love with her yet again, more challenging in his demands this time.

"Definitely still have the hormones." She sighed and then dropped off into a peaceful nap.

He woke her to feed her and then dressed her and escorted her across the street and down Oak to the Reilly Gallery.

"If we were married for twenty years, would we feel the same way?" she asked thoughtfully.

"I think I would lust after you even more."

She laughed, a happy and satisfied woman. Tommy Dineen had been exorcised, temporarily.

Inside the Reilly Gallery they looked at Mike's new exhibition and wolfed down cookies and eggnog. Anne and Mike could have no doubt about what had preceded their visit.

Megan didn't try to hide her self-satisfaction. Even if she had, the glow on her face would have been a giveaway. She hit it off instantly with Annie and, before they left, was offered a job as assistant curator at the new gallery Anne was opening at Huron and Orleans streets over in the River North art district.

"I must rush to catch the Rock Island. The kids are having a party tonight."

"Are you going to accept Mrs. Reilly's job offer?"

"What about poor Joseph?"

"She said three days a week. Joseph will be in high school in another year and a half. You can work out something with Catherine."

"She's already told me that. I'd be scared."

"That doesn't mean you won't do it?"

"It only means I gotta think about it. . . . Thanks for everything."

She ducked into a cab, a teenager rushing home.

I never had a chance, he thought. Once I walked into that church last month, she had me.

And I her.

He smiled. The years ahead would be different from the years past.

Yet somehow, despite the light and warm weather and the soothing taste of Annie Reilly's strong eggnog, he was still afraid.

It was too good to be true.

76

Neal Connor's danger warning system failed him the night before Christmas Eve.

Perhaps a dozen times during his twenty years in television journalism his life had been in serious jeopardy. Half those times he had escaped because the Viet Cong or the Russians or the Cubans in Angola had missed him. The other times he had survived because he'd had time to duck. In both sets of circumstances, he knew a couple of seconds or even a couple of minutes before the crisis point that he was in trouble and had better watch himself.

"Vestigial caveman instinct for danger," his psychiatrist had told him. "Don't expect it to work all the time, especially if you insist on putting yourself in dangerous situations."

Neal had dismissed both the danger and the warning current that seemed to leap through his nervous system. Everyone had to die someday, didn't they?

"Yeah," said his shrink, "you think you're invulnerable? Someday when you find something to live for you'll take an unnecessary risk and get yourself killed."

"If the bullet has my name on it, then that's that," Neal had replied.

He did indeed feel that he was invulnerable—ever since he had rescued Megan from the fire, he knew in the depths of his soul that they would both lead very long lives.

The warning system, if such it was, must be part of the same kink in his organism that produced the slow-motion effect during moments of excitement. Useful but not essential.

Especially useful, he realized now, for seducing and being seduced.

But not essential.

Then, on December 23, 1987, the bullet came which had his name written on it.

In the Oak Street underpass.

After the ten o'clock news, he had ambled back to the Mayfair Regent and decided to walk up to North Avenue Beach on the sand under the crescent moon. Though the weatherman at Channel 3 had pledged a dusting of snow on Christmas Day and a cold spell over the weekend, the temperature was hovering around forty, a soft and gentle December night, perfect for the fantasies of a man in love.

He crossed under Lake Shore Drive in the pedestrian underpass and emerged on the beach. There were a few other people taking advantage of the night air—older lovers hand in hand, young lovers arm in arm, an occasional fiercely penitential jogger.

The lights from Lake Shore Drive cast a benign orange glow over the beach, a fairy-tale warmth that seemed perfect for the Christmas that lay ahead of him, surely the most satisfying Christmas in his life.

He had never had a real family—the winter chill with which his parents were able to exist happily was hardly a family. Now he would be part of a family Christmas.

He had wandered the world searching for excitement and romance. Now, back in his own neighborhood, he had found both—a challenging lover and plenty of adventure.

With such joyous thoughts dancing in his head, he had sat a long time on the bench that he and Megan had shared long ago. Then he glanced at his watch, realized that it was one-thirty in the morning, and stood up reluctantly to walk back to East Lake Shore Drive.

By now the beach was deserted, but the skyline, presided over by the imperial John Hancock Center, seemed to smile down on him, endorsing his happiness with its serenity.

He was vaguely conscious as he approached the north end of the beach that there was someone behind him, but he had no sense of danger, no inclination to glance around and look behind him. After all, this was Chicago and Lake Shore Drive and not the Hindu Kush, even if it was almost two in the morning.

He walked down the steps to the underpass and became conscious that the person behind him had paused at the head of the steps. He paid no attention.

"Neal!" the other shouted softly.

He turned to face the person behind him, stumbled on the last step, and fell forward on his face.

Two bugs swept past his ear, pinging loudly on the concrete wall.

Then, too late by far, the warning system went on. Ignoring his torn trousers and his bruised face, Neal leapt forward from the ground and plunged into the underpass and around the first corner.

Twenty-five-caliber ammo. Silencer. Outfit hit action. A professional contract.

Neal stopped short just around the corner and held his breath.

He heard no footsteps but he knew that the killer was walking toward the bend in the underpass.

He heard his own breathing and imagined he could hear the killer's breath.

In his quick glimpse of the man, Neal had seen that he was short and skinny and dressed in dark clothes and a ski mask.

He carried the gun with its long barrel—the silencer—like it was an extension of his left arm.

Left arm. That means the gun arm will be close to me when he comes around the corner.

He knows I'm still in the underpass because he hasn't heard me run to the street. Maybe I'm lurking in the shadows. Maybe he wounded me with one of those bullets. Maybe I'm bleeding to death somewhere between here and the steps.

Will I be standing, back against the wall, right at the turn, ready to pounce?

He'll think of that because he's a professional and he thinks of everything. But he'll discount the possibility. A fancy TV reporter wouldn't be that cool.

I'll never make it to the street. He's good with that weapon or he wouldn't be using it. He'll fire at the slightest sound. Let's see, they have five bullets in the magazine. Two shots, three bullets left. Not good odds. I'll have to take the gun away from him.

In the distance, seeming light-years away, the noise of Lake Shore Drive traffic rumbled on—never too late in the day.

Early in the day. Christmas Eve. Not a bad day to die.

But Neal did not plan on dying. He had a family now to live for.

Then he knew the man was at the turn and about to come around the corner. This time he did hear the gunman's breathing, quick, anxious, high-strung—a cat ready to leap.

He tensed for the split second he would need.

The killer turned the corner, pistol held firmly in both hands, and poised to fire down the underpass.

Neal brought both his arms down like a hatchet on the killer's wrists. The noise was like tree branches breaking.

There were two more pings as the gunman fired off shots in a reflex action. The gun dropped to the concrete floor.

Neal spun the man around and slugged him solidly in the jaw. The killer sagged, but professional that he was, he jumped for the gun instead of fighting back.

Neal stomped on his wrist and pulled the gun away.

The killer jumped at him, clutching at his hand and clawing to recapture the gun.

"Not this time, buddy." Neal threw the man off his arm.

Does he have a knife?

"Don't come closer or I'll shoot."

The gunman snarled like an injured animal and jumped at Neal again.

Neal staggered back against the wall.

I should have shot him.

The man in black pinned Neal's gun arm against the wall and scratched frantically for the gun.

With a mighty effort Neal shook the killer off again and raised the gun. "I'll kill you," he growled. "I mean it."

But he didn't mean it.

The man in black turned and ran back up the steps and out onto the beach.

Neal raced after him, gun still in hand. "Stop," he yelled, "or I'll shoot."

He had never fired a pistol in his life.

On the dimly lighted beach, the would-be killer turned toward the drive, running awkwardly through the sand.

Neal chased him. His legs were longer and his breathing stronger than the killer's. He grabbed the man in black at the barrier on the edge of the Drive. The man twisted away, leaving Neal holding a torn piece of black sweater, and lurched out onto the drive.

And into an oncoming car.

Neal heard a sick thud as his attacker bounced off the first car. Then a squashing sound as he fell under a second.

Neal's stomach did not react. It had witnessed too many deaths.

The man lay still in the street. Cars swerved around him. No one stopped. Hit-and-run at night.

That was that.

The pistol in his trench coat pocket, he walked back to the underpass and across to Michigan Avenue, in time to see the whirling blue light of a police car. No one noticed him at the corner of Oak and Michigan in front of the Drake. Instead of going to his suite at the Mayfair, he strode down Michigan to the Hancock Center and rang Mr. Casey's room, assuring the polite doorman that he was expected.

A few minutes later, he sat across from the Caseys—both in luxurious winter robes that suggested few if any garments under them—and sipped a cup of Annie's apple cinnamon tea ("Father Blackie's favorite, poor dear man").

The weapon, deceptively small and innocent, an apparent child's toy, rested on the glass coffee table between him and the Caseys. Next to it was the silencer. Not much accuracy except at very close range. That's why the would-be killer had tried to shoot him from the top of the stairway.

"You took the gun away from him?" Mike the Cop ran his fingers through his thin silver hair.

"If I ran, he would have heard me and put those three bullets into me. I know the gun isn't very accurate at anything more than a few yards, but I didn't want three bullets in my gut for Christmas."

Mike and Annie were silent for a moment, more impressed with Neal's feat than he was.

"You sure he's dead?"

"Or badly injured. Probably dead."

"Are you all right?"

"So far, no reaction yet. Not even sick to my stomach. I've been here before. It may take a couple of days."

Mike nodded. "You're lucky."

"Tell me about it."

"Professional. We'll get an ID tomorrow. Out-of-town hit man. Probably no local authorization. Just like Jake Lingle."

"Who?" Annie asked.

"A *Chicago Tribune* reporter who was shot in the underpass down by the IC station in the Capone era. Was in bed with the Mob and then sold them out."

"But why would they want to put me down? I don't work for the Mob."

"That's why it's kind of strange. Who benefits by your death?"

"Dineen?"

"Rumors have it that he's tried killing before."

"The people who put down Pete?"

"Maybe. Young bloods without respect. They'll be in trouble with the godfathers when it turns out tomorrow that they bungled something they were not authorized to do in the first place."

"The dons will figure it out?"

"Oh yeah, they may even let us know that they had no part of it and won't let it happen again."

"Well, I'm safe then."

"Maybe. We'll put some protection on you, too. I didn't anticipate this. It doesn't make much sense. What do you know that they might not want to get out?"

Neal thought about it. "Nothing."

"Strange."

"Do we tell the police about my involvement?"

"I don't see what purpose it will serve. They'll have a professional hit man's body on their hands and will figure either that he blew it or that someone hit him first."

"I think I'll go home now and see if I can get some sleep. Thanks for the tea, Annie."

"Don't you dare leave this apartment till Mike gets you some protection," she said firmly. "Someone has to look out for Megan's interest."

Only when he was back in his suite, did Neal realize that the one secret he did have was the location of the missing money.

But why kill him to keep it secret?

Unless someone else knew where it was and wanted to collect the money eventually?

How would they know? He had told no one but Blackie. And Blackie certainly would have told no one else.

Maybe they were only guessing.

It must be a hell of a lot of money.

In Chicago, Christmas takes place in neighborhoods. So tonight, Christmas Eve, we put our anchor desk in our mobile unit and took it into one of Chicago's most magical neighborhoods, the first of many that Channel Three will visit during the coming year.

Why Beverly tonight?

Because it's my neighborhood—the one I grew up in, anyway. Isn't that enough reason for me to want to anchor the news here tonight?

You often hear it said in a patronizing tone that Chicago is a city of neighborhoods, as if when the city finally grows up, it won't have neighborhoods anymore. But any city worth living in has neighborhoods, whether it be Kinshasa in Africa or London in England. In Chicago we don't pretend that there are no neighborhoods.

Behind us is St. Praxides Church, already lighted for midnight Mass. Or midnight Eucharist, as they make us Catholics say nowadays.

Wherever a family is, there is home. So even if the participants of the first Christmas were on a journey, they were home because they were a family. But Christmas is special when the home is the place where you grew up. I left this neighborhood as a young man with no intention ever to return. I met the present pastor of St. Prax in Vietnam. He bet me that eventually I would return home. It looks like I've lost the wager, although I haven't paid him yet.

When I was growing up here, the lawn decorations were the most elaborate in the city. People from other neighborhoods used to drive through Beverly to admire our displays of lights. Then we stopped them because too many outsiders were staring at our nice homes and our illuminated lawns. Some of us were afraid that black people would admire the neighborhood so much that they would want to come and live here.

Now blacks and whites live together and the lawns are lighted again, if not so spectacularly as a quarter century ago. At midnight Eucharist black and white acolytes will march side by side. That, my friends, is progress. Unless you grew up here like I did, you really don't know how much progress.

Despite the Council Wars, the two peoples can live in peace in a magic neighborhood. The tree-lined lawns, the hills, the curving streets, the bright lights belong to everyone now.

And Christmas, a feast of love yet to be fully achieved, means more here than it used to mean.

In front of St. Praxides Church, in the Beverly Hills neighborhood, Neal Connor, Channel Three News.

His lust for Megan was now a given in his life, a permanent wound, a chronic illness, an incurable infection. His previous enjoyment of her had heightened his hunger. Her ravenous delight in him was gasoline on the flames. The only aim in his life was to take her into a room where they would be alone, undress her, play with her, and make love forever.

Humans could not live that way, he told himself. There had to be a settling down, an achievement of stability, a plateau in which sexual love was a part of life, an important part indeed, but not the whole of life.

Yet she had been not only on his mind but at the front and center of his consciousness all day. The only noticeable effect of his brush with death in the surrealistic setting of the Oak Street underpass was an even greater appetite for Megan.

Love and death.

He could think of nothing but her while he wrapped up the news from the mobile unit in front of St. Prax. Johnny Jefferson told him afterward that the calls to the station were all favorable. The ratings, Johnny was certain, would be "off the wall again."

That was nice to hear, but he joked with Johnny only by concentrating considerable effort. All he really wanted to do was to get out of the mobile unit and hike over to Hoyne Avenue and up to the Lane house.

So it had been all day.

And on Christmas day he would find the missing money and perhaps resolve the puzzle of Al Lane's death.

The *Sun Times* had been cautious:

PRE-CHRISTMAS HIT-AND-RUN ON DRIVE

The story identified the man only as a businessman from out of town.

Yeah.

Mike Casey had called at nine-thirty. They had an ID on the killer, a small-time hit man from Reno. Already the word was coming in from the West Side that the dons were embarrassed and apologetic. It would not happen again.

Then Cos Ventura was on the phone.

"Hey, good buddy, you all right?"

"I'm busy, Cosmo. Deliver your message without any frills."

"You don't have to be nasty."

"Look, some of your friends tried to kill me last night."

"No friends of mine, old buddy. That's why I'm calling. There's some very important people who are disgraced by what happened, very, very upset."

"Yeah?"

"And really impressed with you. They say you are a man of real respect."

"Great, what does that do for my life insurance premium?"

"Neal, I'm trying to tell you, if you'd only listen."

"I'm listening."

"My friends, uh, the friends of my friends say you're a stand-up guy and they want to be friends with you. It won't happen again. Believe me, it won't happen again. Don't ask me how come I'm so sure. Don't ask. You don't wanna know. But it won't happen again."

"I'm happy to hear that."

"It's hard to get respect these days, Neal. Terribly hard."

"So I'm told."

"But from now on you're gonna get plenty of it. The word is out: Don't fuck with Neal Connor."

"Wise advice, as our mutual friend from Reno could have testified."

"No friend of mine. . . . He try to put you down in the underpass?"

"I shouldn't have been walking along the lake that hour of the night."

"Hey, it's a free city. . . . You, uh, took the gun away from him?"

"Yeah."

"You shoot at him?"

"Those toys are no damn good at more than a few yards, Cos, you know that. He fired off a couple by accident when I hit him. I imagine the cops found the bullets down there. Maybe the same gun that killed Pete Keefe."

"Yeah. Maybe. . . . What happened to the gun?"

"I kept it. Souvenir."

Actually he had given it to Mike Casey, but it was none of the Outfit's business what had happened to the gun.

"God, you got balls, Neal."

"Or no brains, Cos. Anyway, Merry Christmas."

"Yeah . . . sure, Neal, Merry Christmas."

"And a Happy New Year, too."

After he hung up, images of Megan's gossamer-white body taunting him all the while, he contemplated the possibility that he had unintentionally avenged Pete Keefe. Not only was the hit man himself dead, but those young bucks who had brought him in were in such trouble that eventually, when the dons were good and ready, they too would "get themselves dead."

Too bad, Neal mentally shrugged his shoulders. Not his war. Even if he were certain, he didn't think he'd brag to the Keefes that he had put down those who had killed Pete.

They might, however, savor the revenge more than he did.

All the more reason for not telling them.

Now he was at the Lane house on Hoyne, with the new family that he had acquired so imperceptibly that he had hardly realized what was happening.

"Mother's on the warpath," Teri greeted him grimly at the door.

"Ah?"

"We're all frazzled. Getting ready for Christmas is such a drag. She and Margaret aren't speaking to one another, and Mark is in his room sulking."

"Merry Christmas!" Neal shouted. "Will some people help Santa with his bags—and maybe provide champagne for his reindeer."

All four children thundered out the door, making as much noise as the reindeer might have made.

"Santa?" Megan appeared, apron around her black sweater-dress (with white trim—a concession to Christmas joy, he supposed) and cookie spatula in hand.

"I hear we're frazzled and fighting."

"An Irish mother preparing for Christmas, what else? I have to teach my daughters how it's done."

They brushed their lips together chastely.

"Merry Christmas, Megan."

"Merry Christmas, Neal."

His lust was now submerged in an even more powerful emotion—loving affection. His desire was not destroyed. Rather it was sent up to its room to wait and to grow.

"Nice family, Megan."

"Gotta make up with daughter. . . . Thanks. I kind of like them, too. Dear God, Neal, it's been a terrible two months."

"I think the worst is over."

It required two trips for the kids to bring all his presents into the house.

Between the two trips, Margaret and her mother hugged each other.

"Frazzled," Neal remarked.

"Too much riding on broomsticks," Mark added.

"Both of you, SHUT UP!" Margaret howled.

"Mostly benign young witches," Joseph chortled.

"QUIET, all of you. That includes you, Uncle Neal." Megan was still in command.

"You sound like Father Ace," Neal replied.

More laughter.

"Uncle Neal, what's in the big box?" Teri demanded. "Is it what I think it is?"

"Go get ready for Mass," he replied.

ST. VALENTINE'S NIGHT

"That's Mother's line."

"Eucharist," Megan corrected, spatula still in hand, and strode back into the kitchen.

So they prepared for the Eucharist. When Neal helped Megan on with her mink, he brushed his fingers against her neck.

"Neal . . ." Momentarily she went limp.

"Just a reminder."

"Lovely reminder. Merry Christmas."

Can you lust for a woman during Mass, ah, during the Eucharist? he wondered.

If God didn't want us to do so, He wouldn't have made us the way He has.

She has, as Blackie would insist.

Father Ace, already dressed for the Eucharist, greeted them at the door of St. Praxides. A light frosting of snow had covered the ground. Snow flurries whipped gently on the air. The chimes were playing Christmas carols.

"Permission to come aboard, sir," Neal requested.

"Permission granted."

They exchanged salutes.

"Hey, recruit." Father Ace pointed at Joseph. "You forgot something."

"Sorry, SIR." The kid saluted with a big grin. "Won't do it again, SIR."

"Carry on."

"Yes, SIR."

"Mean son of a bitch?"

"Seems like a good description, huh, Margaret?"

"Definitely, Captain, SIR!"

"The Trans call you yet?" Father Ace asked Neal.

"Yes, they always do. . . . How do you know that?"

"I know everything." The priest grinned triumphantly.

"You're almost as bad as the exemplary Blackie."

"Worse . . . everyone KNOWS what he is. They think I'm OK."

"Mom, who are the Trans?" Teri asked as they left the priest and entered the church.

"Mr. Tran was a man whose life Uncle Neal saved in Vietnam. He was just a young man then, and his wife was expecting a baby. He worked for Uncle Neal, with his camera, and when he was shot,

365

Uncle Neal carried him back to the hospital. They have a lot of kids now and they live in Boston."

"And cheer for the Celtics. Did Dick, uh, Father Ace tell you that story, Megan?"

"No, I remember it."

"Are you a hero, Uncle Neal?" Joseph asked eagerly, his blue eyes glowing. "Father Ace is. He has lots of medals. 'Course they're only good-conduct medals."

"No, Joseph, I'm not a hero. The heros are all dead. Or like Mr. Tran, they almost died."

The church was awash in candles and poinsettias. The crib—to the right of the main altar—glowed in what might have been starlight. The congregation was brimming with cheerfulness and anticipation. Young people home from college were whispering to one another. The organ was warming up for carol singing.

It had never been quite so cheerful before at midnight Mass, had it, back when it was midnight Mass instead of midnight Eucharist?

In fact, he'd never attended midnight Mass. This was the first time.

Neal had a lot to chew on when the choir began to sing. Not a bad choir at that.

What am I doing in this church? I don't believe in You and I hate this neighborhood. But I'm surrounded by people who believe in You as easily as they breathe. So I'm acting like You're really here. And I've become a member of the neighborhood as if I never left.

You know what? I think that You—if You really exist—are a member of the Wabash Avenue Irregulars.

Do You mind my desiring this woman here in Your church? I'm sorry if it bothers You, but I have no intention of stopping. Not that I could stop even if I wanted to.

Or is she part of the trap You and that troublesome and dangerous priest of Yours have prepared for me?

All right. All right. It's a very nice trap.

Father Ace's homily was clear and to the point, not at all like the convoluted and late-punch style affected by the Cathedral rector.

Naturally he referred to the telecast.

"I suppose some of you saw the church on TV tonight. The only thing wrong with the program was that they didn't ask the pastor to appear. I mean after all, he is an oh-six, that's equivalent to a bird colonel."

The congregation burst into laughter; obviously this was a standing joke in the community.

"Well, we know that pastors aren't important anymore. All they do is requisition the altar boys and the altar girls. . . . Forget I said that. . . ."

More laughter. The Vatican had forbidden altar girls, Teri had told him, but most parishes ignored the rule.

"And the choir and the Sunday collections and the teachers in school and the ushers and everyone else in the parish whom we thank tonight. The pastor even requisitions the gratitude, but he doesn't get any credit for that, either."

More laughter. Father Ace had swallowed the Blarney stone.

"But I'll give the anchorperson—Channel Three News, Beverly Hills—credit. . . ." Not a bad imitation actually.

People were glancing around to check Neal's reaction.

He sensed Megan blushing next to him. Joseph, who had elbowed his way so that he sat on the other side, was nudging him with a sharp little elbow and grinning proudly.

Neal flicked a salute at the pastor and inclined his head. The folks around chuckled. Megan blushed more deeply.

The pastor continued. "He said the neighborhood had changed during the time he was away—he still hasn't paid off the bet, by the way, but now we have witnesses—and he's right. He says it's changed for the better, and I think he's right there, too. He didn't say that the neighborhood, like every community, still has lots of room to improve. We don't change overnight—individuals, families, neighborhoods. We change slowly and gradually, so slowly sometimes that only a person who has been away two decades notices the change. But with God's help we do get better, if only a little better.

"So too our families. We ought to be, each of us, a little better in our family life this Christmas than last Christmas. Not so good that we don't fight—I mean that would be like a total miracle, right?—but we should make up more quickly after our fights than we did a year ago, at least a little bit more quickly, and not let the fights spoil the spirit of the day, not as much as they did a year ago."

Neal nudged Megan, who in her turn nudged Margaret. They all giggled. Most everyone in church was nudging everyone else.

Then Father Ace continued to talk about Christmas as a new beginning for humankind, for the neighborhood, for each family, and for every person. The real excitement of Christmas was that it was an absolute guarantee that it was safe to begin again.

Absolutely safe? What did the priest know about safety?

A lot probably. He'd been shot at, too.

Begin again? Well, that's what I'm doing, isn't it? Maybe I kind of stumbled into it. Or was seduced into it. But I am beginning again, am I not?

In my old neighborhood, with my old girl, and my old friends.

And did Blackie Ryan put his friend the Ace up to that sermon, er, homily?

Is the Pope Polish?

There was kind of an open house at the Lanes' afterward, people stopping by on the way to or from the massive and historic eggnog fest *chez* Ryan, especially young people, kids who apparently only had first names.

A lot of Seans and Marks, and among the older girls, Jennifers and Micheles and Melissas, and among the younger girls an incredible number of Brigids, Fionas, and Deirdres and even a couple of Granias—Brigies, Fees, Dees, and Granies.

Still a few Irish around.

Uncle Neal sat in the corner and smiled benignly as he gave his autograph to those who sought it.

"Maybe you can trade it with one of the Ryans for Cardinal Cronin's autograph."

Then the visitors drifted off. Time to arrange presents under the tree, but not yet to open them. The family rules, laid down by Megan in a tone that admitted of no dissent, were that they were to be opened only after breakfast.

"No, I repeat, no peeking!"

"Uncle Neal," Teri mused, "must have bought out Needless Mark-up like totally."

"Needless Mark-up?"

"Nieman Marcus."

"Next year, Bloomingdale's will be open, so maybe I'll do some shopping there."

"Will you be here next year, Uncle Neal?" Mark asked, his serious young face even more serious than usual.

There was silence in the room, the silence of a graveyard. Or perhaps an empty church.

Megan was watching him carefully, an eyebrow raised.

"If I'm still invited next year, I'll certainly come."

Everyone relaxed.

"That big box." Teri peered at it. "It isn't what I think it is, is it, Uncle Neal?"

"It is too late to think, young woman," Megan ordered. "Everyone to bed. That includes you, Uncle Neal. I think everything is ready for you up in the guest room."

"Yes, ma'am. I'll get my bag out of the car. My IBC News bag!"

"Do you need help in the kitchen, Mother?" Margaret asked.

"One-woman job, kid. Get to bed, you're almost asleep on your feet. You too, Uncle Neal."

As he lifted his IBC bag out of the front seat of the rented Ford Taurus, Neal was filled with admiration for Megan's handling of the Christmas crises. Each of her children had bittersweet memories of the father they had lost. At Christmas you can't forget such memories no matter how hard you try. But you can prevent them from ruining the day. So Megan had thrown herself into the preparations, tree and crèche, tinsel and holly, presents and guests, food and drink, candles and song. She stilled temporarily her own grief and remorse and sustained the children through a difficult day.

How did he fit?

He didn't. He was completely out of place. A new suitor, come too soon. Surely there were tongues wagging after the Eucharist—he got it right this time—at St. Prax. Megan did not care. Nor did the kids, for whom Uncle Neal was an amusing addition.

Megan did not know that the kids thought a voice from beyond the grave had approved his suit, even before he was sure himself that he was a suitor.

Hell, he wasn't sure yet, was he?

Margaret was standing on the stairway to the second floor of the house, looking at the portrait of her father.

"Trying to figure out who he was, Neal," she said, without looking at him. "Only two months and I seem to be forgetting."

"He wasn't an easy man to know, Margaret. I'm sure he loved you very much."

"I know." Her voice was soft, dreamy. "I mean, I was the first child and a daughter and Daddy's little girl and all that, and he kind of spoiled me, I think."

"I'll argue that."

"Mom saved me from being a real brat. . . . But, Neal, he was a little different, wasn't he?"

"We're all different."

"I know that, but still I can't quite figure out who he was and how I feel about him."

"He was your father, Margaret, and you miss him terribly as we all do, all of us who loved him."

She nodded slowly. "I suppose that's enough for now. . . . None of this"—she glanced at him shyly—"is a reflection on you, Neal."

"I'm still reasonably adequate, huh, Marge?"

"Reasonably." She grinned broadly. "A few things to clear up, like 'mostly benign young witches.' But otherwise, we'll take you on approval." The young woman hesitated. "As far as I'm concerned, quite apart from what happened to Joseph."

"I'm flattered, Margaret."

"How could I dislike you when I see how happy you make Mom?" The words tumbled out. "I mean you, like, totally turn her on. She just blossoms whenever she sees you. I want her to be happy. And you'll make her happy."

"She makes me happy, too."

"It's a new thing, your mother dizzy in love, like you are yourself sometimes." Margaret frowned again, like Megan trying to work everything out in her head. "It makes you change your ideas about love and about women and about sex and about growing old and about the kind of man you want and all sorts of things."

"And being your mother's daughter, you must have all those problems resolved by tomorrow morning."

"Right!" She brushed her lips against his. "Good night, Neal. We'd better get upstairs in a hurry. Or we'll be in real trouble with herself."

As he climbed the back stairs from the second to the third floor, Neal wondered what kind of a stepfather he might make to each of the four children, so much alike and yet so different. They probably needed him.

He wasn't sure he wanted to be needed that way.

He was too sleepy to worry about that. He lost consciousness as soon as his head hit the pillow on the single bed in the little atticlike guest room at the top of the house.

As he fell asleep, he hoped that they had installed a fire alarm of some kind since St. Valentine's Day 1958.

Then the lights went on. Megan at the door, clad in a maroon winter robe.

"Are you asleep?"

"No."

"Yes, you were." She glanced around the room. "Everything hung up, too? You frustrate my bustling instincts."

"Sorry about that."

"You're wearing pajamas, Neal. I didn't know you owned any."

"You never give me a chance to wear them, woman!"

"They're cool. Dior, naturally. They match your eyes."

"Naturally."

"You were perfect tonight, Neal. Thank you. The kids adore you." She sat on the edge of the bed. "I don't know how you do it."

"Even Margaret has been won over."

"ESPECIALLY Margaret. I think she's half in love with you herself."

"That's not necessarily bad."

"Not at all."

Megan smelled of shower soap. Deliberately, of course.

"Do the kids know that we're lovers?"

"They don't permit themselves to ask the question, which is fine. Except for Margaret. She watches us like a hawk. She doesn't disapprove, but she's kind of a voyeur, isn't she?"

"That's not necessarily bad, either. At any rate she approves."

"I'll have to have a long, sister-to-sister talk about love with her soon, which might be a big help to her." She smiled ruefully. "Big-deal expert that I am about the subject."

"I think you're pretty good at it."

"I have a good teacher. . . . Neal, I want desperately to lie next to you in that terrible little bed for a few hours, but I'm too tired for lovemaking."

"Be my guest." He moved over against the wall. "I'm beat, too. Besides, cuddling is one form of love—and not necessarily the worst."

"You understand everything." Her eyes shone with admiration.

She stood up, removed her robe, hung it on one of the wall pegs, turned off the light, and slipped into bed next to him. She was wearing plain cotton underwear, a wife wanting a few moments of peace and warmth next to her husband as an interlude during a busy holiday.

An astonishingly well preserved and attractive wife.

Wearing modest white cotton bra and panty and smelling of the shower.

She snuggled up to him. He took her hand. " 'Night, Megan."

She kissed him briefly.

" 'Night, Neal. You keep a nice warm bed."

"I'm glad to be of some use."

He wrapped an arm around her shoulders. She rested her head against his chest. He hummed *Cantique de Noël* softly into her ear.

"Take care of me, Neal," she whispered.

"Always"—he squeezed her—"always."

She was soon asleep.

A wife next to you on Christmas morning. How did that happen?

Well, however it happened, it was wonderful.

"You're even a better wife," he whispered softly in her ear, "than you are a mistress." He kissed her ear. "I think I'll keep you."

She sighed in her sleep, perhaps hearing him from a long distance as in a dream.

He held her even closer. She kept a warm bed, too.

There were still problems, however—unanswered questions, as reporters or rewrite persons would say.

Such as:

Was the money where he thought it would be?

"Uncle Neal!" Teri shrieked, "I KNEW it!"

"Out there!" Mark agreed.

"You were wrong when you said that you didn't think it was what you thought it was?"

"An exercycle!"

"Radical! Totally!" Margaret chimed in.

"Tubular!" Joseph said solemnly.

"You can ride it while you watch TV!"

"Great for stomach muscles!" Teri continued to shriek.

"Not that I observe anything wrong with the stomach muscles in this family."

"Naturally not," Margaret sniffed. "But, Mo-THER, you'll have to use it every day."

"I can take a hint. . . . You're too generous by far, Neal. But I'll say thanks just the same. I'd never have had the nerve to go into the store and buy that for myself."

"You don't buy anything for yourself," Margaret admonished her. "Time you start."

"Yes, Mo-THER," Megan agreed. "Here, let me see if I can work it."

"Kind of hard in that robe," Neal said, "but here, you just release this lock and pedal."

"This is easy. I'll LIKE doing it."

"You'll do it," Margaret insisted, "whether you like it or not."

"Yes, Mo-THER."

When he had awakened, Megan had already left their bed, eager no doubt to return to her Christmas bustling.

He was disappointed. You were supposed to wake on Christmas morning, find your chaste wife next to you in bed, remove her modest cotton bra and panties, and make leisurely love to her.

No leisure on Christmas Day in this house.

The custom was, he had been told, that breakfast is eaten around the Christmas tree, with Boston Pops music playing on the stereo, and presents are then, finally, exchanged. He was rewarded with scarves, gloves, sweaters, and sport shirts—presents for the man in your life who has everything.

Also with a poster depicting Jim McMahon as Douglas Mac-Arthur, promising, "I shall return!"

In addition to the exercycle, he had collected Chicago Bulls jackets and posters for the young men in the family and earrings, bracelets, and scent for the women.

There was much hugging and kissing and expressions of gratitude.

"One more present for the woman of the house," he said, producing a Bonwit box. "For the summer really."

"I don't like the look in your eye." She considered the box nervously. "I won't open it."

"Mo-THER!" her daughters exclaimed in unison.

"All RIGHT!" She sighed. "I'm sure that it's something sexy and embarrassing. Isn't it, Neal?"

"Sexy," he admitted. "VERY sexy, but not embarrassing."

"I'm old enough so that in a few years I could be a grandmother. I shouldn't get sexy presents."

"All right," said Teri. "If you won't wear it, whatever it is, I'll wear it. We're the same size."

"You will NOT!" Megan held the box against her chest. "It's mine. And I commit myself, sight unseen, to wearing it. So there, little Miss Smart Mouth."

"OPEN IT!"

A chorus of "Oh"s and "Ah"s greeted the blue bikini that emerged from the wrapping paper.

An ample bikini of the sort that had been first introduced when they were teenagers, ample compared to the current manifestations of the style.

Perfect for the matron whose figure has been preserved, mostly by accidents of nature.

Megan seemed neither displeased or embarrassed.

"This is Uncle Neal's way of making sure that I use the exercycle." She held the two small pieces of fabric up for all to see.

"I'll introduce you as my big sister, Mom. You'll look fabulous in it."

"Outstanding."

"Really bitchin'."

"Truly?" Megan gulped, still flattered and now mildly embarrassed.

"Truly," they all said in solemn chorus.

"Your mother was the first girl, uh, young woman at Grand Beach to wear one of those."

"NEAL!"

"NO!"

"REALLY?"

"I DON'T BELIEVE IT!"

"Really," Neal assured them all. "One very sexy little chick."

"Nothing has changed." Margaret smiled aloofly as though she had begun to understand and liked what she understood. "Oh, Mom." The young woman engulfed her mother in her arms.

There were lots of tears from the women in the family and a large wink from Joseph.

"Will she really wear it, Uncle Neal?"

"She'd better."

"Cool!"

"Enough of this nonsense," Megan announced, banishing all tears. "Everyone clean this room up."

The tissue and ribbons were cleaned away, the presents were stacked beneath the tree, the piano bench was opened, and the family gathered round the piano, Megan on the keys, to sing Christmas carols.

He noticed that between Mark and his mother there were currents and countercurrents of amusement, the big lug grinning a lot and his mother blushing.

"What's with the big guy?" he asked when the kids had been sent to bring more eggnog and fruitcake.

"He's figured out that the way to cope with his mother is to treat her like an amusing, pretty little woman. It flusters her and gives him the upper hand for the first time in his life. He's imitating you, of course, though he only pats me on the head not the rump."

"What!"

"Caricature, but it works. He doesn't realize that he's imitating you. I've warned his sisters that I'll brain them if they spoil it and tell him."

"I don't pat you on the rump, in public."

"Not physically." She rested her hand on his thigh. "But they KNOW."

Then the kids bounced back with eggnog and fruitcake, and she pulled her hand quickly away from him.

"The glass on the right, NEAL," Teri informed him, "is devoid of rum."

"DEVOID!"

"Anchorman word!"

"Nice eggnog," Megan said, after sipping hers. "Did you make it, Teri? I think we'll put you in charge." She was trying to pretend that she was not flustered. "You know, I think we really ought to bring that wonderful machine downstairs and put it in front of the TV in the game room. It looks kind of odd here in the parlor."

"And some visitors might get the wrong idea," Neal continued her thought.

"I didn't say that."

Neal and Mark carried the awkwardly shaped box down the stairs.

"Never been here before," he commented.

"Half the basement is the TV room—where little kids get sent when they make noise or where teenagers are exiled when they're grounded."

It was the longest sentence Mark had yet spoken to him.

"I'm sure that it will get a lot more attention now," the young man continued. "I think this physical fitness concept for women is wonderful for men."

"You can say that again."

"The other half is the laundry room and storeroom to which my mom banishes all chaos."

They removed the Schwinn machine from the box and wrappings.

"I'll drag this stuff into the storeroom," Mark offered.

"I'll give you a hand. We'll tell her where the mess is and then she won't be affronted by it."

They both laughed together, secret conspirators against the monstrous regimen of women.

Neal glanced around the storeroom—neatly kept by storeroom standards.

What he thought he might see, he indeed saw.

They sang the old carols for perhaps forty minutes, in remarkable harmony, Megan directing from the keyboard with considerable authority.

Heaven on Christmas Day can't be much better than this, he thought, completely content with his charming and lively newfound family.

"Now," Megan said as she finished "In Dulci Jubilo" with a dramatic cadenza. "It's twelve o'clock. Time for anyone who wants to take an hour nap, maybe an hour and a half. Then the college visitors will start to drop by on their way to the Murphys' for Father Blackie's Mass. And we'll get ready for supper."

"I can't sleep a wink," Joseph protested, "I've got to work on this plane Uncle Neal gave me."

"I didn't say you HAD to nap."

"I HAVE to nap," Neal observed. "I'm the oldest person in this house."

"You are NOT," Megan replied. "I'm two months older than you are."

"I stand corrected."

"Sleep well," she said, with barely a hint that he might be disturbed in his room.

Margaret glanced quickly back and forth from Neal to her mother, trying doubtless to figure out whether there was a signal between them. Her expression said that she had decided that there wasn't and that she was kind of disappointed.

She had misread the signs.

Neal had barely settled into bed, when the back door of the room opened and Megan rushed in. She threw herself on top of him.

"Dear God, Neal, you drive me out of my mind."

"How? I didn't say anything. I didn't even touch you."

She kissed him frantically. "It's not what you do or say, it's just that you are here. And I'm worn out and frazzled and anxious and guilty, and I want—no, I need to be loved."

"I think"—he opened her dress and unhooked the front of her bra—"that we can take care of that."

She remained passive and submissive as he removed the rest of her clothes.

He piled them—dress, slip, bra, hose, panties—into a neat stack on the chair next to the bed. Then he imprisoned her meekly squirming body with his own bulk.

"I love you, Neal," she moaned. "I'll never stop loving you."

Their love was quick and efficient, pleasure on the run during a busy family holiday.

What one would expect from a modest wife on a chaste marriage bed.

"You nap," she said when they both sank back into the bed, sweaty, satisfied, and exhausted. "I gotta take care of the turkey."

"I won't argue," he said sleepily. He would have much rather kept her in his arms for the rest of the afternoon, but wives have certain responsibilities on Christmas Day.

He woke up a half hour later. One-thirty. Time to rise and shine.

And check out the basement storeroom.

Four sets of golf clubs leaned against the wall, a picket line of alloy instruments. Dad, Mom, two older kids?

Or maybe Dad, Mom, and the two boys.

It wasn't hard to figure out which set had belonged to Alf. There were more clubs, the bag was bigger, and the covers on the woods more elaborate. The equipment said "serious golfer."

Neal shivered. Al was near, hovering by his golf clubs and his money.

"I think I'm doing what you want me to do. If the money really is here, the only reason I know it, is that you came to the door in your golf clothes."

Did you really come back from the grave to endorse me as your successor?

I don't know whether I believe that scene.

But if the money is here?

He poked around the golf clubs. Nothing in there.

He zipped down the ball bag—a dozen or so balls, some tees, nothing else.

The other compartment—two sets of gloves, nothing else.

So there had been no appearance. No money.

He felt let down. And relieved.

He turned to switch off the light.

Nothing here. Go back upstairs. Forget about this nonsense. There is no money.

Then he saw it.

A plaid duffel bag, propped up against the washer. A golfer's bag.

He hesitated. Again he shivered.

It was none of his business. The bag was a Pandora's box. Leave it there.

He considered the reasons for opening it. A key to the mystery, freedom for Megan, maybe for Al's spirit.

Slowly he crossed the room and picked up the bag.

Heavy. Something stuffed into it.

He hesitated again, then with a single brisk movement he unzipped it.

Hundred-dollar bills, thousands of them, in neat hundred-bill wrappers. Each pile worth ten thousand dollars. Maybe fifty piles. A half-million dollars.

He rezipped the bag, and returned it to its place.

Slowly he walked up the stairs to the kitchen. Megan was fussing with the turkey.

"I want to show you something, Megan."

"Can't it wait?"

"It's important."

"Damn. . . . You're in charge, young woman," she snapped at Margaret. "If it spoils, it's YOUR fault."

"And Uncle Neal's."

He led her down the steps.

"What can be so important?" she demanded irritably.

"That bag," he pointed at it.

"It's Alf's golf clothes. I put it there after . . . after the funeral."

"Open it, Megan."

"I will not! It's a ghoulish thing to do on Christmas."

"I think you'd better."

"All RIGHT. I don't want to, though."

She started to open the bag. The zipper jammed. She tugged at it frantically. It still wouldn't move. Finally with a desperate yank, she pulled it open. Several stacks of hundreds toppled out.

Megan screamed. Hysterically. A wild cry of pain, terror, anguish.

She jumped from the floor and hurled the bag at Neal.

"Bastard!" she shrieked.

"Megan!"

The piles of bills scattered on the concrete floor, like vegetables fallen from a grocer's truck.

"Fucking bastard!"

"Megan." He moved toward her, hoping to embrace her and shake the hysteria out of her.

"Get away from me! You betrayed all of us! You sold us out! You lied!"

"No, Megan. No. You don't understand. Let me explain. Please!"

She stood, as if frozen in place, in the middle of the storeroom floor, the money all about her. Hands over her face, she screamed yet again.

"There's nothing to explain! Go tell the world what you found! Get out!"

"No, Megan. That's not it!"

"Get out!" she wailed. "I never want to see you again! Get out! Leave! This instant!"

Margaret and Mark appeared at the top of the stairs, frightened at their mother's cries of rage.

"Mom . . . Oh my God!"

"We're going to be on the ten o'clock news, a Christmas present from Mr. Connor. Aren't you proud!"

"You have it all wrong. If you'd only let me explain . . ."

Megan didn't want an explanation. Sobbing insanely, she rushed up the stairs and slammed the basement door behind her.

"It's not true, Mark, Margaret," he pleaded. "It's not true."

Ashen-faced, the two young people stared at him, not knowing what to believe.

"The strain on her has been terrible," Mark said tentatively.

"I was afraid she might crack today," Margaret added. "She's been strung out for so long. It's not your fault, Neal."

"I don't know, Margaret; maybe it is. I blew it. But this is not going on the news tonight or ever. I . . . I was trying to help."

"BIG help," the young woman snapped.

"I said I blew it."

"Oh, I'm sorry, Neal." Margaret seemed to crumple. "I don't know what to think anymore. I'd better see what I can do with Mom and the little kids. Mark, help Neal pick up the money."

"Like a good little boy," Mark said lightly.

"We'd better do what we're told, Mark."

"Too right."

They gathered together the bills and stuffed them into the golf bag.

"Joseph said your father was wearing golf clothes," Neal tried to explain. "That's what gave me the idea of looking here. Christmas wasn't the best day, I guess."

"We needed to find it before something happens in court." Mark zipped the bag up. "How much money, Neal?"

"Half million."

"Whose is it?"

"I haven't the faintest idea."

"I believe you, Neal," the big kid said softly. "I trust you. Margaret does, too, but she's torn right now."

"Thanks, Mark. I was a fool for doing it the way I did. She seemed so . . ."

"What should we do with it?" He put the bag in the dryer, a perfect hiding place.

"If your mother calms down, talk her into calling Mr. Curran and telling him. If not, you and Margaret call him. It's dangerous money."

"I understand."

They climbed slowly up the stairs and back to the kitchen. Margaret was fussing desperately over the turkey.

"Neal, I'm not blaming you. Really I'm not. But she's in terrible shape. Maybe we can patch it up later. Not today. I think maybe . . . Oh, God, Neal, I hate to say this. You'll never forgive me."

"No problem, Marge." He rested his hand lightly on her shoulder. "I'll leave quietly."

"Without anything to eat?"

"Without anything to eat."

"I guess you're right. I'm so sorry. . . . She's not like this, Neal, really she's not."

"No way," Mark agreed.

"We'll give her time. Say good-bye to the little kids for me."

"Your bag?"

"I'll get it some other time. My coat and my car keys are in the front closet. I'll let myself out. You get back upstairs to her."

Mark walked him to the door. The Vienna choirboys were singing "Stille Nacht, Heilige Nacht" on the stereo.

"I still trust you, Neal." The big kid extended his hand.

"Thank you, Mark." He shook hands vigorously. "We'll work it out. You try to explain to Teri and Joseph. They'll go to pieces, too, unless you take care of them."

"I will take care of them, Neal. Drive carefully."

Neal shrugged into his trench coat, walked out the front door, and picked his way down the slippery front walk. The rain was a freezing mist. Mark's advice was good: on a night like this, one ought to drive carefully.

An hour ago he thought he had a family of his own with which he would eat a joyous Christmas dinner.

Now, almost without warning and with the best intentions in

the world, he had been thrown out of the house and into the damp winter night.

Why bother to drive carefully?

The pastor himself opened the door of the Cathedral rectory, a book in one hand and an Irish aquamarine tweed shawl hanging around his shoulders, a benign if bewildered leprechaun.

"Neal. Indeed. I thought it would be a hobo."

"You might not be wrong. Are you the only one around?"

"The staff must be permitted to spend the evening with their families. And, in all truth, while I am second to none in my admiration for the Ryan family, there comes an upper limit of noise which no celibate can be expected to survive. Christmas afternoon at the Ryans' and/or the Murphys' is like a high club dance. Only louder. One escapes with gratitude only slightly tainted by guilt. Come up, there may still be some tea, since you do not sip John Jameson's sturdy spirits."

Despite his reckless emotions, he had driven back to the Mayfair Regent without accident or incident—probably, he reflected as he turned the car key over to the doorman, causing great anguish to his guardian angel.

Should there be one such.

Perhaps the angel, like God, had a nasty sense of humor.

That wasn't fair, he had told himself.

"Yes, it is too fair," he muttered half aloud as he rode up in the elevator.

His suite filled him with nausea. Why had he ever come back to Chicago? Why did he go to that thirtieth reunion? Why wasn't he back in the Hindu Kush or some similar place?

Or with Kelly MacGregor in London?

He didn't take off his coat. Instead, he went back to the elevator, rode down to the lobby, strode through the underpass, and as the gray late afternoon turned to a grim misty evening, hiked along the lakefront up to Lincoln Park, then along Clark Street to Fullerton, then to Diversey, and finally to Belmont and Wrigley Field.

His father, a Cub fan although a South Sider, had taken him there to a game once.

He'd seen a few Bears games there, too. Dick Butkus and Gale Sayers.

He turned around and slowly walked back down Clark, lost in his own confused emotions and memories. Somehow he had changed from Clark to State and found himself standing in front of Holy Name Cathedral.

Where he should have come in the first place.

With elaborate care the pastor poured him a cup of tea. Then he disappeared into his bedroom and reemerged a few moments later with a sweatshirt.

"Arrangements should have been made to convey this to the South Side earlier in the day, but our logistics usually break down this time of year. The younger generation seems to have other things on its minds."

Blackie held up a white sweatshirt on which were emblazoned the words NORTH WABASH AVENUE IRREGULARS.

On the reverse side there was displayed a drawing, looking south from the merger of Wabash and State, with the Cathedral spires in the background.

"They are," the little priest continued blandly, "made of moderately high-quality material and ought not to shrink to less than half their present size. Nonetheless, I took the precaution of obtaining for you a double extra large size."

He examined the label at the collar of the sweater, Santa Claus making sure that the elves had not fouled up again.

"I'll treasure it always." Neal doffed his jacket and put on the shirt.

"Yes, it should fit nicely after a couple of washings."

"I assume that only a limited quantity have been made."

"So I am assured by my half sister Trish. Nonetheless, I suspect that every teenaged young woman at Grand Beach next summer will be sporting one, but"—he glanced in bemusement at his watch—"ought not you be celebrating the Yule at the festive board of the Lanes?"

"I was thrown out."

Blackie had gently placed himself in a comfortable position in his easy chair and lifted a Waterford tumbler to his lips.

"What?" He lowered the tumbler.

Neal told him the story.

Blackie leaped from his chair, deposited the whiskey glass on his desk, and shouted, "Damnation!"

"I was kind of surprised—"

"Stupidity, unconscionable stupidity." The priest paid no attention to Neal. "Intolerable stupidity. The brain deteriorates with age, but not this rapidly!"

"Me?"

"Certainly not!" Blackie stopped his pacing and considered him in astonishment. "You did not err"—he jabbed a finger at Neal—"I did."

"You?"

"The woman affects so much self-composure and resilience that one forgets that she is human and has been through sufficient traumas for a lifetime in the space of a few months. All of us should have been there when she opened the money, with explanations and strategies."

"I could have done better."

The priest waved away his objection. "A lover can do only so much. . . . This is all unfortunate, most unfortunate."

"What will happen?"

Blackie sank on to the ottoman in front of his easy chair and recaptured his glass of Jameson's.

"A woman is entitled to one hysterical outburst in her life, is she not?"

"Sure. . . ." But not when I'm the target.

"Still, this is undoubtedly what my sister the virtuous and admirable Mary Kathleen would refer to as a regression, possibly a massive regression. It will require time, I fear. Perhaps a long time."

"And then . . ."

"Much will depend on how you elect to respond to it." The priest sighed loudly. "And you are under no obligation to respond to it at all. The woman, after all, chose to distort your intentions when, hysterical or not, she ought to have known better."

"I thought I wanted to marry her." He had never said it in quite those words before. "Last night and today I began to imagine that she was already my wife." He felt his face turn hot. "I admit, Blackie, that I enjoyed that prospect enormously."

"And now you wonder"—he sighed again—"whether you would in fact be marrying the whole family history of craziness. Make no mistake about it, those were her sisters speaking in her voice."

"I don't know what to think."

"You must make your own decisions. I cannot tell you to discount today's events. They were most unfortunate, most, most unfortunate."

"Megan is only human."

"She strives to be more than human"—the priest pounded the side of his ottoman impatiently—"and persuades us that she is. Hence we are deceived. And then blamed for being deceived."

The phone rang.

Blackie picked it up, changed his facial expression to one of attentive concern, and said, "Cathedral rectory, Father Ryan."

If you had called with any sort of problem, you would already be at least half reassured by the supportive warmth in his voice.

"What?" the little priest exploded. "On Christmas Day?"

He rose from the ottoman, his face red with anger.

"This will surely not go unpunished. . . . Neal? Oh yes, I know where he is—right here in my room. You must speak to him at once. There is another factor that must be considered. The evil spirits are abroad in the land this festive day."

Blackie handed the phone to Neal.

"Neal? This is Nick. You won't believe this, but four carloads of FBI agents appeared at the Lane house late this afternoon, armed with an armful of search warrants. They took every piece of paper in the house. Megan was hysterical. Mark and Margaret engaged in pushing and shoving matches with the FBI and were arrested for impeding the work of a federal agent. The house is a shambles."

"My God!"

"Donny's hardball lawyers have temporarily replaced his softball media consultants. It will be impossible now to prove that some of the papers Tom Dineen gave him were taken beforehand without a warrant. We'll have only Dineen's reluctant admission. It's a slick move in the narrow sense of the word."

"Not when I'm finished with him."

"Precisely, but Donny isn't thinking media right now."

"What's he up to?"

"I think he's going after an indictment next week."

"Megan!"

"She's the only one he can touch. Conspiracy to defraud. Circumstantial evidence. Enough for an indictment perhaps. He might even risk a trial. Juries don't like rich and pretty women."

"My God!"

"He's seized all the papers, so we can't claim that the papers Dineen stole were the grounds for the indictment and plead poisoned fruit. I don't think it will work, but Donny is taking the chance."

"They arrested Mark and Margaret?"

"And dragged them in handcuffs down to the Dirksen Building. On Christmas Day."

"Are they in jail?"

"I think Maynard Leeland, the FBI agent in charge, would have held them overnight in the Federal Correctional Building if I didn't get Ed Meese away from his Christmas dinner. They weren't booked. They're home now with their mother. Catherine is with them. The press is already swarming on their front lawn, murmuring about a 'Christmas Dinner Raid.' They actually pulled the family away from the dinner table. I don't know what would have happened if you'd been there. Even Leeland would have had second thoughts if he'd seen you. Maybe not, though. He is even dumber than Donny."

"He'll regret it, too."

"By the way, why weren't you there?"

"I was thrown out—that's a long story. Nick, did they find the money? The FBI, I mean."

"What money?"

"The half-million dollars in Al's golf bag. Mark hid it in the dryer in the basement."

"Mark? How did he find the money?"

"I found it. How I found it is a long story that you wouldn't believe anyway. I assume the feds didn't find it or they would have been crowing. You figure out what to do with it."

"Did you say a half million?" Nick was shaken. "Whose is it?"

"It may not be anyone's. But a lot of dangerous people think it's theirs. Get it the hell out of there, no matter how hysterical Megan is."

82

Christmas Eve. Morning.

Dear Neal,

I know I'll see you today and tomorrow. But I still want to write to you.

I've never doubted the existence of God. Sometimes, though, like Woody Allen, I think He's an underachiever.

But He's sent you to me as my Christmas present. So I am terribly grateful to Him and to you.

I'll love you always, my surprise in the stocking.

Megan

He tore the letter up and threw the pieces down the toilet.

83

Judge Eileen Mary Ryan Kane studied her fingernails carefully. Doubtless, Neal thought, making sure that her manicure was in keeping with the rest of the perfection of her dress and makeup. One had the impression that even a chip on the clear lacquer would have earned a life sentence for the manicurist responsible.

"Any questions, Mr. Roscoe?"

"No questions, Your Honor. We take the position that the plaintiff has no grounds to seek the relief she requests."

One of Donny Roscoe's brightest assistants was feeding him his lines.

"No grounds, Mr. Roscoe? I find that hard to believe. Surely she seems to have *prima facie* grounds to seek relief. Her lawyer was, after all, a government informant. That would seem to constitute poisoned fruit against your indictment. I am open to persuasion, but you're going to have to persuade me."

"We don't see it that way, Your Honor."

Stonewall, it was called.

"Mr. Dineen, before you leave the stand, let me make sure that I understood correctly your responses to Mr. Whealan's questions. You have testified that at Mr. Roscoe's personal suggestion you removed several cartons of legal and tax papers from Mrs. Lane's home after her husband's death. Is that correct?"

"Well, Your Honor"—Tommy Dineen smiled, convinced that Judge Kane, like all women (as he saw the world), were charmed by his smile—"it was not quite that way. I asked Mr. Roscoe if he would like to see those papers, and he said that they might prove very interesting. So I brought them in."

"And put them on Mr. Roscoe's desk?"

"Yes, Your Honor."

"Oh yes, Mr. Roscoe, I think that there certainly are grounds for Ms. Lane to seek relief."

"If you quash the indictment, we will appeal, Your Honor."

A scarcely veiled threat. Corrupting the attorney/client relationship was surely unethical, Nick had told Neal, but whether it was a sufficiently poisoned fruit to invalidate an indictment was not yet a clear legal principle. A few of the Reagan appointments to the seventh circuit appellate bench could be counted on to overrule almost any decision in favor of defendants. Donny Roscoe's hardball lawyers were willing to gamble on that chance—despite the fact that the evidence against Megan, leaked to the Chicago papers, proved nothing. The media, to the surprise of Roscoe's aides, were on Megan's side, partly because of the horror of the "Christmas Dinner Raid" but mostly because Neal's attack on Roscoe had forced the other media to turn against him.

"It is your privilege to try. Mr. Roscoe. But, once more, I urge you to present your argument in favor of your behavior in this court. An appellate court is likely to mandate another hearing in this court if you do not make your case now."

Eileen Mary Ryan Kane clearly despised Don Roscoe and Maynard Leeland, the FBI agent in charge. But she was leaning over backward not to give them grounds for complaint.

Or, some would say, she was giving them the rope with which to hang themselves.

Judge Kane was skilled at combining her gender with her judicial role. You never doubted for a moment that she was either a woman or a judge.

With Larry Whealan, she became the senior colleague (though she was a few years younger than Whealan), faintly amused by the performance of a talented but mischievous young man. With Donny Roscoe she was the mother superior confronting a boy about to be expelled from the school. With Maynard Leeland and Tom Dineen, she was the tough-minded homemaker confronting two men who had offered to clean her catchbasin. When Neal had slipped into the back of her courtroom and stumbled over a briefcase next to Nick Curran, she had transfixed him with a glare suitable for someone trying to sell pornographic pictures to her children.

The media were not welcome in Judge Kane's courtroom.

Her husband was a columnist, wasn't he?

He'd probably be favored with the same killing glare.

All of these changes of manner were subtle, a curl of a lip, a lifted eyebrow, a flash of sea-green eyes, a finger drummed against the bench, a slight change of voice inflection—nothing that could be reversed on appeal, but still enough to dominate the courtroom.

"She can quash the indictment," Nick whispered in Neal's ear, "if there is valid reason for assuming that evidence obtained in a violation of the attorney/client relationship is inadmissible in a trial. There is no evidence at all against Megan, except for papers in which Al seems to be leaving his secret money to her. So there's two issues: Is the fruit poisoned—does a violation of the relationship ruin the evidence? And is that evidence all Donny has?"

"Can't we get him for corrupting Dineen?"

"One cannot sue the United States Attorney for what he does or says in pursuing an investigation unless he is in clear violation of the law. Violating the lawyer/client relationship is unethical but probably not illegal."

"Stealing papers?"

"Hard to prove right now. But she's a good judge and she knows Donny's way out of line. If she quashes the indictment, the seventh circuit may reinstate it in ten days, but during those days Donny will swing slowly in the wind. Did you see this morning's papers?"

"I did, they're having a field day, aren't they? 'Christmas Dinner Raid!' My line before I could use it. . . . What about the money?"

"Mark came over to my house Saturday afternoon. With the bag. The goons from the FBI didn't think to look in the dryer. His mother didn't care what he did with it. So we have it in a safe in my study. This afternoon it goes into a safe-deposit box at the First Chicago."

"I thought Megan didn't have to come to court."

"She wanted to."

Pale, tiny, taut, Megan was sitting next to Larry Whealan.

"Is she over her hysteria?"

Nick crossed his fingers.

Whealan had toyed with Tom Dineen like a cat with a mouse it plans to kill. Caught between Judge Kane and Don Roscoe, he reluctantly admitted that, yes, he had taken a few unimportant papers from the file of the estate of Alfred Lane and given them to Mr. Roscoe.

"Thus violating the lawyer/client relationship?"

"Objection."

"Overruled. You may answer, Mr. Dineen."

"They were not important papers." Tommy the Clown squirmed.

"That's not an answer." Larry Whealan jabbed a finger at the witness.

"I didn't think of it that way."

"Because you had already been spying on the late Mr. Alfred Lane for the United States Attorney and pilfering papers from him?"

"Objection."

"Mr. Alfred Lane is not a plaintiff in this case, Mr. Whealan."

"I understand that, Your Honor"—Whealan grinned broadly—"but I want to establish that this is not an isolated departure from the path of virtue."

"Very well, you may answer, Mr. Dineen."

"Wow," Nick whispered in Neal's ear. "She's really on our side. We might see some spectacular fireworks before this is over. The virtuous Eileen—as her brother would call her—is one hot volcano when she erupts."

"I can hardly wait."

"I felt it was my duty to help the United States Attorney." Dineen was sweating profusely. "So I did occasionally bring him some documents, yes."

"And on one of those occasions you heard him discuss another case with Judge Forest on the phone in his office?"

"OBJECTION!" Don Roscoe screamed like a pig being castrated.

"Mr. Whealan, really, now. That question might be appropriate in another situation, but is it not terribly distant from the plaintiff's plea for relief?"

"I want to establish, Your Honor, that we are dealing with an intolerable pattern of corruption."

Two very bright lawyers, one a man, the other a woman, sparring with one another and loving it.

"That may be"—the judge frowned, but mildly—"but you are seeking to prove corruption only with regard to the papers of Ms. Lane this morning, and it is hardly necessary to establish the alleged pattern of corruption for that purpose."

"I withdraw the question, Your Honor."

"Thank you very much."

So Don Roscoe's objection, like all his other objections, was not sustained.

At the end of her exchange with Larry Whealan, she turned again to Tom Dineen.

"Mr. Dineen, I want to be quite certain of your testimony before I rule. An occasional paper removed from a client's files may be a violation of ethics, but it hardly constitutes harassment. How many documents did you transfer from the files of the estate of the late Mr. Lane and from the records of his wife"—she glanced at papers in front of her as if she didn't know the plaintiff's name—"Ms. Megan Marie Keefe Lane, to the desk of the United States Attorney for the Northern District of Illinois before his search of the house of Ms. Lane on Christmas night, I believe it was"—she poked through her papers—"on a warrant issued by my colleague Judge Forest?"

All around Neal, reporters were scribbling furiously. The IBC artist was scratching away on her painting of Judge Kane.

Maybe she should wait till the judge blew up.

"A few papers, Your Honor." Dineen squirmed again.

"Surely you can give me a rough estimate. More than ten documents?"

"I think so, Your Honor."

"More than twenty?"

"Probably."

"I see. More than a hundred?"

"Maybe not quite that many."

"I see. . . . Now, gentlemen, I'm ready to hear arguments."

"Your Honor." Roscoe was speaking from his table, an intense younger man feeding words into his ear. "The office of the United States Attorney feels there is little reason to argue. There are no grounds to think that the plaintiff could prevail in a suit against this office. The investigative powers of the federal prosecutor are designedly broad so that he can go about his duties of protecting the laws of our republic with maximum freedom. . . ."

Roscoe paused and snapped at the young assistant, who was obviously not talking slowly enough.

Judge Kane pretended to suppress a mild smile of amusement.

"It may be possible, Your Honor," Roscoe continued, "that at a later date a court will want to rule that we have obtained some evidence illegally. We do not believe that to be the case, but the possibility of such a ruling after a jury verdict is not to be denied. However, a grand jury investigation or a trial ought not to be impeded at this time and in this court. The government, Your Honor," he sounded solemn and patriotic, "is entitled to its day in court."

"I see."

Roscoe was picking up steam. "Moreover, the defendant has made allegations about the investigation being conducted by this office which would not be admitted in a trial hearing. In fact, this whole complaint is irregular and unusual. We think it ought to be summarily dismissed."

"You're suggesting that I ought to have rejected the plaintiff's motion without a hearing, Mr. Roscoe?"

"I am, Your Honor. The very existence of this hearing impedes the work of the United States Attorney."

"Work so important that it must be carried on even during Christmas Day?"

"The laws of the United States must be vigilantly protected, Your Honor."

"I understand."

The press was scribbling even more furiously.

"Mr. Whealan?"

"My distinguished colleague, the United States Attorney for the Northern District of Illinois, seems to think he is above the law, Your Honor. Perhaps he has confused his role with that of the Pope."

Laughter in the court room.

A single authoritative bang of Judge Kane's gavel produced dead silence.

"Really, Mr. Whealan. Such exercises in humor should be saved for the Bar Association entertainments."

"Yes, Your Honor." Larry Whealan strove to sound contrite. "My point is that since the beginnings of common law, shrouded as it is in the dim history of oral traditions, the receiving of stolen goods has been considered a crime as serious as the actual stealing of such goods. Mr. Dineen has testified that he may well have removed a hundred documents from the files of the estate of Mr. Lane and from the records of Ms. Lane and transferred these documents, without a search warrant, to the control of Mr. Roscoe. Does my distinguished colleague really believe that Ms. Lane could not prevail in a civil and/or a criminal action against him? The United States Attorney, Your Honor, is not immune to the requirements of Chapter 38, Article 16-1, of the laws of the State of Illinois."

"That article deals with theft and stolen property, Mr. Roscoe," Judge Kane remarked gently, a Mother Superior explaining the numbering of the Ten Commandements.

"Thank you, Your Honor," Larry Whealan bowed respectfully. "Moreover, Your Honor, all grand jury testimony gathered by the United States Attorney with the aid of Mr. Dineen must be considered poisoned fruit. You know as well as I do that any indictments handed down on the basis of such evidence should be instantly quashed. Finally, the issuance of a search warrant—and the day, Your Honor, is not relevant—by a federal judge against whom certain allegations have been made in this investigation would also weigh in a court's decision."

"Mr. Whealan, really. . . ."

"I withdraw the last sentence, Your Honor, and apologize to the court. My point is that the conduct of this investigation has been so improper that the investigation is now beyond repair. I yield to no one in my admiration for my distinguished colleague's zeal in seeking out criminal behavior in the commodities markets, but in this case the zeal has discredited the investigation. Mr. Roscoe should drop the investigation. If he does not do so, then my client is worthy of relief from further harassment—and certainly from the inconveniences of a circus trial, in which, even if the evidence were not poisoned, there would be no chance of a conviction."

"I see. . . . Mr. Roscoe?"

"We will not drop the indictment, Your Honor. It is too important to respect for law in our country. Young people in Chicago must not be permitted to grow up thinking that commodity traders are above the law. The court must not stand in the way of the efforts by this office to enforce the laws of the United States."

"I understand."

The judge arranged her papers in a neat pile in front of her.

"This is a somewhat unusual matter, though I fear one that might be more common in the years ahead. The lawyer/client relationship, I should think, is almost as sacred as the priest/penitent relationship. The harm done to the legal profession by the routine violation of that sacred trust by prosecutors is incalculable. Does this fact justify the plaintiff's plea for relief from the indictment and from further harassment by the United States Attorney?

"Might a civil suit filed later by the plaintiff win damages against the United States Attorney? Surely there is a possibility of that. Does the United States Attorney have the right to subvert the lawyer/client relationship in pursuit of an investigation? That does seem to me to be a very broad claim. My diligent clerks have been able to find no precedent to support it.

"However, there is the final argument made by Mr. Whealan. There is at least an appearance of dealing in stolen property in this case, an action that goes beyond the rights of the United States Attorney, no matter how broadly these rights might be interpreted.

"I see no reasonable grounds to believe that the government could successfully pursue the indictment against Ms. Lane. I have no choice but to rule that all the papers removed by Mr. Dineen and those removed in the, uh, Christmas Dinner Raid, as I believe it has come to be called, cannot be used in a case against Ms. Lane. The fact that these two sets of papers have been 'accidentally' intermingled suggests only that the United States Attorney and the Federal Bureau of Investigation have certain serious administrative deficiencies.

"Since ALL the evidence against Ms. Lane is in those papers, there seems to be nothing that would sustain the indictment in a trial court. I would also note that even if I were to admit the purloined papers as evidence, I might still have to quash the indictment.

"Therefore, I rule that the indictment is quashed and issue the restraining order requested by Mr. Whealan against the further harassment of Ms. Lane and her family by the United States Attorney and the Federal Bureau of Investigation—on Christmas Day or any other day of the year."

"This order is invalid," Roscoe, ignoring the entreaties of his young assistant, exploded. "We will not be bound by it."

"Invalid?" Eileen Kane contemplated him as she would a new species of insect.

"This office has the right to continue its investigation!"

The gentlepersons of the press were now scribbling with an insane fury.

The network artist was erasing some of her work, trying now to capture the judge just before the volcano erupted.

"You do that, Mr. Roscoe." The judge spoke very softly, so softly that everyone had to lean forward to hear her. "And you, Mr. Leeland. And I'll incarcerate you in the same federal detention center in which you wanted to incarcerate two children on Christmas Day."

"Thank you, Your Honor." Larry Whealan bowed with elaborate Edwardian respect.

"Just a minute, Mr. Roscoe, Mr. Leeland. I have something else to say."

The mitered abbess was now very angry.

The two men reluctantly aborted their hasty exit from the courtroom.

"You are a lawyer, I believe, Mr. Leeland?"

"Yes."

"I didn't quite hear your response."

"Yes."

"Your Honor?"

"Yes, Your Honor."

"I am"—she drummed a single elegant finger on the bench— "going to notify the relevant disciplinary boards concerning your behaviors in this investigation. I must say candidly that I think neither of you are fit to practice law, much less hold offices of public responsibility. Presumably the most that will be done to you is the administration of light slaps on the wrist. The legal profession has yet to face the reality that federal prosecutors are becoming a grave threat, perhaps the gravest threat, to the freedom of all of us."

Her green eyes illumined the whole courtroom. The network artist was dabbing colors wildly. Reporters were bolting for the door.

"Next case," said Judge Kane.

"Well, we win that one." Nick sighed contentedly.

"Now all we have to do is get rid of that damn half million dollars."

"Do you have any comment, Mr. Roscoe?"

"We are going to demand that the indictment be reinstated and appeal this restraining order instantly and—"

"To Judge Forest?"

"To the seventh circuit."

"Do you want to comment on Judge Kane's final words?"

"A woman like her does not belong on the federal bench."

"Mr Whealan . . . Mr. Whealan . . ."

"Yes, Mr. Connor."

"Do you have any comment on Judge Kane's decision?"

"It was wise and prudent, as are all Judge Kane's decisions."

"And her remarks about Mr. Leeland and Mr. Roscoe?"

"I thought they were understated but appropriate."

"Mr. Roscoe just said that Judge Kane is not fit to sit on the federal bench."

"I think that the Bar Association rating of her skills—the highest possible rating, by the way—is a much better indication of how the Chicago bar feels."

"What is your next step, Mr. Whealan?"

"Next? Why, that should be obvious. I'm going to the office of Richard M. Daley, state's attorney for the County of Cook, and swear out warrants for the arrests of Donald Bane Roscoe and Maynard Leeland on the charge of violating Chapter 38, Article 16-1 of the Criminal Code, State of Illinois, a section which, as I'm sure you know, Mr. Connor, deals with the reception of stolen property."

Chicagoans will be disappointed that they will not be able to witness the sight of Rich Daley and sheriff's police coming to the Dirksen Federal Building to arrest the United States Attorney. Late this afternoon, a spokesman for Mr. Roscoe announced that the investigation of the Mercantile Exchange had been "suspended," and therefore there was no need to appeal Judge Kane's rulings.

As a reporter remarked after the announcement, Mr. Roscoe is listening to his media consultants again. Wisely, it would seem from here.

And he obviously does not want to face again the wrath of Judge Eileen Mary Ryan Kane. One can hardly blame him.

The rest of us Chicagoans can sleep a little bit more soundly tonight because such a woman as Judge Kane protects the privacy and freedom of all of us.

Neal Connor, Channel Three News, outside Judge Kane's courtroom.

Another note from Megan.

Neal,

I am so sorry.
Please forgive me.
Please.

Love,
Megan

Again he tore up the note and flushed it down the toilet.

86

"Neal, Joseph has disappeared!"

It was Margaret, calling from Chicago.

"Disappeared?"

"He didn't come home from school this afternoon. Mom's frantic."

"Have you called Mr. Curran or Mr. Casey?"

"Both of them. They say they're doing their best, but they sound worried. . . . Oh, Neal, will it ever end?"

"Does your mother know you called me?"

"Noooo, not really. But please come home and help us. We need you, Neal!"

"I can't do anything that Mr. Curran and Mr. Casey aren't doing."

"Please . . ."

"All right, Margaret. I'll get the first plane out. But don't tell them I'm coming or that you called me."

"I promise."

"Have there been any ransom demands yet?"

"I don't know. I don't think so."

"OK, Marge, keep calm. We'll get him back."

He hung up slowly. Who would it be this time? The Outfit? Lou Garcia? Some totally new actor?

Across his imagination raced images of Joseph—at his computer, working on a model airplane, looking up at Neal with adoring blue eyes, asking if he was really a hero "like Father Ace."

Damn the bastards!

He dialed United Airlines. Flight 363 left at 11:00, arrived in Chicago at 4:39 the next morning. All right, he'd be on the plane.

Then he punched in another number.

"Cos?"

"Yeah?"

"Neal Connor."

"Yes, Mr. Connor."

Instant change. They're still afraid of me.

"I want the kid back. Today."

"We didn't do it, Mr. O'Connor. I swear we didn't do it."

"And you didn't kill Pete Keefe and put out a contract on me?"

"Those were mistakes. Rogue elephants. They wouldn't dare do anything again. Some of them"—faint snigger—"aren't doing anything anymore."

"If you guys didn't do it, then you know who did. I want the kid back or I'll blow the whole Mercantile Exchange caper up all over again."

"We didn't do it. Most likely it was the Garcia family. That Lou Garcia is crazy."

"Are your friends bigger than Lou Garcia?"

"Sure they are," he said proudly. "He's nothing but a punk who's made a lot of easy dough."

"OK, like I say, I want the kid back."

Stir up a war between the Outfit and the Hispanics?

They were going to fight each other anyway.

Neal sighed and stretched out on his bed again. The virus that had plagued him since the day in Judge Kane's court had left him weak, exhausted, and depressed.

The doctor who had seen him warned about the depression and urged him not to make any major decisions for six weeks.

"Six weeks?"

"This bug hangs on."

"Six weeks in my business is a lifetime."

Pompous stupidity. He was beginning to believe the TV news's own press releases.

For a week after the first of the year, he had spent most of the day flat on his back, reading newspapers and Anthony Trollope's fiction—a wonderful cure, he had told Johnny Jefferson, for any viral infection.

He would drag himself over to the IBC Building, put on a thick layer of makeup and smile genially through his anchor role. Then he'd crawl back to the Mayfair Regent, take aspirin and Sudafed, and slip back into bed for ten hours of sleep.

He didn't exactly make a decision to terminate his relationship with the parish and everyone in it. Rather, he did nothing at all about either Megan or the neighborhood, which was as good as a negative decision. He called none of them, they did not call him.

I'm alone and sick in a hotel suite, and none of them even phone me.

That was, he would admit to himself in his better moments,

inexcusable self-pity. They didn't know he was sick. There was not the slightest hint on Channel 3 that Neal Connor was anything but his usual healthy and vigorous self.

"You looked tired, Mr. Connor," Melodi Cain said tentatively one day when their paths crossed in the corridor.

Melodi, like everyone else at the station, was trying to be friendly.

"Only old age catching up, Ms. Cain."

"You're not old, Mr. Connor."

"Old enough to be your father."

"Only if you were a child bridegroom."

Mildly funny line.

Neal did not laugh.

Nothing was funny anymore.

The Lanes had dropped out of the newspapers after a few days of outraged editorials about the Christmas Dinner Raid. Donny Roscoe had recouped his fortunes by launching several drug busts—an action that was about as easy as betting on a horse. Lou Garcia had been arrested on a narcotics charge and promptly released on bond.

The Hispanic Outfit had its own lawyers, too. Irish, and some of them from the neighborhood at that.

Nothing ever changes.

In fairness to the remnants of the North Wabash Avenue Irregulars, it might be argued—and in his less depressed moments Neal did so argue—that they did not want to intrude into his relationship with Megan. They were probably saying that the problem between the two of them was a problem that they had to work out themselves.

At times he was furious at the troublesome little priest. What was the point in having a priest on your case unless he intruded?

Why didn't Megan write so that he could tear up another letter?

Or phone him so he could hang up on her?

But Megan did not call him.

And he did not call her.

The virus proved itself to be an excellent cure for the weaknesses of the flesh, as the retreat masters in high school had called it.

Women did not interest him. On the contrary, their voices reminded him of the sound of a metal-edged ruler being rubbed against a blackboard. He winced and cringed at the sound of a female voice.

Eventually the virus would pass and his normal lusts would return.

Not for the woman who threw him out of the house before Christmas dinner.

Some day in the distant future might see the humor of the incident—out on Hoyne Avenue on his ass as the Vienna choirboys sang "Stille Nacht, Heilige Nacht."

He did bump into Mike Casey once at Michigan and Oak. Mike looked quite pleased with himself, which meant in Neal's judgment that he had either just finished a painting or had just screwed his beautiful wife.

Or both.

Neal envied him—both the craft that was so superior to his and the wife who was so superior to most women.

Rediscovering a wife was doubtless a great kick, so much history between the two of you, all worked out in a furious romp.

Well, I'll never know about that for sure.

"We put the money in a number of CDs," Mike answered the question that Neal had not intended to ask. "We're not sure yet to whom it belongs, if anyone. The government could probably get an order to pick it up, but Donny is gun-shy of the Lanes now. Naturally Megan doesn't want it. We should collect from the insurance company shortly, so you'll be repaid. Probably the money will go into a charitable foundation in Al's honor."

"Appropriate use of the money, I'd say."

"Dineen has become part of the witness protection operation. Disappeared from the face of the earth."

"That's an improvement, I'd say."

"It looks as if all the troubles out there on Hoyne Avenue are over."

"Kids OK?"

"Seem to be."

They chatted briefly and went their separate ways. Clearly the Irregulars had been given their orders to leave him alone.

The troublesome priest was up to something. He ALWAYS was. But now the "something" involved doing nothing at all.

As soon as he had broken the back of the virus, he would consider his future career options. Network wanted him back— Russia and China and maybe another story on Afghanistan as the Russians prepared to desert their own Vietnam.

He didn't find any of those assignments particularly attractive. But he had concluded—despite the physician's advice about making decisions—that he would leave Chicago after his St. Valentine's commitment to Johnny Jefferson ended.

Johnny didn't talk about the subject, but it was pretty clear that he knew the direction in which Neal was leaning.

"Why don't you fly out to San Diego and give us some Super Bowl color. Those folks have gone out of their minds. You call information out there, and they tell you they're the city of Super Bowl XXII."

"People have to be proud of something."

"You've been under the weather, why don't you go out there and do some color stuff and enjoy a bit of the sun. Chicago can be pretty dull in January."

"I don't know, you get used to not seeing the sun."

He came within a hair's breadth of calling Megan and asking her to come with him.

Fortunately reason prevailed.

She would have hung up on him.

Probably.

There was sun in San Diego all right, and some improvement in the virus. But no end to his depression. Or to his resolution to escape from Chicago as quickly as he could.

The Bears contributed to his depression. In subzero cold they had piled up a two-touchdown lead over the Redskins and seemed bound for San Diego. Then in the second half, as Neal watched from his bed, fever mounting, the offensive line forgot to block for Jim McMahon, and the defensive secondary forgot to cover pass receivers.

He told himself in San Diego that he was not really a Chicagoan and hardly a Bears fan. He didn't care about anything. Chicago was a dangerous city, a maelstrom in which you didn't want to get caught.

Now he was flying back into the same maelstrom.

He slept fitfully on the trip from San Diego to Chicago and again in the cab bringing him back to the Mayfair Regent.

He threw off his clothes and jumped into bed for a few more hours of sleep before trying to figure out what he would do to reclaim Joseph.

I'll get him back, Al. Count on it!

Before he could sleep the phone rang.

"Hey, *amigo*, welcome home."

"Lou."

"Look, *amigo,* I don't want to kill the kid, huh? But I do want that money, all of it. It belonged to my brother, so now it belongs to me, huh?"

The laughter was that of a madman. Lou Garcia was crazy, probably always had been. He'd fooled Neal completely. Give him the money, and he'd kill Joseph anyway. He was crazy to kill.

Maybe even his parents . . .

"I don't have the money."

"I know you don't, *amigo.* But you can tell them that I don't joke. And after I slit the throat of the little boy, I carve up the tits of his mother, too. They're not much, I know. But you like them and so does she, so we slice them up a little, huh? Is a half million dollars worth that, huh?"

"No, Lou, it isn't. I'll see what I can do."

"No one has heard a word from him," Mike Casey frowned. "He's enjoying the suspense, trying to break down our resistance."

"The call to me was the first shot in his barrage. He's crazy and he's dangerous, Mike, very dangerous. Joseph might be dead already."

"That's always a possibility."

"What about the police and the FBI?"

"Maynard Leeland? He'd seal the kid's death warrant in the first five minutes. Some of my friends in the department know about it. All they can do is watch and wait."

They were seated in Mike's "studio" at the back of the Reilly Gallery on Oak Street, eating a lunch of ham and cheese on croissant and drinking apple cinnamon tea.

"What's with Garcia?"

"The word is out on the street that he flipped out after his brother's death. Began using some of his own products. Everyone wants him dead—the Outfit, the remnants of his own family, the other drug families, some of the Colombian giants with whom he's been doing business. Lou Garcia, everyone says, is *loco*."

"You suspected him all along in this kidnapping?"

"He's the obvious choice. A half million dollars doesn't mean much to him—the cost of bribing a federal judge—but he's turned it into a matter of personal honor. Crazy, but like they say, he's *loco*.

"There's a teenage hooker, good-looking and I'd say very high priced, who was mixed up with both him and Rickie. Called María Anunciata. I think she's the one who used to phone Megan. Scared but probably not evil, not yet. Maybe you can pick her up. Let me talk to her, not the real cops."

Mike raised a silver eyebrow. "We might have to guarantee her protection."

"Can we promise that?"

"Sure. It costs money, but not a lot. Does she like being a hooker?"

"I don't think so."

Neal wandered over to the IBC studios and into Johnny Jefferson's office.

"Back so soon?"

"Some loose ends to clean up. I'll go back for the Super Bowl, if you want."

"What you want is what I want. . . . You want to go out to Thatcher Woods? Then that's what I want, too."

"What's Thatcher Woods?"

"Forest preserve out on the West Side. Desplaines River. Just west of River Forest."

"River Forest?"

"West Side Irish."

"Worst kind. Why should I want to go out there?"

"You didn't look at the news wire when you came in?" Johnny pushed a flimsy beige sheet of paper across his desk. "The old news hound is losing his touch."

"No more zeal." He picked up the sheet. "Good God!"

"Right. Four Outfit soldiers cut down in a gun battle, cocaine all over the place. Automatic-weapon fire. Probably in the middle of the night with silencers on Uzis and AR-15s. No one on the River Forest side of Thatcher Road heard the shooting. If one of them hadn't lived long enough to crawl out on the highway and stop a patrol car, the bodies would have been buried in last night's snow till a thaw."

"Internal fight?"

"Maybe. Maybe with the Brothers or even the Hispanics. This is an ethnic city, as you know. Even crime is divided on ethnic lines."

"The Brothers? I thought you fellows were following our example and making your money off politics."

"I don't think our kind goes for massacres, to tell the truth. This sounds like the St. Valentine's Day massacre all over again."

"St. Valentine's Day?"

"When Capone wiped out the Bugs Moran mob. There were seven then, instead of four."

"Yeah, I remember now." Neal rose from his chair. "OK, Johnny, I'm on my way to Thatcher Woods."

"Keep your head down."

Deep in snow and ice, this section of the affluent West Side suburb of River Forest looks like a Danish village perhaps or an elfin city in the Black Forest. It is hard to imagine mass murder taking place here last night while the snow was falling. Yet right across this street, only two blocks away from Rosary College, a gangland battle occurred around midnight which old Chicago hands are comparing to Al Capone's legendary St. Valentine's Day massacre of a half century and more ago.

Strange, is it not, that the patron saint of romantic love should be identified with a bloody crime. Stranger still that the similar crime which took place last night might also be named after the Saint, though his feast, as I remember my grammar school religion classes, is a month away.

There is a multitude of clues across the street, tire marks, spent automatic-weapon ammunition, unopened packets of cocaine. State and county police speculate that a drug deal—a very big one—was going down. The Outfit, which has mixed emotions about trading in drugs, was taking advantage of a particularly lucrative deal offered them by one of the Hispanic drug families.

Something went wrong, either by design or chance, and the out-gunned Mafia soldiers were wiped out in a few seconds.

The police probably know who the criminals are. But that does not mean they have now or ever will have any proof. A half century ago everyone knew that Al Capone had ordered the liquidation of the Bugs Moran gang. Despite that knowledge, that massacre went unpunished. Nothing has changed sufficiently in Chicago crime to think that there will be punishment of last night's crime, either. Only Capone kills this way, they said in the nineteen twenties. Only Lou Garcia kills this way, they are saying today.

It does not follow that Luís "Lou" Garcia will be arrested, tried, and punished. In fact, no one seems to know where he is.

The question that worries police authorities today—though you won't get them to admit the worry or even acknowledge its existence—is whether the Mob, the Outfit, the Syndicate, the Mafia, La Cosa Nostra, call it what you want, will take this liquidation of one of their squads quietly.

The Outfit, Chicago's favorite term, has had its share of troubles lately. Most of its elderly godfathers are in federal prisons. The younger bloods are jockeying for position in the struggle for succession, especially should the godfathers live long enough to die natural deaths. Will either group sit still for this insult to its honor?

If the Outfit decides in sessions which are surely taking place today, in the usual back rooms of restaurants here in the western suburbs, that it wants vengeance for the blood of its slain comrades, then the Chicago area will face a gang war which will make Al Capone look like a gentle neighborhood comic by comparison.

Neal Connor, Channel Three News, River Forest, Illinois.

"We're not going to hurt you, María Anunciata," Mike Casey said soothingly. "And we're not going to let Lou hurt you, either."

"He's *loco*," the frightened young woman insisted. "Pretty soon he kill everyone."

"You're an intelligent young woman, María." Neal tried to sound soothing. "And you obviously don't like being a hooker."

"I hate it," she spat out. "He makes me do it because he thinks it's funny to make me do something I hate. He is so *loco* you can never tell what he will do. Sometimes I am his sister, sometimes his wife, sometimes his mistress, sometimes his property to sell on the street."

She was wearing a sweat shirt and jeans and—except for her big brown eyes, which were as old as sin—looked even younger now than Teri Lane.

They were sitting in the bedroom of a nondescript bungalow near Midway Airport. A couple of Mike's men lounged around in another room. Some innocent-looking dark cars were at various places down the street. Even to a keen-eyed observer, nothing said "safe house."

Mike Casey reported that Garcia had now made two calls to Megan, tormenting her with warnings of what he would do to Joseph and then to her daughters and herself if she didn't give him the money. Still no instructions about where to leave the money.

What if the *loco* Lou Garcia should show up at this safe house with his Uzi-toting friends?

Probably Mike Casey's friends were ready for that eventuality, too.

Which did not make Neal's throat any less dry or his heartbeat any slower.

It was a lot safer in the Hindu Kush.

"Do you want to be someone else's property all your life?"

"No way! I want to belong only to myself!"

"We'll give you another chance, María," Neal continued to coo. "A new name, a new place to live, a family to take care of you, a chance to go back to school, even to college, if you want."

"It is too late for me, Señor Neal. You know that. I am spoiled."

"We can unspoil you, María."

"He will find me and kill me anyway. He say, 'María Anunciata, you will not die rapidly like Rickie. You will die very slowly. You will beg me to let you die. And I will spit on your face and piss on your wounds.' He will do that, señor, he will do that. He will kill everyone."

"We won't let him kill you, María."

"Ha, Señor Neal, he fool you once, he fool you again. He fool everyone, even himself. He's *loco*."

"He won't fool Mr. Casey here."

"He fool everyone. Always. No one escapes from Luís. No one."

Luís would have to escape from the Outfit, which was almost certainly searching for him now.

"Tell us about him, María," Mike Casey took over the questioning. "Did he kill his parents?"

"He kill everyone. He imagine they want to kill him. Poor Rickie, he was a nice quiet boy, never kill anyone. He does not want to sell drugs. He try to make some money so we can run away. Señor Alfredo, he has the money and he dies. We try to get the money from his wife. She no give it to us. Rickie will not even let me threaten her. Poor Rickie . . ."

The girl was sniffling. Gently Neal put a tissue in her fingers.

"Did Luís kill Señor Alfredo?"

"No. Señor Pete Keefe was going to do that, but Señor Alfredo had his accident first. He was a good man, no good in bed but not cruel like Señor Dineen."

"I see."

"Luís follow me home from school every day. He promise me gifts if I go to bed with him. I was a virgin, Señor, a good girl. I was, really. He knows I am an illegal. He says he will send all our family back to Mexico. Still I say no. Then he kidnaps me, shoots me with cocaine, and makes love to me." She shrugged her shoulders indifferently. "Nothing is left."

"Did he hook you on cocaine?"

"No, he beats me whenever I ask for it. So I'm lucky I get over it quickly. Sometimes he is very nice to me, gives me presents, treats me very gently, says that he will get rid of his wife and marry me. Then he gives me to men in the store and watches them rape me. It is terrible."

The girl wanted to cry, but there was too much despair in her soul for grief to be possible.

"Rickie see me and he likes me. He is so gentle and sweet. Lou notice and he gives me to Rickie for a birthday present. Then he takes me back from Rickie and calls me a whore and beats me every day till I am covered with bruises. I want to die. I want to die quickly because otherwise he will torture me to death. Then he kills Rickie and I run away. But he will find me like you did, and he will kill me, so slowly that I will beg him to kill me."

"I don't have a daughter, María Anunciata, and I probably never will have one. But when this is over, I'll make you my daughter and give you another life. This I promise."

The enormity of the promise shocked the girl. She studied him carefully, the way Megan did.

"You are a very good man, Señor Neal, but Lou will kill you, too. Still, I think I know where he holds the little boy. Maybe you kill him and I live a little while longer, huh?"

"I only want the little boy back, María, but I promise you I will not let him hurt you."

He had no idea how the hell he was going to keep the promise.

"There is a house in Indiana, near Bass Lake, a farm on the road to Culver, off Highway 35, on Highway 10. It is his most safe house. Only Rickie know about it, and Rickie tell me. It's on a farm two miles from the lake. It's called 'Taunton' on the mailbox."

Neal motioned Mike Casey into the other room.

"She's telling the truth?"

"No doubt about it. Did you mean your promise?"

"Sure. I have a place to send her, in Tucson, people who will take good care of her."

"Then let's get her out of town in a hurry."

They went back to the bedroom. María Anunciata had slumped against the pillows, still trying to cry.

"María, I have friends in Tucson, Mexican-American like you. Good friends. If I tell them, 'Love this girl I'm sending you like your own daughter,' they will do so. But I don't want to break their heart or yours. You must promise to stay with them, let them take care of you, do what they tell you to do, until I say you are old enough to decide on your own. That will be hard to do, but I think if you give your word to me, you'll keep it."

The girl sat up straight on the bed, eyes wide.

"Truly, Señor Neal?"

"Truly."

"Then I promise. I swear on the Bible, I swear on my mother's honor, I swear by all—"

"A promise is enough. One of Mr. Casey's friends will take you to the airport. My friends will meet you in Tucson. I will phone you every day."

"I will be a good girl, Tío Neal. I will. I promise."

Neal called the Hernandezes in Tucson and briefly told them he was sending them a new daughter for whom to care. They were delighted. Then he made a reservation for her on the late-afternoon flight to Tucson.

Shyly she hugged him, promised again she would be a good girl, and left for her new life.

"I'm impressed, Neal."

"Goddamn altruist. Do you think she'll make it?"

"Better than even odds."

"I think so, too. Now one more call to the studio." He dialed the number. "Connor here. Give me John—" Before he could finish the sentence, Johnny was on the line.

"Neal?"

"Johnny."

"Yeah, I told them to put you through as soon as you called. What the hell is going on?"

"What do you mean?"

"A guy named Cos something has been calling you, like he's scared half to death. Who the hell is he?"

"A member of the parish, oddly enough. Did he leave a number?"

"Yeah, hell, it's a Beverly number."

"Thanks, Johnny, trust me and I'll promise you a hell of a story."

Mike Casey raised an eyebrow. "What's happening now?"

"I think there's going to be a Götterdämmerung tonight near Bass Lake," Neal said as he dialed Cos Ventura's number. "You guys better stay out of it."

"Are you crazy?"

"OK, Cos," he barked into the phone. "Let's have it. All of it and quick."

"You still driving that Hertz Taurus, number HZ three one two nine?"

"You got it."

"OK. There's a safe conduct for you and you only. My friends don't want a dead kid on their hands. You pick up the kid and they'll let you out. Otherwise, the kid goes with the rest of them."

"Taunton house near Bass Lake, I presume?"

"Geez, you know everything. I told them you'd find it out. Let me warn you that not everyone wants to give you the chance. They say what's one more dead kid?"

"Do they?"

"But I and my friends say you don't fuck around with this guy Connor. You do him a favor, and maybe he owes you one back, nothing illegal mind you, just maybe a favor someday."

"No deals."

"No deals, no way."

"OK, what time does it go down?"

"Ten-thirty tonight. You bring a camera, get some shots, no one minds, huh? Sends a message, know what I mean?"

"I sure do."

Even the Outfit worries about its media image.

"You're crazy." Mike Casey jammed his hands in his jacket pockets. "Stark raving mad."

"Can you think of a better way of doing it?"

"I guess not. Any messages for anyone?"

Neal thought about it.

"No. No messages."

The moonless sky was clear and studded with a million stars. Highway 10 had been plowed, but snow had drifted back across it. The patches, deceptively innocent in his headlights, had frozen to the road as the temperature plunged toward zero.

There was little wind, which made the wind-chill factor more benign than it might have been.

But, as Neal told every weather person who would listen to him, he didn't believe in the wind-chill factor. Cold was cold.

He had left Mike Casey and two of his men at the Holiday Inn at Laporte (a few miles south of an exit on the Indiana Toll Road). "I'll be back in a couple of hours with Joseph. Don't worry about me."

"Who worries about crazy men who think they're invulnerable?"

"Last time, Mike, I promise."

He navigated carefully down Highway 35 to its intersection with Highway 10—an empty crossroad surrounded by snow-covered farm fields—and then turned left toward the small resort community that huddled around Bass Lake, a summer island in the midst of the ocean of farm country, a resort which had existed since before the Civil War.

He drove slowly through the town of Bass Lake, as deserted under its blanket of snow as an Arizona ghost town. The good citizens would have much to talk about on the morrow.

The homes looked, indeed, as if they too had been built before the Civil War, a set for a film in which the Union army marched off to fight, singing "The Battle Cry of Freedom."

Neal thought about the ghosts that might lurk in the town and then banished such images from his mind. This was not a night for romantic fantasy. There was quite enough real-life adventure going on.

Behind the town, the frozen lake gleamed dully, reflecting the street lights along its deserted shore. Somehow it looked ominous. Was that where the bodies would go after the firefight?

Pleiku all over again. No Tran this time. Only the Minicam on the seat next to him.

Outside the town about a mile, he encountered a car parked halfway across the road. He applied the brakes gently so that he would not skid.

A man in a thick overcoat and a ski mask approached him, flicked a flashlight beam on his license plate, and then walked up to the window on Neal's side of the car, motioning him to lower it.

"All right, Mr. Connor," he said with infinite respect, "we've been expecting you."

"Where do I go?"

"The third mailbox on the left. You drive in, park next to the tree, and wait there. When it's safe, we'll let you go into the house. OK?"

He could have been a vice president in a bank, he talked so smoothly.

"I can take pictures?" He gestured at his Minicam.

"Sure, that's the idea. But if you get out of the car before we tell you, we can't be responsible for what happens to you."

"Never fear."

The man chuckled softly. "You can go ahead from here when I say so. Not before."

He pulled a walkie-talkie out of his coat pocket and gestured with it.

They'd come a long way since Al Capone.

Probably some of the Outfit soldiers had fought in 'Nam. They would know the tactics for a night raid. Garcia, who doubtless also thought he was invulnerable, probably was not prepared for an attack. A smart CO would have pickets on the road and patrols roaming the fields.

"Looks like they're not expecting us," he said to the Outfit soldier, who was still standing next to his car, shivering in the cold night air.

"No military training. Not worth a damn. This is going to be a piece of cake."

"Yeah." Neal's throat was very dry again.

The man's breath was freezing on the air. Bitter cold, almost zero by now.

Neal didn't feel the cold yet. Not scared. Not much!

He thought of Megan and realized how much he loved her.

"OK, sir." The gunman was now a second lieutenant, receiving orders from a higher officer. "You may proceed to that oak tree. Turn off the ignition. Please do not leave the car until you are instructed to do so."

"No way. Carry on."

He put the Ford back into gear, crept down the road, turned the corner and inched through the snow to the massive oak tree inside the open gate.

The farmhouse was outlined against the sky, a dark, two-story, nineteenth-century hulk against the stars, with a window on the first floor and another on the second floor dimly lighted. Garcia's look-outs.

Dummy, he should be guarding the gate and the highway. He was probably so certain that no one knew about the house that he thought it was unnecessary to protect his perimeter. But that was stupid. Nothing was ever that secret. If María knew, then others knew.

It was not clear, however, that Lou Garcia wanted to stay alive.

Neal unlimbered the Minicam and pointed it toward the house. There was another dark shape to the right of the house. A barn probably. He moved the camera gently in that direction. It had been a long time since he'd been his own cameraman.

He put on the earphones, adjusted the sound controls, and waited. The mike was picking up small noises—creaking trees and perhaps stealthy footsteps. He turned the camera on. No point in missing the first shots.

How would they account to the police for the presence of a camera at the shootout? An anonymous caller. Could not reach the local police in time. Something of the sort.

Or maybe the tape was dropped off at the studio by an unidentified visitor. Better.

Then the silence was fractured by sounds of battle. Angola, Afghanistan, Vietnam all over again.

The barn exploded in a burst of incandescent white light. Someone had fired a rocket into it. Tracer bullets, red and white gashes in the night, leapt from fields and converged on the house.

M-16s? Uzis? AK-47s? He couldn't identify the sounds anymore.

As he watched, the walls of the house seemed to crumble and disintegrate. How could anyone survive inside?

What chance did a twelve-year-old boy have in such an inferno?

There was some brief answering fire from the house. It died out quickly.

Then just as suddenly as it had started, the sound of battle died. How long? A half minute at the most. Thousands of rounds of ammunition. A fiery end for the Garcia family.

The house itself was smoldering rubble, miraculously not on fire yet. Next to it, the barn flared like a midsummer bonfire in Sweden, illumining the snow-covered fields.

How soon would the local police arrive on the scene? If they were smart, they would stay away and call for help.

A clatter of gunfire stretched out from the house. Someone still alive inside.

Instantly the roar of battle began again. Angry tracers tore into the house and ripped most of what remained to pieces.

Dear God, keep Joseph alive!

"All right, Mr. Connor, you may go forward now. Exercise extreme caution. Some of them may still be alive. The kid is in the basement. He has been drugged and is asleep."

Neal had flicked off the camera at the first sound of a voice. So his name probably was not on the tape. He'd check it back in Laporte.

He placed the Minicam on the front seat, ducked out of the car, and rushed toward the smoking house.

A picket line of men in flak jackets were closing in carefully on it. One of them kicked open the front door. Two others rushed in, their automatic weapons ready to fire.

No one waited inside for them.

"Must have got all the fuckers," someone muttered. "Serves them right."

"Too bad Garcia wasn't here."

"He's a dead man anyway. We'll get him, too."

So Garcia had escaped.

They must have had moles in his gang if they knew where Joseph was and that Garcia wasn't there.

Inside the ruined house, brightly lighted by the blazing barn, a cloud of dust hung like a fine mist.

"Basement door that way," someone said to him.

Neal kicked the door open.

"No one down there. Don't worry. Hurry up. There's a propane tank somewhere, this place could go up any second."

Neal rushed down the stairs. The basement was nothing more than an unfinished concrete box, gray in the light from the nearby fire. He looked around. No sign of a sleeping kid. Damn, he'd forgot to bring a flashlight.

"Anyone got a light?" he yelled up the stairs.

A man in a ski mask appeared at the head of the stairs and flashed a powerful beam around the corners of the basement. The light came to rest on a pathetically small figure, its head propped up against the wall, the rest of its body resting on an old mattress.

Neal rushed to its side, put his hand on the figure's chest, and breathed a quick, happy sigh of gratitude. The chest was moving up and down, not very vigorously perhaps, but definitely moving.

He snatched Joseph up in his arms, just as he had picked up the boy's mother three decades before. He weighed no more than she had.

Out of the corner of his eye, he saw a streak of flame move across the floor.

He bumbled up the steps and into the ruins of the house.

"Fire downstairs," he said. "Better evacuate double quick."

The three men who were still in the ruins bolted out the front door after him.

Joseph somehow seemed heavier. Neal's feet were dragged down by the deep snow. Behind him he heard sizzling noises. The men were shouting warnings to one another.

It would take until Judgment Day to reach his car, safely behind the oak tree. The propane would go up any moment.

He prayed again, inarticulately but fervently.

Somehow they made it to the car. He dumped the unconscious Joseph into the front seat, grabbed his Minicam, pointed it at the house, and pressed the button.

Just then the propane tank went up. The force of the blast staggered Neal against the oak tree, but he kept shooting. Tran would be proud of me. End of the Garcia family. And as the Outfit soldier had said, Garcia was already a dead man, for all practical purposes.

Maybe had always been a dead man.

Neal drove east toward Culver and then up Highway 17 to Highway 30. Next to him Joseph stirred uneasily, beginning to wake up.

Don't worry, kid, we'll have you safely in your bed on Hoyne Avenue before the sun comes up.

A little more exciting than pulling your mother out of a house.

But not quite as much fun.

Neal met her in front of the Reilly Gallery on Oak Street, where she was working one day a week, as she'd told him on the phone. Two other days were spent, she informed him although he hadn't asked, at the new Huron Street gallery.

"I need a date," she had said briskly, when she called.

"Oh."

"A sixtieth birthday party out in River Forest. Dr. Maggie Ward Keenan. The famous psychologist. Heard of her?"

"Everyone has."

"She's a good friend of the Ryans. Mary Kate especially. They expect me to come. Black tie. Oak Park Country Club."

"I'm supposed to pick you up at your house?"

"Oh, no, at the gallery. I'll bring my car."

Only two more weeks in Chicago. What harm would one date do? Besides, the virus had killed his sexual appetites, possibly forever.

The tape of the firefight at Bass Lake, which he narrated, was a sensation. The police departments of two states, several counties, and the federal government were all incensed that the tape was shown.

IBC News said the public had a right to know.

Neal speculated on the air that the Syndicate had sent the tapes as a warning to those who started gang wars.

The New York Times reported that Luís Garcia was in Colombia under the protection of a powerful drug baron.

The FBI assured everyone that Garcia was under constant surveillance, a guarantee that made Neal uneasy.

No suspects were arrested in either the shootout at Thatcher Woods or the firefight at Bass Lake. Two of the seven men from the Garcia family escaped the latter, Luís Garcia and Oscar Lopez.

Neal was sure that the latter was the Mob's mole inside the Garcia family.

Count up the casualties—Rickie Garcia, Peter Keefe, Keefe's killer, maybe a couple of men who had ordered the elimination of Pete and the attempted killing of Neal Connor, four Outfit soldiers, five members of the Garcia family—all in all somewhere between fifteen and twenty.

Tom Dineen was in hiding, protected by the federal government.

Megan would collect her insurance money. Nick Curran would bring him the check without comment—the Irregulars were still not intruding.

The money from the golf bag would go to a foundation to help needy black students attend college.

He spoke with María Anunciata every day. At first she was unhappy, bored with Tucson and uncomfortable in the Carmelite high school that she was attending.

Then she changed completely, as young people do. She loved her new family, her new school, her new friends.

"*Tío* Neal, we're number one!" she exulted one day on the phone.

"Salpointe?" He thought she meant her high school.

"No! The Wildcats!"

"Northwestern?"

"UA, we won the Great Alaskan Shootout. We're the best in the country!"

"Wonderful!"

So maybe she had a chance.

What did it all mean?

As far as Neal could see, it all meant nothing.

Except that a little boy was alive who otherwise might be dead.

And a young woman saved from the streets. Maybe. Probably.

And he was getting out of Chicago and back to some safe, dull place like the border between Chad and Libya as fast as he could.

Was it immoral for him to accompany the attackers at the Battle of Bass Lake?

He thought of asking Monsignor Ryan, but then decided that he wanted to continue to avoid that troublesome priest, who was also pointedly ignoring him.

He could not have stopped the raid even if he'd wanted to. If he had tipped off the local police or the Indiana State Police, the only result would have been dead cops.

His goal had been to save a little boy caught in the crossfire between crazy killers and cautious, conservative killers.

Her Mercedes was parked on the fourth floor of the lot behind the "Bloomingdale Building."

"How are the kids?" He opened the car door for her.

"Fine. Settled down pretty much, thank heaven."

She was dressed for a formal party, white dress, low-cut in front and, he guessed, strapless underneath her mink. A band of pearls at her throat.

"Joseph?"

She hesitated. "You know about him?"

"Surely."

"He's all right. They drugged him as soon as they took him away. It's mostly just a terrible nightmare."

"Is he seeing Doctor Murphy?"

"Mr. Doctor Murphy. For a few times. Mr. Doctor says he'll be fine in a few more weeks. I'm still seeing Mrs. Doctor Murphy."

"Ms."

"That's right, 'Ms.' And I'm riding the exercycle every day. I like it, actually."

"Good."

"And taking piano lessons."

"A paragon of virtue."

"Not really." She paused. "Making up for lost time."

She was feeling her way toward making peace with him. He did not want to make peace. He wanted only to escape from this crazy city.

"Were you at Bass Lake?"

"Just because I narrated the story?"

"You sounded like you were there. You saved Joseph, didn't you?"

"I'd better not say anything about that tape."

"Have it your way. Thanks, however."

He did not reply.

"There is a certain symmetry, isn't there?"

"Symmetry?"

"Mother, father, child—you saved them all."

"Father?"

"From the man with the broken bottle?"

"Where did you hear that story?"

"You asked me about it, remember?"

"I guess I do."

"I am grateful for whatever you did to bring Joseph back to me."

"I can't talk about it, Megan."

"All right."

But it wasn't all right, not at all.

Why didn't he want gratitude?

Because gratitude was a trap, that's why.

They sparred verbally all the way to the country club, which was only a few blocks north of the site of the Thatcher Woods Massacre, as it was now called.

He'd be in England on his way to Russia before St. Valentine's night. Father Ace would lose his bet.

Oak Park Country Club looked like a castle in St. Petersburg at the height of the Tsars.

"Isn't this the kind of party at which a poor kid like me should be pressing his nose against the windowpane?"

"The West Side Irish"—Megan shook her head in resignation—"have more class than we do, but we're more loyal."

"Can you tell the difference by looking at them?"

"Of course. Just like Belfast."

Maggie Ward Keenan was a pretty, piquant woman—a Megan in fifteen years. Her husband, a big man with white hair, seemed inordinately pleased with her. And himself for having married her.

The Ryans were everywhere.

"You need not have withered so much, Mr. Connor," said Judge Kane.

"I get the same look when I dare to enter her courtroom," said her husband, Red Kane, the columnist.

"And I love him usually. . . . Even my little boy calls it my media look."

All the men seemed happy with their wives.

And all the wives were gorgeous.

Music, dancing, laughter, handsome men, beautiful women.

No, not St. Petersburg. Dublin, maybe at the time of George Fríderic Handel.

Especially beautiful was the woman who was his wife again for the taking. Megan's gown was indeed strapless. She looked exquisitely lovely, a newly finished and cleverly scented and cunningly erotic porcelain doll, an effect which no doubt had been carefully calculated. She probably was using the exercycle every day. Megan would approach fitness with the same logical consistency with which she approached everything.

The virus that had protected him for several weeks suddenly deserted him, frightened off perhaps by the sight of the tops of Megan's fondly remembered breasts. Every motion of her body inflamed him, just as it used to. Would this date end the way the first one had?

It was her car. Would they drive out to Beverly after they left the party? He discovered that he was hoping they would.

I still want you, Megan. You're an incurable disease.

God help him, he still loved the woman. He knew that there could be no future between them, that they would only hurt one another, but still, if there were any chance . . .

There wasn't and that was that.

He was introduced to a tall, striking, beautiful young woman with dark skin, named Diana Clarke. Her husband, it was explained, was flying in from a deal in San Jose.

"He's a venture capitalist, would you believe." She grinned, complacent in their love.

"How are the kids?" Megan asked eagerly.

"Just wonderful. Each of them has a personality that's completely different from the others. It's so much fun to watch them adjust to one another."

"Others?" Neal asked.

She held up three fingers. "Triplets."

"You don't seem unhappy."

"It's wonderful! I love it. God couldn't have been nicer to me."

She seemed to mean it.

"What are your plans?" Megan asked.

Diana shrugged her gorgeous bare shoulders. "Take care of my husband and my kids and my golf game, in roughly that order. Maybe I can beat you at Grand Beach this summer, Neal Connor."

"That would be an interesting possibility. What's your handicap?"

"It was three before my little friends got started. Now it's up to eight."

"I'd be scared." Neal gulped.

"So's my husband." She laughed affectionately.

"Interesting woman," Neal said to his date.

"I saw the way you looked at her boobs."

"Can you blame me?"

" 'Course not. She's spectacular."

It was still being assumed by everyone that he would still be in Chicago next summer. Diana Clarke was certainly some kind of adjunct member of the Irregulars.

"I'll drive," she said when he and Megan left the party early. "You can hardly keep your eyes open. Flu still bothering you, obviously."

"I guess I need a vacation. I'll drive."

"No, you won't," she said firmly. "Give me the keys."

"Damn it, woman, I SAID I would drive."

"I won't get in the car unless you give me the keys."

He gave her the keys.

"What's this street?"

"Harlem Avenue."

"Can't you use the Congress Expressway?"

"Eisenhower."

"Not to Democrats. . . . Why don't you take it downtown."

"Damn it, this is a north/south street that takes us to the Congress."

"Hey, you ran that red light."

"It was yellow."

"I don't like this street, it's too dark."

"Do you want to get out and walk?"

They stopped at the next light even though it was green.

"Satisfied?" she snapped.

He leaned over and kissed her, an angry, assaulting kiss. She joined the passion only at the end.

"Satisfied?"

"No. . . . The light is green again."

The first date had ended in bed. If this one finished in the same place, it would be angry, punishing lust.

I might not mind, he thought, knowing all the while that he would.

They drove down the Eisenhower in silence.

"What's this place?" he demanded as she turned off the expressway.

"It's the lower level of Wacker Drive. Haven't you ever seen it before? I'm taking you to your hotel."

"I thought I was driving you home."

"We'll just bicker."

"We're not bickering."

"Yes, we are. Now we're bickering about the lower level of Wacker Drive."

"What's it for?"

"For taking a shortcut across the Loop to your hotel."

"Couldn't you take Michigan Avenue?"

"This is quicker. What's wrong with it?"

"Those green lights and arches make it look like a road in hell."

"Red Kane calls it a tributary to the River Styx. Claims that you can meet Charon here at night."

"We won't meet anyone else. . . . Oh, God, Megan, I'm sorry for complaining. I don't know what's wrong with me."

"Nothing is wrong with you, Neal. We've just learned how to fight, which you didn't think was possible with me. So we're fighting about meaningless things because we don't want to fight about important things."

"My fault."

"STOP saying that. It's my fault. I've been acting like a bitch on wheels ever since Christmas. You were absolutely right about the money. I don't know why I let myself get so upset about it. Weariness and grief, I guess, and self-disgust for not figuring it out myself. You just happened to be the first available target. Guilt, fear of intimacy, God knows what else. I hope you forgive me, Neal."

He had done everything he could to forestall her request for pardon.

Candid and direct as always, Megan had outmaneuvered him. Doubtless with the help of Mary Kate Murphy's psychiatric vocabulary.

"Sure, I— Hey, look out!"

A car careened alongside of them and pushed them toward the oncoming lane.

Megan held the wheel firmly, accelerated the Mercedes and pulled ahead of the other car, a dark, late-model Olds.

"Dummy," she snapped. "Probably drunk."

The Olds raced ahead of them in the left lane, pulled back in their lane and slowed.

Megan slammed on her brakes. "They're trying to kill us!"

The lead car veered to the right to let Megan pass, and she raced ahead of them. The Olds speeded up just as the two cars turned the corner and headed east along the Chicago River.

This time they hit the Mercedes broadside, jamming it into the opposite lane. Megan now gave the Mercedes all the speed it had and roared away from their pursuers.

"I'm going to try for the South Water Street exit," she yelled.

Neal's throat was paralyzed with fear. This was worse than the Hindu Kush. Much worse.

Megan swerved toward the exit, but the Olds cut them off again and crashed into the side of the Mercedes.

Megan shifted rapidly into reverse and skidded away.

"Cops at Michigan Avenue," she shouted.

Cool as they come under pressure. I can't even talk and she's beating these guys.

She almost did beat them.

But under the Wabash Avenue bridge they began shooting; the firecracker noise of automatic weapons snaked across the empty streets and bullets pinged into the body of the Mercedes.

Instinctively Megan swerved the car again to avoid the bullets. The Olds followed them, crashing into the side on which Neal was sitting.

But the driver of the other car had lost control, too. Both cars leaped forward toward the guardrail, slammed over it in tandem, and plunged toward the chunks of floating ice in the Chicago River.

This is the end of it all. "I love—" he yelled, though whether God or Megan he did not know.

The car hit the river with a dull, sickening crash, water swirled up around the windows. Neal's head hit the roof, and he lost consciousness briefly. Somehow he felt that Megan had been thrown free.

I hope she makes it, he prayed. The kids need her.

Then, burning like a gasoline fire, the cold water welled around him.

How long can you survive in this water? Not long, but I'll probably drown first.

Automatically he shoved at his door. It wouldn't open. The collisions on the lower level had jammed it.

Sleepily, as if he were in a dream, he reached for the door on Megan's side. It too was jammed. She wasn't there. So she had made it.

Dear God, help someone find her.

The car was still floating. He saw the green lights on the shore and blue twirling lights of a police car. Good, they would save Megan and nail the killers. Lou Garcia, gone completely mad? Probably.

He'll die, too, and he doesn't care.

I care. I was in love.

The thought of love made him shove hard against the door on the driver's side. It moved a little.

As the burning ice water crept up his waist toward his chest, he shoved again. No more give.

It was too late. Another few moments and the car would sink. They would fish it out the next day, and Melodi Cain would report on the five o'clock news that his body had been found inside.

He gave up. Only a few seconds, a minute at the most left to his life.

What a terrible waste. Blackie Ryan had been right all along.

Strange, he thought sleepily, he could not quite remember about what Blackie was right.

Then he felt something tugging at his hair, pulling him out of the burning water and off the front seat.

Someone was holding him under his shoulders and tugging him violently upward.

He wasn't moving. Still strapped in by the seat belt.

A hand groped at the seat belt and missed the buckle.

Too late now, the water was at his chin, the car was going under.

The hand hit the belt again, the buckle popped open.

A second or two at the most.

He was yanked firmly upward once more.

But there was no room up there, no opening.

Suddenly his head was out of the car and above the river. He heard voices shouting on the riverbank.

The sun roof!

He tried to kick his feet and lurch further out of the car, his feet moved, so they were still working and his body propelled itself out of the car as far as his hips, but the auto was sinking now and his hips were jammed against the frame of the sun roof.

Whoever was tugging on him gave one last savage pull. Neal flew free from the car and into the frigid river. The car slipped away and sank. He wanted to swim, he tried to swim, he knew he had to swim, but he was just too tired.

Let me die peacefully, he thought—and he gave up.

Then he asked himself the important question he had forgotten: Who's trying to save me?

He couldn't quite figure it out.

A lifeguard was pulling him toward the shore.

Teri Lane. They were at Grand Beach in the summer, a lovely humid day with white cruisers and multicolored sailboats and wind surfers all around. Teri wouldn't let him die.

No, not Teri. She wasn't here. Now it was Megan. Saving his life as he once had saved hers.

Can't expect the poor little kid to do it all by herself, must help her. Kick my feet.

He was so sleepy. He hadn't enjoyed a good night's sleep in five years. Why not fall asleep now and rest till Judgment Day?

But his feet, numb and heavy, continued to push. Ought to have kicked off my shoes.

The voices were close now, men shouting and cheering, hands reaching down, grabbing him firmly.

Then nothing at all, for a long time.

He was before the judgment seat of God.

92

No, it wasn't quite God. It was the troublesome priest, with a purple stole at his neck and a little gold container in his hand, a confused druid witch doctor who had forgotten the precise words of his incantation.

"I'm not going to die," Neal insisted, "I don't need Extreme Unction. I don't want it."

"While you were away"—Blackie sighed loudly—"we had a vote to change the name to the Sacrament of the Sick. And you've already received it."

"You're not going to die." A woman's voice, a young woman's voice. "But you are like TOTALLY sick, NEAL!"

Margaret.

The lovely blond girl floated in and out of his vision. He concentrated. At first there were a pair of Margarets—too much altogether. Then there was only one, triumphantly ticking off on her fingers what was wrong with him.

"Brain concussion, broken arm, two cracked ribs, shock, exposure, hypothermia, and assorted cuts, abrasions, and bruises. Isn't that true, Doctor Murphy?"

Joe Murphy. So this was Northwestern Hospital.

He searched for Joe's white hair and beard and kindly blue eyes.

"I'm only a shrink, Margie, but I think that's a fair description. He's lucky to be alive."

"VERY lucky," Margaret agreed.

Then he remembered the Olds and the guardrail and the river and the sunroof and someone saving his life.

"Your mother!" he screamed.

"Oh, she's like totally all right, just terribly proud of herself because she's such a great heroine," Margaret said, and nodded her head to the right.

He followed the trajectory of her nod. Sitting on a chair, fully dressed, wan and pale, and indeed like totally proud of herself, was Megan Keefe, as radiantly beautiful as the highest seraph of heaven, a self-satisfied seraph who had just pulled off a major miracle and was waiting for praise from the Lord God.

"You saved my life, Megan."

"No big deal."

"How did you ever get me out of the car?"

"Teri taught me some lifeguard holds last summer, like I told you. You are one very heavy ape, I must say."

"I saved your life from fire"—somehow this seemed to be a profound and important statement—"and you saved mine from water. Are we quits, Megan Marie Keefe?"

"You and I will never be quits, Cornelius Stephen O'Connor."

Someone, either her daughter or the troublesome priest, added, "No way."

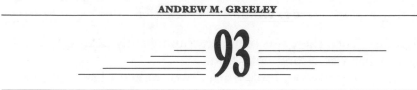

The management of Channel Three insists that I earn my paycheck before I end my stint here in Chicago. They say I must do one editorial. So I want to talk about my colleague Dan Rather and Vice President Bush.

If you remember, the Vice President's camp proclaimed the encounter a major victory for Mr. Bush. And many of us in the industry were more than a little embarrassed by Mr. Rather's loss of temper.

I claim no objectivity in the matter. Mr. Rather is both a rival and a friend. My roots are Chicago Democrat. But it did seem to me that the Vice President's refusal to answer legitimate questions about Iran would make a saint lose his temper.

In any event, the polls are all in now and they show two things:

First, the people of the republic are evenly split on who won the fight. Mr. Rather apparently did better than many of us in the industry thought.

Second, Mr. Bush's victory, widely hailed especially in the print media, which unaccountably still seem to exist, was nonexistent. His standing in the presidential popularity polls moved neither up nor down.

What does this prove?

I almost hate to say it.

It proves that the confrontation was a nonevent.

It proves that the public does not take us media personalities nearly as seriously as we take ourselves.

And, as I prepare to leave this admirable but dangerous city, that strikes me as very good news for the health of our republic.

I'm Neal Connor, with bittersweet emotions, ending my season for Channel Three News.

His last night in Beverly. The last ever. A Sunday night in February. The groundhog had not seen his shadow. The swimsuit issue of *Sports Illustrated* had created its usual stir. Throats and candles, he presumed, were still blessed in Catholic churches. The "Presidents' Day" long weekend had come.

All vain protests against winter blahs.

The night was crisp and cold, the star-drenched sky sparkled cheerfully, apparently smiling benignly on Father Ace's St. Valentine's night "romantic dance."

Of which Neal Connor had no intention of being a part.

He parked the car in front of the house on Hoyne. St. Valentine's Day 1958. Thirty years, he glanced at his watch, thirty years and fourteen hours.

He had thought of calling her on the phone to say good-bye. But that would be running away as they had both done before. This time they should put closure on their relationship.

She was a wonderful woman, but she no longer had need of him. The insurance check had arrived. She was working several days a week at the new Reilly Gallery now. The mystery of her husband's death had been solved. Threat and danger had been removed from her life. She had been blessed with the grace of a new beginning.

Without him.

He had helped to salvage Megan Keefe and her children. He had discharged his last responsibility to Al Lane's memory. It was time to leave. He was an inherently rootless and alienated person, condemned to a life of wandering about the globe. Realism demanded that he accept who and what he was.

Intimacy was a burden he could not sustain for long.

The flu, then hypothermia from the Chicago River had extinguished his passions long enough for him to realize that he simply could not live in a sustained relationship with a woman, much less a family. He was too old to change and to adjust to a family.

To say nothing of a neighborhood.

The troublesome priest would doubtless disagree—which was the reason that there was no way Neal Connor would stop by the

Cathedral rectory to bid farewell to the Captain-General of the North Wabash Avenue Irregulars.

There was a risk in a face-to-face meeting with Megan, too, but only a coward would refuse to face the risk. Theoretically, he could come back to Chicago after the ten days the network wanted him to spend in Russia. With Kelly MacGregor as his producer. The network grapevine reported that Kelly had broken up with her English lover. Maybe they could put it back together again.

His love affair with Megan had been bittersweet. Like an orgy on chocolate chip cookies, only when he'd stopped had he realized how much he had gorged himself. Now it was over and they both knew it. If they said so honestly to one another, they would both be freed for the rest of their lives from a burden that they had carried for three decades, a silly childhood crush.

The doctors at Northwestern insisted he needed a week of rest when they released him from the hospital. So he had flown to Tucson, put up at the Hacienda del Sol (no Arizona Inn this time) and permitted the warmth of the desert sun to heal his body and, as he told himself, his soul.

He took his foster daughter to lunch at El Charro restaurant. The son of the house, it turned out, was a classmate of hers at high school. María loved everything in her new life. Especially the UA basketball team and its superstars, Steve Kerr and Sean Eliot.

"Thank you for the second chance, Uncle Neal," she said.

Uncle Neal indeed.

Lou Garcia and his driver, whose bodies were fished out of the river the next morning, were given no such opportunities for a second chance.

While he was in Tucson, the network had called with a renewed Moscow offer: half and half with Channel 3 so that Johnny Jefferson could still keep his claws in him—with the added attraction that his old love Kelly MacGregor would be waiting for him at Intourist in Moscow.

He told them that he was leaving Chicago. They sounded disappointed.

"You stirred up a lot of action there, Neal," the relevant vice president (news) said to him.

"Almost got myself killed."

"Great ratings."

"I'll take Moscow, thank you. Or Beirut."

They bid him a fond farewell at Channel 3. Melodi Cain cried, an emotion to which he responded with a perfectly straight face.

Once he was freed from Northwestern Hospital, he avoided Blackie Ryan like he really was a plague.

He sighed and pushed himself out of the Hertz car. Better get this over with so that both our lives can go on.

He strolled up to the house on a neatly shoveled sidewalk. The half inch of snow which had fallen in the morning had laid a blanket over the dirty brown ugliness of the February thaw that had occurred the day before.

A lot better weather than thirty years ago.

Inside, someone was playing the piano. Megan, surely.

He told himself that she was playing every day and riding the exercycle, too.

Certainly she didn't need him.

Megan, wearing a red and gray sweater-dress, in the spirit of the feast, no doubt, and no wedding ring, met him at the door.

"On time, as always." She smiled. "Come in. The tea is ready, I'll be right back."

He felt an enormous relief. Megan was going to be civilized. No pleas, no recriminations, no backward glances.

He tossed his coat on the couch and sat next to it.

"What's happening over at the parish tonight?" he asked when she returned. "The parking lot is filled with cars and there's a red glow coming from the hall."

He knew full well what was going on in the parish hall, but he wanted to hear her version of it.

"Did you forget what day this is?"

"Hardly."

She was prettier than ever, vibrant with the excitement of her new life—like a college student home on her first winter vacation.

"Well, it's Father Ace's St. Valentine's Night Dance—Eucharist in church, renewal of marriage vows, then a very romantic dance. Every woman in the parish has dragged her husband over there."

"Something else they took a vote on when I wasn't around."

"Probably." She poured the tea.

Neal Connor was bathed in soothing warmth, no, a converging assault of warmth—the warmth of the burning logs in the fireplace, the warmth of the tea, the warmth of the woman with the amused gray eyes sipping tea across the table from him, the warmth of a home, with music on the piano bench, kids' boots at the door, and a stack of video cassettes on one of the chairs.

Why the amusement in her eyes? She had never looked at him that way before. As intense as ever, Megan was now entertained, too.

He shifted uneasily on the couch. "Nice tea."

"Earl Grey."

"Naturally."

"Marshal Field's. Loose tea, not bags."

She did not need him. Nor did he need her. They would both be happier if he left as soon as possible.

"Megan . . ." He took a narrow box, wrapped in gold tissue and red ribbon from his trench coat pocket. "This is not exactly a Valentine, though it does kind of fit, but . . . well, open it."

She blushed and tore eagerly at the wrappings. She knew, surely, that it was too big to be a ring!

"Beautiful!" She held the watch up to a lamp to examine it closely. "Too beautiful ever to wear when I swim in the river."

His brain filled itself with images of her at the height of sexual pleasure.

"It's waterproof. I insisted."

"Thank you, Neal." She fastened it around her wrist. "I'll think of you whenever I wear it. Oh! It's so beautiful!"

So I chose wisely.

He drank his tea and nibbled on the fruitcake—"left over from Christmas," she joked.

Megan Keefe Lane was remarkably self-possessed for what she must know was a farewell.

How else would I expect her to act?

"I have a Valentine for you, too," she said. "Suddenly, I'm afraid to give it to you."

"Now that you've mentioned it, I won't leave without it."

"WELL . . . I suppose I'd better get it." She bounced enthusiastically out of the room.

What was happening? Uneasily Neal began to smell a very large rat. The North Wabash Avenue Irregulars were up to something, make no mistake about that.

She returned, flushed and breathing rapidly, as if she had climbed to the third floor and back. She held out a flat package, perhaps a foot and a half square. It was wrapped with the same kind of paper and ribbon as had protected his gift to her.

"Coincidence, I guess," she snickered. "Here, take it, before I lose my nerve and run."

Carefully, so as not to tear the paper, he opened the outer wrappings and eased away the tissue inside.

It was certainly a Valentine he had never expected.

"Megan," he could barely speak.

"It's a Catherine Curran original. It's a miniature, more or less. The larger one will hang in her next show. I asked her to keep this one small, so that it could be carried around. It's a very thin frame, too, so that—"

"It's you," he gasped.

"Well, I think so, but if you don't see the resemblance, then maybe Cathy and I are both wrong. It was a very interesting experience. . . . I wish I had agreed to it long ago."

Just as Catherine had promised, it was not a misty nude. No man with hormones could possibly look at it for long without his imagination running rampant. Not quite porno—in fact nowhere near porno—but certainly powerfully erotic.

What an ingenious strategic ploy, he was forced to admit to himself.

"It is," he said, "a little different from a watch."

"Do you like it?"

"A unique Valentine."

"Absolutely original."

Run now, Cornelius O'Connor, while you still have a chance.

"I'm supposed to take it with me and hang it wherever I go?" He could not take his eyes off the picture.

"That's the general idea. It's up to you, of course. You could throw it in a trash can or sell it or—"

"It will certainly make me think of you," he admitted, realizing that he should wrap the picture back up, but unable to do so. "The kids see it?"

"Only Margaret." She was watching him carefully.

"What did she say?"

"She said that it was really excellent, completely radical, truly outstanding, and totally bitchin' besides. She also made some remarks about your reaction that were totally inappropriate."

"Well, it won't make it easy for me to forget you." He pulled the tissue back into place.

Damn the woman, it wasn't fair.

"There was some discussion in the family whether I ought to give it to you. We took a family vote. Even without the other three kids seeing it, you lost, five to zero."

Margaret, Teri, Mark, Joseph. I don't want to lose you, either.

Then Neal Connor realized that he was a heel, a cad, a louse. He arrived at that conclusion with considerable happiness.

He had not come to say good-bye at all.

He had come to see how she would try to hold on to him. She was performing brilliantly.

"You don't play fair, woman." He removed the tissue paper from the painting again. Damn Catherine Curran, too. She had captured Megan's appeal perfectly; she had seen her just the way Neal saw her.

"Neal"—she breathed deeply, her brash confidence slipping—"neither of us will ever know what would have happened if you had run after me at O'Hare twenty-one years ago."

"That's right."

"But I'm running after you now. I give you fair warning. It would be a terrible mistake for both of us if I let you get away. I'll pursue you to the ends of the earth."

She looked like she was about to unbutton her dress. Not quite yet, woman.

It was an extremely attractive proposal. Network should be able to get someone else. Johnny would be overjoyed to keep him in this crazy, dangerous, exciting city.

Megan.

Megan!

MEGAN!

MEGAN!

"That sounds like pure delight, but I can't permit the woman I love to do that."

In saying it, the sentence became truth.

"Oh?" She didn't understand.

"Did Blackie tell you what your chances were in life alone?"

"By a generous estimate, to quote his exact words, not above three or four percent. He give you the same odds?"

"Marginally higher. But he wouldn't make an estimate of our chances together, not when I asked him before Christmas. He said there weren't enough data. Do you have a revised opinion from him?"

She smiled uncertainly, beginning to understand what was happening, but afraid to trust the good news. "He said that absolutely he would not under any circumstances consider pushing his estimate higher than ninety-seven percent."

He placed the Catherine Curran painting next to his coat on the couch and covered it with tissue.

Mine, the painting and the model both.

He wanted the model. The painting could wait.

First there was love. Then, desire—absent most of the time since the onset of his viral infection—reappeared, alive and well. And with desire came tenderness and affection.

He wanted her now and forever.

"He said that Megan? Truly?"

Tentatively he touched one of her wondrous little hands. She clung to his fingers like she would never let them go.

"Truly." Tears were forming in her eyes and in his.

"What we could do tonight is go over to Father Ace's romantic St. Valentine's Night Dance and sign up for an early morning wedding Mass next Saturday. Make an honest man out of me." His voice choked.

"Yes, we could do that." She bit her lip as the tears ran down her cheeks. "Couldn't we?"

Truly they could.